EMILY OWEN studied English Language and Literature at the University of Leeds. Since completing her Masters by Research, she has worked as an Archives Assistant at the University of Huddersfield. She lives in Wakefield, West Yorkshire. *The Mechanical Maestro* is her first novel, and is the first book in an upcoming series following the adventures of the Abernathy family and their clockwork creations.

The Mechanical Maestro

Emily Owen

To Amy,

E. Owen

SilverWood

Published in 2020 by SilverWood Books

SilverWood Books Ltd
14 Small Street, Bristol, BS1 1DE, United Kingdom
www.silverwoodbooks.co.uk

ISBN 978-1-78132-967-2 (paperback)
ISBN 978-1-78132-998-6 (ebook)

British Library Cataloguing in Publication Data
A CIP catalogue record for this book is available from the British Library

Page design and typesetting by SilverWood Books

For Mum

Acknowledgements

I am hugely grateful to my family and friends for their continued love and support. I particularly want to thank my parents for their encouragement. I am immensely grateful to my partner Marcus for his input on early drafts and his endless patience. Special thanks to Teresa for proofreading the first full draft and giving me the confidence to share the novel with others.

Chapter One

Old Mr Abernathy's workshop was a rather peculiar one. As a newly married man, he had fled with his bride to London and rented a narrow, three-storey property at the corner of Peter Street, near the bustling Berwick Street Market. He soon discovered that there was insufficient room for his private projects in what became his clockmaker's shop on the ground floor. Mrs Abernathy, a woman of considerably better breeding than her husband, would not permit him to litter her house with all his 'grubby pieces of machinery'. With no chance of expanding the property outwards and with nothing resembling a yard, he had followed the example of the rest of London and built upwards. Protruding from the second storey was a trapezoid-shaped structure of wood and metal. He had used anything he could find to build it as long as it was sturdy. His wife believed that the extension would collapse within two weeks of its completion. The landlord had only granted him permission to execute his project as he did not believe that it would succeed, anticipating great amusement in seeing the clockmaker's efforts turn into a pile of scrap and splintered wood. However, William Abernathy's knowledge of mathematics and engineering served him well, and the extension, which became his workshop, was still standing at the time of his death over twenty years later. Its only source of natural light was a large, circular window lacquered in dust and cobwebs. Candles supplemented the supply of light from within. Inside the workshop, great sloping shelves ran along the walls at such steep gradients that they zigzagged all the way down to the ground, their nails having rusted overtime. Naturally, this meant that all of the trinkets and dissected clocks, which Mr Abernathy placed upon them, simply slid down to the bottom in a matted clump of metal.

After he had succumbed to the ailments associated with old age, his two sons had inherited the family house and business. They tore out the old shelves and scrubbed the window until there wasn't a single thread of cobweb left and the yellow-tinted glass gleamed once more. It was only then they discovered that the window was actually patterned like a clock face with the numerals in black lead. They quickly set about filling the workshop with all sorts of strange clockwork contraptions of their own, for they had inherited their father's natural aptitude for anything mechanical. It was here, just before midnight on a Tuesday evening, about a year after their mother's death (Mr Abernathy's rest had not remained peaceful for very long, as his wife joined him in their shared grave a little more than a year after he was buried), that the two young men were hard at work on their latest project.

The candles lighting the room were little more than wicks bobbing about in watery pools inside their holders, giving the room a low orange glow like the inside of a stove where embers are still pulsing with life. Notes and drawings were spread out along the bare wooden floor or hung on the walls. In a square metal tray upon the worktable beneath the window was a grey, diced-up hunk of rubbery meat with a pungent, vinegary odour. Its dryness suggested that it had been there for some time.

Seated nearby was the eldest brother, George, filing a metal disc smaller than a half farthing with the aid of a loupe positioned over his left eye. In one hand he held a pair of tweezers that had the disc clamped firmly between their jaws. His eyes felt strained from having to concentrate on such a small thing by the dying candlelight for so long. Once he had filed the piece until the corner was smooth, he brought a segment of machinery, about the size of a snuffbox, closer towards him, carefully inserting the newly cut piece in amongst all the other equally delicate metal parts. A small click informed him that it was in its proper place. Laying the loupe aside, he placed the completed segment on his palm and carried it over to the wooden table behind him where his brother was at work on the main body of their creation.

Sitting upon the table was a humanoid automaton. Although it had a head, arms and upper torso, its body abruptly ended there. The torso was a patchwork of copper plates welded together, with two ball-shaped joints at the ends of its shoulders where the skeletal arms were attached. Its eyes were mismatched in size and shape, the right being far larger than the left. Both had black, glassy lenses with steel shutters; the larger eye was wide open while the other was partially shut. The top of the gaping head revealed its inner workings, its glass, domed crown resting on hinges at the back of its head. Attached to the left wrist was a metallic hand skinned in copper. The iron joints, rubber tendons and steel springs allowed it all the flexibility and dexterity of a human hand. The right hand was lying on Douglas Abernathy's lap as he finished tightening a catch controlling the middle finger. Two years George's junior, his face was longer, and its features more angular and expressive than his brother's, although he was just as lean and, at that moment, just as dishevelled and tired-looking around the eyes. His auburn hair had more of a wave than a curl to it and was parted slightly to the side. One thick curl swung down over his forehead and stuck out at an awkward angle at the side of his head.

He tugged at the metal fingers to make sure that all the mechanisms were connected before reattaching the hand to the android's wrist.

'Is the last bit finished?' he asked George.

'I believe so. Hold it in place while I attach it to the rest.'

Douglas held the chunk of mechanical brain between his thumb and forefinger while George fixed it in place inside the android's head. When he was finished, Douglas removed his fingers and flipped the glass dome over its brain, fastening the latch on the side of its head.

'That's it.' Douglas turned towards his brother. 'Ready?'

George held up a small wind-up key and inserted it into the slot in the machine's back, giving it four stiff turns. As soon as he released his hold on the key, there came the grinding and creaking of the wheels moving inside of the machine, the sound reverberating through its metal torso. Inside the glass dome, they could see the intricate mechanisms beginning to flicker and pulse. Their movements were fluid and graceful somehow, like a faultlessly choreographed routine. The shutters over the android's eyes began rapidly snapping open and closed. Its black eyes briefly met those of its makers and then it stared fixedly at an unknown spot past their heads. It raised its arms and let them hover in mid-air, flexing its fingers.

'Fetch the board,' said George, without taking his eyes off their creation. Douglas hurriedly brought a chessboard to the table and, seating himself in front of the android, began to arrange the pieces. George positioned himself adjacent to the two of them and watched proceedings with his arms folded across his chest. The throw of a dice determined that Douglas was to be black and the android white. Douglas slid one of the centre black pawns one square forward. The android's eyes followed his move and after a second it deliberately raised its hand and slid a white pawn from the corner of the board two squares forward.

'It knew to take advantage of the first turn even when I didn't.' Douglas glanced eagerly at George, whose passive expression remained unaltered.

'Don't make it easy for it, otherwise it's pointless running the test.'

Douglas proceeded to put another pawn into play. The android responded to his move accordingly. After three turns it took one of Douglas's knights. Douglas bit his lip and studied the board with his elbows propped on the table and his hands pressed together, the fingertips brushing his lower lip.

He felt it watching him.

He slid a piece forward and watched the android's eyes roll from side to side as it calculated its next move. The metal fingers cranked open and Douglas felt a gleam of triumph as it proceeded to make the exact move that he had predicted. Douglas then moved his bishop and swiftly plucked the knight that had defeated his own from the board. The game went on for some time, each player steadily capturing the other's pieces at an even rate. George drummed his fingers against his upper arm. He wished they would hurry it up. This was only intended as a simple, straightforward exercise; there was still much more testing to do afterwards. Eventually, only five pieces remained on the board: the two kings, a black queen, a black bishop and a white pawn. These pieces had been continually shifted around the board in what was looking increasingly like a stalemate. Then Douglas looked the android in the eye and a smile spread across his face as he deliberately moved the black queen to a square adjoining the white king. The black bishop backed the black queen from the north-west. There was no help available from the white pawn, which was stranded at the other end of the board. The white king was trapped.

'I think you will find that is checkmate,' he declared, although his victory was tinged with disappointment.

However, this was nothing compared to the android's reaction.

Its shutters began blinking wildly and its limbs made spasmodic, jerky movements. One arm swept the board onto the floor, the pieces scattering and rolling away. Small streams of white smoke drifted into the air from between its joints. A grinding, screeching sound like tearing metal could be heard from inside its body. Several cracks formed in the glass dome housing its brain. George quickly pulled Douglas back by the shoulder just before the dome smashed. The force of the blast spat out splinters of glass and metal in every direction, George shielding their faces with the chessboard. The android's half-emptied head swayed a little from side to side a moment and then drooped. Its arms clattered listlessly onto the table.

George lowered the chessboard, and they both watched the android cautiously for several minutes.

'Well,' said Douglas eventually, 'I'd say it was a bad loser.'

'You must have done something it didn't expect that caused it to break down.'

George hesitantly approached the android and inspected it from all angles. He then turned his attention to one single drawing fastened onto the wall and continued to stare fixedly at it. 'Where was it we went wrong?'

'Wrong? It was working fine up until then. It almost had me beaten.'

'But it *should* have beaten you.'

'It was able to counter my moves to prevent me winning much earlier in the game. It *was* actually making calculated decisions,' Douglas pointed out. 'Besides, no one has ever beaten me at chess, not even you.'

'I have beaten you on several occasions and you know it.'

'I let you win to stop the game going on for too long.'

'That is a poor excuse,' mumbled George, although that was precisely what he had done himself on every occasion Douglas *had* won a match.

'Well, next time you can play it and see how it performs against you.'

'There must have been a fault in the brain somewhere.' George's eyes travelled back to the drawing. He seemed not to have heard Douglas's last remark.

'George, it could have been something as insignificant as a screw that came slightly loose.'

'I wouldn't call it insignificant if *this* was the result.' George indicated the defective android. 'And that was only meant to be an initial test. We didn't get on to any of the real experiments. If we can't even make something as simple as a machine that can play games, how are we to hope of achieving anything greater?'

'Making a machine that can actually make its own decisions is still an achievement in itself.'

'The brain is still too limited,' muttered George. 'A child of average intelligence can play chess with a reasonable degree of skill. Was our objective not to build a device that could surpass the capabilities of the human mind?'

'Well, I suppose that was the idea, yes. But perhaps the reason we're having difficulties with it is because our own minds have not been working at their full capability recently, what with all the additional work we've had to take on.'

'You mean mending pewter tea sets and brass ornaments?' returned George curtly, as he sat down on a chair. 'Hardly trying work.'

While George brooded over a diagram of the failed mechanical brain, with his pencil hovering over the paper, Douglas went to a lever in the wall and pulled it. Moments later a small automaton scarcely fifteen inches high came speeding through the little flap in the door adjoining the house. It was made of tin and had a leather pouch on its back. One of its arms was shaped like a funnel while the other clutched a small broom. It slowly made its way around the room sucking up the fragments of glass and metal.

Stifling a yawn, Douglas took out his pocket watch and flipped the lid open. 'We can get about five hours' sleep before we have to open up shop. There's not much use in stewing over it anymore tonight at any rate. We can try to find out what went wrong in the morning.'

'It's already morning.'

Not wishing to justify this remark with an answer, Douglas snapped the watch's lid shut and began blowing out the last few remaining candles. The little cleaning machine completed its sweep of the room and retreated through the door flap. All the while George had not moved. The back of his dark head and the arm that held the pencil could be seen in the moonlight leaking in from the landing as Douglas held the door ajar with the only remaining lit candle in his hand.

'Are you coming or do you plan on sitting there in the dark until sunrise?' Douglas asked, as he stood in the doorway. After a moment George disappeared from view, leaving only the empty chair and the pencil upon the worktable. He emerged onto the second-storey landing and stood there with his hands in his pockets and his head cast down while Douglas locked the door. He headed for the stairs.

'Aren't you going to bed?' asked Douglas, slipping the large brass key into his pocket.

'I don't feel that I can sleep just yet. I think I'll stay up a while.'

'Mind you don't wake Molly and me when you come up.' Douglas advanced downstairs a couple of steps after his brother. 'Just remember you are not a machine, George.'

He wasn't sure whether George made any response – he had already disappeared further down the stairs. Douglas stopped at the first floor. There were two doors on the landing. Their younger sister's room was the smallest one on the right, which the family's long-serving maidservant, Anne Snell, had formerly occupied. The second room on the left, which the three of them had shared as children, was now solely occupied by Douglas. The largest bedroom, which had been their mother and father's, and where both their parents had passed away, was on the second floor. After their mother's death, George had ransacked it and moved himself in; its contents he either assimilated, sold or threw out.

Douglas softly shut his bedroom door and set the candle down on the pine chest of drawers beside the bed. The additional space was useful as it meant that he could work more freely on projects of his own, yet there was something in the hollow ring of his footsteps on the floorboards that even now still seemed strange to him. He changed into his nightshirt and snuffed out the candle before he lay down under the cold bedclothes.

Douglas blinked in the dark, finding like George that he too could not sleep.

The ear that was not pressed against the pillow caught the ticking of the clocks from the shop directly below the bedroom. He was sure that he could faintly hear the creak of George's boots crossing the parlour floor, followed by the sound of glass clinking. In his mind's eye he watched George pour brandy from the decanter on the table into a tumbler until it was a quarter full, replace the stopper with a soft chink, and then carry it over to their father's old wooden chair. Its familiar creak just about registered with Douglas's ear. He saw George sitting there taking the occasional sip of brandy as he stared fixedly at some spot on the wall, his mind elsewhere.

The ticking seemed to grow sharper, each strike of the second hand cutting into Douglas's eardrum and causing the blood in his ear to give a giddy leap. The sound built up and up until all the clocks burst into a chorus of chiming to welcome the new hour, each clock in perfect synchrony with the others. After the second chime rang out and dissolved away, the ticking resumed steadily. Douglas tried to smother it by putting his pillow over his head.

His past, present and future was in that sound, that one, ceaseless, monotonous sound forever marching onward, indifferent to the affairs and systems of man. He'd had it in his ears for the entire twenty-two years of his life. He removed the pillow and sat upright. Gradually his eyes grew accustomed to the dark, and vague, grey shapes condensed out of the black. George's words had stirred up the fear that had been sleeping in the back of his mind. Was this really all their future was to be? Perhaps they were to remain poor clockmakers forever after all. It had been their parents' desire that he and George remain tethered to the family business and now, when they were finally no longer bound by any small sense of parental duty, it seemed they had nowhere else to go. They were just about scraping a living repairing watches or whatever else people happened to bring their way – they'd fixed everything from candlesticks to antique guns. (Hardly anyone ever actually bought the brothers' watches, even though many remarked that they were some of the most exquisitely crafted timepieces in all of London.) It was not the nature of the work they minded – clockmaking was in their blood and was second nature to them both, after all – but they were greatly frustrated at not being able to afford the time or the resources to exercise their full capabilities. They had certainly never been encouraged by their parents or anyone else to make something more of themselves besides simple clockmakers. In fact, their father had conceived a deep-seated jealousy of his sons' natural gifts. Although Mr Abernathy had once been on his way to making something of a name for himself as a talented clockmaker and inventor, what George and Douglas were able to produce transcended anything he had been capable of. By the time they were at an age where most children were still learning to string their letters together, they had mastered the art of watchmaking and outstripped their father's abilities. They could produce mechanical animals that moved, acted and sounded identical to the real creatures themselves. They built machines that simulated all manner of human behaviour, and others that could perform complex calculations with remarkable accuracy. They designed larger devices that were powered by wind, steam and electricity, which (if they worked) could revolutionise public transport and industry. While they were still boys, the two of them had actually gone as far as to steal the clock in the church tower so they could harvest it for parts. It was George's idea of course. Douglas smiled to himself as he recalled the memory, even though he had been sure that they would be thrown into prison or transported to Australia at the time as he was helping to pull the wagon containing the stolen clock through the backstreets and alleyways of London. It had been a risky escapade but they had been in desperate need of parts for the android they were building. They wanted to build a machine to replace the family's maidservant. They had actually managed to get it working rather well until they came home one day to find it with a poker through its chest and Snell sat knitting by the hearth with a smug look on her face.

Feeling his eyes grow heavy, Douglas let his head sink back onto the pillow and his memories were succeeded by dreams.

Chapter Two

Douglas found George fast asleep in their father's chair when he came downstairs to the shop the next morning. After repeatedly calling out his name and shaking his shoulder, Douglas had tipped a glass of water over his head. He took great delight in watching him start up and look about wildly, flinging water droplets from the ends of his black hair. George then shut himself in the workshop for the rest of the day. An explosion from upstairs at around two o'clock told Douglas it was not going well.

Towards late afternoon, Douglas was sitting in the shop tinkering with an old mantel clock a customer had wanted fixing. A broken mainspring in need of replacing was the cause of the problem. It was a simple job that occupied his mind just enough to prevent him from falling asleep. Clocks of every shape and variety filled the wall behind him and two grandfather clocks towered above each side of the counter. Several of their inventions were also displayed throughout the shop alongside the clocks and watches. More timepieces were arranged in the shop window. Pocket watches were sitting on, or dangling from, the glazing bars. One or two had card tags attached to them on which was written a customer's name followed by 'to collect'. It had been a reasonably slow morning, although a gentleman had come in to enquire about a device in the shop that had caught his attention. It was a more advanced version of the prototype 'washing machine' in their kitchen, only this one washed, rinsed and then pressed clothes. He had wanted them to build him six such machines – only when Douglas informed him that they would need a deposit to cover the cost of making that number, he had frowned and said he would have to call at the bank. He hadn't returned.

After fitting the spring, Douglas happened to glance out into the street where two ladies in bonnets lavishly decorated with ribbons and flowers were pointing at a silver watch in the shop window, when a gentleman in a top hat and dark greatcoat passed by. Breaking his firm, purposeful stride to briefly scan the contents of the window, he retreated several paces and approached the shop door. The shop bell gave a shrill little tinkle as he entered.

'Good afternoon, Mr Maynard.' Douglas greeted him amiably. 'How can I help you today?'

'You can give me some advice to begin with.'

'About what, sir?' Douglas put down his tools and wiped his still slightly greasy fingers on his trouser leg. The cloth he'd been using was already saturated with oil.

'It's my wife's birthday next week and I am caught between two of the watches I saw in the window just now as to which would make a better present for her.' He pointed towards the window with the tip of his cane. 'She has been making remarks about her own watch being broken for several weeks now.'

'I happened to see Mrs Maynard pass by the window earlier today, sir, and I noticed that she distinctly lingered in front of the silver watch with the rose head on the case.'

'Ah! That settles the matter then. May I see it?'

Douglas retrieved the watch from the window and held it before Mr Maynard.

'There is also something else that I require,' said the gentleman as he inspected the watch and nodded approvingly. 'Although the second matter concerns your sister.' He withdrew a small, dark brown glass bottle from his coat and placed it on the counter. 'That tonic of hers seems to be doing wonders for my gout, which is more than can be said for my doctor. I would like to request another bottle from her.'

'I will mention it to her, sir.' As Douglas's fingers made contact with the bottle, he realised that he had forgotten to take Molly the bag Mrs Blakeslee had left her that morning.

'I admit I was sceptical at first,' continued Mr Maynard as he drew out his purse, 'when my wife showed me that bottle your sister had sold her. She persisted in getting me to try it, saying it was made with natural plant extracts, unlike the strange pills and tonics you see those quacks trying to pass off to desperate fools. But I swear that within two days of having applied it, I began to see the swelling go down!' He took the small brown-paper parcel, which Douglas had just finished tying the string around with well-practiced efficiency, and knocked the brim of his hat a little higher up his forehead with his cane. 'Tell her I will be willing to pay her more than a farthing for the next bottle. I dare say she could sell it for twenty times that amount.'

Tucking the parcel safely into the pocket of his greatcoat, he bade Douglas a good day and exited the shop as swiftly as he had entered it. Watching Mr Maynard flit past the window in the direction he had come, Douglas retrieved the cloth sack that had been sitting beneath the counter and turned to a device set in the wall behind him. It consisted of a flat, square, steel plate with a circle cut out of the middle and a screen of hessian fabric stretched across the void. On the left side of the plate was a small lever and two glass bulbs. Resting on a stunted little arm branching out from the wall, and attached to the device by a plaited cord tail, was a hollow metal cone. Douglas took the cone in his hand and flicked the lever down, causing the bulb below it to light up with a soft white glow. A muffled buzzing could be heard coming from the device as though an incensed wasp were trapped inside.

Douglas spoke into the wide end of the cone, which he held near his mouth. 'George, will you mind the shop a moment, please?'

A red light flickered into life beside the white one and a faint, exasperated sigh rattled through the hessian. Douglas flicked the lever up, cutting off both sound and light.

Several moments later, George appeared at the black door that led to the back of the house.

'At least try to appear human for a few minutes while I'm away,'

Douglas warned, before swinging his legs nimbly over the counter with the sack in one hand and exiting the way George had come.

To the right of the hallway at the back of the shop was the room their mother had referred to as the parlour. Its faded Chinese wallpaper was riddled with small tears and marks, while the floor was covered by a large and heavily patterned carpet. Most of its furnishings and ornaments had been sold, yet it still wore a sad air of grandeur like some destitute old dame. They had held onto the portraits, a small redwood table and two chairs, now stripped of their cloths and doilies. On the left of the hallway was the kitchen and staircase. Douglas suddenly froze as he planted one foot on the bottom step and heard a crunch under his boot. All along the stairs were huge, thick grey roots that crumbled away to dust where he had trodden on them.

'Molly!' he called, as he marched upstairs, the roots crackling and snapping under his boots. Their source appeared to be underneath his sister's bedroom door. 'Molly, what have you been—?' He reached out to grasp the door handle, but it turned sharply downward of its own accord. The door swung inward and a messy-haired girl bolted out of the room, holding up a small corked vial of pale green liquid.

'I've got it! I've finally got it!' she cried, waving the vial around in front of him.

She was a fresh-faced, petite girl of sixteen with wild, mousey hair. Her long cotton dress was starting to become tattered around the hem and the sleeves had been rolled back along her thin arms so they sat above her elbows. Brown leather gloves covered most of her forearms, and a leather toolbelt was strapped around her narrow waist.

'I'll ask about what it is you've got in a minute, Molly. First of all, can you account for why there are roots all over the stairs?'

'Roots? Oh, I see.' She bit her lip as she followed Douglas's gaze. 'I didn't realise they had spread that much. Ah, you see here?' She retrieved a small flowerpot from behind her door; the thick roots were sprouting from the drainage hole. 'This is the result of the last experiment I ran. Hopefully this next one should produce a different result. Come take a look, then you'll see what these roots are all about. Is that another lot of clothes? *Urgh.* Just leave them on the bed for now.' Douglas dumped the sack he had been carrying on the bed as he followed her inside. The air in Molly's bedroom was thick and muggy, possibly due to the quantities of pollen and plant toxins floating around in it. It made Douglas's nose itch every time he came in. A threadbare rug was stretched over the wooden floor and a narrow little bed was pushed up against a wall on the left. Every inch of shelf or table space was covered with peculiar plants, books and things pickled in glass jars. Opposite the bed, beneath the only window, was a long table mounted with chemistry equipment. A series of large glass, bubble-like bulbs were held in place by clamps and stands, communicating with one another by a series of glass arteries. The largest bulb was filled with vivid green liquid with a long, narrow cylindrical tube sticking out of its bottom. A small dial at the base of the bulb regulated the flow of liquid. Molly placed a glass beaker beneath the end of the tube and turned the dial to allow some of the green fluid to seep into it.

'What is that, Molly?'

'A new growth serum I've been developing. It came out rather stronger than I intended it to be. What you're seeing there is a really diluted mixture, about two parts water to one part of my formula.'

'Are you sure you've found the right concentration now?'

'That's what I'm about to find out.'

She placed a flowerpot filled with soil beside the beaker and dipped a pipette in the latter. A small amount of green liquid was sucked up inside it, forming one or two little air bubbles. 'Watch this.' She squeezed three drops of green liquid onto the soil. Nothing happened.

'What are you—?'

'Just keep watching...there!'

A tiny green shoot uncurled itself from the soil and rapidly began to grow and sprout leaves. A beautiful, sumptuous pink flower bloomed right before their eyes.

'Months' worth of sowing, watering and waiting condensed into a matter of seconds.' She looked up from the plant to Douglas so he could see her glowing face. Her emerald-green eyes, a mirror of his own, were glittering brightly. 'Imagine if we could grow crops as fast as this. There would certainly be no more famine like there was in Ireland, that's for sure.'

'I can see your line of thinking, Mol. I really think you could do something with this.'

'All the other seeds I tested it on either didn't sprout or grew into monsters, but I think I might finally have landed on the right concentration after—'

'Um, Molly, I think you might want to turn around.'

Molly spun her head around to see that the flower head had swollen to twice the size it had been a moment ago and its roots were spreading onto the ground. The long yellow filaments wriggled about like tentacles.

'No, no, no. Damn!'

She seized a metal watering can sitting by the table leg, but before she could do anything with it one of the filaments wrapped itself around her wrist. Quick as a flash, Molly drew a tool from her belt and severed the filament in two before Douglas could do anything to help her. Her hand now free, she poured the contents of the can over the roots of the plant. On contact with the liquid, the roots instantly died away, the flower and leaves shrivelling up and changing from green to brown in the blink of an eye.

'I was really hoping I wouldn't have to kill another one,' she sighed, as she let the empty watering can clatter to the floor and pulled off her gloves. Her white hands were speckled with dry soil and stained with green blotches, most likely the tissues of various plants. Her fingernail ends were blue-black. One of her worst sins as a girl, which her mother had catalogued with unwavering diligence, had been to pick out the dirt from underneath her nails when she was sat at the dinner table or meant to be doing her needlework. She wasn't consciously aware she was doing it, but her mother always caught her at it, even if her hand was under the table or if she was sitting with her back to her. Even though her mother and Snell were no longer around to reprimand her for her 'faults', the memory of having her fingers scrubbed with a scrubbing brush until they were red raw stung keenly enough in her mind to still make her sometimes hesitate before her thumbnail dislodged a particle of dirt.

'I'd say you almost had it right, Mol,' said her brother kindly, as he eyed the dead plant, 'but how much weaker does the concentration need to be? Perhaps the problem lies in the composition of the formula itself.'

Molly tossed away the gloves and dropped onto the edge of her bed beside the sack of clothes. 'Let's see what you've brought me then.' She undid the string tied around the top of the bag and peered inside. 'It's full of costumes.' She pulled out a sailor's hat. 'Who did you say dropped it off?'

'Mrs Blakeslee. She just about managed to squeeze herself through the door.'

Molly attempted to screw the hat on over her unruly hair and gave a salute.

'Mr Blakeslee must have got hold of some old costumes from somewhere and thought he could sell them.' Douglas winced slightly as he caught the faint, stale odour starting to escape from the bag.

'With that glib tongue of his he could sell gin to the British Temperance League,' said Molly. 'I've seen all sorts of things turn up on his stall. Oh, there's a velvet sheet that could possibly be a curtain in here as well, and...' Molly's eyes widened and she held up between her thumb and forefinger a pair of enormous drawers trimmed with drooping lace.

'Mrs's Blakeslee's no doubt.' Douglas smirked.

'She probably threw in a few things that she wanted mending because she was too idle to do it herself and then her husband dumped a load of his second-hand costumes in here as well. There're at least three pairs of drawers in here with holes or loose lace. I think this sheet might actually be a dress rather than a curtain.' She started pulling garments out of the bag. 'Most of these are probably beyond repair. I'll patch and stitch up what I can at any rate.'

'She said some of the shirts were badly stained. I think she was wanting you to wash them too.'

They could certainly use a wash but I'm not the one prepared to wash them.' Molly thrust the clothes back into the bag. 'It's bad enough I'm her seamstress without being her washerwoman. And I still don't trust that bloody machine of yours not to shrink everything again.'

'And Mr Maynard wants another bottle of that tonic.'

'Does he? It'll take some effort to find all of the ingredients I used in the first batch.' She sighed as she fell back onto the bed and closed her eyes.

Douglas began examining the contents of her shelves until he spied something behind the jars of pickled flower heads and the dusty old books. 'Ah! I remember when George and I made this for you.' He smiled as he brought down a large metal lotus flower in his hands.

One of her eyes flickered open. 'You gave it to me for my sixth birthday.' She half-smiled. 'Don't think I'd just got bored with it and thrown it away. I always keep the things you make me. Well, the ones that work at least.'

'The things we make you always work.'

'Most of them do. Let's see if she still dances like she used to.'

Molly pulled herself up and wrapped her arms around her knees as she watched Douglas set the metallic flower on the pillow and turn the handle. A tinkling tune started to play as the petals unfolded, revealing a little mechanical dancer with a prettily painted face in the middle of the lotus flower. Extending her white, winged arms, she began to twirl around in her floaty, sage-green skirt with the tails of her pale pink sash spinning after her. She gracefully raised one leg and leapt lightly from the flower's centre onto a petal, then danced across the bed en pointe. Molly spread her hand out on the bed and the little dancer stepped onto it. The tiny feet tickled her as they pitter-pattered on the flat of her palm. Molly's eyes glittered brightly, and she could not resist laughing as she watched the dancer pirouette as she had done when she was a little girl. There was a sweet smile on the dancer's face and a circle of red paint on each cheek, which had mingled with the white while the paint had still been wet and made milky pink swirls. Two large, if blank-looking and unblinking, eyes were framed by delicate, curling lashes.

On hearing the change in the tone of the song, Molly set the dancer down and watched her prance back to her place in the centre of the flower. Both the song and the dancer began to wind down as the petals closed around her. The final notes of the song dripped away and dispersed as the tips of the petals touched, the dancer now completely hidden from view.

'Poor girl, she gets to come out and dance so rarely nowadays,' said Molly. 'I forget that she's sitting there on my shelf gathering dust.'

'As long as she gets to see the light of day every now and then,' said Douglas, returning the lotus flower to its place on the shelf.

Molly uncurled herself from her sitting position and sprang lightly to her feet. 'I'd better go clear away those roots. I'll add them to my compost heap so at least that way it won't be a complete waste. Then I'll see about Mr Maynard's tonic.'

'What about Mrs Blakeslee's clothes?'

'They can wait.' Molly pulled on her gloves and gave Douglas a sidelong glance. 'I can always burn the midnight oil like you and George were doing last night.'

'Did we wake you?'

'I was woken up by all the racket going on up there around midnight. I'm guessing it didn't turn out as it was supposed to.'

'No. George has been in there all day trying to fix it.'

'No doubt he has. I feel slightly better about my own failure now at any rate.' She grinned. 'After all, that is how knowledge is won, frustrating as it may be.' She gave the flowerpot the roots had sprouted from a swift kick. 'Although I don't intend to be stitching Mrs Blakeslee's bloomers for the rest of my days.'

'Molly, you don't need to do so now. George and I can just about earn enough to—'

'I will earn my keep,' she said firmly, looking him straight in the eye in her bold, frank way. 'You and George did enough when you saved me from having to marry the undertaker's son.'

'You owe us nothing for that, Molly,' said Douglas. 'Do you really think we would have stood back and let Mother marry you off against your own will? Although you would've had something of a comfortable life compared to what we can give you.'

'I wouldn't choose any other sort of life if I could. Oh, and another thing,' she said gravely, holding up a warning finger, 'if Laura Blakeslee calls to pick up the clothes, try to engage with her as little as possible, even if it is difficult for you.'

'There's no need to warn me, Mol. I discovered you were right about her being a shrewd, cunning and dispassionate girl.'

'How did that come about?'

'It happened last Friday.' He looked away from his sister before resuming speaking, recalling the details of the painful affair. 'I made my feelings known to her and she said in a matter-of-fact way that she could not possibly consider courting me and that my family's circumstances didn't make me a suitable candidate for a potential husband in the future.'

He pictured how she had continued to briskly sort through the merchandise on her market stall as she spoke, her eyes occasionally gliding over him. He had protested that he would not contest her rejection if she genuinely did not return his feelings, but that she shouldn't let such practical matters influence her decision. Then she finally looked him squarely in the face, with all the usual lustre gone from her pretty brown eyes.

'Where does feeling come into it?' she said. 'It is a financial transaction. You cannot expect one to enter into an arrangement where the other party has little to offer in the way of collateral. That is not a sound investment.'

'I did try to warn you,' said Molly, shaking her head gently. 'Although if she ever tries to pursue you for whatever reason, I'll wash her clothes in nightshade solution after I've finished mending them.' With that concluding remark, she marched briskly from the room.

Douglas smiled to himself when she had gone, although he didn't doubt that Molly had been sincere in her threat.

As Molly cleared the landing, Douglas trod downstairs. Something skittered past him in the opposite direction. A little clockwork mouse. It paused momentarily to contemplate him, standing on its hind legs.

Molly called from above. 'Ah! So you're the little blighter that's been nibbling my gowns!' The mouse narrowly missed the trowel, which came flying towards it, and retreated into the kitchen.

Douglas quickly slipped through the black door. 'All right, George, I'm here now. You can go back to—'

The shop was empty, the bell still trembling above the door as if someone had just gone out. The drawer on the till had not been shut properly and when he tallied up its contents, Douglas found that a half-crown appeared to be missing. He slammed the tray shut and shook his head. He had feared as much. It was always the same when George had something he couldn't get out of his mind.

Chapter Three

There was a unified groan across the table as George set down his final card. Each of the three men he was playing with slammed their own cards on the table.

'That's the fifth time in a row,' growled a large man by the name of Mussel to George's left, rubbing his bristly upper lip. He was built like a barge with a dark beard and ruddy face coated in a film of sweat. There were dark patches on his shirt around the underarms, neck and in the small of his back.

'I know,' said the carpenter to the left of him, as George swept the pile of coins and notes from the middle of the table towards him with one arm and took a swig from his beer glass with the other. 'And he's had about twice as much to drink as the rest of us.'

Anyone sitting close enough would have observed that there was a slightly clouded look about George's eyes as they inspected the notes before he deposited them into his pocket. He would usually only take a half-crown out with him when he went to the public house, but he would win his drink playing cards and bring a few shillings back home with him. He won every time. When the other men grew tired of him always beating them, he simply moved on to another drinking hole.

'Well, I've had enough of this.' The legs of the carpenter's chair scraped against the wooden floor as he rose from the table and took his glass away with him.

George's eyes hovered between the two remaining men: Mussel and the silent, sandy-haired man. Their irises were a striking shade of blue, like pale sapphires, and just as keen and sharp.

'Well gentlemen,' he said after a pause. 'Shall we continue playing?'

'Damn right,' grunted Mussel. 'Your luck has to run out sometime or another, and I want to see it when it does.'

George raised a finger. 'No, not luck.' He paused a moment to drain his glass. 'Luck is little more than a superstition. It is simply a matter of recognising patterns.'

'Well, there's only one pattern I can see and that's you winning every hand.'

Mussel squinted his beady, bloodshot eyes like two yellow and red marbles at George. 'That's a pretty damn suspicious pattern if you ask me.'

'If my style of playing bothers you so, go play against someone else.'

'Oh, I'm playing.' Mussel folded his thick arms across his chest. 'I'm not watching you walk off with every last penny I have.'

'I'm still in too,' whispered the sandy-haired man.

'Very well. You call the game.'

'Whist. You deal,' Mussel snapped at the sandy-haired man, who cowered a little in his seat, although he reached out one trembling hand towards the cards scattered on the table nonetheless. 'I'm going to get another drink. I'll try to get the carpenter to come and play again.'

The table shuddered as Mussel wrestled himself out from his seat in the corner and rose unsteadily to his feet. George held up his empty glass by the base towards Mussel, who clenched his fist and spat on the floor in the opposite direction to George as he marched straight past him.

As the sandy-haired man began to shuffle the deck, the door to the public house opened. The man who entered was a tall, graceful figure shrouded in a purple cloak, which flowed down to his feet and hung in two rows of rippled pleats around his shoulders. Through the folds of silk one could see that he wore tight-fitting, narrow leather trousers, which clung to his legs like a second skin. His heeled leather boots reached halfway up his calves. On his head, tilted at an odd angle, was a plum-coloured velveteen flat cap with a plume of speckled feathers and two looped strings of pearls on one side. Seeing his eccentric costume, the drinkers nudged one another and leant their heads together, talking in hushed whispers. Many broke out into wheezing laughter that was hastily checked when the second man entered after him.

He towered over every other man in the public house in stature and presence, looking as if he could take on every man in the room all at once. He was a marvel of physical perfection with exquisitely sculpted features, like a Greek statue made flesh. Here was Narcissus or Adonis dressed in a black frock coat, his curling waves of golden hair shining forth.

With movements so fluid that even the slightest step commanded dignity and testified to the aura of grace that seemed to envelop him, he followed the first gentleman as he waltzed up to the bar, cutting directly across Mussel's path. The gentleman began to ask the barman, without much success, if he could direct him to a street on the fringes of Soho, oblivious to the giant man stood silently glaring at him.

'Oi, you there,' snapped Mussel. 'I was here first.'

The gentleman blinked his pale silvery eyes at him, one hand pressing against his lace collar. 'Sir, I find your manners most offensive. I will be courteous enough to overlook your language on this occasion, but you must show due consideration when addressing your social superiors.'

'My *what*?' A purple vein stood out against Mussel's greasy forehead.

'My what, *my lord*,' corrected the gentleman, fishing a silk handkerchief from the ruffles of lace at his wrist. 'I am Lord John Josephus Leyton, the Earl of Banbury, and so I expect you to wait your turn.'

'I don't care who you say you are. I won't be pushed aside by a fop like you.'

The man in the black frock coat placed himself firmly between his master and Mussel.

'*Move*,' Mussel growled at him.

The man made no answer.

'You deaf? I said *move*.'

'And what will you do if I refuse?' he said in a hushed, silvery, yet commanding voice.

Mussel clenched his huge, hairy fists. 'Then I'll make you.'

'That is not wise,' the manservant replied.

'Oh dear,' the sandy-haired man swallowed beside George. 'That'll be enough to set him off for sure.'

Mussel snorted and charged at the manservant, who remained stock-still in the face of this seething bull. With one deft movement of his arm, he flipped his attacker over and brought him crashing down through the nearest table. Glasses and bottles smashed onto the ground, sending the drinkers scattering and the nearby barmaid screaming. For a moment the inhabitants of the room remained motionless and open-mouthed. George widened his eyes very slightly but made no other show of amazement.

Mussel groaned weakly. The manservant straightened the collar of his coat and flexed his leather-clad fingers.

'That will do, Bellamy.' Lord Leyton waved his silk-gloved hand and turned to the bartender. 'I assure you I will pay for any damages, sir.'

The bartender made no reply. His glance flitted back and forth between the manservant and the man spread out on his back. One of Mussel's huge feet twitched.

'Th – that won't be necessary, your lordship,' he stammered. 'No harm done, no harm done.'

'What sort of wine do you serve?' the nobleman asked, flicking a lock of his pale, flaxen hair away from his eye.

'We have sherry.'

'Good lord,' sighed Lord Leyton, shaking his head as he stuffed his handkerchief back down his sleeve. 'That will suffice. We might as well remain a while, Bellamy. It will be something of a novelty and I am so bored by the talk at the Athenaeum. All they discuss is politics now. It is dreadful to hear.'

'Mrs Delcott is expecting you to dine with her at eight, my lord.'

'Oh yes, I had forgotten about that. Now you have brought that to my mind I am even surer that I wish to remain here.'

Once Lord Leyton had been served his drink, Bellamy carried both it and his cap while he scouted for a table. Gradually, as the talk and noise resumed their normal level, the man who had been sitting at the organ took up his position again and jauntily rattled his fingers along the battered keys.

‘I must say,’ Lord Leyton said, as he looked around keenly, ‘this place has a certain charm to it, in a quaint sort of way. Imagine what my father would say if he knew how often I frequent such places – it would finally put him in his grave. I am certain he only remains alive to prevent me having his dukedom and estate.’

George’s table had the misfortune of being the one he approached.

‘Pardon me, gentlemen, I happened to notice you are playing cards. Would you mind if I were to join you?’

‘N – no, your lordship,’ squeaked the sandy-haired man, hastily rising and bowing before the nobleman. ‘You would honour us by your presence.’ His eyes glided over the god-like man looming above him.

Lord Leyton slid into the place formerly occupied by the carpenter before the little man had finished speaking, the manservant having simultaneously relieved him of his cloak and placed a lace-trimmed square of silk over the seat the exact second before he sat down. George lowered his head and tried to keep his eyes on his cards.

‘What game is it you are playing?’ Lord Leyton asked, as he slid off his jewelled rings to remove his gloves, showing two long, lily-white hands beneath.

‘Whist, my lord.’

‘Ah, I must warn you gentlemen, I am quite the whist player.’ His thin lips flattened out into a smile but then he arched one pencil-line eyebrow. ‘But do you not already have two other players?’

‘Our third man is currently lying on the shattered table over there,’ said George, whose mouth was gradually losing communication with his brain and running freely on its own accord. ‘And we are lacking a fourth.’

‘Oh, I do apologise, gentlemen. I will compensate by putting your drinks on my bill. Bellamy here also happens to be a deft card player, although not quite as talented as myself.’

Bellamy switched places with George so that he was partnered with Lord Leyton and George with the sandy-haired man. (Neither of the latter objected to this breach of the rules as the nobleman upheld his promise to purchase their drinks for the remainder of the evening.)

Once the deck had been shuffled, it was offered to the manservant to determine the trump suit. Bellamy delicately reached out his gloved hand

and lifted the ace of hearts from the top of the deck between his long, elegant fingers. The sandy-haired man then dealt each player thirteen cards, Lord Leyton labouring to arrange his in a perfect fan. While he was thus occupied, George took the opportunity to examine his manner of dress. The lord wore a heliotrope and black fern-patterned frock coat with large lapels, lined with vibrant pink silk. Beneath was a white shirt and a violet waistcoat heavily embellished with embroidered flowers and silver thread, the silver buttons inset with diamonds and amethysts. A clump of lace engulfed his throat and the unnatural broadness of his shoulders was obviously the result of padding. His hair was parted down the centre and fell in natural waves, which just brushed against his shoulders; his delicate moustache was of the same colour and cast light charcoal shadows on his wan face. The darkness of his eyelashes and the rosiness of his hollow cheeks were most likely painted by a hand other than nature's own.

Bellamy led the first trick, laying down a five of hearts, which George followed with a king, both Lord Leyton and the sandy-haired man placing down a card of a different suit. George won the first two tricks for himself and his partner, but Lord Leyton and Bellamy won the next.

'This is so much more entertaining than sitting in some crusty old dame's house or going to Almack's as one is expected to do during the season. Thank God this year's season is almost at an end,' said Lord Leyton as he placed down the ten of diamonds and sipped his sherry. 'Watching those girls and their mothers hunt after eligible men is quite fascinating and the ensuing scandals are, I grant, rather delicious, but it is so repetitive. It is like watching the same play performed one year after another. The conversation is as stale as the cake and flat as the lemonade. They either talk about themselves or other equally uninteresting people.'

No one offered a response to this. The sandy-haired man thinned his lips and placed a two of diamonds on the table. George tossed down a card after Bellamy played his turn, then propped his elbow on the table and rested his head on the ball of his fist.

'And the gentlemen's clubs are even duller,' resumed Lord Leyton, as if they had answered him in the affirmative. 'The ones I know of are anyhow, of which the Athenaeum is probably the best. Most of them are filled with my brother's sort of people. They talk forever about politics, social reforms or the East India Company. No, the only subjects really worth indulging are those of beauty and the arts. Everything else is meaningless.'

His voice gradually became more affected as he delivered this soliloquy. The sandy-haired man trained his eyes on his cards although he was visibly bewildered. The first set of six tricks having been won by George, Lord Leyton claimed the second point so the score stood at one all.

'For all their talk of efficiency and progress, these industrialists are slowly sapping this century of its soul and vitality. Their senses are stunted to the more refined things in life. Instead they delight in watching a steam-driven engine pumping mindlessly round and round.' He spun small circles with his hand as he spoke.

George watched the nobleman's reflection flicker on the side of the glass mug beside him. It was half-filled with dark amber liquid. The weak beer wasn't producing the desired effect of subduing his hectic mind. One of his fingers absently drew symbols in the spilt foam that had dribbled onto the wooden table and dissolved to water – the solution to an equation some part of his mind was at work on without him being consciously aware of it. His brain felt heavy. It pulsed at each word that fell from the earl's mouth as if they were tiny hammers knocking against the walls of his skull.

'They are becoming more like the machines they worship all the time. They only value a Turner for the price attached to it with no notion of the elements of its composition or the feelings it can stir in one's breast. I say to them that, although they may spin cotton faster and better than a hundred workers, I would like to see a machine that is able to paint a better masterpiece or compose a more touching sonnet or symphony. That is beyond the reach of these great machine-makers, for they cannot replicate the very essence of the human soul and mind. No machine can ever possess imagination or creativity.'

'Wrong,' said George abruptly.

'I beg your pardon?' Both the earl's thin eyebrows and the pitch of his voice shot up. Bellamy brought himself up higher in his seat and his attention gravitated towards George. George saw the fabric on his shirt grow taut as his great, muscular chest expanded.

'My lord, I believe that there is no reason why a machine can not only emulate but also surpass man in every way, including in the arts,' said George evenly, keeping one eye on the manservant as he spoke.

Lord Leyton seemed to recollect himself and smoothed down the lace at his throat before speaking. 'What is your name?'

'George Abernathy, my lord.'

'Explain yourself, Mr Abernathy.' Lord Leyton twisted a lock of pale hair between his fingers and spoke in a calmer manner. 'You seem awfully affected by this matter. What makes you so sure?'

'I am a designer and builder of what you would call automata, although I believe that is putting it too simply.'

'An automaton-maker you say?' Lord Leyton's shining grey eyes stared intently at George. 'You know, I would never have guessed it from looking at you. You have the look of a physician or a banker about you. Yes, there is something about the shape of the brow, although the shape of the chin…it is rather a puzzle. I confess I am stumped by your countenance, and I pride myself on being an amateur physiognomist. Instinctively so, you might say.'

'To think you can read one's inner characteristics from their countenance is nonsense. But just about all phenomena, even what makes a piece of music brilliant, can be broken down into mathematical formulas and complex patterns. Quite easily in fact. It is simply a matter of unravelling them.'

'Well, I dare say *your* mind is very complex. You certainly have the air of a philosopher about you, and you build wind-up toys for a living, of all things.' Lord Leyton chuckled. 'Oh, how delightful!'

'That does not quite describe what I do accurately. To be more exact, I am in the clockmaking trade, but I also create machines that are infinitely more advanced than the clever puppets you have in mind.'

'Well.' Lord Leyton smiled, taking his eyes off George and picking up his cards once more, 'I have heard of human-like machines that can play musical instruments as well as a man. That is quite a well-worn phenomenon. There is little novelty in it nowadays. But I have never heard of one that could actually *write* music *and* perform it.'

'I believe one can. I even dare say I could create such a device myself.'

'I see.' Lord Leyton wrapped an end of his moustache around his index finger and the corner of his mouth slid into a smile. 'You mean that earnestly?'

'Yes.'

'Then how about we have ourselves a little fun?'

'What do you mean, my lord?'

'I mean a wager. If you are as clever a designer of automata as you say you are, do you think you could build me a machine that can compose music?' Lord Leyton raised his arched eyebrows.

'I have already said that I can.'

'And you are willing to put that to the test?'

George studied him intensely with his keen eyes as he deliberately placed the ace of spades upon the table, claiming the trick and the third point. 'There is no doubt in my mind.'

The sandy-haired man watched the exchange between the nobleman and the clockmaker with fascination.

'What would be the terms of this wager?' George continued.

'The terms are quite simple. I will give you until I am to return to London, which will be six months from now, to build the device. If at the end of that period you have managed to achieve such a feat, I will pay you an agreed sum. If you fail, you will pay me the same amount.'

'What sum?'

'How does forty pounds sound?'

'I will need materials.'

'Then I will add another ten pounds to cover costs, which I will pay you now in advance. If you lose you will owe me fifty pounds.'

'I don't intend to lose.'

The terms of the wager were drawn up on the back of the bill, which both men signed, the sandy-haired man acting as a witness. Lord Leyton then withdrew several bills from his purse, which, along with the slip of paper, George tucked into his pocket. Lord Leyton was visibly more animated, his eyes gleaming like polished platters and his cheeks blushing a rich red underneath their rouge. He ordered a fresh round of drinks with relish.

'A toast, sir.' Lord Leyton smiled as he raised his glass, eyeing George over the brim. ‘I sincerely hope you do not disappoint me. Either way, I will be most interested to see what you come up with.’

‘As I said, Lord Leyton,’ said George, as he raised his own glass, ‘I don’t intend to lose.’

Chapter Four

The surface of the worktable was hardly visible beneath the scraps of paper and metal covering it. The stack of dirty crockery in one corner was slowly spreading outwards too. Many of the diagrams and rough notes that covered the worktable were crumpled, torn and stained. Some were speckled or ringed with a faint brown substance like dried ink, more likely coffee. They spilled out onto the floor and formed a papery puddle around George's feet. Inky figures began to drift up off the papers in front of him and swim before his eyes. He blinked until they'd resettled onto their pages again, and rubbed his eyelids. How long had it been since he'd last slept? Possibly a day, or maybe two days now he thought about it.

He glanced at the prostrate form laid out on the long, narrow table behind him, now shrouded in grey cloth, as he just couldn't stand the sight of the damn thing anymore. A softened outline of it remained. George's eyes traced the rise and fall of the fabric. The deep caverns, folds and peaks were suggestive of a head, feet and limbs. He returned to the drawings before him and rested his chin on his fists, feeling the weight of many months' worry and sleepless nights pushing against his heavy eyes. There had to be a way to do this. Not that he had any doubt as to whether it *could* be done, of that he was certain. It was simply a question of time. The earl had given him six months and George had already spent five, along with most of the money the earl had supplied for tools and materials. The basic structure of the android was, at least, sound enough and when activated it performed according to his design.

Well, not quite.

George detected the sound of boots on the stairs, growing louder with each step. He recognised Douglas's footfall. The boots fell silent outside the door, followed by the tinkling of keys and then the begrudging grinding of tumblers. George didn't raise his head as Douglas entered.

'God Almighty, George!' Douglas covered his nose and mouth with his shirtsleeve. His eyes began to water a little. 'It smells absolutely horrendous in here! I dare say you're the source of it. Do you realise the state you're in?'

George raised his head and looked at his brother from beneath his matted black hair. His face, even paler than usual, had taken on an ashen hue and there were dark, purple-grey half moons beneath his bloodshot eyes.

'What do you want?' he asked hoarsely, twiddling a coiled spring between his fingers.

'Molly asked for matches and I thought you might have some.'

'Is that the feeble excuse you've come up with to finally come aggravating me?'

'No, although I must admit we're both becoming a bit concerned about you.'

'And I suspect Molly is listening at the door, is she?'

'She's in her room setting fire to her geraniums actually.'

'But I thought she needed matches?'

'Look, George,' said Douglas sharply, somewhat anxious not to lose face, 'since I'm here you might as well give me an explanation about what it is you've been doing, while you've locked yourself away from the world, and precisely what that covered-up thing is on the table over there.'

The two of them stared at each other from across the room. George found himself cornered. He drummed his fingers on the tabletop, hearing the papers crackling underneath them. At length he stopped, exhaled deeply and rose from his chair. He strode over to the table and began to peel back the cloth, teasing off loose threads, which had become attached to odd bits of metal here and there as he worked. From the cotton cocoon emerged a skeletal figure, just under five feet in height and constructed almost entirely out of gleaming brass, the dense mass of cams and gears inside its head and chest fully exposed. Inside its head and abdomen was an engraved metal cylinder, and a pair of bellows was seated in the chest cavity.

'So this is what you've been working on all this time then.' Douglas leant over the dormant android. 'What is it meant to do?'

'It plays music,' said George stiffly, looking away. 'And not only that, it composes too. As good as Mozart or Beethoven, if not better.'

'George, do you mean to say that you've actually created a machine that's capable of creative thought?' There was a rising note of excitement in Douglas's voice.

'Yes, although its creative capacity is limited solely to musical composition.'

'Even so, think of the potential! George, if what you're saying is true, then this could be the first step to creating an android that possesses all the capabilities of the human mind, and who knows what else? Maybe even consciousness itself!'

'I wouldn't use the word "consciousness". That's something of a vague cover-all term, second only to the notion of the "soul". Still, I don't see why a machine possessing something approximate to sentience is such a hard thing to imagine.' George shrugged. 'After all, what is creativity when you boil it down? It's simply a matter of making connections between seemingly unconnected things. A human brain and nerves are not so different from a cam and a cam follower, something you should know all too well.'

'But you make it sound so simple!' Douglas scoffed. 'Then again it is you after all. *I* could never hope to better you,' he added sarcastically.

'Indeed you couldn't,' said George, as if Douglas had been sincere. 'But you're missing something even more significant.'

'What's that?'

'That *this* will be the thing that saves us.' George jabbed his finger in the direction of the android and spoke vehemently. 'With this machine, we will be poor clockmakers no longer but celebrated inventors. No longer will we have to slave away under this crumbling roof and waste our gifts mending simple pocket watches and clocks.'

'What are you talking about, George? Just what precisely do you intend to do with it?'

'Sell it. A considerably wealthy nobleman commissioned me to build it for him.'

'And just how did this commission come about? Not many wealthy noblemen happen to come into our shop. There must be more to it than that or else you wouldn't have kept it a secret for so long.'

George was mute.

'I'm right, aren't I? There's something about this nobleman.'

Douglas watched his brother's expression darken. George's hand delved inside his trouser pocket, producing a grubby, creased slip of paper. He held it out to Douglas, who plucked it lightly from between George's fingers.

'It was at the Duke of Wellington one night several months ago. I was playing cards with a few of the regulars when this queer-looking gentleman walked in. He and his manservant joined us. We made a wager between us that I could build a device capable of composing music and he paid me a sum for the materials. He said he would return in six months' time to see my finished effort.'

'And how much exactly did you bet? I can't make out the figure, it's been smudged a great deal.'

'Fifty pounds.'

'George, are you *mad*?'

'I wasn't exactly in an entirely sound state of mind at the time,' said George curtly. 'In fact I might not have remembered anything about it if I hadn't found that bill in my pocket the following day.'

'Oh, and then where would we have been when this nobleman of yours rolled up on our doorstep in his carriage to see his automaton composer?'

'Well, think us both fortunate that I did find it and that I've been slaving over the infernal thing for the best part of five months now.'

'Why didn't you tell me what you were up to? Not out of sheer pride surely?'

'I didn't want you interfering like you always do.'

'Oh, heaven forbid that I should contaminate your genius.' Douglas rolled his eyes. 'Will you at least permit me to hear it play?'

'No.'

'Why not? I'm assuming it works?'

George folded his arms across his chest. 'It can play.'

'How well?'

'Flawlessly.'

'In that case let me hear it.'

After a moment's hesitation, George pushed past Douglas and bent over the android. He produced an oddly shaped key and unlocked the rectangular panel in its chest, beneath which was a second keyhole. He flipped the key around and inserted its handle into the second slot. Winding it a couple of times, he resealed the panel. No sooner had he done so than they began to hear clicking and whirring sounds coming from inside the android, and watched the tiny brass gears starting to turn. Wheels and shutters sluggishly began to move. The bellows stretched out briefly and then folded in on themselves with something like a yawn. Soon the whole mass of machinery inside the android was wriggling about like a hive of insects and giving off golden shimmers in the candlelight.

The android's fingers twitched.

The hoods of its glassy yellow eyes drew back and it slowly raised itself to sitting. The pockets of tension released from the joints in its spine produced a rapid, creaky ticking. It blinked as it swivelled its head between the two brothers, its gaze settling on Douglas.

George rummaged through the mass of paper until he uncovered a violin and bow. He held both before the android. 'Play.'

Upon his command, the android gingerly curled its fingers around the neck of the violin and placed it against its chin, taking up the bow with the other hand. It rested the bow against the strings and, after an expectant pause, began to play. Its nimble fingers flickered along the strings, the bow darting jaggedly across them as the violin's warbling melody poured forth. Douglas knew it was Paganini, although he couldn't recall the number of that particular caprice. Yet he felt the renditions he had heard of it up until then to be diluted, clumsy imitations compared to the automaton's performance. It was as if the piece was in its pure, concentrated form, distilled straight from the composer's inner ear. The speed with which the automaton played was rather astonishing in parts, yet it also held the pauses at precisely the right time and played the softer sections very movingly.

When the automaton had finished playing and given a modest bow, Douglas could not resist applauding. 'Bravo! Well, George, I can't deny it played the piece exceptionally beautifully, but I confess I was expecting it to play something of its own devising.'

'You didn't ask for something original,' muttered George, his gaze aimed at the ground as he spoke. He fiddled restlessly with the key in his hand.

Douglas was quick to catch on. 'That's the problem, isn't it? It can play any piece of music set to it and it can choose a piece from its repertoire, but it can't compose music of its own.'

'But I don't understand *why*!' George exclaimed. Both Douglas and the automaton started as one. 'I have gone through every scrap of my notes and scrutinised every single part inside it, but I cannot understand why it won't perform as it ought to.' He sank into his chair.

'Will you permit me to look over your notes?' Douglas asked calmly.

With one sweep of his arm, George cleared the papers from the worktable; they came cascading around Douglas's feet. Rolling his eyes, Douglas gathered them up and sat down on the cold wooden floor. He remained there for some time silently scrutinising every last line of scribble.

'Incredible,' he breathed at last. 'Why, George, the design is absolutely flawless. I doubt anything like this has been conceived of by anyone before.'

'As I said, I have every confidence that there is nothing wrong with the design. It only took me three days to have it fully worked out. That's why I simply don't understand where the problem lies.'

Douglas looked at the automaton, which was tuning one of the strings on the violin. The machine's eyes met his own with a deep and, he reckoned, inquisitive gaze. He felt as if they really were looking at him as opposed to just following his movements. Had he not known better, he would have sworn there was a living, thinking intelligence operating behind them.

Douglas rose to his feet. 'Would you consider lending it to me for a little while? A second pair of eyes might help.'

'You might as well. I'm at a loss as to what to do with it.'

'I'll take all your notes as well. Maybe something will reveal itself in them after all.'

'Just tell it to carry the notes and follow you. It might be capable of thinking creatively but it is still bound to obey human commands.'

'Oh, in that case, *Could you gather up all these bits of paper for me, please*?'

The automaton promptly, but carefully, laid the violin on the table and did what Douglas had asked of it.

'How much time do we have before this nobleman arrives? Four weeks by my reckoning.'

'Three weeks, six days.' George's eyes fell on the automaton as its hand reached for a piece of paper trapped under his boot. It turned its face up at him, looking as if it was about to retract its hand when he leisurely lifted his foot. 'Do you know what it is you plan on doing with it?'

'Just leave it with me. You'll see soon enough. In the meantime, you can go back to mending clocks and pocket watches so we still have a roof over our heads a month from now. Oh, and George?'

'What is it?'

'Before you do anything else, make sure you have a wash and change your clothes. If any of our customers catch you looking and smelling like that it may drive them away for good.'

Douglas stood at the top of the stairs and waited for the automaton to appear around the corner. 'This way. Be careful not to trip.' Balanced precariously on its outstretched hands was a great stack of George's notes that reached to the ceiling, preventing the automaton from seeing where it was going without tilting its head to the side. The little cleaning machine had been following them and gathering up all the loose sheets that strayed from the pile. Douglas had the larger rolls of paper under his arm and held a candle in one hand to guide the way to his room. When he paused on the stairs to relight the candle, he glanced up to find the automaton was lagging several paces behind him, examining its surroundings. It occurred to Douglas that it had never before ventured outside the workshop that, until that moment, had been its whole world.

'This must be all a little daunting for you, but it's quite all right. You'll soon adjust to everything. Come along, there's not much further to go.'

It made its way downstairs at a painful pace. Douglas would hear one of the floorboards make a long groan, then there would be a momentary pause before another one started. A great deal of time seemed to have passed before they finally reached his room.

'You'll have to excuse the mess, I'm afraid,' said Douglas, as he held the door open for the automaton. 'Set them down there.'

The automaton placed the stack of papers in the corner of the room that Douglas had pointed towards, and then looked about its new surroundings. Douglas pried the strayed sheets from the cleaning machine, which then scurried back upstairs, before shutting the door. When Douglas swivelled his head, he expected the automaton to be stood in front of him awaiting instruction, but he saw that it was near the window.

'Have you seen something of interest outside?' Douglas asked, as he approached the automaton from behind, even though the sun had just about set. But when he followed the line of its gaze, he realised that it wasn't looking at what was on the other side of the window. It was looking at its own ghostly reflection in the darkened glass. 'Oh, you've never seen what you look like before, have you? Hold on a moment.' Douglas went over to the chest of drawers by his bedside and removed the small, round shaving mirror that had come apart from its mount and was now lying on top of the chest amongst his other scattered possessions. After giving it a wipe with his sleeve, he held the mirror before the automaton. 'Look here.'

It twisted its brass head towards Douglas and peered intently into the glass. Then it laid one finger on the surface of the mirror and lifted its other hand to its face. 'My God,' Douglas breathed, 'it really does recognise itself.' He let the automaton take the mirror from him and watched in fascination as it turned its head from side to side so that it could examine itself from different angles. When it was finished, it handed the mirror back to him. Douglas's mind was in a whirl. The excitement grew inside of him until he laughed aloud. 'You might not be a composer yet, my metal friend, but you are certainly something special.'

The automaton only blinked its yellow eyes at him.

As Douglas replaced the glass, he caught the smell of something burning and saw faint curls of grey smoke slithering in from underneath the bedroom door. He burst out onto the landing to find it thick with hazy, charcoal-coloured fog. Pressing his sleeve over his mouth and nose, he flung open his sister's bedroom door, quickly shutting it behind him as he was instantly engulfed by a dense cloud of leaden smoke.

'Molly!' He stumbled into the room as the smoke attacked his eyes and throat. 'For heaven's sake, Molly—' He choked on his words.

'Hold on, let me try to find the window!' called a muffled voice that sounded a lot like his sister's. Not waiting for her to find it, Douglas fought his way through the smoke and made out the dim shape of the chemistry apparatus. Feeling his way along the table, and hearing the smash of one or two glass instruments that he knocked over, his hand groped along the wall until it landed upon the window pane. Once he found the latch, the smoke rapidly spilled out into the dark, dank night and dispersed. Relief washed over him as his lungs drank in the cool air. But when he turned around, the skin on the back of his neck bristled on seeing the hazy figure that was gradually materialising in front of him. It reminded Douglas slightly of a plague doctor. Its face was made of metal with something resembling an elephant's trunk in the middle of it. The trunk was attached to a leather bag on the figure's belt. It had two dark, glassy round eyes and no ears. Only when it yanked down its leather hood, there was something very familiar about its mane of bushy, light-brown hair.

'You shouldn't have just come barging in like that,' Molly cried as she tore off her mask. 'You could have been unconscious in a matter of minutes!'

'There was smoke coming from your room. What did you expect me to do?' demanded Douglas with a faint cough. 'I had no idea what had happened.'

'It was an accident. The rug caught fire but I managed to put it out right before you came in.'

'Really, Molly, I wish you'd be a bit more careful when you do things like this.' He furiously blinked his stinging, watering eyes to try to clear his vision.

'Well, it would be easier if I had a bit more space. This room is crammed full enough of my specimens already, and I don't have anywhere else in the house where I can do my experiments. You and George won't let me use any of the rooms downstairs.'

'Not after that incident with the explosive pollen.'

'I admit that was a very bad miscalculation on my part. I didn't expect them to spore that quickly – or as much. Or to blow the glass out of the windows – but I promise it won't happen again.'

'I would be willing to take your word for it, although this gives me reason for doubt.' Douglas pointed towards the floor. The rug was a blackened ruin and many of the floorboards were also badly charred. Standing not far off from them was a cracked flowerpot filled with bright dahlias, their spiky petals like little orange flames.

'But not *that* much of the floor caught fire. Besides, you knew that rug was a fake. It was a cast-off from the parlour.'

'Yes, but that's beside the point.'

'Well I'm just glad you're all right anyhow, and it looks as if it wasn't for nothing either. My experiment seems to have worked.' She knelt beside the dahlias and leant her head close to them. 'Not so much as a scorch mark on them,' she said delightedly, as she brushed her hand against their petals.

'You mean you've managed to make flowers that are fireproof?'

'Yes, although I'm thinking of trying it with trees next. It might be useful for construction and things like that. If we had wood that didn't burn, two hundred years ago, then the Great Fire of London might never have happened.' She beamed, brushing down her hands on her skirts as she got up off the floor.

'But what if you wanted to light a fire? It wouldn't be much use then.'

Molly opened her mouth to reply but suddenly stopped. She looked past Douglas and cocked her head to one side a little. Following her gaze, Douglas saw the automaton had followed him and was lingering in the doorway.

'So is that what George was working on all this time?'

'Yes, it's an automaton that can compose music.'

'Really? Can I listen?'

'Well, the thing is that it doesn't seem to be able to at the moment. I'm hoping to try to fix it.'

'Do you know what's the matter with it?'

'I might have an idea.'

'Which is…?'

'You'll see.'

'Humph, you're no better than George sometimes with your little secrets. You both always have to prove how clever you are.' She blew a wisp of hair out of her eyes, set her flowers on the table, muttering under her breath about all the broken glass instruments, and approached the automaton. She placed her hands on her hips and sucked her cheek as she contemplated it. The expression on her face was rather grave as she thrust her hand out at it. But when the automaton gingerly took it, a broad smile melted her stony look and she shook its hand.

'It does look a little funny,' she concluded, 'but I still don't understand why George was so determined to keep it a secret.'

'You know what he's like when he's caught up in something. If we didn't leave his meals at the door he wouldn't even think to eat.'

'True, but there's something different about this. I can feel it.' She looked up at him sharply, narrowing her eyes. 'You know what it is, don't you?'

'I don't know what you mean, Mol,' he returned, a little too promptly. What was the use in worrying Molly unnecessarily with the knowledge of George's predicament?

'You don't fool me one bit, Douglas. But I suppose I'll find out sooner or later,' she sighed, returning her attention to the automaton. For some time she picked and chewed her thumbnail in silence. 'Is that how it's meant to look or does the outside of it still need finishing?' she asked suddenly.

'What do you mean?'

'I'm just saying it looks a little, well, naked.' She shrugged.

'To be quite honest I hadn't much thought about that. I suppose

I could make it a casing for the outside.' He just managed to stop himself from adding, 'if there's time'.

The automaton had stepped over the threshold of the room and was prodding the leaf of a plant, which immediately curled inward on itself at its touch and the little purple flower heads fluttered along the stem. The automaton looked like it was going to try the next plant when, sensing the two pairs of eyes watching it, it instantly stopped and drew itself upright.

'Go on back to my room. I'll be there shortly.'

The automaton instantly obeyed Douglas's command. Its joints could be heard clicking as it moved along the corridor.

'It's a funny thing, that machine,' said Molly. 'And very curious I'd say.'

'You think so?'

'Well, it looked like it was examining that mimosa just then. Why, is it important?'

'George is beginning to have doubts about the machine and fears that it can't be curious. No more than a plant can.'

'Why can't it be? And plants are smart, y'know. They'll turn themselves during the day to capture more sunlight and their roots can dodge obstacles in their path as they spread. Take that mimosa over there – they even have a very primitive nervous system. I'm hoping to advance it along a bit. When they're touched, the electrical impulse is transmitted through the plant, from the leaf to the base, and then to the other leaflets, running along the rachis. This causes water to flow out of the cells at the base of the leaves, making them less turgid, so the leaves collapse. It means they're quite sensitive and shy little things.'

'Very well, I take it back. You're the expert after all.'

'Too right, I am. Now get on out of here and fix that automaton of yours while I sort all this out. I expect to hear it play as soon as you've got it working.'

'All right, as long as you promise to be a bit more careful in future.'

'I will,' she said inattentively, having just struck a match.

Douglas backed out of the door and shut it, shaking his head as he made his way to his own room. The thing was standing in the middle of the room looking up at him expectantly. Douglas ran his eyes over its stick-thin metal arms and legs. Its exposed innards were still visibly rotating and palpitating away beneath the thin brass caging that encompassed its torso. It was not really a dignified appearance for a musician.

'Molly?' Douglas stuck his head out of the door. It was only a moment before his sister emerged from her room. 'Do you remember that growth serum you were working on several months ago?'

'Yes, of course. I actually managed to perfect it in the end. In fact, that's how I was able to grow six batches of dahlias and geraniums all at once. Why?'

'Well, how fast do you think you'd be able to grow a maple tree?'

A grin spread over her face. 'Is that a challenge?'

Chapter Five

For almost three weeks Douglas kept the automaton hidden away in his bedroom and refused to let George see it. Instead he had to gauge from Douglas's smirking at him every time he passed him that he was on the right track. More often than not, however, George would lose patience and demand to know what exactly his brother was up to.

'You'll see soon enough,' was all he ever got in reply.

'But how soon? That rich fool will be here in less than a fortnight.'

'And when he does,' replied Douglas coolly, 'he will have to concede defeat to us.'

This was payback on Douglas's part, of course, for George's arrogance and for having been kept in the dark for so many months. He took a somewhat wicked delight in watching his brother wringing his hands and pacing the length of the house. Perhaps it would teach him a little humility – to not put too much faith in his own genius and accept the help and advice of others when he needed it. Then again, he knew George too well to hope for that. At least George had shaved and rediscovered soap and water. Not to mention that he was keeping the business ticking along while Douglas worked on the automaton.

On the night before Lord Leyton was due to arrive, Douglas told George to fetch a candle and follow him upstairs. The candle's feeble flame only devoured a small patch of darkness inside Douglas's room but George could make out great stacks of books, some towering up to the ceiling. He also caught a glimpse of their mother's small pianoforte, which Douglas must have taken back out of the pawnshop. George felt his shoe scuff against something and picked it up. Looking over the title of the battered book in his hand, *A Book of Nonsense* by Edward Lear, he threw it back into the darkness, which readily swallowed it whole.

'There.' Douglas raised the candle so the light shone on a figure seated on a chair at the far end of the room, facing towards the window with its back to them. The candle's flame was flickering precariously so the figure flitted in and out of sight, but George could make out chestnut-brown hair, probably a wig, with the ends curled into tight rolls. It was only when George took possession of the candle and got closer that he realised the wig was made of wood. Walking around the seated gentleman, George saw that it was a dummy with polished maple skin. It was dressed in an old-fashioned style, wearing a blue velvet coat, green waistcoat and grey breeches. Its feet wore wooden clogs. Only the hooded yellow eyes testified that it was, in fact, his android.

'I like your choice for the casing, maple like a violin,' said George eventually.

'I confess I may have used a little artistic licence.'

'But I doubt simply dressing it up like this will serve much purpose. The man might be a foppish fool, but it's unlikely this will convince him of anything.'

'I haven't only made cosmetic changes. Watch.'

Douglas took the key from his pocket and unbuttoned the square flap of material on the front of the automaton's shirt that concealed the panel. After he had wound it up, a ticking came from inside and the automaton stood upright. It started a little on beholding George standing there.

Douglas presented it with the violin once more. The automaton took its time composing itself. Finally, a tender, plaintive note was drawn from the violin, quickly followed by another and then another, the mood of the melody gradually lifting. It was as if each note were a silver bubble that rose and burst in the air in a shower of golden sparks. The violin was possessed of an ethereal voice that spoke to the very soul and seemed to come from somewhere beyond the material world in a language that was beyond words and was not quite music. Suddenly the song grew much more rapid in pace. The bow feathered across the strings with the utmost delicacy and the automaton's fingers flickered across the strings in a blur, hardly touching them. No human could have ever played with such speed or vivacity. It was unlike anything Douglas and George had ever heard before. The effect it produced on them was indescribable. George had the most peculiar sensation, as if something had gripped hold of his heart, which pulsed away erratically, while the rest of his body seemed to have dissolved away, leaving him floating adrift.

As the song was nearing a climax, it came crashing down again and melted into a slow adagio. The automaton let the last note fade away, lowered the violin and bowed. It was only as it rose that it noticed the bow was a shredded mess of horse hair.

'Well, George,' Douglas's voice quavered with stifled emotion, 'I'd say it works, wouldn't you?'

George failed to reply, continuing to stare wide-eyed at the automaton. Even when Douglas snapped his fingers before his eyes, and poked him in the arm, he made no response. He remained in this state for a minute or two and then all of a sudden his hand shot out and grabbed Douglas by the front of his shirt.

'What did you do? What was it I missed?'

'Nothing. All I did was simply provide him with inspiration.'

'Inspiration?' exclaimed George in disbelief, as he released his hold.

'Yes, you try working without it.' Douglas smoothed down his shirt. 'You said it yourself that creativity is simply about making connections between things, but this automaton of yours had no reservoir of knowledge that it could make connections from. What I did was open up the world to him. I showed him books and pictures not only about music, but also about history, nature and literature. I even managed to smuggle him into a music hall to see a performance there.'

'You mean to say that while I was at my wits' end, you were reading to it and taking it to concerts?'

'Correct.'

'Putting the matter aside of precisely *how* you managed that, you mean to tell me that you taught it all of this in the space of three weeks?'

'Yes. It only took him around a week to learn his letters.'

'You taught it to *read* as well?'

'Yes, he's a remarkably quick learner.'

'I notice you repeatedly refer to it as *he*.'

'Yes, I do. Your point being?' Douglas spoke in an insouciant manner calculated to irk his brother.

'My point being that it is senseless to ascribe a sex to an inanimate thing. It cares nothing for your choice of reference.'

'Well, you may disapprove of my choice of pronoun amongst other things, but you can't deny that I managed to achieve what you were unable to do. He has been churning out all sorts of wonderful and ingenious music this last week. What you heard just then was merely a prelude. There are scores of music here written in the android's own hand. And that's not all.' Douglas dipped down somewhere near the automaton's chair and rustled around in the dark. He retrieved a piece of paper. 'What does that look like to you?' he asked as he handed it to his brother.

'A child's crudely drawn ship,' answered George, as he inspected the drawing. The lines were irregular and the proportions far from accurate, but the basic impression of the drawer's objective had been achieved, even if they had not mastered adequate control of their pencil.

'The automaton drew it. From a picture he saw in one of the books I showed him.'

'Why did you make it do that? Did you mess around with its input system?'

'No. I didn't touch anything inside of it. I came upstairs one afternoon to find him sketching. At the time I thought he was writing down a score but then he got up, tapped me on the shoulder and presented me with the drawing.'

'But how could…?' George frowned at the automaton. 'Impossible. You must have done something to it. Did you alter the parameters of its mental capacity?'

'No. Not that I'm even sure whether I could do that…'

'Then either you're not telling the whole truth, or you drew this yourself to try to fool me.' George pushed the drawing at Douglas, whose hand mechanically reached for it while his mind was elsewhere. He laid the crumpled drawing aside and stuck his thumbs into his pockets. He held himself uneasily, thinning his lips and looking down at his feet. At length he took a long intake of breath and exhaled sharply through his nose as he worked himself up to speak.

'George, I don't think we should hand it over to the earl.'

'What do you mean? How could we possibly not do so? '

'I mean that, well, I don't think you realise exactly what you've created. He's more than just a mechanical composer. I truly think this android is unlike any of the other models we've constructed in the past. I believe that it actually has consciousness.'

'Consciousness? You are serious?'

'Deadly.'

'Why, just because you claim it drew a boat?'

'No, not just because of that. It's done other things too.'

'That it could operate beyond the parameters I determined in its design is inconceivable.'

'Can it not learn?'

'Not to such a great extent as that. This is all a mere fancy of yours. You are seeing what you wish to rather than what is really there.'

'But do you not see? When you look into its eyes, do you really not see it?'

'See what?' George looked the automaton hard in the face as Douglas continued speaking.

'When you look into the eyes of an automaton, even an advanced one, it does not look back at you. Even a bird does not look at you in the same way an intelligent creature would. But he's different. When you look into *his* eyes you feel there's really something *there* behind them. George, it's alive. Not just alive, but a fully self-aware, sentient being. Look here.'

Douglas brought out a slate that was leaning against a stack of books and held it before George. 'I've been using this to try to get him to communicate. I ask him a question and he writes a response. For instance, this morning I asked him, "Which instrument would you like to play for

Master George this evening?", and he chalked the word *violin*. Look, you can see it's right there.'

'That proves nothing. Clearly you suggested a desired response to it somehow and it was merely mimicking you. That does not prove that it can think for itself.'

'But sometimes he even indicates that he wants me to give him the slate because he wants to try to tell me something. Yesterday he pointed rather insistently at it and when I handed him a piece of chalk, he wrote, *Master, do not go out. Pieces are falling away from the sky*. You can see the faint outlines of the words underneath if you look carefully. I soon realised he was trying to tell me that it was snowing. How could I possibly have prompted him to do that?'

'A few faded words on a slate are insufficient proof to support your claim.'

'What reason would I have to lie about it to you?'

'I didn't say you were lying to me. I think that is what you truly believe happened, as misguided as that belief may be. Why not offer it the slate now and see what it does?'

'All right, you try asking it a question then.' Douglas exchanged the violin for the slate with the automaton and took a small piece of chalk out of his pocket. 'Go on, George. Try asking it something.'

'I'm thinking of something,' George snapped. He shifted his stance, causing the floorboards to whine weakly. He watched the automaton from behind the soft flame of the candle in his hand.

'Can one believe in a truth without evidence?'

The automaton stared down at the slate with the chalk poised. They waited for it to apply it to the board but it didn't move a fraction. Douglas repeated the question but still the automaton did nothing.

'That will do,' said George at last.

'I'm sure there is a reason for it.' Douglas retrieved the slate. 'Maybe it's because you deliberately chose an awkward question. But you said yourself that an automaton with all the faculties of a human being wasn't that hard to imagine. It's what we've been striving towards ever since we were boys. Why is it that when it's staring you in the face, you deny its existence?'

'Because, as I said before, this device cannot possibly achieve anything resembling human consciousness. Yes, the replication of consciousness is plausible but achieving it will take a great deal of further experimentation and research. This automaton marks a step towards that end but only one small, single step and nothing more. And as of tomorrow it will be the property of Lord Leyton.'

'So you would really let it go as easily as that?'

'Yes, I would. However, I will see to it that we get the technology patented. The designs for it will still be in our possession – we can simply replicate it.'

'I'm not so sure we could, you know, George.'

'There is no use talking with you when you are in a fanciful mood as you are now. I am done discussing the matter any further. As long as the earl is convinced that the automaton composer is genuine and gives us what is due, that is all that matters at present.'

'If you take the pragmatic view of things, I suppose you are right,' sighed Douglas as he looked across at the automaton, who was busily writing what was presumably the score to a piece of music. What was the use in trying to persuade George of anything? Although he knew his brother was right on some level, they had no choice but to hand the automaton over. 'I will admit I'm intrigued to see what this nobleman of yours looks like. The picture you painted of him was a rather eccentric one.'

'And quite accurate as you shall see for yourself. Now I'm going to bed. I suggest you do so too.' George made a motion to go, but then his step faltered. He stared at the automaton. 'What do you do about it?'

'About what?' asked Douglas as he sat down on the bed.

'I mean what do you do about it when you retire for the night? You only just wound it so it'll run for a good few hours yet.'

'Oh, I hadn't thought of that. Usually I make sure he's fully wound down before I go to bed. Well, how about we let him have free run of the house for once? He can go downstairs and compose without disturbing any of us.'

'I don't see why not.' George shrugged as he leant against the wall beside the doorframe.

'All right, you can go down to the parlour as long as you're quiet, but I know that won't be too difficult for you. Understand?' Douglas said.

The automaton nodded and sidled past George. They heard its footsteps creaking on the stairs.

'I'll leave you the candle. I have enough light in my own room.' George set the candle on the chest and turned to go.

'You know what I think?' said Douglas suddenly, as he crossed his leg across his lap and screwed off his boot. George paused in the doorway. 'I think you feel exactly as I do, but you just don't want to admit to yourself that you've really outdone yourself with this one. Building a clockwork composer? *Pfft* – too easy for *you*.' The boot whumped against the floor and he started on the other one. 'So part of you wanted to push further. And without realising it, you did – ' Off came the second boot. 'And now you don't want to admit to yourself that by this time tomorrow your greatest creation will be the plaything of some vain, pompous aristocrat.'

George looked at his brother a long while without moving. 'You may think what you want to, Douglas. But either way it changes nothing,' he said coolly.

'Fine.' Douglas lay back on the bed and rolled away from George, even though he had not begun undressing. 'You had just better hope he keeps his end of the deal and agrees to pay us then. Goodnight.'

'Goodnight.'

Although George didn't shut the door with a great deal of force, the candle still went out. The bedclothes rustled as Douglas sat up and groaned in the pitch black. He raised his head. 'Molly! Lend me a match, will you?'

Douglas heard the floorboards creak in his sister's room. Molly appeared at his door moments later, looking like a ghost in her nightdress. The light from her candle sharpened her angry features.

'I heard everything,' she said.

'Molly—'

She rushed into the room and thrust the candle close to his face. 'You're going to tell me what's going on right now.'

Douglas hastily explained.

She whacked him around the head when he'd finished. 'And you didn't think it wise to tell me sooner?'

'We were going to tell you everything in the morning,' Douglas protested. 'We didn't want to worry you.'

'I had every right to know that George has potentially ruined us! I'm not a child in need of protecting. Do you understand how significant this is?' she cried furiously. 'We could lose everything!'

'You don't have to remind me. It's been tormenting me these last three weeks. I wanted to spare you from the same torment, but you're right, we should have told you.'

'You'd better be bloody confident that George will win this bet.'

'He will. I have every faith,' said Douglas.

Molly cursed under her breath as she left. She repaid Douglas for keeping her in the dark by leaving him without a match.

Chapter Six

At eleven o'clock the following morning, a grand coach rolled up outside the shop. It managed to wedge itself into the narrow street, having just about enough room, so it almost touched the window casements of the houses on either side. Despite the weather being bitterly cold and the ground being glazed with ice, people still came out into the street to see what was going on. They made sure to keep a few yards away from the coach, as if mindful of the aura of greatness emanating from it.

'Oh Lord.' Douglas widened his eyes and grinned as he and George watched from his bedroom window. 'I see you weren't exaggerating in the slightest, George.'

The fair man descending from the coach was clad in a crimson coat with a fur trim and a broad hat. Another man who was taller and dressed in a black coat, which made his golden locks of hair shine all the brighter, closed the coach door after him.

'Yes.' George smiled faintly. 'And he seems to be causing quite a commotion.'

'Well, I suppose we had better go greet him.'

The two of them swiftly made their way downstairs and glanced in at the parlour. They had tried to make some effort to prepare it for the earl's arrival. The room had been swept and dusted early that morning and the windows cleaned. Molly was absorbedly arranging a bowl of her brightest flowers on the table, frequently trying to stop their heavy heads diving headlong over the edge of the shallow crystal bowl. Standing in the middle of the room was a white shrouded form, like a ghost.

'I still think the cloth is unnecessary,' said George.

'It adds a touch of drama. From what I can tell of this gentleman, I think he will appreciate a bit of showmanship.'

'Hmm, perhaps.'

Molly raised her head. 'Is he here yet?'

'His coach is outside now.'

She ran past them out of the room and hollered from the shop, 'Good Lord! Would you look at that?!' before bounding back into the parlour. 'I don't have to stay, do I? I mean, I am curious to see what he makes of the automaton, but I don't really see the point in my being here. It's not like I have anything to say to an *earl*.'

'You can watch and listen from the hallway, Molly if you think you'd feel uncomfortable,' Douglas offered.

'I just don't want to sit there like a statue the entire time he's here.'

'Might I be so impertinent as to mention that he has knocked twice on the door this last minute?' cut in George. Douglas and Molly paused to look at him.

The next instant Molly flitted into the kitchen and Douglas rushed past George into the shop and wrenched the door open.

'Ah! Good morning, sir. I was beginning to fear I had the wrong address,' said the strange, sumptuously dressed individual who stepped into the shop, his servant following behind.

The soft, heavy scent of violets wafted towards Douglas, as he stood there stupefied. Quick to recover his senses, he bowed and said, 'We are terribly sorry to have kept you waiting, Lord Leyton.'

George joined him and made a very brief, stiff bow.

'Oh, it is no trouble,' replied the earl offhandedly, as he removed the dark, blue-tinted glasses he wore and shook his wan hair free from his hat. A small sapphire dangled from his right ear like a crystalline teardrop. 'I always find it amusing to mix with the lower orders of society, granted one is not close enough to be able to smell them.'

The rings on his fingers blinked all the colours of the rainbow as he brought his hand up to his face and smoothed back his hair. Beneath the glasses, his silver eyes gleamed brightly and a strange, excitable expression illuminated his pale face. His comportment was dignified, with his chin slightly raised. His movements were refined and suggestively self-conscious, as if he were watching himself in a mirror.

'You must be the other brother.' His eyes landed on Douglas while George closed the front door to shut out the blatantly curious gaze of their neighbours, although the crowd outside was beginning to dwindle away now that the coach had driven on. Snow was starting to fall in thick clumps.

'Mr Douglas Abernathy at your service, my lord.' Douglas smiled, bowing once more.

'How charming.' Lord Leyton knocked back a wisp of hair with his long, thin fingers, which were clad in mulberry-coloured silk gloves. 'And it is good to see you again, sir.' He looked over his shoulder at George, who was standing hunched over with his hands in his pockets. 'Although I dare say you are a lot less…high-spirited than the last time we met, shall we say?' His laugh was shrill.

'Maybe so,' said George sullenly. Douglas shot him a warning look.

'But all these pleasantries aside, I must ask whether you were successful. Do you actually have something to present to me?'

'If you would please come through to the parlour, my lord,' said Douglas with a sweeping gesture. 'I think you will be most satisfied when you see the product of our efforts from these last six months.'

They led the way to the parlour, with Lord Leyton exclaiming how quaint and charming everything was. 'These blossoms here, what are they?' He peered at the bowl of flowers on the table and lifted a petal with one gloved finger. 'I don't recall ever seeing flowers such as these. And they smell positively divine! Like the scent of rose otto.'

'They are a unique variety our sister created, my lord. They adapt their scent to each individual's own preference.'

'How exquisite! I think I should like to meet this sister of yours.'

'I am afraid she is out at the market, Lord Leyton.' Douglas's eye flitted towards Molly, who was concealed in the doorway to the kitchen.

'Oh, that is a shame. It would have been interesting.' He smiled, crestfallen, as he seated himself in their mother's armchair and declined tea when Douglas offered him it. Douglas subtly shook his head at Molly, who was dangling the copper kettle at him from her vantage point.

'So where is the automaton you promised me?' Lord Leyton raised his thin eyebrows at George. 'I do not see it anywhere, unless it is hidden beneath that sheet over there.' He pointed to his right and slid his eyes along the length of his finger.

'Ah! Why yes, there is indeed something hidden beneath the cloth, my lord.' Douglas smiled artfully. 'As you will soon see.' He positioned himself to the side of the shrouded automaton and cleared his throat. Lord Leyton crossed one leg over the other and supported his jaw on the fingers of one hand, his elbow resting on the arm of the chair.

'Lord Leyton,' Douglas grasped one end of the cloth while George took hold of the other end, 'may I present to you the world's first and only mechanical composer.'

They whipped away the cloth to reveal the dormant automaton beneath.

'Oh, my word!' Lord Leyton instantly sat upright, clasping his hands together and pressing his fingertips to his smiling mouth. 'That is it? Oh, it is a curious sight to behold!' He rose and examined the automaton from all angles, sporadically bursting into shrill, delighted laughter.

The brothers opened the panel in the automaton's chest and gave a heavily diluted explanation of how it worked, which Lord Leyton listened to with a glazed expression even though he directed his gaze towards them the entire time. 'I confess I only understood a fraction of what you just said, most of which I am likely to forget,' he said, as he resumed his seat and took a pinch of snuff. 'However, I shall reserve judgement until I have heard it play.'

'Of course, my lord.' Douglas signalled to George, who wound up the automaton. There was the usual second's delay before a shudder ran over its body and its eyes shot open, now fully animated once more. Lord Leyton made a sound that was somewhere between a squeal and a gasp, seemingly transfixed by the way the automaton moved, with a fluidity approximating a human being.

Upon realising there was a new gentleman in the room, the automaton bowed politely in the visitor's direction and then looked at Douglas enquiringly.

'This gentleman is here to listen to you perform,' said Douglas gently. 'Would you play him a couple of pieces of your own on the piano or the violin? You can play whichever and whatever you choose as long as it's your own.'

The automaton dutifully sat down at the pianoforte (which Douglas and George had had considerable trouble getting downstairs earlier that morning). It carefully lifted the lid but then just held its fingers suspended over the keys. Douglas's heart bumped against his ribcage. He didn't breathe in the intervening silence. It was impossible to gauge George's feelings from his face, although his attention remained riveted on the automaton, which still hadn't done anything. Was it broken? Douglas wondered. What on earth would they do then? At length, the automaton closed its eyes and let its hands drop to the keys. The notes fell, soft as white snowdrops, and then swirled up into the air from the pianoforte. The tension inside Douglas evaporated in an instant. Even though he knew to expect it by now, it never ceased to amaze him how the automaton's playing took possession of the listener's entire being. The melody was unspeakably mellow and tender without being too sombre, although it still caused one's eyes to water involuntarily. Douglas looked across at Lord Leyton, who was similarly entranced. His face wore a dazzled expression and he had one hand pressed over his heart. The second melody imperceptibly melded into the first, strikingly different as it was in tone and tempo. Jangly and disjointed in places, with frequent pauses, it was much, much faster. It sent the blood racing and nerve ends throbbing as if every part of one's body came into a life of its own. It took all of Douglas's self-control to restrain himself from being carried along with the music, which commanded him to dance, as if a million imperceptible little strings had been looped around various parts of him and repeatedly tugged. At one point the overwhelming energy that had been charging his limbs almost spilled over, and he caught himself as his body was about to lunge forward. He had to content himself with tapping his foot.

'That's enough,' said George abruptly. From the strained, slightly flushed look on his face, Douglas wondered if he had been similarly afflicted and in danger of losing control of his own body. George shot Douglas a dark, clouded look. The ragged rhythm ceased and the automaton closed the pianoforte, rotating itself before its audience.

'Would you care to hear it play the violin as well, my lord?' Douglas asked. 'It can play just about any instrument, but those are the only two we have.'

'No,' returned Lord Leyton breathlessly. 'No, I think that will do for the present moment.' He lifted himself from the chair and walked in a trance-like manner towards the automaton. On perceiving his approach, it gave a swift but handsome bow and blinked up at him.

Lord Leyton spoke in a faint whisper. 'I have seen that it is only wood and metal, and yet…' His voice faltered. 'And yet the effect its music has, how it touches the soul, is such that one would only have thought it possible of a mortal being! Why, it is utterly impossible!' he cried.

Douglas felt a stab of panic, fearing the worst.

Then Lord Leyton let out a shattering laugh. 'Impossible, and yet it cannot be denied!' He clasped his hands and turned to face George. 'Sir, I concede defeat to you. I am fully convinced that there is no trickery involved and that this automaton not only creates music but possibly the most divine music I have ever heard!'

Douglas's shoulders sagged with relief.

Lord Leyton spun back around to the automaton, whose hands he seized in his own, and cried out, 'You are going to be a sensation, my mechanical marvel – yes, *mine*. Oh, that I could ever possess such a wondrous thing as this! Bellamy,' he addressed the manservant over his shoulder, 'please see to it that Winston has brought the coach around. I said he was to be back within the hour.' He released the automaton's hands and addressed the two brothers. 'Gentlemen, I cannot tell you enough how overjoyed I am that you have provided me with this machine of yours – but can he be called so? It does not seem an adequate word to describe him. What pleasure he shall bring me and how he will serve to while away the weary hours! You can be most certain that I shall see to it that all of London knows who is responsible for this marvel. I shall sing your name to every person of significance.'

'And my winnings, sir?' said George.

'Oh yes, of course.' He snapped his fingers and Bellamy placed a purse into his waiting hand. He pulled out a great wad of bills and handed a number of them to George.

'But Lord Leyton,' said Douglas, craning over George's shoulder as he counted the notes, 'there must be three times the promised sum here.'

'Shut up,' George hissed out of the corner of his mouth.

'Take it. I would gladly pay four times the original wager for it,' said Lord Leyton, as he beamed at his new acquisition.

George opened his mouth, but Douglas elbowed him in the back.

'And I hope that we shall become better acquainted over the course of future commissions I may have for you.'

'Oh, uh, that is very kind of you to say, Lord Leyton,' Douglas faltered. But the nobleman's eyes were already cast down and his hand hovered over the bowl of flowers. 'I say, would your sister mind terribly if I were to have one of these for a buttonhole?'

'Oh no. In fact I think she would be most delighted to be favoured by such a great personage as yourself.' But when Douglas caught his sister frowning at him darkly, he simply held his hands up in apology as the nobleman plucked one of the flowers from the bowl and fixed it in his lapel. It was best not to refuse any request the earl made.

Having now secured his purchase, the delighted earl bade the automaton follow him to his coach where the manservant was unfastening the trunk attached to the rear.

'Leave it, Bellamy. He shall ride alongside me.'

'Yes, my lord. As you wish.'

Lord Leyton called to the two brothers, as Bellamy handed him into the coach, 'I will be sure to show him off at the earliest opportunity. He will be the talk of the season!'

The automaton tentatively attempted to mount the coach steps and lost its footing on the first rung, eventually managing to pull itself up once Bellamy had taken charge of the violin, which it carried under one arm.

'Adieu, dear gentlemen!' Lord Leyton cried with a wave.

Once Bellamy had also entered the coach, the driver yanked on the reins of the four handsome horses, two black, two white, and the brothers watched from the shop doorway as the coach rolled on down the road and turned the corner.

Douglas held out his hand.

'What?'

'There's no chance I'm letting you hold on to all of that money.'

'I think you'll find that it was my name on the wager, therefore I am entitled to hold on to it. Besides, what does it matter who keeps it? You're as equally entitled to it as I am.'

'Yes, but I don't trust you not to spend a considerable portion of it on drink.'

'You should know I wouldn't be as reckless as that,' said George indignantly, as he took the bundle of bills out of his pocket and rapidly spread them out in his hand. They smelt faintly of violets. 'You will only waste an equal amount on parts for whatever those designs in your room are for,' he said, as he held out a portion of the bills to Douglas.

'Well, since he did pay us three times what was owed, I say we split it three ways. You do what you please with your third, I the same with mine, and Molly can have the remaining third. How does that sound?'

'That is reasonable. And if you must know, I don't intend to spend every penny of my winnings at the public house. It would be put to better use funding our projects.'

'I agree with you there,' said Douglas, as he tucked his share of the money into his trouser pocket. But as he looked towards the horizon, he sighed. 'I can't believe it – our greatest achievement just driven away like that.'

'Might I remind you that I was the one who technically built the machine?'

'Oh, all right I'll give you that. But still…' Douglas trailed off, not knowing how to finish. He shrugged instead. 'I only wish I'd had a bit more time to properly study him.'

'The android or the earl?'

'Which do you think?'

'Well, Lord Leyton is something of an interesting study. He is definitely a peculiarity.'

'I can't disagree with you there.'

'Besides,' George added, after a brief silence, 'if he does intend to show it that can only be good for us. It will get our name out in the higher circles of society.'

'Hmm, I hope so,' said Douglas, although without a great deal of enthusiasm.

George went inside. Inquisitive neighbours were threatening to approach. Casting one last glance in the direction the coach had driven away, Douglas let out a sigh and followed him.

Chapter Seven

The automaton watched as the two small figures, one waving and one looking down, slowly shrank to almost nothing in the distance. The coach turned the corner onto a busy street and he gazed with wonder at all the buildings and things he had only seen in books or been told about by Master Douglas. The far-off building with the tall point on top of it he knew to be a church, and he recognised some of the different kinds of shops. The uneven rhythm of traders' cries, children's shouts and horses' hooves clashing against the cobbled road built up into a bewildering tumult that made his head spin. A little round man in a strange hat stood on a street corner playing an accordion. Children were running along the street and dodging in and out of the streams of people, although some were sitting on the edge of the road or on the steps of houses. He studied them with great interest. A small one glanced up at him as the coach rolled past.

Absorbed by the spectacle before his eyes, the automaton leant his face closer to the window, when he found himself being forcefully jerked back by a large, black leather hand. The view of the street abruptly vanished behind a purple curtain.

'We can't have anyone seeing you. Not yet,' said the gentleman, reclining in his seat opposite the automaton with his hands resting on his lap. Master Douglas had explained to him the previous day that he was to have a new master and go live with him in his big house. When the automaton had scribbled *Why* on the slate (which he realised was still in Master Douglas's room), a change had come over Master Douglas's face. He had rubbed his neck and said, 'Because it was for this gentleman that you were built. It's all very complicated. But tomorrow he will be your new master and you must do whatever he asks of you. Understand?'

The automaton had nodded to show that he did and he had not asked any more questions after that.

The coach veered sharply to the right and the automaton held onto the side to prevent himself sliding down the seat. The gentleman opposite managed to remain almost perfectly stationary and continued to look at him rather peculiarly. His grey eyes sparkled brightly and his mouth was curled into a smile as if he anticipated something extraordinary was about to take place at any moment. The other man in the black frock coat was a lot more solemn-looking. He had one leather hand on the violin.

'Do you want your instrument? Bellamy, give our maestro his violin.'

The servant, for that's what the automaton reasoned the man in the black coat was, leant forward and held the violin out to him. A ripple of light from a gap in the curtain slid along the violin's polished face and then fell across his own maple-skinned hand.

'And the bow, Bellamy. Don't say that it isn't here.'

But before the gentleman had finished speaking, the automaton had already positioned the violin against his chin and had begun plucking the strings delicately with his fingers. (Master Douglas had once told him that the pads of his fingertips were leather to make them more sensitive, as wood or metal would have been too heavy to handle the instrument with any great degree of delicacy.) He made up the tune as he went along without a great deal of thought; it was enough to distract him from the gentleman's ever-present gaze. Gradually, the notes began to slide into a jaunty rhythm, mimicking the chaotic clamour going on around him outside. But the violin's harmonious chords seemed to unify them and provide some sort of backbone to the disjointed rhythm of everyday life beyond the coach.

'Oh, it seems he does not require the bow after all. What a pretty little tune.' The gentleman clapped both of his hands together, his voice and face rising with irrepressible delight until a high-pitched noise burst from his lips. 'To think that you really are mine – the world's first and only clockwork composer!'

His eyes fell upon the violin, which now rested on the automaton's lap, and he waved his hand in a dismissive gesture. 'You will not have to be content with that old violin for much longer once we reach your new home. I have a surprise in store for you that I think will be much to your liking. Oh!' he exclaimed, as the coach bumped to a stop. 'It appears we have arrived at last!'

The servant opened the door on his side of the coach and glided to the ground. The automaton heard the crunch of gravel as he walked around the back of the coach and opened the door on his master's side. Extending a leather hand, he assisted the gentleman to alight. Tightening his hold on the violin, the automaton shuffled himself along the seat and cautiously planted one foot on the coach step, a little unsteady on his feet, as he had one hand on the violin that was tucked securely under his arm. He dropped down from the bottom step and landed with both feet on the ground. The coach door was shut behind him and it rattled on.

He found himself in the middle of a circular courtyard, a gravel island amid a sea of green grass. Before him was a huge house, which easily dwarfed the other buildings around it. It was the same colour as piano keys, with white columns between the windows on the third storey and a roof like an isosceles triangle. There was a stone man on the highest point of the triangle and two smaller statues at the other two points, with a balcony running around the roof. The windows on the top floor were the tallest and narrowest. They too were topped with triangles like they were wearing small, three-pointed hats, and each had a balcony. One long balcony ran along the squat windows on the second floor. The windows on the ground floor were slightly different. They were oval-shaped on top.

A servant in black with a white front and white hair stepped forward and bowed before the earl. 'Welcome home, my lord,' he said in a whispery voice, as he straightened, 'although we did not expect you to arrive until—' He stopped. His eyes boggled at the sight of the automaton, which was hovering behind his master, hunched over the violin, which he held protectively in both arms.

'My business was concluded early, as you can see here.' The earl beamed with delight at the automaton once more. 'He is an automaton, which both plays and composes music. Is that not remarkable? I had him built especially for me by two rather extraordinary young men.'

'Indeed, my lord.' The servant rose to his full height, without taking his eyes from the automaton. There was something in the hard line of his mouth and his dark eyebrows that the automaton did not like a great deal.

'Everything is all right with the house I trust, Gilbert?' continued the earl.

'To tell the truth, my lord,' Gilbert stammered, 'since we did not expect you until later in the day, there are one or two things that are yet to be made fit for your lordship's comfort.'

'I trust my own chambers are ready at least? And that most of the rooms have been made clean and had fresh-cut flowers put in them. No lilies?'

'There are no lilies in any of the rooms, my lord. And most of the house has been cleaned and made presentable.' Gilbert followed his master up one of the two stone staircases on either side of the entrance, which led into a reception hall. In two neat columns on either side of the doorway were more servants, each bowing or curtsying as their master passed by them. Yet when they caught sight of the automaton, as he stood in the mouth of the doorway, a wave of unnameable emotion struck them, like human dominoes. Many gasped aloud, one girl turned as white as her apron, and some even neglected to pay their respects to their master as he passed, not that he noticed as he was firing questions at the unfortunate Gilbert.

Bellamy breezed past the automaton, his appearance also having an observable impact on the servants, although of a different kind. All turned their eyes reverently towards him, and many of the women turned red (as did one or two of the men). The automaton decided it might be wise to remain close at his heels. He looked timidly up at the servants' faces as he passed them, quickly darting his head away when he saw that their gaze had once more reverted to him. He took in the hall around him. It was all grey-beige stone with a black and white tiled floor, which was arranged in a rather eccentric pattern. A crystal and gold chandelier winked above him in the mild daylight. He could hear the soft, delicate tinkle of the lustres. On his left was a staircase with a stream of purple carpet trailing all the way down the middle of the steps.

'I trust that my furs were accounted for as I asked? And my silk robes?' persisted the earl, as Bellamy relieved him of his fur-trimmed coat. 'The last time I made the journey to London only three of them followed me down.'

'All five made the journey unscathed, I personally made sure of it.'

'Good. Don't you be going off anywhere, Bellamy. I may want you for something yet. As for the rest of you, you may return to your work. Oh, and Gilbert?' He called the man back with a twitch of his finger as the other servants began to disperse. 'I intend to hold a little soirée tomorrow night for a few close friends, and I'll require a decent dinner to be prepared, the good wine to be taken out of the cellar, and fresh linen in all of the guest rooms.'

'Entertaining so soon, my lord?' Gilbert's eyebrows shot up. 'But we did not receive word—'

'Well, I have already sent out the invitations, Gilbert. It would look rather ridiculous to retract them now! Oh, just bring out a few bottles of the good claret and the rest will take care of itself. And as for *you*, my maestro, yes, do not linger there like a shadow! Wait until you see what a surprise I have in store for *you*.' His shrill voice rang with excitement across the hollow hall and he waltzed over to the staircase on his nimble feet. 'Come! Come along! I am absolutely dying to show it to you!' His coat-tails flew out behind him as he mounted the first step, sliding his hand along the glass banister, which had gold leaves, snakes and flowers entwined around it. On the railings were golden winged figures and animals. The automaton tentatively raised one foot onto the plush purple runner that smothered the echo his wooden feet had been making on the hard, tiled floor. He rubbed his foot experimentally against the fabric, his acute ear detecting the wood rubbing against the thick material. It was very fine indeed. Turning his attention to the banister, he reached out his hand and stroked its smooth, transparent spine.

'Come along! Do not dawdle!'

The automaton was bumped from behind and almost tripped over the next step as the manservant pressed his hand on his back.

'Now, Bellamy, don't be rough with the poor thing. He is nowhere near as strong as you are.'

'Forgive me, my lord,' said the man in hushed tones like a spring breeze. 'I will try to exercise more restraint in future.'

'But enough delaying, let us get on!' The earl flew up along the staircase, the automaton matching the rhythm of his footsteps to his master's light, quick step. The manservant progressed slightly ahead of them with fluid strides, seeming to glide along effortlessly. The walls were crowded with oil paintings of noble-looking gentlemen and ladies.

They climbed to the second storey and passed by a series of sumptuous and elaborate rooms, which the earl named as they went along. 'This is the morning room, the drawing room, the smoking room (although I abhor smoking, it ruins the wallpaper), the reading room...'

Some aspect of each room, be it the colour of the walls, carpet or furnishings, was coloured purple. There was a lot of black too. One corridor they passed through was lined with black marble statutes. There were all sorts of exotic-looking treasures too: richly worked tapestries, huge chunks of glittering stones, stuffed animals and many, many paintings. In one of the rooms there was the white and black striped pelt of a slain animal spread out over the black marble floor in front of the fireplace. A mirror bordered in an ivory, flaky, swirling frame was hung above the mantel. In another room the walls were papered with a pale pink wallpaper covered in painted trees budding with pink flowers, and a number of vibrant birds were perched on their branches or swirled about the treetops. There were huge blue and white vases with long, scaly blue creatures painted on them, and screens covered in birds and trees and buildings, as well as funnily drawn people in odd robes.

'The Chinese room,' remarked the earl as they were passing through it. 'The decor is something of an anomaly compared to the rest of this wing of the house, but it had the most exquisite wallpaper that I simply couldn't bear to cover. Ah! Here we are, the music room!'

Before them was a white door. The earl wrenched the crystal handle and flung the door wide open. 'Well, my wooden friend, what do you think?'

The automaton blinked. His feet shuffled across the wide, circular rug that covered most of the floorboards. He stood in the middle of the room, gazing every which way, wide-eyed. The room was filled with instruments of every variety. A slender, elegant golden harp stood in one corner and a black grand piano in another. There was also a cello, a silver flute and several instruments he had no names for. Some did not even seem to bear a resemblance to instruments he was familiar with. One of them, a rectangular, slightly convex piece of wood with strings running along its length, lay on the floor near the back wall. Above the mantel on his left was a painting of a young woman in a loose white gown with a bright blue shawl draped loosely over her elbow, trailing down to the ground, and a wreath of flowers entwined in her hair. She was standing in a garden, one arm resting on a stone block with a gold flute in her hand. Her other hand brushed against the scroll lying on top of the stone. With a dreamy expression, she gazed to her left at something beyond the picture's frame. The automaton turned his eyes to her and wondered who she was to have had someone paint her portrait.

He dimly heard the earl say, 'Bellamy, go make sure my chambers are in order. I will remain here with our mechanical maestro a while,' as he drifted from one instrument to another.

After the manservant's footsteps had died away, the earl waltzed into the centre of the room and threw his arms out wide, as the automaton continued to gaze around, seemingly stupefied. 'This is for your use whenever you like.' He then flung himself into a chair, crossing one leg over the other, and watched the automaton with a rapt gaze.

The automaton approached the harp first and, after carefully setting his violin down on a chair, ran his fingers delicately over the strings.

'Oh, do try some of them out. Please do!' the earl exclaimed. The automaton blinked at him and then sat down on the little stool before the harp. Glancing up briefly at the earl, who was watching him with acute anticipation, he stroked the strings, which came alive under the coaxing of his fingers, and began to sing with a heavenly sweet voice that caused the earl to pull out a silk handkerchief and dab his eyes with it. Gradually, he worked his way around the room, moving from one instrument to the next. Despite never having laid hands, or even eyes, on most the instruments he played, it was as if he had practised them for years, and each performance he gave was flawless and often startlingly original. When he came to the cello, he even lashed and beat the bow across the strings, or simply beat the back of the cello itself, producing a strange, deep twanging sound that rumbled through the cello's belly. One moment he would be sliding the bow along the strings in a relatively conventional manner, and the next he scantily struck the strings in quick succession in a most extraordinary, erratic manner that reduced the bow to a tattered mass of hair, prompting the earl to exclaim, 'My word,' and leap up a little in his seat each time the instrument was struck. The earl became more and more enthralled with each performance the mechanical man gave, crying out, 'Marvellous! Wonderful!', and clapping frantically.

Last of all, the automaton tried the piano. Having lifted its glossy hood, he could not help pausing to look at the pristine ivory keys. He pressed down on a key and the note rang out sharp and clear. His hands hovered over the keys and the joints clicked as he slowly opened and closed his fingers. The earl drummed his own fingers on the underside of his chair. With a final quick wriggle of his fingers, the automaton sent them dancing across the keys with a flourish, and a torrent of music poured out. The earl started violently in his seat. This piano was different to the smaller one the automaton had played at the old house; the sound was much more bold and powerful. But after a while, his fingers failed to keep up with the music that came tumbling from his mind. He felt as though his mind and body were becoming slower and more sluggish by the second, his fingers striking wrong notes until they had all but seized up completely. He fell heavily to one side onto the piano, and was just able to prop his arm to break his fall, although the sound that came out as his arms struck several bars at once was dastardly and went right through him. How heavy his body felt – he could scarcely support himself much longer.

'What is wrong?' cried the earl, starting to his feet and dashing over to him. Yet the automaton, being no stranger to this sensation, managed to crank his head in the direction of his master and make his trembling finger point at the gentleman's coat pocket. It took the earl a moment to realise why. He put his hand into his pocket and pulled out the automaton's key.

'Oh, but of course! You are in need of winding up!'

The earl opened the flap in the automaton's shirt and, after initially inserting the wrong end of the key on his first fumbling attempt, wound it round several times. The automaton instantly felt the wheels inside him begin to turn more quickly until all his parts were moving at their usual pace. His movements became fluid and easy once more. He raised himself upright and, after a quick flex of his fingers, finished the piece he had been playing with relish.

'That was most fortunate indeed!' exclaimed the earl, as his hand flew to his own chest. 'We must be careful not to let you wind down, my wooden friend. I want you to be in perfect working order tomorrow night, for I intend to show you off to my closest friends. None of them will have seen anything quite like you before and, since they are well-connected people about the town, no doubt word about you will soon spread. You will be the highlight of the season!' So overcome did the earl appear to be by this prospect that he immediately sank into the seat that the automaton had just vacated and let out a lengthy sigh, although his face was glowing. He gave a little toss of his head, flicked a lock of hair away from his forehead, then looked down at his hand, which still held the key. 'Oh yes, I forgot to put it away.'

The automaton watched as the key disappeared back into the coat pocket before the earl rose to his feet and swept across the room. 'I will leave you to play with some of the different instruments,' he said, as he laid his hand upon the crystal door handle. 'I am expecting great things from you, my mechanical maestro.' Casting one last look at his prized possession, with a shrill, silvery laugh the earl shut the door behind him.

After the sound of the earl's footsteps had died away, the automaton remained standing upon the rug in the middle of the room. He looked about him and blinked at the instruments. For his own use! He could play and play as much as he liked, that is what his new master had said. He looked from one to the other, not entirely sure what to do or what to play first. Instead, he found himself drawn to the window, which looked out onto a busy street at the rear of the house. Roofs and trees and chimney tops crowded his vision. Beyond the stretch of lawn and the tall iron railings that guarded the grounds of the house was a road filled with carriages and pedestrians. Evening was just beginning to descend. The sky was a pale blue, melting into yellow in the distance. Sunset. Like he had seen from Master Douglas's window, only the sky had been pink and blue and orange then. Everything else about this place was so different, perhaps the sunsets were no exception. How strange it all seemed. Yet if this somewhat peculiar gentleman were to be his new master, then he would do just what Master Douglas had told him to and obey his wishes. Turning away from the window, he went back to the piano and stroked the keys with a touch that was gentler than the brush of a dove's wing. The yellow sunlight laid its golden fingers over the keys also. Where they caught the automaton's hand, they brought out the grain in his maple casing. He pressed down on one of the keys and let it resonate. It seemed to express the mood of the evening rather well.

Presently the sound of footsteps retuned, only a heavier tread than the earl's or the manservant's. A female servant entered carrying a small wooden table.

'His lordship says you will be needing this,' she said, as she set down the unusual-looking table. When she drew back up to her full height, she looked at the automaton, shook her head and muttered, 'I'm talking to a flaming wooden doll,' before she went out again, locking the door.

The table had a protruding slanted top, supported by two curving columns, and four drawers down one of its sides, inside which the automaton found paper and writing materials. He assembled these on the tabletop and took up a clean slip of paper. But when he dipped the pen into the ink and let it hover above the paper, his teeming ideas seemed to vanish. His mind was as blank as the paper. He had wanted to capture all the sights and sounds that had caught his attention while he was in the coach earlier and translate them into music. But how was he to go about doing it? After trying out one or two things on some of the instruments, he finally settled on an idea and set about writing down the score. He sat and composed for hours until he was summoned by the earl, by the means of a butler, to come play to him while he took supper.

As he laid aside his pen, and followed the servant, the automaton took one last glance at the instruments and at the painted woman with the flute before the room was shut up behind him. Perhaps, he thought to himself, as he was led back through the sumptuous rooms, perhaps he should like having the earl for his new master after all.

Chapter Eight

The following morning the house was filled with activity. The automaton wandered about the many rooms and hung around on the great staircase, where he observed the commotion. Every which way he turned, servants were scrubbing floors, washing windows or dusting surfaces.

Maids hurried in and out of bedrooms with towers of fresh bed-clothes in their arms. Down below, he could hear voices quarrelling in the kitchens and the clattering of cooking utensils. Master Josephus, as the earl had asked to be addressed, had said he was expecting a party of around eight ladies and gentlemen to arrive in the evening. He had explained it all to him while he was opening letters in the morning room, even though it was past midday and Master Josephus showed no intention of changing out of the purple silk robe he was wearing.

'And *you*, Maestro, will be performing for them,' he said, pointing at him with the tip of the silver letter opener, which had a purple stone set in its handle. Since Master Josephus often referred to him as *Maestro* or *My Maestro*, the automaton had taken it to be his name. A smile spread across Master Josephus's thin mouth as he stretched out languidly against the back of the sofa. 'I will call you to the drawing room after dinner. They will have quite a surprise waiting for them. Oh, I cannot wait to see the expressions on their faces when they behold my mechanical wonder!'

Having eventually resolved to dress, Master Josephus had gone out to buy necessities for the occasion, accompanied by the servant, Bellamy, whom Maestro had ridden with in the coach the previous day. Since he found that the door to the music room had been left unlocked, he was at liberty to roam wherever he chose. Even though he was eager to experiment with the instruments and some of the new ideas he had come up with during the night, he found it somewhat stifling being confined to the same room for hours on end. Besides, his acute hearing had detected every scuffle and clatter going on below and above him, and he was curious to know the origin of the cacophony of sounds. He was certain Master Josephus would not mind his wandering about – after all, he had said to him that he should go in search of inspiration and he was certain that he should find it in this enormous house with all its goings-on. Many of the servants were far too absorbed in their tasks to notice him much. The one or two who did observe him, however, underwent a visible change in their behaviour and would momentarily stop whatever it was they were doing to look at him. Maestro would attempt to bow politely before them, but this did not appear to be the correct thing to do as they always jumped and then hurried away. By mid-afternoon he had decided to try to avoid the servants and keep to the parts of the house where it was quieter. His acute ear would alert him to any human presence nearby and he would alter his position accordingly.

Maestro wandered onto one of the balconies on the second floor where he took out a few slips of paper from his coat and scribbled notes as he listened to the birdsong. A small brown bird landed on the black railing right next to him. It twitched its head to one side and seemed to watch him with its little black eye. But when he raised his arm towards it, it instantly flew away. Soon after that, he tucked the paper back into his coat and turned indoors, determining to explore the other rooms on the floor. His head was still whirring with birdsong as he gently pushed open the door leading to the next room and happened upon a maid who was busily polishing silver with a cloth.

She did not hear him enter at first, but when she lifted her head to find him standing in the doorway, she gave a violent start and knocked several items of silverware from the table, which clattered onto the bare wooden floor with a harsh sound.

He had started at the same moment as she. He should have expected that he would startle her. How thoughtless he had been.

The maid automatically stooped to retrieve the fallen silver, continuing to keep her head down as she rose and fanned the objects out on the table with a noisy blatter, her hands trembling. Maestro noticed something winking at him from near the table leg and saw she had missed a teaspoon. Slowly he made his way towards it, hearing the soft shuffle of his wooden feet along the plush carpet. The maid watched him all the while. She looked as though her heart was thumping a lot quicker inside her chest. Meeting her gaze, Maestro bent to pick up the spoon between his fingers, his joints creaking faintly as he brought himself back up to full height. The maid's face was hard and white as alabaster, the mouth set into one line as if it had been chiselled straight across. When he held out the teaspoon towards her, she recoiled from it as if it were a lit matchstick. With some confusion, he withdrew the spoon, but as he did so, his eyes landed on the fork that was teetering on the edge of the table. Even with his quick reflexes he could not stop it from diving headlong towards the floor. Grabbing a wine glass, he managed to catch it just before it hit the ground, sending out a *ching* sound as the fork's teeth bit the glass. But the moment he had shot out his arm to catch the fork, the maid had let out a small cry and run out of the room. Maestro stared after her, cocking his head to one side a little. He carefully set down the spoon and glass on the table and turned his attention to the vase of flowers sitting in the window bay. He examined the red flowers whose name he did not know and tried dipping his index finger into the water. The wood that had been submerged was a lot darker when he drew it out again. A little drop of water like a liquid crystal trembled on the end of his finger and then fell back into the vase. He tapped his finger on the glass and it made a very blunt sound. He ran his finger around the rim of the vase but the crystal hardly made a sound. An idea struck him. He carried the vase over to the table, lifted the flowers out a moment and dunked the wine glass into the water. He filled four more glasses and transferred the liquid between them until he got the pitch just right. Wetting the leather pad of his fingers once more, he ran his finger over the rim of the wine glasses and they sang out beautifully. His fingers danced across the glasses with astonishing speed. The water inside them juddered slightly from the movement. Suddenly, he heard approaching footsteps, which he recognised as Gilbert's. His suspicion was confirmed when he heard Gilbert call out, 'Sarah! Sarah! Aren't you done with the glasses and silverware yet?'

Unsure what to do, Maestro swiftly retreated to the adjoining room and closed the door so it was only ever so slightly ajar. He watched the man burst into the room. His eyes boggled as he took in the sight of the glasses upon the table. He scratched his white head and put his other hand onto his hip.

'What the blazes? Does she think she's here to lark about? At a time like this? I'll have her guts for garters when I get hold of her.' With those words he marched out of the room. Maestro crept back into the room and looked down at his makeshift harmonica. Perhaps if he were to put things back as they were, then the maid might be spared the house steward's anger. He poured the water back into the vase and carried it over to its seat by the window. He dried the glasses on his coat and mopped up the small ring of water on the table left by the vase, replacing the glasses in the exact positions they had been before he had interfered with them. Once all was put right, or at least as much as he could manage, he went out of the room and turned in the direction of the music room. As he made his way along the corridor, he saw another maid with a tower of bed things piled high in her arms. He could hear the rustling of the fabric on her clothes, the brittle stream of breath she was emitting and the heavy tread of her boots. Master Douglas had told him his hearing was a lot better than that of most humans. 'Where you hear the world come alive, we hear almost nothing at all.' When the woman, the same woman who had brought him his desk the night before, craned her head around the side of her load and saw him, she stiffened and then bustled straight past him with great haste.

He stayed in the music room until the sound of Master Josephus's high voice rang out from below and he presently arrived at Maestro's room, the manservant carrying a stack of parcels and boxes behind him.

'Oh Maestro, wait until you see what I had made for you. I had a servant take your measurements while you were wound down this morning. Pray forgive me, I thought it necessary to take such a liberty – but *look* at these!'

From one of the boxes he produced a coat of deep peppermint green and from another a purple striped waistcoat. 'Aren't they divine? Imagine how you'll look in them before the party tonight!'

Maestro was imagining it, although he doubted the image he had in his mind was quite the same as that in his master's.

Late that evening, Maestro detected the talk and laughter of a number of people down below as he stood waiting in the music room. He reckoned there were seven or eight people, a mixture of bass, tenor, falsetto and soprano voices. His master's rang out high above them all. After some time, a servant conveyed him to the drawing room and bade him stand on the rug before the hearth. He was still standing there a quarter of an hour later, listening to the ticking of the clock behind him, which was out of synchrony with the sound coming from the machinery inside of him. He could feel it vibrating against the inside of his chest casing. Maestro tapped out a tune with his foot, his fingers moving behind his back as if they were strumming invisible strings. He studied the details of the room but did not dare move from the spot. The walls were covered in a dark blue wallpaper with a fern pattern and adorned by several pictures in gold frames. There were two long yellow and cream sofas facing one another and an odd assortment of chairs before him. His harp and cello had already been brought down from the music room, and there was also a small piano in the far left corner of the room. He twisted his head around to look at himself in the mirror above the mantel. Master Josephus had looked ever so pleased when Maestro had been dressed in the new coat and waistcoat, along with a pair of breeches to match the coat. A light green silk bow was tied under his stiff collar. Maestro still wished he had been allowed to wear his blue coat, or just any coat that wasn't so...loud. As the clock chimed eleven times, voices and footsteps advanced along the corridor outside towards him, Master Josephus's clambering above the rest. He suddenly bade them hush until their whispers and titters died away.

'Now, now, my dears, pray be quiet a moment. What awaits you in here is a wonderful marvel that I picked up near Soho – no, not like that, Hugo!' A gentleman's snigger had started up, ceasing almost as soon as it had begun. 'Goodness, what a child you can be sometimes. No, this is something quite different altogether, and nothing of *that* nature as you shall soon see. For I have in this room the world's first and only clockwork musician *and* composer.'

The door burst open and Master Josephus appeared, dressed in a dark blue coat paired with a slightly darker waistcoat, both decorated with gold embroidery. It was very similar to the wallpaper. He wore a large cream-white rose on his lapel and a black and blue striped necktie. He turned his head in profile towards the door, showing the gold star that had been painted near his left eye, and waved his hand, on which sparkled a large yellow stone.

'Come, come! Do not be shy. My dearest friends, I present to you – ' he threw his arm out towards the automaton ' – *the mechanical maestro*.'

Maestro detected the loud rustling of fabric as the company entered the room, each gaze becoming instantly riveted on him. Maestro bowed politely. For a moment there was no sound but the ticking of the clock, the rustling of fabric and a gurgling noise that Maestro recognised as the sound humans make after they have taken nourishment. A small, rosy lady in white and pink made a shrill yelp and leant on the arm of the gentleman beside her, her gloved hand flying to her mouth. She blinked and then let out a high, trembling laugh.

'Oh! It moves like a real person! I thought it would be all stiff like those machines I once saw at a waxworks show when I was a girl.' She detached herself from the gentleman's arm and peeked over Master Josephus's shoulder. There were even streaks of pink in her fluffy white-blond hair, which hung in little rows of curls around her face, and was woven with pink flowers, bows and butterflies. 'Is it dangerous, Cephus?'

'It is nothing worth screaming about,' said the tall gentleman with light grey hair and a square face whom she had been linked to. 'I have seen automata like it many times before. A whole orchestra of them and a monkey that could hang from its tail and play a drum. You could have sworn they were real living creatures until you got closer to them and saw their faces were pasteboard or wood and utterly dead. After watching them a while, you grew to notice how there was something not quite right about their movements. Their timing would be slightly off, or they'd be a little too stiff and jerky. Then the illusion was swiftly put to an end. I have seen that show played out many times before.'

'Not like this you haven't, Basil!' interjected Master Josephus. 'Pray, please sit down all of you. Maestro here is going to give us a little performance in a short while, but please take a moment to look him over, just to settle any doubts you may still have.'

'Is this a trick, Cephus?' asked another young gentleman with a smile, who was the only one of the guests to remain standing. 'I know how fond you are of deception.'

'You have my word, Gregory, this is no trick. I had him built by two rather interesting young men. He is the genuine thing.'

'How do we know there isn't a boy or midget stuffed inside that thing?' continued the man, pointing his glass at Maestro.

'That *thing*?' Putting the hand that wasn't holding a glass on his hip, Master Josephus gave the blond gentleman a long look and raised his chin as he thinned his lips. 'Humph. Very well, Gregory, I will answer your scepticism.' Master Josephus slid his hand into his pocket and held Maestro's key aloft. Placing his drink upon the sideboard, he strode up to Maestro and opened the panel in his chest to expose the whirring clockwork inside. His guests gasped and leant forward as one, some of them adjusting their monocles or spectacles.

Master Josephus waved his hand. 'You will observe that there is no trickery involved and that he is indeed purely mechanical. Surely you will all agree that not even a small dwarf could fit inside there? There is no human intelligence communicating with him anywhere.'

'What about through the floor?' asked a curly-haired gentleman. 'There could be wires or pipes controlling him from underneath the floor.'

'Very well, Theodore, I will show you what a ridiculous idea that is. Stand on one leg, Maestro.'

Maestro did as his master bade him, and then switched legs when commanded to do so.

'Now, are you convinced?' said Master Josephus with a conceited smile.

'Nor is he connected to thin strings through the ceiling as Hugo suggested earlier, or by magnets as Eliza suggested. He runs entirely on his own.'

'Oh, do get on with it, Josephus!' snapped a woman with heavy, dusky eyes and skin the colour of walnut, only far smoother. Her rich, bronzy voice rose and fell in places where one wouldn't expect, her vowels longer, and the quality of her voice was a lot more nasal. 'If you mean to have it play for us, let it,' she continued, languidly sweeping back her cascade of loose dark hair and causing all her gold bangles to slide down her arm, making a dry chinking sound.

'But it is all merely good showmanship,' said the man called Basil with a hoarse chuckle. 'One must warm up one's audience first before the main show. It builds anticipation.'

'It builds irritation, you mean,' the dark lady muttered sharply into her glass.

'My dear Christina, you are absolutely right. I have dilly-dallied far too long. In which case, Maestro here will play a short piece on the cello that he has composed especially for your pleasure.'

Master Josephus lowered himself onto a plush chair nearby and tossed one leg over the other, his hands folded in his lap. 'Please begin when you are ready, Maestro.'

Maestro moved over to where the cello was standing and bowed before the company, who watched him with looks wavering between curiosity and suspicion. Maestro sat down behind the cello. He made sure that the instrument was properly tuned and took up the bow. Someone swallowed in the brief interval and he heard someone else drumming their fingers on their glass. He drew the bow across the strings, adjusted his seating position, and then swiped it across the strings in a similar fashion to what he had done before Master Josephus the previous day. The music soon built up as he played faster and faster. The company gasped and drew themselves up as they watched. Maestro's arm was a flurry of green as the music continued to build in a torrent of ecstasy. The dark lady widened her eyes and pressed her hand to her straining chest. Then, when it seemed to reach its climax, the music stopped. The next time he played, the music was a lot slower and more tender. Instantly the guests' looks softened and tears rolled down their cheeks –

but they seemed wholly unaware of them, transfixed as they were by the automaton. When he ceased to play, they cried for an encore and after he had played again the cello and then the piano, they beat their hands together with such vivacity that Maestro feared their finger bones might snap – human fingers were a lot easier to break than his brass ones after all.

'Incredible!' exclaimed Theodore, the curly-haired man. 'I declare I have never heard anything like it!'

Maestro gave a bow and looked across at Master Josephus, who was beaming at him broadly with flushed cheeks, their colour genuine on this occasion.

'Such speed!' cried Theodore.

'No human could hope to play that fast.' Master Josephus smiled.

'Wasn't that good, Basil?' The pink and white lady beamed as she tugged at the gentleman's arm. 'Wasn't that the most splendid thing you've ever seen?'

'I think your cousin is made of stone, Rosemary,' remarked Gregory, 'for he appears to have been rendered insensible.'

Rosemary's cousin did indeed appear to be in deep thought as he stroked his square chin. At last he cleared his throat and spoke gruffly. 'Well, I'll admit that was rather something, Cephus. But you have yet to convince me that it is what you claim it to be. I mean, how do we really know that machine composed the music it just played for us?'

'Oh, but it must have done,' said Rosemary. 'Like Cephus said, no human could have played that fast.'

'Yes, but it doesn't mean that a clever human composer could not write an impossible score that the machine could then play.'

'Oh, I quite agree,' said a gentleman with fuzzy orange hair and a rust-coloured beard. 'In fact I know of several such pieces that are said to be impossible to play, many by that great unnamed Renaissance composer—'

'Oh, you are no fun, either of you!' cried Rosemary in dismay, curling her bottom lip like a tiny rosebud. But the next instant she uncurled it, appeared to ponder something a moment, and glanced up quizzically at her host. 'But he has a point, Cephus. How do we know that he did make up all those little melodies by himself?'

'Rosemary, you have my word that all of those wonderful melodies come from his very own head.' Master Josephus glided over to the lady and took her gloved hand. 'Why, he has been up in the music room composing all day long.'

'Then how *does* it do it? Compose music I mean.'

'Oh, well...it's a rather complicated business. All to do with cylinders and such things. The two young men I mentioned explained it all to me but to be quite honest with you, I failed to absorb the best part of it.' Master Josephus waved his wrist vaguely.

'Now that I do believe,' Gregory laughed. 'I never knew you to fix on one thing for very long, Cephus.'

Master Josephus raised his long index finger and said something in a language Maestro did not understand. All of the company laughed at the remark, however, save for Gregory, who merely smiled tightly. Some of the guests, apart from Basil, approached Maestro and scrutinised him with their eye-glasses, some even going as far as to raise his arm and move it about. But when he actually moved it himself most of them flinched and then burst into laughter, even though there was a quaver of some other emotion underpinning the sound. They laughed and danced merrily as the clock went round. They must have been terribly thirsty from all the dancing for they all drank many glasses of sparkling fluid. Some asked him to give them a little demonstration and he of course obliged them. The gentleman named Gregory swaggered up to him and dared him to put a tune to Rosemary, like a musical portrait. The gears inside Maestro instantly began to whir around rapidly and after a minute or two he played a chirpy little piece on the violin, which all the company said was very pretty and an ideal likeness. For her part, the young lady bopped up and down in her seat as her little hands fluttered rapidly in applause. While all of this was going on, Basil, after remaining motionless a while, got up and sat beside Master Josephus.

'That machine of yours is quite miraculous, Cephus,' he said in a low voice that went unheard by all but Maestro.

'Indeed, is he not the most miraculous thing you have ever beheld?'

'You should exhibit him, you know. People would pay good money to see him.'

'Oh, and I suppose you'll propose that *your* theatre be the venue?'

'I said no such thing, Cephus. Yet, if you *were* to consider showing him, of course I would—'

'You might as well save your words, dear Basil. I will part with him on no account.'

'Not even for, say, three nights? I would see to it that he was taken care of. Think what a sensation it would generate!'

'And how much money it would generate.' Master Josephus looked him squarely in the eye. 'I have known you since you were an unknown actor scraping for parts as an understudy, Basil. I know your agenda.'

'But you said yourself that you intend to show him to the whole of London, my dear friend.' Basil leant closer to Master Josephus. 'What better way than on the stage of one of London's most promising theatres? There will be journalists and all manner of people there.'

'People of significance?'

'Undoubtedly. And besides, don't you think it is what your musical maestro over there would want? What musician does not desire to perform before a great audience?'

'Well, truth be told, I had not thought of it in that way before.'

'Cephus! Of course your maestro would want it! If he were built to perform, well, why do you hinder him?'

Master Josephus continued stroking the yellow stone in his ring with his thumb. 'Three nights you say?'

'Three nights, three performances. You can come backstage as often as you like to satisfy yourself that he is being looked after properly.'

'Oh very well, Basil.' Master Josephus sighed. 'But mark my words, I will hold you accountable should any harm come to him.'

'I will treat him as my own.' Basil placed his fist over his heart. 'I shall even take out insurance on him, against any unfortunate accident.'

The two gentlemen then shook hands.

It was past midnight when the company retired to their rooms and Maestro was conducted to his. He stood before the music-room window gazing up at the yellow moon that was half-hidden behind the cloud, thinking about what Master Josephus had said, that he was to perform on the stage of a theatre. His musings were interrupted when that familiar feeling of stiffness closed in on him once more. As he wound down, a dim thought floated through his head that maybe it was something akin to human sleep.

Chapter Nine

Two nights later, Maestro found himself inside a very large building, although not quite as large as Master Josephus's house. He remembered a music hall that Master Douglas had taken him to once – this building was much like that only it was far larger and grander, and he was seeing it all from the other side of the stage. All manner of people were constantly coming and going around him. He heard the chatter of their voices, but he saw hardly anyone as he was made to wait inside a place called the dressing room for a very long time. After that, they brought him to stand on the wooden stage behind a deep-red curtain with a lot of ropes dangling above. He had his new violin held firmly in his left hand and his bow by his right side. His maple had been polished until it shone with a glossy sheen in the candlelight. Master Josephus had had his tailor make him another new coat and waistcoat that were both red with gold thread. He thought this suited him a lot better than green and purple, although he had been careful to stow his old garments away in his room, tucking them safely inside the grand piano. There was a lot of noise coming from the other side of the curtain, but when he tried to peer underneath it, setting his instrument down first, he felt himself being pulled back by the collar. He looked down at his feet, which were dangling about a yard from the ground.

'Keep away from there,' said a gruff voice behind him. He recognised it as belonging to one of the huge men whom he had seen pulling the ropes. 'Bloody thing, it's a joke that they're letting it on stage at all.'

'Mason! Put it down this instant!'

That was Mr Basil's voice. Maestro's feet re-established contact with the floor.

Basil was red in the face as he marched up to the man. 'You hear that?' He jabbed his finger towards the curtain, from behind which seeped the clamour of the audience. 'That's a sold-out house that has paid to see this thing perform, and if you damage it, then we will have to reimburse the cost of the tickets, part of which will be made up of your wages. Is that clear?'

The man scowled and looked down. 'Sorry, Mr Griffin,' he muttered, and then strode off, the boards creaking heavily under his boots.

'Damn sailors, no class about 'em, not any of 'em.' Basil sniffed, clicking open the lid of his pocket watch. 'Five minutes. That fool, Cephus, reckons you'll understand just about anything I say to you, so listen closely.' Basil dragged Maestro into the centre of the stage by the arm, picked up the violin and thrust it at him. 'Don't move from the middle of the stage and don't start playing until the applause has stopped, got that?'

Maestro nodded, but Basil had already turned his head to bellow at the other men managing the ropes. He then disappeared, leaving Maestro standing all alone again. Suddenly Basil's voice resumed from the other side of the curtain and the hum of the crowd subsided.

'Ladies and gentlemen!' he bellowed in a commanding voice that silenced the audience completely. 'Tonight we have a most spectacular show for you. A concert performed by not only the greatest musician in the known world but also the greatest composer. *However* – ' The last word drove back the murmurs that threatened a resurgence '– What is even more remarkable is the fact that he is made entirely of wood and metal. He is a clockwork automaton capable of creativity! Something once believed to be solely the possession of man! Do not think this is some clever deception, for I promise you that both your eyes and your ears will assure you that no trickery is at play. So, without further ado, may I present to you the Mechanical Maestro!'

As rather modest applause commenced, the curtain rose. Maestro was greeted by a room filled with finely dressed humans. Some were seated in the pit before him, while many more were seated in the tiers of seats that rose up to great heights. A few were watching him from boxes with red curtains that rose above either side of the stage. The ceiling was painted with human figures in colourful robes and there was gold on the moulding of both the ceiling and walls (both of which were peeling). Yet the most magnificent thing of all was a glassy, pale gold chandelier hanging in the middle of the ceiling, twinkling and shining. Upon beholding Maestro's small figure, the humans gasped, and their applause faltered. Whispers rippled across the audience. A lady screamed and there were even one or two outbursts of harsh laughter from the pit.

'What the bloody 'ell is that thing?' someone shouted. 'It's either a puppet on strings or a dwarf in a costume!'

Maestro turned his head to the side where Basil was watching, only to see him gesticulating wildly to turn back to face the audience. The sound of Maestro's footsteps rang out as he took a few paces forward and bowed. As he raised his head, he happened to catch sight of Master Josephus and his manservant, Bellamy, in the box nearest to the stage on the left. Half his face was hidden behind a white fan or handkerchief, which he then waved at Maestro. The automaton looked down at his violin. The reaction from the humans confused him, but he had been told to perform so that was all he could do, and so he raised the instrument into position. He twitched a fraction as the cylinder inside of him clicked and shifted itself about. The wheels in his head and chest spun around faster and faster until he could hear them hissing like sand streaming through an hourglass. A great pressure began to pile up and up inside him. The wheels spun and the sound grew more insistent, turning from hissing to a harsh screeching. As its pitch and the pressure grew, it was accompanied by another high, yet far softer sound, which broke through the air like a flash of lightning – the long note that was being emitted by the violin. His arm shot into motion, dispelling the pressure almost instantly, as he feathered the bow across the strings with such delicacy that the hairs hardly seemed to brush the strings, although the sound rang out clearly, the fingers of his left hand darting dizzily across the strings at the same time.

The sequence of notes streamed forth like starlight. The violin's voice was sweeter than the most alluring siren's and had ten times the magnetic pull on all those who heard it. Each change in the melody pulled at the heartstrings inside the crowd, who held their faces up (or down in the case of those in the boxes) to the wooden figure who was the source of this ecstatic cascade of music. Many burst into tears and quivered all over as the music became unspeakably tender, their hearts soaring or sinking to the rise and fall of the music. They were completely and hopelessly in its power. The automaton, which had but minutes ago appeared so pathetic and measly, now seemed to have grown in presence as he stood in the middle of the stage and commanded the attention of all. Yet beneath the music was another sound, as if coming from somewhere beyond the strings of the violin, whispers of a preternatural voice that wavered in and out of hearing like the flickering flames of a fire. This was music unmediated, in its purest form. A peculiar atmosphere suffused itself over the theatre like a cloud of glimmering golden dust as the song poured forth. All who heard it found themselves carried away on a wave of bliss, as if their souls were drifting above and away from them, while still curiously remaining attached to their bodies. It was as if they could feel themselves melting, drowning, sinking, and gladly so.

When the music ceased, Maestro's arm lashed back and sent the bow skidding across the stage. Recollecting himself, he hastily went to retrieve it and bowed once more. He looked out over the crowd, who seemed immersed in some sort of stupor. Had he done something wrong? They were all unnaturally still. He might have thought they were sleeping save that their eyes were still open. Suddenly, frenzied applause broke out from one of the boxes above and the theatre soon recovered itself. Soon every member of the audience had risen to their feet and was applauding furiously.

The next piece Maestro played was briefer and more energetic, producing an altogether different effect on the audience. For this second movement, he was joined on stage by a human pianist, who thrashed out thundering notes to bolster the violin's rapid, unbelievably high-pitched notes, which Maestro was able to create by placing his left hand lightly over the strings in carefully calculated places, while bowing. In other places the slacker, tinkling notes glided between the feathery arpeggios from the violin. The final movement featured the piece that Maestro had written on the day he entered Master Josephus's house and pushed the timbre of the violin to its utmost limit. The voices contained in its strings were innumerable.

The crowd was in raptures at the end of the performance. Maestro felt something knock against his arm as Basil came past him to the front of the stage and raised his hands. 'Ladies and gentlemen, I hope you have been entertained by my marvellous machine. He will be performing here each night this week with a fresh repertoire and—'

'*Your* machine?' All heads turned in the direction of the shrill, and impossibly loud, voice that wounded Basil's speech. It had come from one of the boxes on Maestro's left. Master Josephus was leaning over the edge of his box and staring down at Basil. 'Why, my good sir, I think you might wish to amend part of your last statement.'

'Oh, I don't see where I have made an error, Lord Leyton,' Basil called up to him with a grin, 'since it is I who am exhibiting the automaton.'

'Well, in that case I regret to inform you, although you know this all too well already, that he belongs to *me* and furthermore – ' Master Josephus spun his head around. 'Pray wait a moment.' He vanished from Maestro's view, Bellamy following him. Several minutes passed. Basil looked at his watch and the audience at one another, then Master Josephus's white form reappeared from the side. He marched right past the people seated in the stalls and, with Bellamy's assistance, mounted the stage. He was dressed in a glittering white tailcoat with a purple jewel embedded in his ruffled lace necktie. There was powdery purple around his eyes curling out in feathery little swirls.

'Since you are my friend, Basil,' he said, his voice possessing far greater composure now, his head held high as he looked down at Basil, 'I will ask you once more, did you claim just now that Maestro is your possession?'

Basil did not reply immediately. He smiled coolly at his friend and slid one hand into his coat pocket, but suddenly his calm expression was swept away and his arm contracted as he became aware that Bellamy was now standing directly behind him with one gloved hand upon his shoulder. Even Maestro's quick eyes had missed how he had come to be standing there, for a moment ago he had been standing behind Master Josephus.

'Why – I, of course, I did not mean to offend you, Cephus. Come now, surely you want to avoid making a scene—'

'Because if so,' Master Josephus continued, 'I consider it my duty to inform your audience of the truth.'

'Please, Cephus, for God's sake it was only a joke!' A wheezy sound came out of his windpipe as the manservant's grip on his shoulder tightened, causing his arm to jerk oddly.

'Bellamy, please. You need not go as far as that.' Master Josephus waved his white-gloved hand for Bellamy to release Basil, and then turned to face the audience. 'What this man has told you, whether in jest or otherwise…', he cast a glance towards Basil, '…is not true. For, I, Lord John Josephus Leyton, the Earl of Banbury, am the rightful owner of this automaton.' He extended his arm towards Maestro and beckoned him to step forward. 'And as to who built him, he was created by two clockmakers by the name of Abernathy, two gifted brothers whose name is as of yet all but unknown. What these young men can do with clockwork is beyond belief, and Maestro, who stands before you now, is their latest and greatest creation!'

Astonished murmurs arose from the audience. This gave way to renewed shouts and cheers. One or two made questionably rude remarks at Basil and attempted to throw things at him. Master Josephus smiled and raised both hands outspread over his head as if he were distributing something down into the crowd, going right up to the stage edge. 'Remember their name!' he called above the growing frenzy. 'Remember the name of those two marvellous inventors and spread it far and wide! Abernathy! Abernathy!'

Chapter Ten

Small flecks of snow were beginning to fall, melting away to nothing as they touched the wet cobbled ground. It was hardly enough to settle. The few flakes that stuck to Douglas's new greatcoat lasted considerably longer as he made his way through the street. His fingers curled around a crumpled note and a few coins inside his coat pocket, a small fraction of the payment they had received from Lord Leyton. Immediately after his departure with the automaton, they had got all of the family heirlooms and valuables out of the pawnshop and that evening the three of them had enjoyed a plentiful supper. Most of the money that had already been spent was used to buy parts for the new machines they were planning on building. George had actually been true to his word and hadn't drunk any of his share away. Douglas had only spent a relatively small portion of his share so far on bits of clothing and parts for a machine of his very own that he was constructing. He had managed to buy some old, disused livery stables to store his construction in, and now he was on his way to procure the materials he needed for the engine. True to old habits however, he had still sourced most of the parts for it from scrap metal littering the streets, or things from the rag and bone man. He still found a familiar pleasure in scavenging for scrap like he and George had spent hours doing as boys. There was no telling what you would land upon.

It was still early morning and the fog was very thick, but already people were beginning to fill the streets. There were maids with baskets slung over their arms out shopping for their mistresses, even though it was not yet nine o'clock and many of the shop owners were still setting out their merchandise. There was a grubby little girl at the corner of Portland Street holding up clumps of violets to passers-by, ignored by just about all. A policeman appeared around the corner and she instantly scuttled away. Douglas felt for the bit of paper that was curled up with the pound note inside his coat pocket. Molly had given him a list of things to buy, saying someone else besides her could do the shopping for a change.

He saw a great crowd was gathered outside a newsagent further up the street, each person with a newspaper in hand. Amongst them, he recognised the Maynards and some of their other old customers, including old Mr Spencer with the paper held so close to his face that it was brushing against his puffin-beak nose. Douglas could see the puffs of vapour blasting from their mouths as they conversed and gesticulated amongst themselves, pointing at something in the paper. Many, for some reason, were taking out their pocket watches to show one another. Mrs Maynard was displaying the watch with the silver rose that Douglas had sold her husband many months ago.

'World's first mechanical composer performs at Gryphon Theatre!' exclaimed a boy as he brandished a paper in his hand high above his head. All Douglas could see of him was a hand waving from side to side at the centre of the crowd as the disembodied voice cried out again and again, 'The Mechanical Maestro gives first concert of music composed by an automaton at the Gryphon Theatre last night!'

The nerves at the back of Douglas's neck prickled, as if a clump of snow had slid down below the collar of his coat and shirt. Walking as casually as he could, grateful for the gauzy cover of the fog, he crossed the street a little further down and dived into a narrow alleyway between two buildings. The vagabond with his head leant back on the slimy brick wall nearby didn't stir. Douglas judged that it was better to avoid being seen by anyone he knew until he understood exactly what was going on. Douglas took what looked like a squat, fat loupe out of his pocket. He twisted the head, which came apart with a crack, and it sprang out into a telescope. He held it against his eye and adjusted the magnification, the crowd blurring in and out of view before the image became sharp and clear. Even when he had exhausted the magnification dial, he still couldn't make out the print on the paper beyond the headlines. When he aimed the lens down, he noticed one or two discarded papers lying on the ground, their corners dipped in the pools of dirty, sludgy water that formed where there were gaps in the cobbled road. He also happened to see a number of small hands slipping into pockets or snatching purses and handkerchiefs right from their owners' hands while they were engrossed in the paper.

Catching the eye of the small boy attempting to fish his hand into Mr Spencer's pocket, Douglas signalled to him with a movement of his fingers. Like a little fox terrier, the boy scurried along the street to where Douglas was.

'Would you like to earn yourself a couple of shillings?' Douglas asked him. The boy nodded. 'See if you can find a discarded paper that's reasonably dry. Try to avoid stealing one if you can. Offer to purchase it off someone if needs be. Here, I'll give you a half-crown for the purpose. If you're back in less than five minutes, I'll let you keep the change plus the same again as interest.' Douglas dropped the money into the boy's small, dirty paw.

The boy tucked it into his pocket and jerked the brim of his cap up away from his eyes. 'I won't be long, sir.'

As the boy scurried off once more, Douglas continued to watch what was going on (glancing intermittently at his pocket watch), having given up on the lens. Many of the people began to peel away from the main body of the crowd and he caught snatches of their conversation as they passed by him. He slumped down upon the cold ground with his head turned away from them, burying the lower half of his face inside his turned-up coat collar in imitation of the man beside him, even if his coat was nowhere near as shabby and filthy.

'...the clockmakers down Peter Street. Yes, I am certain it is them. Two brothers...yes, I always thought it rather peculiar. Since the mother died, their sister has been little better than a gypsy.'

'...they say it can actually compose music, and it actually thinks for itself. This journalist says it does. It's all right here. Imagine that!'

'Utter nonsense, of course. A machine that can make decisions for itself? Whoever heard of such a thing?'

In four minutes and fifty seconds, the red-faced boy returned with a newspaper tucked under his arm. 'I got one, sir. Bought it off an old gentleman. That's three shillings what you owe me.'

'I make it out as two, if the paper was sixpence.'

'No, I'm sure it's three, sir,' said the little street arab adamantly, stopping his cap sliding over his eye.

'I don't suppose you ever learnt proper arithmetic, did you?'

'What's 'rithmatic?'

'Never mind, here you go,' sighed Douglas, as he exchanged the copy of the *London Illustrated News* for three silver coins.

The boy swiped the coins from Douglas's hand and scarpered, calling, 'Thank you, sir.'

'Little capitalist,' Douglas muttered under his breath, as he took up the newspaper and began reading it there and then. As he did so, his grip on the paper tightened and his eyes widened. A short spurt of disbelieving laughter escaped his mouth. Hastily bundling the paper under his arm, he bolted out of the alleyway and crossed over into a side street, taking a longer, but more discreet, way home. Breathless with excitement, he ran as fast as he could, narrowly bobbing and weaving his way past anything and anyone in his wake, catching the startled faces of one or two people who recognised him as he ran past them. He thought he probably looked slightly mad; his mouth was open and fixed in a grin, allowing in a rush of cold air that sucked the moisture from his mouth and made his teeth tingle. His route took him through the crammed rows of crumbling houses. He decided to use the back door, which led into the hallway. Molly was just on her way out. She looked questioningly at his glowing face as he stood panting heavily, sending small spurts of steam out through his still smiling mouth.

'What is it?' she asked.

'What?' He swallowed, regaining his composure for the moment. 'We are famous, that's what! Our automaton is in all of the papers. "The

Mechanical Maestro", they're calling him. Come take a look for yourself.'

Molly came to Douglas's side, drawing her cloak tightly around her. Her green eyes flitted across the page, blinking rapidly every now and then. Finally, she broke out into an excited yell and threw her arms around his neck, almost pulling him over sideways. Her hair bounced around her wildly. 'What did I tell you? You and George are famous!' She hung onto his arm, still grinning from ear to ear. 'Does George know yet?'

'No, but he's about to. Whereabouts—?'

Before he had finished the question, George himself appeared in the doorway. 'You both might want to come see this.'

Exchanging perplexed looks, Douglas and Molly followed their brother into the house and up the stairs to the little window at the corner of the first storey. All three looked down at the scene beneath them.

'Oh, my word…' Molly strained to see on her tiptoes. People were crowding around the shop door and filing down the street.

'They have been here since eight o'clock this morning,' said George. 'My only guess is that word of our automaton has gotten out.'

'Your guess is right. Here, it's on pages three *and* seven.' Douglas passed him the newspaper. 'It is the talk of London. He gave a performance at a theatre last night and brought the house down.'

There was an etching of what was meant to be their automaton beneath the chunk of text recounting the performance. The drawing was rather crude. It was like a plump gentleman with wooden skin, the grain of the wood being heavily etched, smiling benignly over the crowd of caricature people with comically shocked expressions. It held a violin and had a large wind-up key in its back.

'An artist's impression?' George frowned. 'It is hardly accurate. Grotesque rather.'

'Yes, but never mind that, just read what it says.' Douglas jabbed the paper from behind George's shoulder. Both he and Molly watched George's keen eyes dart back and forth across the lines of print.

'Still, it is not all good news,' said Douglas. 'Some of them are saying it is a fake. The most popular theory is that there's really a small dwarf in the torso controlling it.'

'That is to be expected,' said George vaguely, his eyes fixed to the newspaper.

'Well, what are we going to do?' said Molly, peering through the window again. 'We can't leave all those people standing out in the cold.'

'We let them in, of course,' cried Douglas excitedly, whipping himself around. 'Molly, you go and make sure the shop is ready, but don't open the front door yet.'

Molly shot off down the stairs like a whippet. When she had gone Douglas shook his brother by the shoulders, hardly able to contain himself. 'This is it. This is what we've been waiting for our entire lives, George.' His green eyes shone brightly.

'Will you please get a hold of yourself,' hissed George, pulling away. 'You're acting as if you have lost your mind.'

'Perhaps I have lost my mind. Who knows?' Douglas laughed. 'But can you really blame me? Are you not in the least excited by what is happening? I mean just *look* at the number of people outside our door.'

'I don't want to celebrate prematurely, that's all,' said George, trailing after Douglas down the stairs.

'Don't be such a pessimist, George. The world knows about us now. We can only go upwards from here!'

'What I meant was that we can hardly base our expectations on one piece in the *Illustrated News*. They will have found something else to excite the public's attention come tomorrow.'

'Even so, I think a music-making automaton will sustain people's interests for a little while, don't you? Speaking of which, I wonder how all this attention will bear on Maestro himself.'

'What do you mean? I thought I warned you against projecting a personality onto it.'

'Oh never mind,' Douglas sighed, as they reached the foot of the stairs. The chorus of voices fiercely chattering away outside was now quite clearly audible.

Molly quickly slipped through the black door and pressed her back against it. 'It's getting a bit mad out there. I don't think they're prepared to wait much longer.'

'Then they'll wait no longer,' declared Douglas with a commanding air and strode through the door. George just managed to catch his sister's eye before passing through also, long enough for a wordless exchange to pass between them. *Yes, I know. Make sure he doesn't get carried away with himself.*

George gave a stiff nod at her and then stepped into the shop. The people filled the window; some shook the shoulders of those beside them upon seeing the brothers enter and pointed towards them. Arms were waving and patches of condensed breath blotted the window as the crowd grew even more restless. Molly positioned herself against the door and placed her hand on the handle, trying to avoid looking at the people on the other side.

'Well, here we go.' Douglas rubbed his hands together and raised a finger like a pistol trigger. 'Now, Molly!'

Molly flung back the door and the tide of people rushed into the shop, filling it in a matter of seconds. They jabbered and rattled ceaselessly. Above the din, a few individuals could be heard shouting, 'That's them!' They immediately swarmed around the two brothers, who were barricaded behind the counter. Molly had slipped into the window and was hugging her knees tightly to her chest. George's face tensed, like one braced for an assault, although he managed to maintain his impassive, stonily calm exterior. Douglas seemed unfazed by the disorderly crowd and raised his hands, as if to batter down their noise.

'Ladies and gentlemen! I thank you all for your patience,' he cried, but to little use. George, who was half distracted by something that kept nudging against his foot, could see his brother wasn't going to get anywhere. Still the crowd pressed on with their questions.

'Is it real?' demanded an old crone in a black bonnet.

'Did you really build it?' pressed a fresh-faced journalist with note-book and pencil in hand.

'Could you make a mechanical doll for my daughter? One that walks and talks?' said a smartly dressed gentleman with a tall silk top hat, elbowing his way past the old crow, who beat the wings of her black shawl at him and cried out, 'Eh!'

'If you could all just please quieten down a moment, we will be happy to answer all your questions.' Douglas stood on the counter but it produced little effect. 'If you could please just—'

A high-pitched, piercing screech cut off both Douglas and the crowd. The lights on the sound transmitter were on and George was holding something in his hands up against the speaking tube. He had a little clockwork tin mouse in one hand and a tight grip on its tail with the other, enough to cause it to give an ear-splitting squeak if pulled. He set the little mouse down on the floor. It lifted its head and twitched its wiry whiskers before scuttling off into its hole. The people in the shop seemed stupefied a moment, their hands raised over their ears.

Douglas seized the opportunity and cleared his throat. 'We thank you for your patience, ladies and gentlemen. Those of you who have read this morning's papers will no doubt be wondering whether the story of the Mechanical Maestro is in fact true.' Here he paused to allow sufficient suspense to accumulate. 'But I can assure you that it is very true, and it all started right here in this very shop.' The ensuring mutters of astonishment were not quite at the level he had anticipated, but he continued with his routine, unfazed. 'The musical automaton is just the latest product of Abernathy Brothers clock and watchmakers, where we sell all varieties of exquisitely crafted timepieces, miraculous inventions to ease the strain of everyday life, *and* custom-built androids, each a one-of-a-kind masterpiece. So please feel free to look around the shop and if you have any questions, my brother George and I will be happy to answer them.'

Good show. Molly nodded from her nook in the window as she observed the resurgence of people around Douglas as he hopped down from the counter. One or two people had already diverted their attention from him and were looking at some of the inventions on display. Yes, today was going to be quite a long day.

It was gone seven o'clock before the last of the people were out of the shop. Even then it had taken some effort to make them leave, most of whom were journalists by this time. Douglas practically had to shut the door on a particularly persistent pair of Grub Street hacks, who were asking questions about them and their mother's history. He leant his back against the door and let out a long breath. The shop was completely emptied out, down to the last pocket watch. His steps had a hollow ring as he swooped over the counter and examined the shop's till. The till's drawer wouldn't shut properly as it was filled to the brim. They had emptied it twice throughout the course of the day. After trying in vain to ram it shut, Douglas strode into the back of the house with an elastic stride. A straggly trail of steam was coming from the kitchen, carrying the faint whiff of onions and other cooking smells. Some small part of his brain recalled that he hadn't eaten since breakfast, and the moment it did he felt painfully hollow inside. Through the steam he distinguished Molly sitting by the stove, stirring a large pot that was bubbling away furiously. He sat down on a chair by the table, only to instantly rise again and start agitatedly pacing about the room.

'I haven't seen you in such a good mood since you found those giant cast-iron wheels in a rubbish tip and somehow managed to roll them all the way back home.' She smiled, turning her head over her shoulder without moving her body.

'Is it any wonder, Mol?' he said as he came over to where she was. He slapped his hands down on her shoulders and swiftly kissed the top of her messy head. 'After the day we've had? Hopefully it'll be the first of many more like it.' He looked down into the pot, his face quickly becoming damp. His smile contracted. A reddish scum floated on the top of the pot's contents and tails of vapour of the same colour waggled in the air. Every now and then there came a deep *plop* as a thick bubble burst. The heat clawed at his eyes. 'Um, what is that you're making, Molly?'

'The stew for our supper,' she answered simply, as she stirred it round and the scum melted back into the red-brown liquid. Indistinguishable beige chunks bobbed to the surface and then sank again.

'And what exactly did you put in it?'

'Mainly vegetables. Don't let the colour put you off. Here.' She dunked a spoon into the pot. It retrieved two orange lumps in a steaming red pool. 'Taste it.' Douglas thinned his lips.

'Don't be such a baby, you've eaten my vegetables before.'

'Yes, but that was when I could actually tell what vegetables they were.'

'I'll tell you once you've tasted it,' she said, offering him the spoon once more. Douglas eyed it dubiously as he took it and brought it slowly to his mouth. Looking at Molly's expectant face, he rolled his eyes and then bolted the spoonful quickly down his throat. He felt its heat sear through him on its way down, leaving a strong, spicy aftertaste in its wake that wasn't entirely unpleasant.

'Well?' She handed him a glass of milk. 'How was that?'

'Not bad,' he admitted, after glugging down the entire glass and leaving a cloudy white smear down its side. The heat at the back of his throat had receded.

'You didn't really taste it though. You swallowed it down whole.'

'I got a bit of its taste, and I still ate it all the same. Now tell me what was in it.'

'Carrot, potato, onion, ox tongue, various spices…and a variety of pepper of my own making.' She smiled wickedly. 'Five times stronger than any natural variety. I only used a tiny sliver. A whole one would probably burn you to cinders from the inside out.'

'But it's perfectly edible in small doses, isn't it?'

'Yes.' She rolled her eyes at him. 'I always try eating them myself first before cooking with them. I had to knock up a stew from whatever was to hand since no one went to the grocers or the butchers today, did they? I thought adding the pepper to it would make it a bit less bland.'

Just as she rose and reached up to the china cabinet, a loud squelch caused her to turn her head and see a flotilla of large bubbles hovering in her direction. At the far end of the room, a squat, cylindrical machine with lots of tubes, pumps and a porthole window in the middle of its body, like a huge, glazed eye, shuddered and rattled. Thick soapy scum oozed out of its joints.

'Blasted thing.' Douglas struck the machine on the side. It jittered about and sent another stream of bubbles into the air. 'It's worse than the old one. Our clothes won't be fit to wear.'

'It doesn't matter,' said Molly offhandedly, popping bubbles over her head. 'We can afford new clothes now.'

'Those *were* our new clothes.'

'Well, we can afford *new* new clothes then. I'll go call George down for supper. You be serving it up.' Molly dumped three china bowls on the table with a heavy thud and went out of the room.

'Can you make sure I locked the door to the shop, Molly?' he called after her. 'My head isn't entirely in the right place at the moment. I can't remember if I locked it.'

'*All* right,' she sighed.

It was still a bit of a shock seeing the shop so empty. The floor was covered in dried, muddy footprints and litter. The clockwork mouse had come out from its hole and was nibbling a fallen threepence as if it were a piece of cheese, but on seeing Molly it quickly scarpered. She wasn't up to scrubbing the floor, not after rushing around all day and then cooking supper, since nobody else would have given a thought to doing it. Maybe they could afford to hirc a maid now, or build one. She laid her hand on the cold door handle and gave it a firm tug. Douglas had locked it after all. As she turned to go however, an insistent knocking sounded sharply against the other side of the door. Narrowing her eyes, she passed back through the shop and went to unlock it again.

She found Laura Blakeslee standing on the doorstep.

'Good evening, Molly.' Laura smiled. She wore a smart blue dress with her blond hair arranged in neat bunches of curls beneath her bonnet. 'I was wondering if your brother was home?' She peered over Molly's shoulder into the shop. She held a small blue, beaded purse embroidered with red and green leaves in her right hand and a newspaper in her left.

Molly replied coolly, 'Douglas is not home. I can take a message if you wish.' The cold air outside was starting to seep into the shop, but she was glad she didn't shiver in front of Laura.

'Oh, that's a pity. No, I was hoping to speak to him directly. When might I call again?' Laura said briskly.

'You mayn't.'

'Oh?' Laura's corn-silk eyebrows pinched and her smile grew taut.

'I know what your game is, Miss Blakeslee.' Molly lowered her voice slightly as she placed one hand on the door and the other on her hip. Her eyes were like two dark jade stones. 'And I don't intend to let you try to manipulate my brother for your own ends.'

Laura wasn't smiling any longer. She raised her chin a little. 'I will tell my mother not to let you mend her clothes any longer.'

'Well, if what the papers are saying is true, I think we'll survive without her patronage.' With that, Molly slammed the door fast.

'Did I just hear the door slam, Mol?' Douglas came out of the kitchen as Molly re-entered the house, his voice thick as his mouth was filled. He was holding a half-eaten piece of bread in his hand.

'Oh, it was just some beggarwoman at the door asking for money.' Molly shrugged. 'I gave her a sixpence but she stuck her foot in the door as I tried to close it and started making a racket. I think she was drunk. She reeked of gin anyway.' The lies came off her tongue smoothly enough. The trick to a good lie was in the detail, something she'd practised on old Snell a thousand times. Usually successfully.

'You shouldn't really have answered the door after dark, Molly. It seems the minute you manage to come into some money, someone is trying to pry it from you again.' He swallowed another mouthful of bread. 'At least we can actually spare the odd sixpence here and there now.'

'I would be careful if I were you though. All sorts of people will try to manipulate you now you and George are rich.'

'I wouldn't say rich, Molly. Besides, you're rich too by the same logic.' He pointed the hand that held the remains of the bread at her before cramming it into his mouth.

'It isn't *my* money, what did I do to earn it?'

'You've kept us going with your hybrid vegetable stews for one thing. Otherwise, we might have starved to death.'

'Humph, I'm glad I have my uses, even if only as a cook and washer-woman. Not that you and George can't do those things for yourselves.'

'If you two don't cease quarrelling our supper will be cold.'

Both Douglas and Molly started at hearing George's voice. He was stood on the bottom step of the staircase with his arm leaning against the banister. 'And you cannot give away money to every beggar and vagabond that comes our way, even if your intentions are good.'

'Oh, have some heart, George!' cried Molly light-heartedly as the three of them made their way into the kitchen. Three bowls of steaming stew, cutlery and a loaf of bread were set out on the table.

'Yes, I'm with Mol. That did sound rather cold,' said Douglas as they sat down, sensing an opening to have a jab at his brother.

'I am merely being practical,' George replied as he took up his spoon. 'Philanthropy, as it is practised by so-called Samaritans, is an empty gesture. More often than not it is concerned more with the emotional and social benefits gained by the benefactor rather than those he purports to help. And even when it is done earnestly, it is ultimately futile. They will never eradicate poverty without changing the structure upon which the country is built, which privileges a competitive market and inevitably leads to a grossly disproportionate distribution of wealth. What is the work of a few individuals in the face of such a fact? One might do better to look out for their own interests. On another note, I was just adding up our takings for today and they are considerably less than you might expect, once the costs have been deducted. It should see us through for a few weeks at any rate.'

'Since when did you become so fixated on money?' Douglas raised his eyes at him.

'I'm not. Money is merely a means to an end. For us it is a means to continue our research.'

'And keep a roof over our heads,' said Molly, biting a crust of bread. 'Practically speaking. We must look out for our own interests after all, mustn't we?'

The scraping of spoons filled a brief interlude.

'Anyway,' said Douglas brightly all of a sudden. 'We got something even more exciting from today besides money.' His chair scraped back as he got up and disappeared from the room.

Molly drew her spoon from her mouth very slowly and watched after him until he came back with slips of paper bunched up in each of his hands. 'What's all that?' she asked.

'Commissions!' He smiled. 'Just take a look at them.' He scattered them on the table amongst the supper things. George and Molly gathered them up and began glancing over them.

'This man is offering us twenty pounds to build him a mechanical clerk since his *is a lazy oaf who hardly ever does any work and sneaks off to go to the public house at midday*,' Molly read, widening her eyes.

'This woman requests us to build her an automaton to serve as a companion, specifying that it must *speak intelligibly and wittily, and respond to whatever is said to it*. There is no mention of a sum,' said George, flicking through them rapidly. 'The rest are a little more promising.'

'I know. Can you believe it?' Douglas cried excitedly. He had been rapidly perusing one piece of paper after another and slapping them down on the table (one unfortunately landing in Molly's bowl, which she fished out between her fingers and shook about). At last he seemed to no longer be able to contain himself and simply threw them up into the air, laughing aloud as they rained down over him. Unable to help herself either, Molly joined in his laughter and flung the handfuls of papers on the table into the air one after another.

George watched the two of them and shook his head.

'From *you* I would expect such behaviour, but I'd expect more of Molly.'

'But, George!' Douglas scrunched the slips of paper between his fingers in front of George's face. 'To think yesterday we were lucky if we sold two or three pocket watches in a week and today we are flooded with orders for our automata!'

'I am as thrilled about all this as you are,' said George, as he got up from his seat and knocked Douglas's hands away. 'In fact, I've been devoting a great deal of thought to how we are going to take on some of these commissions and replenish the stock of timepieces in the shop.'

'Restock the timepieces? George!' cried Douglas exasperatedly. 'You aren't looking at the bigger picture. We don't have to confine ourselves to pocket watches anymore. From now on, we can earn our living doing what we have always dreamt of – building androids and machines.' He suddenly became much more serious. 'If we divide our time between the two, we divide our focus as well. We can't play it safe by falling back on pocket watches and clocks that nobody ever bought anyway.'

George said nothing. He only continued to look at his brother. A change came over his face and his stony exterior fell away. It was as if a light had suddenly dawned upon him. Yes, they could do this. This was really happening. The thing they had always hoped for but never seriously imagined had come to pass. He had to admit to himself that Douglas had a valid point. If they split their time between making watches and building automata, it meant they were only devoting half as much energy to their real pursuits.

'Well, perhaps we ought to continue with the watches in the short term, just until the first lot of orders are completed and we have established ourselves. Even if it means working through the night.'

'We can take shifts,' said Douglas eagerly. 'One of us works on the watches, the other on the automata. We can switch between them depending on how tired we are, since the watches won't require as much concentration.'

'Yes, that might be best.'

The two of them hastily gathered up all the papers off the floor.

'So which ones do we take on first? What about this one here?' Douglas showed George the paper.

'No, too easy. What about this one here?'

'Hmm, perhaps. Although there's one here that looks good and pays well.'

This exchange went on for some time until they had collected every single scrap of paper, setting aside seven that they both settled upon in the end.

'Right, so we'll start with that one. Who's taking the first watch-making shift then?'

'Shall we toss a coin for it?'

Douglas took a coin from his pocket and flicked it into the air.

'I call heads,' said George, as Douglas slapped it down on his arm and lifted his hand away.

'Heads it is. All right, I'm on first shift then. We'll switch in six hours' time. Let's see how many pocket watches I can churn out by then. I bet you it's more than twenty.'

'Twenty is no great feat.'

'Well, I bet I can do thirty then. I bet you can't match that.'

'We'll see when it comes to my turn. Just don't go making a bad job of them.'

'I'm just as good a clockmaker as you are, and you know it,' Douglas taunted, as he slipped out of the kitchen.

'And a far greater braggart,' George muttered, as he followed.

'But wait, what about your supper?' Molly called after them as she heard the door to the shop slam shut and boots trudging upstairs. 'Oh, what's the use?' she muttered to herself as she scraped the last dregs of stew around her bowl. The machine behind her whined and sneezed out another cloud of soap bubbles. 'And you can shut up as well,' she snapped. 'There's enough madcap machines around here already without adding any more to their number.'

Chapter Eleven

Life fell into a regular routine for Maestro. His days comprised working on fresh material in the music room for each new performance he was to give at the theatre. It seemed it had not taken much for Basil to persuade his friend that he had meant no ill, and he not only made Master Josephus hastily repent his actions, but also got him to agree to have Maestro perform at his theatre for three nights each week. Each night the crowd grew larger and more ecstatic, some practically flinging themselves at the stage. There was a set of several songs that the human musicians knew well and usually played each night, but Basil was constantly insisting that Maestro devise new melodies to be slotted between the old, should the audience tire of them. When a new song was introduced that was not a solo piece, the human musicians were given two or three days to learn it before it was performed for real. Any of them who failed to keep up were swiftly replaced. Maestro couldn't help but feel that the material suffered from the small amount of time in which he was expected to produce it. In all truth, it often wasn't terribly good, but Basil, and the audience, did not seem to mind. Although, when he struggled to churn out a tune, or attempted to communicate to Mr Basil that something was not quite right and in need of changing the night before it was premiered, then Mr Basil did mind. Terribly in fact. On one occasion, after Maestro had attempted to tell him he was struggling to find the right notes for part of a sequence, he had gently muttered, 'Well, perhaps we ought to try forcing them out then,' and had struck Maestro's head and sent it whirling round. Not knowing what to make of the incident, Maestro had not mentioned it to Master Josephus or anyone else, and the melody was performed later that night, without any changes. A subsequent attempt by Maestro to approach Mr Basil with another such entreaty had resulted in a similar response.

And of course, between performing and composing, he tended to the wishes of Master Josephus. He often played to him if he could not sleep at night or in the afternoons when there were no callers and he was afflicted with a bout of ennui. Master Josephus never seemed in danger of tiring of Maestro's music and was often content with the same melodies that Maestro had played him previously. Maestro had become used to the rhythms of the household. He could identify which of the servant bells corresponded to which room by its individual tone and knew the voices and footsteps of every occupant in the house. Master Josephus was, he could not help observing, rather out of synchrony with the rest of the house, which ran smoothly and punctually to the hours of the day as if they were driven by similar gears to those which turned inside of him.

Master Josephus rose at any time from six o'clock in the morning to the middle of the afternoon, depending on whether he had been out the previous evening, and whether he was affected by a bout of limitless energy or listlessness. There was often no in-between. When it was a case of the former, he would usually be possessed by an impulse to go out dancing or to the theatre. Alternatively, he would entertain his friends and have Maestro come down to the drawing room to play for them. But when the latter mood possessed him, he was altogether different. He would not see any callers, or sometimes even leave his room at all. He refused to eat and only drank coffee or claret. These moods could be occasioned by something as triflingly small as one of his favourite garments that he intended to wear having been damaged, his having failed to receive an invitation to a gathering, or having discovered a number of silver hairs in his engraved silver comb. He would then summon Maestro to restore his good humour so that by the evening he was lively and gay once more.

Master Josephus had told him on many occasions, 'You, my dear Maestro, are worth more than the entire legion of doctors my father insists on frittering away part of my inheritance on. Why, I feel as though your music is balm for the very soul!'

One morning, Master Josephus had risen unusually early and had bade Maestro keep him company in the morning room, having ordered a servant to bring his writing desk down too, so that Maestro might compose while he took tea or chose to speak to him. As the servant brought in the tea things and the morning paper, Maestro sat at his desk with his pen in hand, intermittently scratching away – although more often his gaze was directed outside at the grey morning, the sun a silvery disc behind the swathes of cloud and mist. He had been trying to pen a new piece for the end of the week but was struggling.

Suddenly Master Josephus grew excited, and cried out, 'Why, you are the talk of London, Maestro! Everybody adores you!' He lightly tapped the review of his performance from the previous evening, which he had been reading. The pen in Maestro's hand ceased scratching across the scoresheet. He looked at his master and then back at the pen. He very much hoped that they would like his music, but as for whether he himself was adored or not, he was not entirely sure how he felt with regards to that. Mr Basil and a number of men, journalists, had said he was something called a 'phenomenon'. Mr Basil had even talked of getting a man he knew who owned a factory to start producing wooden dolls of Maestro and to paint his face on tea sets and all sorts of other things. He had displayed a few teacups in the theatre foyer the last couple of nights and apparently they had sold out in minutes. But why anyone would want a tea set with his face on it was a mystery to him. It had not escaped Maestro's eager eyes how some of the faces in the crowd looked as blank as a wooden doll's and, quite frankly, uninterested in whatever it was he was playing. Some even looked hostile towards him. He had once glimpsed his name in the Letters section of the evening paper. The letter's author, one Reverend Clarke, had said that he was an 'insult to God'. What he had meant by that, Maestro was unsure. Master Josephus had tossed the paper into the fire when he attempted to ask him about it.

'You know you have been receiving more post than I have this last week?' Master Josephus continued. 'Letters from your legions of admirers. I confess I opened some of them. I was sure you would not mind. I have tasked two of the servants with sorting through them all and writing out the same line in reply, but they will be wanting your signature of course.'

Maestro's eyes fell on the hand holding the pen. His cuff had slipped down his wrist to show the faint crack that was crawling up along his casing. Perhaps he should mention it to Master Josephus. It seemed to grow worse after each concert, and his shoulder joints were becoming stiff. If he attempted to sign all those letters, his arm might fall off.

At that moment there came a tentative knock on the door.

'Come in!' called Master Josephus, his teacup clinking against its saucer.

The old house steward entered the room. 'Mr Griffin is here to see you, my lord. I have shown him into the reception room.'

'What? Now? Oh gracious. At least it is only Basil. I needn't dress for him. You might as well show him in here, Gilbert,' sighed Master Josephus, with a vague motion of his hand. In the same instant the house steward had spoken the visitor's name, Maestro's pen contracted in his hand. There came a sharp scrape and he saw that a skewed black line had shot across the page.

'Maestro, is something the matter?' said Master Josephus once the servant had left. He was standing over him with a look of what Maestro thought was concern on his face. 'Is there something wrong with your hand?'

Maestro shook his head. The truth was he wasn't entirely sure what had caused his hand to move so suddenly like that upon the mention of Mr Basil's name.

Just then Gilbert returned and announced, 'Mr Griffin,' the man himself appearing a moment after.

'Basil,' said Master Josephus crisply, folding his arms across his chest. 'And to what do I owe this visit?'

'I am afraid this is strictly a business call.' Mr Basil smiled easily, seating himself on the sofa opposite Master Josephus.

'Business? I don't have the slightest idea what you're referring to.' Master Josephus's voice prickled with annoyance. 'Would you care for tea?'

'No, I shan't keep you long. There's just a small matter that needs clearing up regarding this automaton of yours.' He aimed his gaze at Maestro, who involuntarily flinched a fraction.

'And what might that be? The change in the days he is to perform next week? I assumed that had been cleared up.'

'No, something more important than that. You see, there is a discrepancy with regard to who has rightful ownership of him.'

'Ownership?' exclaimed Master Josephus. 'Why? Who can possibly have a claim to him besides me? Pray tell me who is saying such things, Basil, and I'll sink their name so fast they won't be able to show their face to anyone ever again.'

'Well, you see, Cephus, the one who has a rival claim to him just happens to be me.'

'*You*?'

'Yes. And I intend to take him with me when I leave here today.'

Master Josephus let out a laugh. 'Surely this is a joke, Basil! You cannot possibly mean what you say! Is this your way of getting around me so you can have him for another three nights? Because I assure you it won't happen.'

'No, I am quite serious,' said Mr Basil gravely, his smile vanishing. 'And I can back it up too.'

He reached into his coat pocket and spread a piece of paper on the table before Master Josephus.

'What is that?'

'The agreement you signed on the night before the automaton premiered, transferring ownership to me. That is your signature at the bottom, is it not?' Mr Basil folded his arms over his chest and leant back onto the sofa. Master Josephus took up the piece of paper and read it over.

'But you told me this was to insure Maestro against damage.'

'I may have embellished the truth somewhat. I meant to present it to you at the theatre that night you caused something of a stir, but of course your servant manhandled me before I had a chance to.'

'So you seriously mean to take him from me?' Master Josephus looked up sharply at the other man. 'With *this* as your only proof?'

'It is a legal document. It would be considered as evidence in a court of law.'

'But surely you recall that I was...out of my head ever so slightly, shall we say, when I signed this? I had no notion of what I was agreeing to.'

'And how could you prove it?' Mr Basil grinned. 'I banked on the likelihood that you wouldn't have read it even if you had been as sober as a priest. I know you, Cephus.'

'Perhaps,' returned Master Josephus coolly, his grey eyes hardening. 'But I perceive it is only now that I am getting to know you, Basil.'

'That is your own fault if you made a misjudgement of my character.' Mr Basil shrugged. 'Does this mean I won't be receiving an invitation to the birthday celebration then? Dear little Rosemary will be ever so put out.'

'Was she implicated in this scheme of yours to steal Maestro from me as well?'

'It is not stealing if he is my property. In fact, it is you who are in the wrong in the eyes of the law, I think you will find, Cephus. That wooden thing is going to make me a very rich man and I'll have it perform twice a day, seven days a week if I want it to.'

Master Josephus rose to his feet. He sounded graver than Maestro had ever heard him sound before. 'Sir, I regret to inform you that I will no longer be in need of your services. I am grateful for the pains you have gone to with Maestro and you will receive due payment, but now that your business with him is concluded, I ask that you leave. You may show yourself out,' he said coldly as he rang a small bell, which made a tinny little chime.

'What? You cannot be serious, Cephus!' said Basil laughingly.

'I assure you, Mr Griffin, that I am quite serious.'

'But what about the performances I have already sold tickets for? I have a full house of people for Friday night wanting to see the automaton!'

'That is no concern of mine.' Master Josephus sniffed. 'I am afraid they will be disappointed for there will be no automaton for them to see. I am sure you can reimburse them. It was foolish of me to let you use

Maestro as you have been doing, but that stops today. Now once more, sir, I must ask that you leave.'

'Then if I am going...' The man narrowed his eyes at Master Josephus and spoke in a lowered tone. 'I am taking it with me.'

'I think not.' Master Josephus looked down upon the other man with a look of utter contempt and clenched his long white hands.

'Oh yes.' Mr Basil grinned as he rose. He was a good head taller than Master Josephus and had a great deal more flesh. 'What is there to prevent me simply taking it? You speak fine words, but they are nothing but air. You are really quite powerless.'

At that moment the door clicked and Bellamy entered. Mr Basil barked a laugh. 'I see you've called your guard dog to your aid as usual. But I'll have it, by whatever means.'

'The automaton belongs to *me*,' returned Master Josephus sharply, in that same steely tone of voice. 'There was nothing in our agreement that entitled you to claim him, nothing whatsoever. And if there were, I would contest it even if it meant losing my entire fortune. I am acquainted with some of the best barristers and men of law in the country and I assure you, Basil, they would not even think this scrap of paper of yours fit to wipe the floor with.' Saying so, he pinched it between his fingers and let it limply twirl to the floor.

'You are a fool, Leyton. If you think you're frightening me then you're even more deluded than I imagined you to be! If you are unconvinced by the document, might I remind you that I know plenty of your little secrets. I'm sure a journalist would be very interested to hear them.'

'Bellamy, please show him out.' Master Josephus flicked his hand, only a slight rise in the pitch of his voice betraying his otherwise unruffled appearance. Bellamy instantly grasped Mr Basil by the shoulder and arm and began to manoeuvre him towards the door.

As he was wrestled out of the room, he twisted his head around to Master Josephus. 'I will get it. I promise you that, Leyton. I will get it.'

Even after Bellamy shut the door behind him, his shouts could still be faintly heard.

'Well,' said Master Josephus exasperatedly, his proud posture slumping, 'that has taken care of him. What an exhausting and wearisome affair!' He fell back weakly onto the sofa and pressed his fingertips to his forehead, his temporarily steely demeanour now having softened to his usual state. 'Play me something soothing, Maestro. That encounter has frayed my nerves. I feel something on the harp would help. Go retrieve your instrument from upstairs.'

Maestro more than readily obliged this request, glad to at last be free of that horrid gentleman. Yet as he played, a thought struck him that caused his fingers to slacken on the strings and his pace to slow.

'No, not like that, that is far too – Oh, does something trouble you, Maestro? Pray tell me what.'

Maestro went over to the desk and dipped the pen into the ink before scribbling down a line and showing it to him. *Do you really think he was sincere about coming after me, Master Josephus?*

'You are afraid that he really will come after you? What nonsense! Take no heed of it. There is no way he could possibly enter this house (although that will be irrelevant in a few weeks' time anyhow). Now don't let such things occupy your thoughts, and resume playing. I feel a resurgence of my headache. Please do continue.'

But despite Master Josephus's conviction, Maestro could not help dwelling upon the look of intent on the man's twisted face. A good deal of time passed before Master Josephus was satisfied that the state of his nerves had been fully restored. He lay with a vacant expression on his face, wafting himself with his fan, following its movements from under half-closed eyelids. The fan suddenly remained suspended in mid-air and Master Josephus stared fixedly ahead like someone who has just awoken from a vivid dream. He snapped the fan shut and sat bolt upright.

'You know, Maestro, it has just occurred to me that you have never seen an opera before. Well, we shall soon remedy that. You will come along with me to see *La Favorita* tomorrow night.'

Maestro stopped playing and blinked at his master. He took up another leaf of paper, hastily writing out a message that he then held before Master Josephus.

'Why of course they will allow you in! Your being made of wood should not matter in the slightest. Why, half of the people there are more paste, padding and cloth than anything else. Although,' he added in a muttered undertone, 'since you are not technically a flesh-and-blood being, you will not require a ticket, which saves a lot of bother, since it is practically impossible to lay hands on a ticket at this hour! I have a private box so you will be away from prying eyes. Oh, I am so glad I hit on this plan. How delightful it will be! You will need evening attire. I wonder if my tailor is available at such short notice? I will send word to him. Bellamy, go lay some of my new evening wear out in my chambers for me to select. Oh, this will be a grand evening!'

Chapter Twelve

That night, the dining hall was occupied by five of Master Josephus's friends who then, along with Maestro, got into the coach (two of the guests following behind in a hansom) and drove through the gas-lit streets of London. Maestro stared at his faint reflection in the coach window. He was wearing a black coat and trousers with a white shirt and a white flower in his buttonhole.

'What a charming little gentleman he makes!' said the lady in the green dress, smiling at Maestro.

'Yes, how tastefully and fashionably you have dressed him, Cephus!' conceded the companion beside her. They looked and sounded exactly alike, except that one wore a green dress and the other pink.

'Unlike yourself,' said the third lady.

Master Josephus was dressed in a sharply fitted, lacy black coat, with a chiffon necktie that swathed his throat and billowed out in soft waves like flower petals. He wore narrow black trousers with a black band of minute jet studs along the outside of the legs that glimmered faintly in the dark coach. In his buttonhole was a large yellow rose.

'And what of it?' said Master Josephus as he crossed his arms over his chest. 'I never pay attention to what is fashionable. Fashion is for those with little imagination, and it repeats itself tediously. What was outdated one season will be quite the rage the next. Besides, you can hardly say anything about being out of touch with fashion, Caroline. You are a dedicated follower of Mrs Amelia Bloomer.'

The coach pulled up outside a very large and very grand building that towered above the android as he stood on the pavement gazing up at it. Four stone columns loomed above the doors like sentries. There was a plaque with the words, HER MAJESTY'S THEATRE, written in gold letters above the columns. The inside was much like that of the theatre Maestro was used to performing at, only it was a lot larger and seemed a lot newer. None of the paint was faded or peeling, nor the curtain frayed. All seemed bright and clean and glossy.

Every person they encountered stopped and stared at him as they passed. They all whispered furiously to one another, although Maestro could hear plainly what they were saying. His own name was voiced by a great many people, like an echo chamber. Some of them squealed or screamed upon seeing him and rushed towards him. Many pressed him with flowers, ribbons or some such token from their dress, while others asked if he would write his name on the back of their programmes. The young ladies became quite excitable; a number actually fainted. But there were some who laughed or muttered remarks in gravelly tones that were not entirely pleasant and turned their backs on him.

'Pay them no heed, Maestro,' said Master Josephus, as they mounted the stairs. 'Mere sycophants and leeches most of them. One should never acknowledge one's admirers or else they'll quickly lose interest.'

They made their way to one of the boxes at the very top of the theatre. Some of Master Josephus's friends were occupying the neighbouring box. The theatre attendant gave Maestro a rather strange look. Maestro peered below him where people were taking their seats in the stalls and circles. He glanced towards the red curtain and then back down again. It was funny how often he had looked up at the people seated in the boxes when he was stood on the stage, only to find now that the view was not quite what he had imagined. In fact, he fancied the people who were squarely facing the stage in the dress circle had the better view.

'One does not have a private box for the best view,' said Master Josephus from behind, as if reading Maestro's thoughts. 'One does so to be noticed.'

What really captured Maestro's attention was the orchestra, whose members were tuning their instruments in the pit. He leant right over the ledge of the box to see what they were doing more clearly until Master Josephus called him back. Maestro took his seat beside him and retrieved the programme that he had initially sat on. His attention became wholly occupied with it until the lights dimmed and the overture commenced. The music fell and rose in waves. Slow at first, before breaking into something far lighter and chirpier when the flute's melody entered, then becoming dark and brooding once more. When the curtain drew back, the deep brassy ring of a church bell sounded faintly as the scene of a monastery and two robed figures appeared before them, presumably Balthazar and Fernando, who proceeded to sing a duet. The bass voice of the man playing Balthazar was as deep and resonant as the church bell, as powerful and pure as thunder, while the lighter tenor's voice was even more striking in the richness of its tones and the clarity with which it rang forth. Its power seemed to grow as the performance went on, until it electrified the air of the theatre. Maestro felt one of his wheels jar inside his chest as the tenor hit the higher notes, and struck it repeatedly until it settled. When the heroine, Leonora, began to sing in a voice that was sweet and elastic in tone, but more modest in volume, Maestro almost found himself lifting up from his seat, but Master Josephus bade him remain where he was. Maestro did not understand the words being sung but he did not need to – the anguish or elation of the characters was felt through the melodies that poured from them, and from their gestures and facial expressions. The blending of the liquid bass and tenor, or mezzo-soprano and tenor tones, was superb, one answering the other, and the music shadowed their voices almost perfectly. Master Josephus frequently watched through binoculars (or at least Maestro thought he was watching, as he occasionally heard him mumble, 'Oh my, look at the dowager countess over there. She has gained at least twenty pounds since I saw her last'), but Maestro did not need such enhancements. His eyes were more than adequate to see everything clearly. Even so, at some point he left his seat and watched with his arms leant on the ledge until he was pulled back by Bellamy. At the end of the performance, the audience applauded wildly, Maestro beating his wooden hands together with zeal. The ballet that followed the opera was almost as good, although the ending was far less tragic. The dancer playing Esmeralda was especially graceful as she leapt and pranced about the stage, carried along by the music. Again, the fervent applause sounded from across the theatre as the performers disappeared behind the curtain.

The melodies he had just heard were still swirling around Maestro's head as the two parties united and decided to go somewhere where they could sit down and drink. They made their way to a supper club not far from the theatre. Maestro did not pay much attention to the conversation that they were having initially, being still far too entranced by all he had just seen and heard. His mind was ticking over rapidly. Ideas began to flit across his mind without him being able to fully make sense of them. He began wondering, although he was hesitant to let the idea fully flourish, whether he could create such a thing as an opera. Perhaps such an attempt would be little more than a poor copy of what he had just seen; he knew little of opera still. Yet if he were to become better acquainted with the genre, maybe then he could. His pondering was interrupted by Master Josephus's addressing him.

'So, what did you make of the opera, Maestro? You have had the look of another world about you since the curtain fell. I take it that you enjoyed it.'

Maestro nodded keenly. There was so much that he wished to convey about what he had thought of the opera, but all the thoughts welling inside him were without an outlet, so the subtlety of his true opinion was lost in that one single gesture.

'Oh, how charming, like a little dog,' said Caroline drily, eyeing Maestro as she sipped her drink. She had the shortest hair of any lady Maestro had ever seen – it was even shorter than Master Josephus's. She pursed her dark lips as she lowered her glass. 'How do I make it stop looking at me, Cephus?'

Maestro hastily turned his head away from her before Master Josephus could reply.

The lady in green, Lilith, cleared her throat. 'Well, we thought Signor Giuglini—'

'—was absolutely marvellous,' chimed in the lady in pink beside her. In the better light, Maestro noticed the lady in pink, Lydia, had slightly lighter hair than her twin Lilith.

'Yes, but Mademoiselle Spezia was a little lacking. Her inexperience showed itself too clearly at first. You could tell she was nervous by the way her voice trembled to begin with,' declared the man with the dark beard whom Maestro had heard the others address as Bailey. 'Now, Rosina Mazzarelli on the other hand, now she is a great soprano!' Bailey continued. 'one of the best of all time, in my opinion. In fact, last year I had the opportunity to meet Luigi Astoff who is married to her younger sister, Fanny, when I was wandering through Italy. It was the same gathering where the celebrated Professor Gottfried gave the most fascinating lecture on the necessity of removing feeling in achieving a perfectly calibrated dance, so the dancer is like a puppet on strings following the forces of nature. "Human error" was a phrase he was rather fond of. I even had the opportunity to speak with him afterwards for a considerable length of time. After telling him I was an art dealer, he entered into the subject of attribution, namely the techniques involved in analysing the chemical elements found in the pigment of unsigned works. He said he had been in Italy specifically for the purpose of hunting works by lost masters, using a new technique he had recently developed with great success. Such a marvellous man! A little eccentric, I admit, but very clever and most interesting to talk to.'

'Professor Gottfried?' Master Josephus knitted his thin brows together. 'Pray, who is he?'

'Why, don't tell me you have not heard of Professor Charles Gottfried?'

'I cannot say I have.'

'Why, I am surprised at you, Cephus!' said Caroline, with a taunting leer as she set down her glass. She began rolling a cigarette. 'Why, he is simply the most ingenious, clever and marvellous man in all of England. Surely you must have heard of him?'

'My darling, I have spent these last three months of the year tucked away in a quiet corner of Bedfordshire and before that I was abroad and quite out of touch with England. It is not impossible that one or two noteworthy persons escaped my attention,' returned Master Josephus coolly with a dismissive flick of his wrist, yet his eyes hovered over his glass with a thoughtful look. 'But pray enlighten me as to who this remarkably clever man is.'

'He's a professor of chemistry at Cambridge, but he has a proficient knowledge of just about every branch of the sciences and is highly respected and sought after,' said Bailey, 'yet he is also a devoted art collector – many a lost masterpiece is said to be locked away in his house. He speaks a dozen different languages, is a first-class engineer, and has a reputation for being something of an eccentric who delights in astonishing and astounding all around him with feats of the impossible. They are no mere clever conjurer's tricks!'

'Although an exceedingly charming eccentric all the same,' Caroline added, 'he insists his illusions have a scientific explanation but he never divulges what.'

'No one knows how he made his fortune,' said Lilith, then, almost as if the two sisters were performing from a script, Lydia picked up where she had left off. 'Some say he was in the military, some that he travelled to the East and learnt alchemy and sorcery.'

'And some say that he came up with a new method for weaving cloth and sold it to a manufacturer in Lancashire,' put in the blond man, Gregory, whom Maestro remembered from a previous gathering, with a smile playing on his mouth. 'You women delight in the marvellous.'

'Thankfully we have you to provide the dry, common-sense view of things, Gregory,' Lydia teased.

'Professor Gottfried also has the most wondrous collection of oddities under the sun,' continued Mr Bailey. 'My friend dined at his house once and he showed him a few specimens from his collection. Rare animal bones and minerals, stuffed animals with two heads or four pairs of limbs, misshapen skulls from the mountains of Peru, dolls said to be possessed by spirits and rooms filled with impossible mechanisms and devices – many of which he himself invented. In fact, my friend was left positively shaken by the uncanny things he saw there. The professor is particularly known for having a marvellous collection of automata, although I dare say not as marvellous as this one of yours, Cephus,' he added, indicating Maestro. 'Although I'd lay a guinea that he'd trade his entire collection to acquire him.'

'In which case, I would have to inform him that the entire contents of his collection would not even begin to compensate me for the loss of my Maestro.' Master Josephus twisted his moustache thoughtfully before releasing it. 'I have half a mind to invite this Professor Gottfried to my little gathering near the end of the month. It would be most interesting to meet him.'

'Oh, I doubt you would get him to turn up to one of your parties, Cephus.' Caroline smirked.

'Au contraire, my dear Caroline.' He held up a long white finger. 'I have my methods of persuasion.'

'You mean you will bribe him?' She raised an eyebrow with a half-smile.

'Did I say anything of the sort, Bailey? Lydia? Lilith? Did I say such a thing? There are other methods of persuasion besides outright bribery. I mean first to write to Professor Gottfried and attempt to persuade him through the sheer charming eloquence of my language.' Master Josephus tossed his head back and swept his hair from his shoulder as he finished speaking.

'And if your charming language fails to convince him?' Gregory smirked.

'In that case, I shall simply provide further incentive,' he said off-handedly into his glass.

Gregory sniggered.

The subject of Gottfried was dropped soon after that as the company began a lengthy discussion about a famous new poet and a lady by the name of Madame Bovary before agreeing to part for the night. Bailey offered to escort Caroline home in a hansom, amid much teasing about what a scandal they would cause by riding alone together, and the rest were to travel in Master Josephus's coach. Master Josephus handed Lydia into the coach and was about to be handed in himself by Bellamy when something suddenly caught his attention.

'There it is!' The cry came from a little way up the street. A large mob of people were marching in their direction. Their faces were hard and angry-looking.

'Abomination!'

'Burn it! Smash it!'

'Reverend Clarke says it is an insult to God and that we must destroy it!'

The mob brandished axes, torches and clubs, letting out cries like wild beasts. Some were chanting, or rather droning, hymns that were rapidly picked up by the others as they drew closer to the coach. Master Josephus, standing beside Maestro, clutched his chest and his fan fell to the ground. His companions were similarly affected. Their faces turned pale and many cried out in horror at the sight of the advancing mob. From inside the coach Lilith screamed and huddled with her sister. Maestro suddenly felt a gust of air blow up his coat and the manservant Bellamy leapt before them. The tails of his black coat fanned outwards as he landed with one fist on the ground before drawing himself up to full height.

'No, Bellamy! Get back!' cried Master Josephus in a high, trembling voice. But still the servant remained standing where he was, like an obelisk, and seemingly just as impenetrable. The mob slowed to a stop, their chanting evaporating. They seemed to be in a state of confusion. The next instant, Bellamy flung something like a discus that appeared as a white blur before Maestro's eyes until he realised it was the fallen fan, which struck a nearby cart outside a public house, loaded with wooden barrels. The fan slashed the ropes that secured the barrels and sent them rolling into the road, cutting across the mob's path. In the same instant that the fan had hit its target, there had been a peculiar creaking sound and Maestro saw that Bellamy had struck one of the gaslights and sent it plummeting to the ground. No sooner was the soft, reedy hiss of unfettered gas audible than the lamp came crashing down on the barrels and an enormous ball of flames burst up before the mob, dispersing them instantly.

'Into the coach, Master. Quickly,' Bellamy said in his usual hushed tone as he looked over his shoulder. His face was as calm and unmoved as ever, silhouetted against the sharp yellow-orange glow of the fire. Master Josephus's friends scrambled into the coach and Master Josephus was lifted off the ground by Bellamy, who also got hold of Maestro by the collar with his other hand, and deposited them safely inside. It was very cramped with Lilith, Lydia, Gregory and Master Josephus in the coach, plus Maestro, who was crouched against the door. Lilith was sprawled out on the floor, so Maestro saw up her hooped skirt without meaning to and politely averted his eyes. Bellamy finally mounted the rear of the coach and the driver yanked the horses' reins. The coach gave a violent jerk that sent everyone reeling forwards and backwards inside. As they passed the mob, missiles pelted the side of the coach: rotten fruit, eggs or stones. The window was smeared with red, brown and yellow so Maestro couldn't see out of it clearly.

'Oh! Oh!' moaned Lilith with her hands over her head. 'Make it stop! Make it stop!'

A larger stone then shattered the window and glass plinked onto the floor. The two sisters screamed as they were sprayed with glass shards, although most of them hit Maestro and hardly touched the human passengers. Lilith had her face buried in her hands and was sobbing loudly.

'Lilith, my dear,' said Master Josephus, gently lifting her by the elbow. 'It is quite over now. You can squeeze onto Gregory's lap, can't you? Oh, don't act as if you've never done such a thing before, my girl. I saw you in the orangery that time at Godfrey's.'

Lilith's face turned from white to scarlet and she meekly squeezed herself beside Gregory. The other passengers were stark white and silent as they sped on, having now left the mob far behind them. Maestro looked down at himself. Shards of glass were caught in the folds of his coat, like chips of diamonds. He had carefully started to brush them off when Master Josephus's voice suddenly broke out.

'Oh, I do not think my nerves can sustain the shock,' he said, clutching at his hair. 'I can practically feel my hair turning grey. Dreadful brutes! I will see to it that they're locked up somewhere where the light of day cannot reach them for going after my Maestro like that!'

'Who cares about your wooden doll, Cephus?' Lilith wailed. 'They could have had us all killed! We should have just left it there so they won't come after us.'

'Now see here, Lilith,' said Master Josephus gravely. 'I will put that last remark down to the shock of this whole affair and willingly forget it, but I would never – I say, *never* – give up my Maestro. I should sooner have my whole head of hair turn snow-white and fall out.' He sharply looked out of the window. Lilith hiccupped and stared at him with wondering eyes. Maestro blinked at his master's face, now pale and hard as alabaster beneath its light coating of powder. No one spoke for the remainder of the journey, although Master Josephus seemed to regret being so harsh towards Lilith, as he clasped her hand and muttered delicate entreaties to her. The coach dropped Master Josephus's companions off at their residences before they finally arrived back at the mansion, and the night's misadventure came to an end.

Chapter Thirteen

The following morning was bright and airy. The dew dripped slowly from the roses outside the music-room windows and birdsong flickered through the air. But inside the music room, the cello warbled a melancholy tune. Maestro sat hunched in the chair as he absently drew the bow across the strings, his eyes turned upwards towards the picture of the girl in white. The names the people had called him still seemed to be ringing in his ears. *Abomination. Puppet. Monstrosity.* He felt a heaviness inside him, as if his parts had suddenly become very stiff. They seemed to grind more slowly, even though he had only just been wound up by a servant. What looks those men and women had had on their faces. Why was it they had wished to dismantle him so fiercely? Was he really an abomination? What truly was he? He was more than an automaton, but not quite human. Something there was no word for.

Putting down the bow, he crossed to the window and stared out over the garden. The cracks and splinters in his casing showed up clearly in the bright light. A glint of brass was visible beneath the largest crack on his left hand. It seemed to have become even worse since the previous day. If only he could have explained himself to the mob, or have asked them why it was that they wished to destroy him, he would have told them that he meant them no harm, nor wished to offend anyone. He was, after all, still largely ignorant of human customs and behaviours. The fact that what one person said or did often contradicted what another would say or do under the same circumstances made it even more perplexing for him to know how to act sometimes. Was he even bound by the same rules, anyhow, given that he wasn't technically human? If only he could communicate this to Master Josephus or someone. He felt that perhaps if people were only allowed a chance to explain themselves, it would prevent much misunderstanding. All one had to do was listen. But that was just a thought of his; it probably meant nothing. Unfortunately, it was rather difficult to put all of what he was thinking onto paper or slate, or express it through his music even. As these were the only methods of expression available to him, he was at a loss as to know what to do.

Something clicked inside his head. A song. It had set the wheels in him turning and was urging him towards the piano. Obeying the impulse, he connected his fingers to the keys. The Minervian song was there, fully formed like the goddess, just waiting to be released from his head. It fell softly from his fingers, enveloping him. The mood was wistful and dreamy to begin with, threatening to break into forlorn melancholy as his hands travelled across the sharper keys, before gradually growing more raw, the accompanying words he spoke inside his mind in time with the music.

His fingers stopped a little abruptly, his smallest finger accidently brushing the G-sharp key. He felt this was only a prelude to something greater. The something that had been covertly assembling itself in the back of his mind since he had seen the opera, this was it. It was only now that he truly acknowledged the strength of the idea that had been lying dormant all that time. He *would* attempt to compose an opera of his own. Everything was there: story, music and all. An untapped seam. But was it any good? He really knew so little about opera. Perhaps the idea was unsuitable. Master Josephus would know. Yet, if it were a feasible idea, maybe it could even help overcome some of the anger and mistrust that burned within some humans towards him. Perhaps, although he could not be sure.

There was a tap on the door and a servant entered. 'Master wishes to see you.'

Maestro got up and followed him to the large white door of Master Josephus's bedchamber. He could hear his master's voice coming from the other side, as well as crisp ruffles of silk or cotton swishing against one another. 'Why does my aunt insist on coming to stay the whole weekend of the birthday? She talks as if she is doing me a great privilege! The best thing one's distant relations can do for one is to die, granting they have left a legacy in their will. Then again, if there's a chance of them asking for your money or time, then perhaps they should just die all the sooner regardless—' The servant swiftly rapped on the door. 'Yes! What is it, Samuel?'

'Maestro here to see you, my lord.'

'Send him in right away!' called Master Josephus's reedy voice.

Maestro entered. Master Josephus was sitting in the middle of the great bed with a purple quilt and paler purple sheets beneath, propped up on pale lavender pillows with ruffled edges. The wall behind the bed was black with purple draperies, and hung on it was an oil painting of two figures half reclined against a rock on the ground, surrounded by purple flowers. The figure in the red robe had his hand over his eyes and the one in white looked to be sleeping. Maestro had seen the interior of Master Josephus's bedchamber many times before. The panelled walls were burgundy and adorned with gold stencils. Candelabras holding a great many candles were positioned about the room and heavy purple draperies fringed with gold tassels shut out the sunlight. There was a cream-coloured sofa in the far corner of the room with indigo cushions, and a number of golden chairs upholstered with purple fabric were scattered about the room. To the far right was a dresser with a large, oddly shaped looking glass with a gilt frame. With a degree of imagination, it might have resembled a pair of open lips. Amongst the various bottles and combs on the dresser was a gold figure of a seated man that had always captured Maestro's interest; the man was holding up one hand and had a smiling mouth. The pale lavender carpet was patterned with white thistles or ferns. Seated in an upholstered chair to the left of the head of the bed was Bellamy. He had turned his head towards Maestro as he entered but looked back towards his master before the automaton took another step.

'Come closer, Maestro. I have something I wish to say to you,' said Master Josephus, not looking up from the letter he was opening with the silver letter opener. His face took on an intense yet tranquil and far-off look as he perused the letter. Several others slid along the quilt as he shifted his position, the rustling being the loudest noise in the room. Maestro stood near the foot of the bed on the same side as Bellamy. 'I hope you are not affected in any way by our encounter with those ruffians last night.' He lowered the letter and looked Maestro directly in the face. 'I have seen to it that they will be severely dealt with by the law. Even so, I still feel that I am somehow to blame for all that transpired.' The letter drooped in his hand and he tossed it aside with the rest. He rearranged the quilt around himself before resuming, letting out a long sigh and picking at a loose thread.

'Perhaps if I had not insisted on you attending the opera then you would not have had to endure such an unpleasant affair. You must not think about those horrible things that they said. It was all utter nonsense stirred up by that dastard cleric, Clarke! Why, you are not a monstrosity in the slightest! You have more heart and mind than any of *them*. Anyhow, let us leave the matter aside.' He instantly brightened. 'I have some exciting news for you. As you may have gathered, in less than a fortnight I will be giving a ball here in honour of my birthday, and you are to give a concert to my guests. Is that not something exciting to look forward to?'

Maestro nodded, unable as he was to do anything else and unsure what Master Josephus expected of him.

'It will be a spectacular affair!' Master Josephus continued excitedly. 'I will spare no expense. I want people to be talking about it many seasons from now! The celebration I gave last year was rather disappointing on reflection, but I am determined to surpass it this year. And in what better way than having you to provide the music?' He smiled as Bellamy handed him his tea, which he had been preparing on a small table beside the bed. 'I am sending all the invitations out today to two hundred of the most fashionable and interesting people in the known world. I mean to invite your makers also,' he added. 'As my guests of honour in fact.'

Maestro's head jerked up and he blinked twice in rapid succession. The masters *here*! He would get to see Master Douglas once more.

'Ah!' Master Josephus's voice trilled as he tapped his spoon on the side of the teacup. 'I thought that might please you. But of course – ' Master Josephus's voice suddenly became grave, and he grimaced, ' – we cannot have you appear before my guests in *these* shabby old things.' He plucked at Maestro's old blue coat and shook his head. Maestro had changed back into his original garments since he thought no one would see him except for the servants until the evening. 'I already have a few designs for your attire of my own. Have faith, my dear friend, I will not have you looking anything less than perfect on the night!' He held out his hand and the manservant placed a sketchbook into it. He began rapidly flicking through a series of pencil and watercolour drawings. 'Oh, perhaps I could coordinate it with my own attire. Yes, what a brilliant idea!' He reached for a pencil and hurriedly began scribbling. It was some time before Maestro was allowed back into the music room, where he hastily returned his old clothes to their hiding place.

Chapter Fourteen

There had been an argument that morning. Again. The separate shifts had been a good idea, Molly reflected, as she made her way back home from Berwick Market. But even so, they were bound to end up at odds with each other at some point. It was true that they were both at their best when they worked together and bounced ideas off of one another, that is if they didn't kill each other first. Molly had heard their voices from upstairs when she was preparing breakfast.

'It is a complete and utter waste of time!' George shouted through the roof.

'I'm telling you there is nothing wrong with the calculations,' had been Douglas's slightly sharper and louder reply.

'It was *your* idea in the first place.'

'Well, you were all in favour of it earlier.'

'No, I said it had potential. It was you who insisted on putting our other projects on hold to pursue it, and now it's stuck up there—'

Something crashed against the floor upstairs, and the whole altercation showed no sign of subsiding anytime soon. Not willing to have to deal with it, Molly put on her cloak and slipped out to deliver her medicines and try to sell a few of her fresh vegetables. She still felt the need to earn her own pin money, even if she was now in command of fifty pounds courtesy of her brothers. Having just about emptied her basket in only an hour, she was taking a deliberately labyrinthine route home, in case the hostility between her brothers had not yet entirely subsided. She knew which alleyways to avoid and which streets would be teeming with people. Besides, she was quick on her feet and her load was only an empty wicker basket.

Emerging into Wardour Street, she was met with the glances of a few people who recognised her. She still received scathing glances from her mother's old acquaintances who shook their heads at one another as she passed by. (They'd always thought that she was a wild and ill-tempered child. They had been polite to Molly in front of Mrs Abernathy but privately discouraged their daughters from associating with the girl.) Then there were the boys who used to try to make her cry by pulling her hair or squishing her flowers, now having morphed into six-foot grunting creatures with scabby beards who would whistle at her and snigger as she passed. She sailed past them, sucking up the saliva that was welling in her mouth. She wouldn't have hesitated to spit at them and box their ears as a girl, but now she exercised more restraint. It wouldn't exactly help her brothers' fledgling reputation if she went around picking fights with the furniture-maker or frame-maker's apprentice. And her brothers' reputation certainly had been growing rapidly. Every day more and more commissions and begging letters arrived in the post – they'd even resorted to building a sorting machine to deal with it all. The house was constantly crowded with machines of all shapes and sizes. There'd be bits of automata, odd arms or legs, covering the kitchen table or just lying on the floor. Her brothers would forever be sat tinkering at something, just sitting there with that look of deep concentration, oblivious to everything else. She'd even once managed to get hold of the clockwork mouse and slipped it down the back of Douglas's shirt while he was working away. She had watched the small bulge migrate across his back and down his sleeve, her brother still unaware of its presence even when a nose and whiskers poked out of the end of his sleeve. She'd had to cram her fist into her mouth to stop herself laughing. It was only when it nipped his finger that he let out a loud yelp and Molly burst out into uncontrollable laughter.

The air was a lot milder now it was April, she thought, although the London air was just as stifling and fetid as ever. She hated it with a passion. She knew it was slowly suffocating her and everyone else who dwelt in the city. Nothing grew and everything withered, including its residents. She passed by St Anne's church where her mother and father were buried, slowing her pace a little as she tried to make out which headstone was theirs. She didn't notice the gentleman in the black greatcoat and top hat until he was right in front of her. She instinctively drew back a step.

'Miss Abernathy,' he said in a brittle, hushed voice as he tipped his hat at her. He wore white gloves that made his large, spindly fingers look positively skeletal.

'Mr Underwood.' She gave a shallow curtsy and was about to hurry on past him when a further remark of his arrested her step.

'I hear your brothers are making something of a name for themselves.'

She half-turned towards him and looked straight at his cadaverous face, grey and dour as ever. Yet there was something in the voice or the lines around the eyes that was akin to a smile.

'Yes. They have been rather fortunate as of late.'

'Send my regards to them. I shall tell my son that I happened to run into you today.'

Now she could definitely detect a ghost of a smile in his voice. 'That is most kind of you, Mr Underwood. I trust that both you and he are well. I must be getting home. Good day, sir.'

'Good day, Miss Abernathy.' The hand that held the walking stick touched his hat once more and he went on his way.

Molly's pace quickened as she drove for home. Fancy that she should happen to meet Mr Underwood of all people, whose boorish son her mother had wanted her to marry, but it was no reason for her to feel agitated. She peered around the building at the street corner to check whether any journalists or other unwanted persons were gathered around the front of the house. Seeing the way was clear, she briskly made her way down the road and took out her key. But as she drew nearer, she saw there were shards of glass on the ground like blue-white snow. One of the window panes had been smashed. She curled her fingers around the door handle and braced herself as she turned her key and pushed it gently.

Silence. Save for the ticking of clocks. Lying on the floor, having smashed a pocket watch or two on its descent, was a brick. A note was fastened to it with string. Letting out a sigh, Molly retrieved it and went through to the back of the house. On the floor was a muddle of sooty footprints leading from the parlour to the kitchen, most of them about the size of a small child's, although a number had been made by two larger sets of fainter, smudgy feet. Through the archway to the kitchen, she saw George sitting at the table surrounded by bits of machinery. He did not acknowledge her presence as she set her basket down beside him and added the brick to the stack by the hearth. There were four in total.

'They smashed another window pane.'

'They actually managed to hit their target this time?'

'Unfortunately, after the last two missed. There was another note attached.' Saying so, she unknotted the string around the brick.

'I'll see about getting the glass replaced. What does the note say?'

'The same nonsense about us being blasphemers and how we'll burn for our sins et cetera.' She shrugged, tossing the note into the fireplace.

'Devotees of that fanatic Reverend Clarke,' muttered George.

'How is it again that they refer to themselves?'

'SOAL,' George replied. 'The Sons of Adam League.'

Molly rolled her eyes. 'I hear there's been gangs going around smashing up factories now too, like Luddites. I doubt *that's* to do with machines usurping humanity and more ruffians looking for an excuse to cause trouble. What is it you're doing?' she added, as she removed her cloak.

'Making a part for a machine I'm working on,' was the vague reply. She'd noticed how he'd attempted to cover bits of it up with the morning paper while her back was still half-turned. Typical George, secretive as ever. She had hoped he'd been attempting to fix one of the machines that had been steadily filling the kitchen. Maybe she should start leaving notes by the decanter in the parlour or the coffee-making machine.

'What was all the noise about this morning?' She sat down opposite him and rested her arms on the table. Hopefully this question would produce a lengthier response.

'Douglas had this idea for an automaton chimney sweep, although we were supposed to be working on a number of other projects at the time.

I eventually agreed to it as I thought it might be quite easily marketable. Then, when it failed to work as it ought to have – it would go up inside the chimney but not come down again – he had the nerve to blame it on me and accused me of not giving it my full attention. Then I also discovered he'd used components that I had intentionally saved for something I was privately working on for a project of his own.' He didn't take his eyes off of what he was doing as he spoke.

Molly attentively watched him and nodded to herself. George had not reached for the brandy or gone down to the public house nearly as often since he and Douglas had become so busy. She could only hope that it would keep up. 'So are you going to get one back on him?' she asked, as she slid the open pages of the paper towards her and scanned the columns for anything of interest.

'Such an action would be foolish and petty,' said George, as he turned the piece of machinery around in his hands.

The next moment there was a violent crash from above and they heard Douglas yell.

'Although I may have made a few adjustments to that alarm-clock of his,' he muttered.

'You're very deceptive, you know. And not half as logical as you make out to be.' Molly smiled. She turned her eyes towards the ceiling. All was silent from the floor above. 'Maybe one of us had better go up and make sure he's not hurt.'

'He'll be all right. Go see for yourself if you're concerned. You can fetch me down my coat while you're at it.'

'Why? Where are you going?'

'A meeting with a potential client.'

'Does Douglas know you're going?'

'I decided not to tell him.'

'I'd be quick if I were you then, because if he catches on that you're going somewhere he'll—'

Before she could finish speaking there came the sound of hurried footsteps thudding down the stairs and Douglas bolted into the room, his face oddly bright. 'Did I hear you say you were off to a meeting?'

'Yes, but I know what you're going to ask and—'

'Oh please, please, *please* let me use the airship.' He clasped his hands together in a deliberately melodramatic begging gesture. 'I haven't tested it properly yet and I want to have a passenger.'

'I've told you a hundred times no.'

'But *why*?'

'Because I'm certain you'd kill us both.'

'I promise I won't go too high. It'll only be a short flight.'

'The altitude and the duration of the flight make no difference.'

'Oh, just do as he's asking, George.' Molly rolled her eyes. 'I'll come too if that'll make any difference. I wouldn't mind the opportunity to fly.'

'It would be at your own risk,' said George gravely. 'Are you sure?'

'Positive.' She nodded firmly, smoothing back the strands of hair that had tipped over her face.

'Thanks, Mol!' Douglas squeezed his sister and then ran back upstairs, calling, 'I'll go get our coats.'

'He's like a little boy sometimes.' Molly smiled as she retrieved her cloak.

'Are you really certain about this?' asked George.

'Well, not entirely. But I don't think he'd try it if he thought there'd be a chance of it crashing on the maiden voyage. Besides, he'd only keep asking.' She slipped the cloak over her shoulders and fixed the gold brooch she used to fasten it at the centre of her collarbone.

'Hmm, I suppose that's true.' George put his work aside and they waited until Douglas returned with two coats, one black, one brown, draped over his arm, and a wide grin fixed on his face. He flung the black one at George, who caught it deftly in his right hand.

'So where is it you're off to?' asked Douglas, as he thrust his arm into his coat.

'The Queen's Inn,' said George, as he shrugged on his own.

Douglas frowned, with still only one arm in the sleeve. 'Isn't that where we were supposed to be meeting Mr Clayton Cobb?'

'Yes, that is who I'm meeting there.'

'But wasn't it—?' He twisted around to look at the old clock on the mantel. 'Of course, I set my clock to go off at half past eleven so I'd be ready in time and you messed with it. I would have missed the meeting.'

'That was my intention.'

'Who is Mr Clayton Cobb?' interjected Molly in an attempt to diffuse the rising tension.

Douglas and George fell silent and turned to look at her. George adjusted his collar and cleared his throat. 'Mr Cobb is a textiles manufacturer from the north who's hoping to establish himself in London,' he replied. 'He wrote to us with an interesting proposition – to create a factory that is completely mechanical in its operation. He invited us to come and discuss it with him today at the hotel in Whitechapel where he is residing.'

Molly whistled. 'That sounds like a huge commission. Are you seriously thinking of accepting it?'

'That remains to be seen. It depends on how today goes.'

'So let's get going then! Come on!' said Douglas, who was already out of the kitchen and making his way to the front door.

George and Molly followed their brother down a narrow bystreet, snaking through a series of blackened brick streets until they reached a boarded-up building of scabby brickwork practically slouching on a street corner. The sign hanging down over the doorway was illegible, save for the faded 'L' in peeling yellow. Molly could just about decipher LIVERY AND BAIT STABLES on getting closer.

'How much did the man sell it to you for again?' asked Molly.

'I gave him a sovereign for it.'

'I don't think anyone in their right mind would have given a shilling for it, judging by the outside.'

'Yes, but I didn't buy it because the exterior looked attractive. Come on.'

He led them to the front door and took the key from his pocket. It took a bit of twisting in the rusty lock, but eventually he managed to get the door open. Molly's nose twitched. The musky air still very much had a horsey smell to it. It was a low-ceilinged space with whitewashed walls, the stalls having been removed and propped against the far wall, although some pieces had been converted into a makeshift table. It was undeniably clean in spite of the smell. Douglas lit a lantern, which threw a weak puddle of light over the room. 'I did have an electric light in here, but the generator's broken,' he said apologetically. 'But you can still make it out over there even in this light. What do you think?'

Sitting in the middle of the room was something, Molly fancied, like the offspring of a bird and a locomotive. Its body was of bolted metal, but its wings and fanned tail were canvas, its face glass and its pointed beak metal. There were a variety of wheels, pipes and valves attached to it, with two enormous metal barrels sticking out below each wing.

'Well?' Douglas stood there smiling expectantly.

'It's...different,' said Molly carefully, as she came closer to inspect it. One of her shoes squelched, and she feared she'd stepped in a leftover patch of manure, but when she looked down she saw it was a puddle of gloopy oil. She inspected the glass bubble that contained what was presumably the controls and red, leather-backed seats. 'I hope you don't mind me saying, but I can't imagine something this heavy getting off the ground.'

'Oh, she'll get off the ground, I don't doubt that.' Douglas patted her steely hide, which rang with a clear, metallic purr. 'She has twin four-cylinder hybrid steam engines that can generate up to one-eighty horse power. Do you want to sit in the front or the back?'

'Hmm...back. If George doesn't mind sitting in the front.'

'I have no preference,' said George, who had been examining the engines. 'You do realise that your biggest error was using steam-powered engines.'

'Oh, go on, say your piece. I knew you'd been silent too long.'

'Steam is inefficient. The power-to-weight ratio required is simply too impractical. You might get us airborne, but you have no means of controlling it once in flight.'

'Thought of that. You'll soon see how for yourself once we're in the air. All right then.' Douglas clapped his hands. The sound bounced off the ship's side. 'If you'd like to step on board.' A rectangular panel on the bird's side opened with a hiss of steam. (Whether Douglas had opened it with a valve on the bird or with a hidden device Molly didn't know. She just saw his right hand disappear behind his back.) He extended his hand to his sister with a crooked grin. 'The lady can go first.'

Molly mounted the ship without accepting his hand and slipped into the backseat. George seated himself once Douglas was sat at the controls. There were great lengths of copper pipes surrounding the driver's seat, as well as all manner of valves, dials, gauges and handles. Some handles were wood, metal or crystal, and a telescope dangled down from the roof. At the centre was a wheel, rather like a ship's, but it was leather and metal rather than wood. The door closed of its own accord and there came a sound like oysters being shucked as it sealed itself shut.

Molly felt she'd sat on something and lifted up a red, cloth-bound book.

'The manual,' explained Douglas. 'There are so many different parts to operating this thing that I thought I'd better jot them down as I was going along.'

'Well, looking at this, I'd say that was a good idea,' said Molly, as she began thumbing through the manual. 'Does the ship have a name?'

'Well, to tell the truth, I've been stuck on what to christen her.'

'How are we to get off the ground without blasting a hole through the roof?' interrupted George. 'Unless you mean to—'

Suddenly the rear of the ship began to tilt downwards so the beak was pointing skyward. Up until this point, Molly had been fairly calm, but now her insides started to knot. On the other side of the glass, she could see two huge wheels turning on either side, the clacking sound muffled from inside the dome. Slowly, the wooden ceiling parted inch by inch and the sky opened up before them. Something bumped the ship from behind. There was a harsh, tense creaking from outside as they sank down a few inches.

'I also added a spring-loaded mechanism for a bit of extra propulsion. All right, ready?' Douglas turned a small key in a slot beside the wheel. The engines roared into life and sent waves of vibrations through the bird, which Molly could feel chugging through the back of her seat. A number of coloured lights sparked into life and the faces of the dials lit up. The shuddering and growling grew louder and fiercer until bits of the bird actually began to rattle. It was only then that Douglas curled his fingers around the large, red lever by his left leg and thrust it back. Molly's stomach lurched violently as they shot upwards and were hurtled into the sky at breakneck speed. It was a peculiar sensation that she experienced.

She felt light-headed and her ears were stuffy, as if they had been crammed full of wool. Stars swam before her eyes and she was insensible to anything that was going on around her save for this feeling of acceleration and the hard blue that filled her vision. For a brief moment she was certain she'd be sick but the nausea retreated down her throat. When the metal bird straightened itself out and was sailing serenely, as if it were travelling along an invisible stretch of track laid out before it, Molly peered out over London. How strange everything looked from above. There was the clocktower they were building near the Houses of Parliament, and there was Westminster Abbey.

'This is amazing!' she cried out, looking over at George, who was equally engrossed in the view from his side. A flock of birds passed them overhead, and behind them two white ribbons of smoke stretched out seemingly endlessly into the distance.

'Shall we go higher?' said Douglas, not waiting for an answer before he pulled back a lever, causing them to gently rise. Now they were flying amongst a sea of clouds. Molly's ears began to crackle and she had to tense her jaw and press her teeth hard together until they cleared, as if she had a head cold. The air felt thinner but somehow purer, far preferable to the fusty atmosphere of the city below. It had grown colder inside the airship and she pulled her shawl tightly around herself to stop her shivering. But the view was a breathtaking sight, and something nobody had ever seen before. Molly placed her palms against the glass and the window began to fog from her breath. She wiped it away with her sleeve.

'I see how you've achieved it,' remarked George. 'It's the shape of the wings and rudder. You've made it so that they can be altered, thus allowing the ship to roll and change direction.'

'Precisely. Just like a bird does. I ran a series of hollow canes through the wings, which I can control with these levers here. See? I'm not quite as foolish as you believe me to be. Right, I'll lower her back down again and come in range of our destination. It should be a steady descent, and then—' But as they sank below the cloud bank, the ship gave a violent jolt. The engines spluttered and the vibrations from the back of Molly's seat ceased.

'What was that?'

'That was the sound of the engines cutting out.'

'*What?*'

'It's all right. Let me just try something.' He pulled a sideways-facing lever and a second pair of wings sprouted out from either side of the ship. 'Hopefully that should steady us for now until I can restart the engine.' But even as he was speaking, they had begun to drop out of the sky, rapidly picking up speed. The ship tipped forwards and was hurtling headlong towards the earth.

'Douglas! Do something!' yelled Molly, seeing fragments falling away from the ship's body.

Douglas was frantically trying to turn the key, which only made a wheezy noise, and then fiddled around with the various controls, swatting away George's hand when he tried to interfere. Molly began rapidly flicking through the manual. One engine coughed back into life and stalled their descent, although they were now flying at an angle, tilting towards the right.

'I think one of the engines has an oil leak. I could try cross-feeding the fuel valves, then she'd fly straight!'

'Do that then!'

There came a deep thunk and the bird suddenly reared up. Douglas then pressed down forcefully on a pump and the remaining engine gave a powerful roar. He fed as much fuel to it as possible and gradually they slowed back down to a much gentler pace and resumed their correct angle. Molly's heart was still thumping away in her chest. They descended steadily, circling the city. Molly could see the upturned faces of people below.

'What part of London are we in?' she asked.

'We're in Whitechapel,' said George.

'I have *this* to tell us where exactly we are.' Douglas tapped at a round, glass-covered image of a map, about the width of a teacup, on the control panel. It was moving, a grey dot being visible beneath one of the veins of road. 'This device detects signals coming from the Earth's magnetic field. I aligned the map so the magnet slides along as we do; that way we'll never get lost. The next thing I'm hoping to do is allow us to plot a course in advance with it. I call it the Gravitational Pull Sensor, although I've been meaning to find a better name for it. And according to this we're in…'

'We're in Whitechapel,' said George flatly.

'Shoreditch,' said Douglas almost simultaneously. He frowned at the GPS and tapped the glass again, which made a disappointingly blunt sound. 'No, that's not right. It must have become misaligned somehow when the engines cut out.'

'I recognise the area. The hotel is further up Commercial Street. Just fly straight and keep following the road,' said George impatiently.

'Where should I land her?'

'Somewhere out of the way. You've attracted too much notice as it is.'

'How about that alleyway down there? It should be relatively quiet.'

'I suppose it'll have to do.'

'You all right to guard it, Mol?' Douglas craned his neck over the back of his seat. 'She has ammunition in case anyone does try to go for her. And the glass is quite thick. It'd take a lot to smash it.'

'It's not like I have anything better to do, is it? But just hurry up and land or you'll be late to your meeting.'

The airship gradually sank lower and lower until it was hovering over the dingy, narrow lane. It snagged on a washing line as it landed, just about managing to fit into the street.

'If anything happens, press this big rubber button here. That's connected to a rather loud horn. We'll hear it and come running,' Douglas told Molly, as he and George climbed out.

'I won't need to,' she said breezily, as she swung herself into the front seat. She held up the red book and grinned. 'I'll be able to fly this thing better than you can by the time you come back.'

She was already contentedly reading when Douglas and George emerged into the main street. Despite her confident demeanour, Douglas was still a little uneasy about leaving his sister – and his ship – in the middle of Whitechapel, albeit in one of the more respectable parts. The hotel was only around the corner from where Molly and the airship were hidden, or rather, it was an old coaching inn masquerading as a hotel. The sign on the outside read QUEEN'S TAVERN AND FAMILY HOTEL, but once inside, as far as Douglas could see, it was occupied solely by gentlemen.

The sitting room was worn, outdated and shabby. The furniture and the paintings looked like poor copies. They were shown through to the dining room where one or two men were sat with a pipe and a paper while two waiters were setting the tables for the luncheon. Seated near the back corner of the room was a rather corpulent man who looked as if he had been formed from lumps of raw clay. His face certainly had the same sickly ochre shade to it as unfired clay. He had been stuffed into a celadon sack coat and a waistcoat of the same colour was stretched over his bulging stomach. Upon catching sight of the two brothers, he struggled to his feet, being somewhat tightly wedged into his seat against the wall.

'Mr Cobb.' Douglas nodded as they approached the table and offered his hand.

'Mr Abernathy,' Mr Cobb said emphatically, as he slapped hold of Douglas's hand.

A twinge shot up along Douglas's arm at the touch, as firm as steel yet clammy and slimy like an autumn leaf on a rainy day. How George managed to maintain his usual passive expression under the same treatment he didn't know.

'It is a pleasure to finally meet you both at last. Pray have a seat,' Mr Cobb said, gesturing to the two chairs opposite his own. Now they were closer to him, Douglas could see the wet sheen on the man's face lit by the weak sunlight streaming in from the window. A few wisps of yellow hair were spread thinly across his crown but his moon-shaped face was otherwise as plump and hairless as an infant's. His wide neck was ringed with fat. He didn't have a double chin but triple or quadruple chins, for they would divide into finer rings when his head sank down into his body, as if the flesh had not properly set. They were also now close enough to smell the dense, keen stench of bodily odour and stale sweat that was being emitted from him. A waiter came over to the table and they ordered drinks before Mr Cobb mashed his doughy hands together and cleared his throat with a grunt.

'So, you're the two gentlemen who built the automaton that can think for itself?' He spoke with a northern accent that reminded Douglas slightly of their father, only he supposed their father's pronunciation had been somewhat diluted by comparison.

'Well, it doesn't think, as such,' said George. 'But rather it has a system of gears that—'

Cobb held up his hand. 'I don't want all the particulars of it, Mr Abernathy. I'm a man of business, not an engineer. It's all Greek to me. All I want is definite proof that it's not some clever fraud.'

'I promise you that it is genuine, Mr Cobb,' said Douglas firmly, as the waiter returned with their drinks. They would not be serving luncheon for a while yet. He suddenly thought of poor Molly sitting in the airship. It'd be a while before she could have her luncheon. 'We have even secured a patent for the technology,' he continued.

'Do you have any documentation to back up that statement?'

'Yes, as it happens, I have it right here.'

Douglas prided himself on his foresight as he took the papers from his coat pocket and placed them in Mr Cobb's hand. Cobb scrutinised them with his flinty little eyes as he took out a handkerchief and dabbed his dripping forehead with it. 'It all looks fine.' He returned the documents to Douglas with four translucent, circular impressions in the paper. 'You've satisfied me for the time being. Now,' he leant forward, 'about the proposition I outlined in my letter. How feasible is it?'

'Well, that depends, sir,' said Douglas, 'on what exactly it is you want us to do. You said that you wanted to completely mechanise every aspect of production in your textiles mill. How exactly do you mean?'

'Let me explain a little about what it is I intend to do.' Cobb sank back into his seat and his face assumed a more placid, self-assured look. The rings on his neck increased to three. 'I started out in ceramics, y'see. That was my family's old trade. I joined the firm with my brother and father when I was still just a lad and after only two years, I'd helped increase production fivefold. But I wanted to try my hand at another trade and see what I could do with it, having conquered one already. And, well, I suppose you could say I have a golden touch, since everything I try my hand at instantly becomes more efficient and profitable. I tried steel next and became a partner in a company in Sheffield. A year later, they'd gone from churning out a sorry amount of poor-quality steel to being one of the leading producers in the area. Recently I decided to enter the textile trade. I bought an ailing woollen mill and transformed it outright – scrapped all the old looms and replaced the waterwheels with a steam engine. But now I want to take on an even greater challenge.' A smile split across his face and he rubbed his lips together as if savouring the pause. Then he leant forward again and bent his head low, as if he were communicating a great secret. He even lowered his voice a fraction when he spoke next. 'Silk.'

'Silk, sir?' said Douglas promptly.

'Aye. Where we are now is only a stone's throw away from Spitalfields. It was once the thriving heart of the British silk industry, and still very much is, even though a lot of it's done in the country now. And of course it's been crippled by cheaper silks coming in from abroad. I don't reckon French silk is half as fine as they make it out to be compared to what comes out of Spitalfields. If it weren't for the government propping it up, the industry would've collapsed altogether decades ago. Most of the weaving is done in the weavers' own homes. You ever seen Spitalfields – no? It's not a particularly pleasant sight. But the days of hand-looms are numbered. Takes a lot more skill to weave silk than it does cotton or wool, too much for a machine to be able to do it. Right now those power looms over on the Continent can still only produce simpler, lighter fabrics like taffetas, and the quality isn't as good as the handwoven stuff. But give it a few years and they'll be able to produce any sort of fabric as good as a human weaver. And if the duty on French silk goods is lifted, then that'll be the final nail in the coffin, unless we can beat the froggy buggers at their own game. They might have their Jacquard looms, but if we could have English machines churning out high-quality silk and lots of it before they catch up, they won't be able to compete on price or quality. That's what gave me the idea.' He nodded with a smug, self-assured air. 'The idea, gentlemen, is to completely mechanise production from the spinning of the raw silk to wrapping the finished product. Which is why I bought a factory here in the capital, thinking I'd test out this idea of mine that I've had in mind for a long time. Two birds one stone, eh? I mean, textiles are a prime example of how replacing human workers with machines can transform an industry. Yet there still remains some human involvement, doffers, piecers, and overlookers to keep 'em in line and so on. And where you introduce human involvement, you introduce potential error – that's how I see the matter anyhow. The weaver lets his fingers or foot slip for one minute, and there! The whole thing is ruined. What I envision' – he tapped his temple with a porky digit – 'is a factory of clever machines overseeing every stage of production – machines building other machines even! Each one designated for a specific task, which it performs perfectly and unceasingly day *and* night. And intelligent machines to come up with new patterns and fix problems as they arise, but not so intelligent as to question their work. There'd still probably be an overlooker or two. Yet ultimately, there will be no need for any workers.'

'Thus maximising efficiency while lowering the overall cost of production and the price along with it, meaning English silk can compete with foreign markets,' said George with his arms folded across his chest.

'Precisely! No wages to pay, no mistakes, and the machines will pay for themselves in no time. A better quality product for a lower price, and lots of it. The French will never know what hit 'em!'

The brothers remained in astonished silence for a moment until, certain that the soliloquy was at an end, Douglas cleared his throat. 'That is quite an ambition, Mr Cobb. But what of the weavers?'

'What of them?' Cobb raised an eyebrow. 'They'd all be out of work since I'd 'ave no use for 'em. Don't tell me you're one of them humanitarian sort, are yer?'

'No, I was merely curious,' Douglas muttered into his beer.

'But what I want to know is, could you design such machines?' persisted Cobb. 'And if so, how long they would take to build and at what cost?'

Douglas and George exchanged a look.

'It is...feasible,' said George. 'We can produce a prototype and see if it meets your expectations.'

'Can you give me an estimate of the price?'

George's eyes turned upward a brief moment. 'Six hundred pounds.'

Cobb's head sank down into his neck and the rings multiplied. 'Are you certain?'

'Absolutely. If you want us to do it correctly then that is how much it'll cost, and we would only just be making a profit. We should be able to manage it in less than four weeks.'

Douglas widened his eyes at his brother, who sharply kicked him in the ankle under the table. Cobb regarded the two of them with a dubious stare.

'And you can guarantee it'll work?'

'Yes.'

Cobb's stern expression did not alter, and then the cracked smile spread across his face, exposing small, rounded teeth like tea-stained china.

'Very well, gentlemen. We have a deal then.' When he raised his hand, Douglas feared he was about to shake theirs with it again, but instead he signalled to a waiter to bring George and he fresh drinks. Douglas's was still a third of the way full. 'Now, let's discuss the details. I'll arrange for you to have a tour around the factory at your earliest convenience. I'll give you a rough sketch of the layout, and what I envision to go inside of it.'

Douglas glanced at the other diners who were beginning to drift in. As Cobb laid out his grand vision before them over a plate of chops and fried potatoes, Douglas listened with one ear for the impatient bleat of a horn. It was only when Cobb was enquiring about pudding that it sounded.

Chapter Fifteen

A whole sack of mail had arrived by the morning post. Douglas heaved it onto his shoulder and just managed to tip its contents into the top of the sorting machine. It vaguely resembled a stove; a rectangular shaft at the top fed each item into a device like a waterwheel, and from there it was fed into one of the sorter's three stomach chambers labelled Junk, Commissions, Other. The lever on the side was jammed. After opening the panel at the top, Douglas found a bill from his tailor jammed in the pivot. He removed it and tried the lever again. This time it clicked and there came a chugging sound from inside the machine as each letter whizzed around the wheel and was deposited into one of the three chambers. The Junk file belched a jet of flames and a wispy trail of smoke curled up into the air. Douglas popped open the trays of the other two compartments and carried the remaining letters through to the kitchen. It was still a sizable stack.

George was still in his dark burgundy dressing-gown with the black sash, his hands deep in his pockets, as he stood over the automated coffee maker on the kitchen table. Made of steel, it was a distant relative of the kettle, with lots of tubes and nozzles and a compartment at the bottom where the cup was placed. It rattled and sweated – a sound like gravel being churned was coming from inside the drum. George tapped the side impatiently.

'Don't say it's broken?' said Douglas.

'No, although I think it's in need of cleaning. The grounds must be clogging the nozzle.'

'I thought my coffee had been a little gritty recently.'

Yesterday's debate about Cobb's commission now seemed forgotten. They had argued about it all the way home. Douglas objected on the grounds that, if they accepted it, it would put all of the Spitalfields weavers out of work. George dismissed this point as redundant and insisted it would be foolish to pass up the opportunity. They ultimately failed to reach an agreement and had not spoken for the rest of the night. But the implications of building automata to replace human workers had pricked Douglas's conscience. Perhaps there was a grain of truth and sanity in Reverend Clarke's preaching.

'Is that this morning's post?' asked George, as the machine gave a gurgle and steaming brown liquid shot out of the spout into the waiting cup.

'Yes, not so great a load today,' replied Douglas brightly, dumping the stack of letters onto the table.

'Just as well. We have a large enough back catalogue of work as it is.' George sipped his coffee. The next second he grimaced into the cup and poured its contents over the coals.

Douglas started sifting through some of the letters until he paused over one and held it up nearer to his face. He recognised the handwriting.

'What's that?'

'A letter from our patron.' Douglas turned it over and broke the seal. There was a single page of elegantly written script, a faint scent of violets uncurling from the paper. Nestled inside the folded letter was a stiff square of rose-gold-coloured paper bearing the same crest that Douglas had seen on Lord Leyton's coach. It was a black shield with a white heart and stripe inside of it. Above was a knight's helmet with a winged golden star on top. On either side, stood on hind legs with claws raised, was a tiger.

'What does he want?'

'Two things. First of all, he wants us to build him two mechanical tigers.'

'Two tigers?'

'Yes. He wants them to sound, move and act just like real ones.'

'And the second thing?'

'A bird. He doesn't specify what sort, he only requests that it *do something extraordinary*. He says he will pay us handsomely for both but they must be completed for a gathering he is hosting in two weeks' time. What do you reckon we should do?'

'We've got enough commissions coming in to be able to choose between them.' George plucked the other letters from Douglas's hand and began riffling through them. 'We don't need to waste our time making wind-up trinkets for aristocrats.'

'You really don't want to accept it?'

'I don't see any reason why we must. We are not in any immediate want of money and two mechanical animals are hardly testing our abilities.'

'He is our first and foremost patron – it seems disloyal not to,' said Douglas, following his brother into the parlour.

'What has loyalty got to do with it? You think he wouldn't go to another maker of automata if they could offer him some novelty?'

'Well, I dare say he might, although I'd like to think—'

'As far as I'm concerned, our dealings with Lord Leyton came to an end the moment he collected the android. If he needs us to repair it at any point in the future, then that is fair enough, but I don't feel any sort of obligation towards him in the slightest.'

George threw himself into an armchair. On the table beside him was a little plant with oddly shaped pink petals like a pair of lips. It raised its head as he sat down. 'All these requests for golden elephants and life-sized mechanical dolls are distracting us from our real work.' He held up the letters he had already opened. 'Do you realise what will happen if we continue to take up commissions like this? We'll secure a reputation for ourselves as nothing more than makers of playthings for the rich and decadent. They have served their purpose, they were merely a stepping stone to something greater. They got us noticed, now we can leave them behind and get on with—' There came a moist little noise. George froze. The plant had pressed a little kiss on his cheek. 'I wish Molly would stop leaving her specimens lying around the house.'

Douglas, hiding the smile on his face, snorted with laughter behind the letter. 'Yes, as do I.'

George edged away from the plant, which leant inwards after him. 'But as I was saying, I am entirely for refusing this commission. I think it would be an utter waste of time.'

'Wait, I haven't finished reading the letter to you. I think this next part might give you some incentive. The gathering he wants to display them at is a ball in honour of his birthday and he has invited us to attend – as his guests of honour, no less.' Douglas looked up. 'And it won't just be aristocrats who will be there. It will be all sorts of people, like intellectuals and people of business. You said yourself that these noblemen are stepping stones and you know that Lord Leyton, for all his eccentricities, is very well connected.'

'Undoubtedly. I see your point.'

George held up the letters as if he meant to strike the plant with them. It retracted its head and hid it beneath its top leaves.

'I think you hurt its feelings a little.'

'It's a plant.'

'I don't think Molly will appreciate you hitting it at any rate,' said Douglas, as George got hold of a newspaper and began rolling it up.

'Having considered the matter a little more, I think perhaps we should take up the commission after all. Although I know you really want to go to this ball because you want to see the android.' Tossing the paper down on the table, he went over to the decanter of brandy and poured out a measure.

'Well, it would be nice to see him again. You do know it hasn't gone eight o'clock yet?' he said with slight disbelief as George added the soda water to the glass and took a swig from it. Douglas weighed up the benefit of rebuking him further, deciding it wasn't worth the effort.

'Oh, I thought I'd left it in here!' Molly suddenly flew into the room and picked up the plant.

'It seems very fond of George. It even gave him a kiss a moment ago.' Douglas smirked at his brother, who glared at him from beneath his dark brows.

'Oh yes, it'll do that.' Molly stroked the plant's head with her little finger and it reached up to kiss her cheek. 'That's how they make sense of things around them, and how they catch their prey. Be thankful it wasn't one that had red petals instead of pink.'

'Why's that?' asked George.

'Because if it had been, you would have been paralysed for the next twelve hours.' She readjusted her position so she had one arm around the plant's flowerpot and the other on her hip. 'What was it the two of you were discussing before I came in? I heard you both through the floorboards.'

'An invitation from Lord Leyton. He has invited us to a ball and he wants us to build him three automata for the occasion – a bird and two tigers.'

'That sounds exciting. I can't imagine it being to George's liking though. Being confined in a big room filled with lots of people, having to dance and converse with real humans! How'd you get him to agree to that?' She grinned roguishly at George.

'He's invited you too, Molly.'

Her grin swiftly sank. 'Me? What for?'

'He requests that we *bring along our darling sister*. He seems keen to meet you, plus there is a shortage of young ladies to pair up with the gentlemen, it seems.'

Setting the kissing plant down again, Molly snatched the letter from Douglas and perused it briefly. 'Humph. What is it to me if he is short of young ladies? I refuse to make a spectacle of myself.'

'Oh, come on, Mol. It might be interesting.'

'I don't doubt that. In fact, I am rather curious to see what a ball is like. But I'm not curious enough to spend an entire evening in a room filled with people of *importance*. I won't know what to do with myself.'

'Mother taught you dancing and etiquette from the age of three.'

'But I didn't expect that I'd ever actually have to use any of it, and there is no way I am dancing with one of your lord's friends,' she said flatly, folding the letter. Then she knocked her head back to clear a wisp of hair from her eyes. 'Besides, I don't have anything to wear.'

'Lord Leyton probably has an interesting collection of plant life,' said Douglas in a wheedling voice, as he nudged her arm with his elbow. 'He might have a hothouse full of rare specimens.'

Molly cast her eyes down and sucked her lip. Douglas could sense that she was wavering.

'You'd be doing me a favour as well, Molly. Otherwise you'll leave me stuck with Mr Social over there all evening.' George glowered at him. 'Please, Mol. I promise it'll be fun. I'll make sure no strange gentleman makes you dance with him. You'll have me or George with you the entire time. What possible danger is there?'

She pushed back her hair and groaned. 'Urgh, fine then, I'll come – for you, not for Lord Leyton. But *you* had better not abandon me.' She jabbed her finger at Douglas.

'I'll be right by your side the whole night,' said Douglas firmly. 'The only time I'll be away from you will be if the automata he wants us to build are in need of seeing to.'

'Speaking of which...' George purposefully set down his empty tumbler on the sideboard and his hands slunk back into his pockets. 'We had better come up with the extraordinary thing this bird must do, and what sort of bird it'll be, for that matter.'

'A peacock?' offered Molly, dangling her arms over the back of the sofa. 'They are quite impressive birds anyway.'

Douglas and George exchanged looks. 'What do you think?' asked Douglas.

'A peacock will suit. If we make a start on it now we can have it finished by Saturday.'

'I was thinking for the tigers we could adapt the design for the mechanical kitten we drew when we were boys. All we need to do is increase the scale and make a few adjustments to their behavioural sequences.'

'Hardly a challenge though, is it?' said George. 'If we *are* going to do this, we might as well try to make something worthwhile that'll really push us. If he wants something extraordinary, we will give him it.'

'What do you mean?' Douglas detected a suggestion of a cunning smile glinting in George's blue eyes.

'You will see. I'll make a start on the bird, you dig out the plans for the cat.'

'Right. But what about these?' Douglas pointed to the pile of letters George had abandoned.

George ran his eye over them indifferently. 'They can be put to one side for now, we can always return to them later.' He shrugged.

His brother and sister watched after him as he disappeared upstairs.

'You worried about him?' asked Molly, the volume of her voice carefully calculated to be below George's level of hearing.

'Oh, no more than usual,' Douglas lied. 'Why? What is it that worries you?'

'Nothing in particular, it's just—' Molly looked at the empty tumbler and gave it up. 'Just a feeling.' She flopped down on the sofa and returned to Lord Leyton's letter. 'So what do you plan on doing about the dress code?'

'The what?'

'Didn't you read the letter all the way through? It says here that guests are required to wear at least one item of purple.'

Douglas's brow furrowed. 'I don't think I own a single thing that is purple.'

'I could easily conjure up a couple of purple buttonholes for you and George if you think that'll count.'

'Maybe, although it might specifically mean an item of clothing. What about you?'

'I'll come up with something.' She let the letter fall, but as she reached for her plant, her attention was caught by the bowl of apples on the sideboard. She crossed the room and took one of the apples. It did not look quite right. The rosy sheen that it cast seemed abnormally bright. She felt that the apple was almost grinning at her, daring her to take a bite.

'Douglas, where did these apples come from?'

'From your tree. I picked a few of the ripest to put in Mother's antique fruit bowl. I didn't think to tell you, but it would have been a shame to leave them to rot.'

'But no one has actually tried to...eat them, have they?' Molly asked apprehensively.

'No. Why?' Douglas laughed lightly. 'You don't normally mind us picking the odd piece of fruit from your trees. What's so special about those apples?'

'Nothing,' Molly said quickly, dropping the apple she was holding back into the bowl as if it was burning her. Then, to Douglas's confusion, she picked up the bowl and said over her shoulder, as she hurried from the room, 'Just don't pick any more of my fruit without asking me in future, all right?'

'Oh, all right Molly.' Douglas was left scratching his head after she'd gone. He couldn't make his sister out sometimes.

Chapter Sixteen

Douglas hollered up the stairs, 'Hurry up the pair of you, we're running late as it is!'

George took no notice of him and carried on tweaking the cylindrical drum of the device he was testing on his bedroom worktable. It was part of the prototype they were developing for Cobb. What was his brother so concerned about? They were not expected to arrive until eleven o' clock and it was not yet quarter to. The house was only a fifteen-minute drive away.

Douglas's footsteps grew louder on the stairs and he burst into George's room. 'Will you stop messing with that thing and come downstairs? The cab is outside and the driver doesn't seem at all happy about the boxes.'

'What are you so flustered about? We're both practically ready,' said George coolly, adjusting one of his cuffs as he rose.

He was wearing a knee-length black frock coat with white piping, his waistcoat and trousers also being the same severe black. A neat violet cravat was fastened onto his white collar. Douglas's coat was longer and lighter than his brother's, ending at the ankle, and charcoal grey in colour. His waistcoat was lavender, a silvery fern pattern showing when it caught the light. His trousers and bow tie were both black, the tie having been slackened slightly on account of his repeatedly jerking it away from his throat.

'You and I are ready, but I don't know what state Molly is in. You go see how the driver is getting on with the boxes and I'll see about her.'

George made his way downstairs while Douglas rapped on his sister's door. There was no answer so he knocked again.

'What?' demanded a low, irritable-sounding voice on the other side of the door.

'Are you ready yet? The cab is already outside.'

'I'll be down in a moment. I just need to finish sticking pins in my hair. Ah! Do all well-bred women go through this much trouble every day?'

'They go through a lot more than that, I should imagine. Just make sure you're downstairs in the next five minutes.'

Downstairs, Douglas saw his brother standing in the middle of the parlour. 'Are the boxes loaded up?'

'Yes. Is our sister ready?'

'Not quite. George, do you really have time to be doing that?' George was pouring himself a measure of brandy.

'I reckon so if Molly is still getting ready. The driver is tending to his horses anyhow.'

Douglas crossed his arms and sighed, his foot rapidly striking the floor. Was he the only one with any sense of urgency? He eyed George's cravat. 'You do realise bow ties are the thing now?'

'I am not wearing a bow tie.'

There came the careful tread of light footsteps on the creaky stairs, progressively accompanied by the rustle of fabric. Both sounds suddenly ceased and Douglas saw a shadowy figure lurking in the dim passage. 'Let us see you.'

'I feel thoroughly silly in this costume.'

'I'm sure you don't look it. Now come on, you can't hide there all night.'

After a moment's hesitation, Molly stepped out into the light. She wore a simple, light lavender gown with short sleeves that sat just below her shoulders, with a fitted bodice and a full skirt arranged in elegant folds.

The skirt wasn't as full as it would have been with a crinoline underneath like all the ladies were wearing now. It was more likely being supported by a starched petticoat. Her unruly hair had been fastened into two smooth plaits that met at the back of her head, entwined together in a neat bun. Cosmos, carnations and other flowers of purple and white decorated the plaited coronet. One or two loose ripples of hair framed her face. She wore fingerless white lace gloves that, by the way she was chafing her hands, were evidently irritating her. Together the various elements of her dress worked to highlight her slender form, the round shape of her face and her delicate, fine features. She was like a nymph or a fairy queen. The effect was only spoilt by the fact that she was sucking her cheek.

'Molly, you look positively beautiful. Quite the young lady, isn't she, George?'

'Yes.' George's reply was as apathetic as ever, but he looked at his sister with a directness that he was not normally accustomed to bestow. He even set the soda bottle and tumbler on the sideboard and moved his hand away from them.

Molly shrugged one shoulder and half-smiled as she raised her hanging head. 'Oh, I almost forgot.' She bounded up first to Douglas and then George, fastening a purple carnation in each of their buttonholes. 'There.' She nodded with a satisfied smile. 'That looks better.'

'Can we please get going now?' Douglas sighed. 'The driver will be losing what little patience he has left.'

'He agreed to the arrangement and will be paid adequately for it,' said George as he retrieved his top hat and ebony cane. Its topper was a glass disc in the middle of a silver ring like a magnifying lens.

'Ah, hold on.' Douglas paused as they were at the shop door. 'We almost forgot to set the alarm system.' He pulled a lever beside the door and there came a rattling within the walls. A great, thick steel plate came down sharply over the black door, a series of gear-shaped locks shifting and writhing about until they each shunted and clicked into place. 'Not even the world's greatest locksmith could figure out that combination.'

'What about the front door?' asked Molly, as she slipped a light wrap over her shoulders. She had not seen the new system her brothers had only recently installed.

'Once I lock it, it'll activate a series of defence measures hidden beneath the floor,' Douglas explained, as they stepped outside and he twisted the key in the lock. A grinding sound came from the other side of the door, along with the noise of a tense spring being wound.

The driver had been slouched against the growler, smoking a clay pipe, but when he saw the two brothers emerge from the house, he threw it to the ground and vented his indignation at having to drive *these two bloody boxes all the way to St James's*. The two wooden boxes in question were secured to the roof of the carriage by many lengths of thick rope. The roof was visibly dipping in the middle under their weight. George wordlessly tossed him a sovereign and then mounted the carriage, seating himself beside his sister. The driver fumbled to catch the coin, stared wide-eyed at it for a moment and then, jerking his hat down, grumbled under his breath as he hauled himself into his seat and took up the horses' reins.

'I wish we didn't have to take a cab,' said Douglas, as he climbed in after his brother and sister. 'If only I could get my airship working as it ought to.'

'We wouldn't have travelled in that contraption of yours even if you had managed to restore it in time,' said George firmly, sharply directing the tip of his cane at him.

'You won't get me back in that thing in this lifetime,' Molly chimed in, as she folded her arms across her chest.

'But we would have made a much grander entrance, and it would have been a lot easier to transport all three machines.'

'And it wouldn't have cost us eightpence a mile, I will allow you that.' George adjusted the angle of his hat with the head of his cane. 'Plus the extra it took to pacify him about the boxes.'

'I told you we should have taken two cabs.'

'And risk one becoming separated from the other? Not to mention it would have cost even more to do it that way. You know I have to say that I still have reservations about going to this gathering.'

'You didn't really *have* to say anything,' muttered Douglas. Why was George becoming increasingly obsessed about money? He had said himself that it was only a means to an end and they had a sufficient supply of it, so why fuss over every last penny?

'It'll be an experience, I suppose.' Molly shrugged as the cab began to move. 'Hopefully the supper is good. I've had nothing but a crust of bread since mid-afternoon.'

'I'm sure it will be up to scratch, Molly. I shouldn't imagine Lord Leyton will have spared any expense.'

'At least I'll know which fork to use and everything, although I'm sure I'll expose my lower social standing some other way.' She sniffed, rubbing the side of her nose.

'I just hope I have a chance of seeing Maestro,' Douglas said. 'I'd like to hear from him how he is getting on.'

'Your persistent attachment to that android is bordering upon delusion,' said George curtly. 'I fail to understand what you mean by "getting on". You have read all the papers.'

'I know what he has been doing and where he has been these last few weeks, but I can't help feeling concerned that he is – that it is all too much for him. His parts cannot take such excessive wear as they must have suffered from performing each and every day for hours on end.'

'If that were the case would Lord Leyton not have said so in his letter to us? You are bent on convincing yourself that this machine possesses a fully working consciousness after I have repeatedly tried to explain to you that it cannot possibly have one. I even replicated it in an attempt to show you.'

'No, that thing you constructed was a poor, stripped-down copy of Maestro.'

'Well, even if I had rebuilt the machine in its entirety, I doubt it would have been enough. You would more than likely have insisted *that* machine also possessed a soul or whatever you might call it.'

'Then why don't you try it and see if I do so? It might prove that you're right and I'm delusional, *or* it might just prove *me* right,' taunted Douglas.

George muttered something under his breath that was unintelligible to Douglas, although Molly thought she could distinguish the words *impossible* and *idiot*. That put an end to the conversation. Every now and then the roof groaned under the strain of the burden placed upon it.

They had left Soho well and truly behind. After journeying down

Princes Street, they were passing by Piccadilly on their way to Pall Mall. The street consisted of two long rows of immeasurably splendid classical mansions with finely dressed people going to and fro in hansoms. The cab turned into a street near St James's Square a little further ahead, and they saw in the distance the lights from a particularly grand mansion casting a phosphorescent purple gauze over the house's facade. Molly whistled and leant her head out of the window, gazing at the magnificent stone building. The house was surrounded by a wide square lawn and a great many trees, some of which were moulded into human and animal shapes. There was a circular, gravel courtyard with a square water fountain. In the middle of the fountain there was a golden Atlas bearing a black marble globe upon his shoulders. At each corner of the fountain bronze male figures spurted jets of water onto the god.

Scattered about the grounds were a number of toweringly huge lamps, about fifty feet high, that appeared to be projecting the purple light onto the house.

'Each lamp has a Fresnel lens to refract the light into a powerful beam, just like with a lighthouse,' remarked Douglas.

'I doubt the earl thought of it himself,' said George from the dark recesses of his corner of the cab.

Extravagantly dressed gentlemen and ladies, each attended by almost as finely attired servants, all in purple, were descending from several fine carriages, which were already lined up before the entrance to the house around the back of the fountain. When the Abernathys' cab lurched towards the house and squatted between the twin staircases, it prompted both servants and guests to stop and stare, many raising their eyebrows and giving a jingly little laugh. The cab's horses, panting and wheezing dreadfully, hung their heads low and their trembling legs were all but ready to give way. The cab itself let out a groan and seemed to sink a few inches, its belly almost touching the gravel. Without waiting for any assistance, George swiftly alighted and addressed two footmen.

'Inform his lordship that the mechanical animals he requested for tonight have arrived and that we will require assistance unloading them.'

The two footmen exchanged a glance and slunk off into the glowing open mouth of the house, presently returning with two more men who informed George that they were to be unloaded at the tradesman's entrance.

'I will make sure they take sufficient care with them. I'll join you both inside later,' George told his brother and sister, getting back into the cab.

'Are you sure that's necessary, George? After all, I doubt they would mishandle the automata lest should they displease his lordship. Besides, Lord Leyton will want to introduce you to all of his most distinguished friends. Wasn't that your sole motivation for coming?' said Douglas, folding his arms over his chest.

'I want to make sure they don't drop them or anything of that sort. A significant amount of effort went into those animals and I want to see to it that the job is carried out properly. They might accidently set one of them into motion.'

'Oh, I think you're shy, that's all. What do you reckon, Molly?'

'Oh, undoubtedly.' Molly smiled at Douglas, her mischievous look answering his.

'That is preposterous,' said George curtly, adjusting his hat and taking out his pocket watch. 'Yet seeing as it is now fifteen minutes past the hour and the earl is expecting us, we will have to take our chances with the servants as you suggest.' He swept past them and made for the right-hand staircase before he had concluded this remark.

Grinning at one another, Douglas and Molly followed on their elder brother's heels. 'Well, here we go,' said Douglas, as he took Molly's arm.

'Just promise me that you won't leave me to fend for myself with these people.'

'I will be by your side the whole night,' Douglas said firmly, placing his other hand over his heart emphatically. And then in a more offhand manner he added, 'There's no need for you to feel anxious.'

'Who said I'm anxious?'

'Well, I can feel your arm trembling slightly.'

'I think you'll find it's *your* arm that's trembling,' she said stiffly, staring straight ahead with a fixed, stony expression, although she couldn't maintain it for very long. She couldn't fool herself that her arm wasn't trembling a little, nor that her heart wasn't hammering away inside her chest. 'But you're sure you won't have to leave me for very long to see to the automata, right? And you'll stay with me the rest of the time?'

Douglas squeezed her hand. 'You know I wouldn't break my promise to you.'

Driving back whatever it was that was creeping its way up inside of her, Molly nodded and prepared to be engulfed by the warm yellow light seeping from the entrance.

They found themselves inside a grand reception hall. The floor beneath their feet was of black and white tiles like a chessboard, that gradually became more fragmented and deranged as it spiralled outwards from where they were standing. Candles in silver candelabras burned brightly, only serving to make the deep shadows in the corners of the room all the darker. White marble busts stood on speckled marble columns. Purple flowers decorated the room and swathes of silver fabric hung along the walls. Someone had placed a wreath of purple flowers on the head of one of the busts, making the dead old duke's irritated expression very fitting.

Lord Leyton was waiting to greet them. He wore a white coat with a purple silk waistcoat embroidered with a Chinese willow pattern. A lock of his fair hair was curled at the side of his head and the rest was tied back, fixed with a violet ribbon and little purple flowers. A twin ribbon curled tightly around his throat, an oval amethyst set in silver holding the choker together in the centre. His eyes were adorned with purple and indigo at the corners, forming spirals like a butterfly's wings around the rim of each eye, the pattern spiralling down onto one of his hollow cheeks. His lips were almost bleached of colour, although the bottom lip was tinged pale blue.

When he saw the Abernathys, he gave a loud, 'Oh,' and clapped both hands together as if in prayer. He then threw out his arms and advanced a few steps towards them, ruffled silver silk flowering from each of his wrists. 'Thank goodness, you are here at last!'

'Sorry if we are late, Lord Leyton.' Douglas stepped forward and bowed pleasantly. George made a movement that could just about be called a bow.

'Oh it is quite all right. I myself always make a point of either being late or early to any gathering. It gets one noticed. I take it the mechanical beasts made the journey all right?'

As the strange nobleman talked, Molly found herself being relieved of her wrap by the very beautiful Grecian-like man wearing a coat the colour of deep wine. Molly recognised him as the servant who had accompanied Lord Leyton when he came to their house. She blinked up at him wide-eyed, somewhat dazzled.

'Oh yes. Your men are seeing to them this very moment,' Douglas assured him.

'Marvellous! I cannot wait to see what you have created!'

Douglas was about to introduce Molly when Lord Leyton exclaimed 'Oh! This charming little creature must be your sister!'

Molly snapped out of whatever trance it was she had slipped into just in time to see the earl's gaze and inclination had turned on her. Some impulse in her brain made her curtsy and extend her hand, which he took readily. She saw he wore the most extraordinary rings on his long, white fingers. All were silver with carved semiprecious stones, cameos, glittering jewels or fine metalwork.

'My dear,' he said, pressing her hand with both of his. 'You look exquisite in that gown and with those blossoms in your hair.' One of his hands wavered over the flowers, perhaps just brushing a single petal ever so slightly. Molly felt the skin on the back of her neck prickle icily as if he had touched the bare skin there. 'These are purple marigolds if I am not mistaken.'

'Yes. I bred them myself, my lord,' she said frankly, her eyes flitting to Bellamy, who was disappearing behind a door with their cloaks.

'Oh yes, that's right. You're a budding botanist, aren't you? It appears talent runs thick in this family! You know, I happen to have the most remarkable collection of orchids in one of my greenhouses, which I simply must have the honour of showing you. I think you will find it much to your liking.'

'That is most kind of you, my lord. I should like that very much,' she said simply, not doubting for a moment that he would do no such thing.

Lord Leyton's expression suddenly stiffened as if some alarming thought had struck him. He gave a flick of his hand, and said, 'I have been absent from my other guests for far too long. There are a great many people I mean to introduce you to. Come, come.'

Douglas nudged George's arm with his elbow as Lord Leyton led them down the corridor. The manservant, now having returned from the cloakroom, followed closely at his master's heels. The sound of Lord Leyton's indigo boots clipping the floor echoed across the room.

'This is a fine old house, Lord Leyton,' said Douglas, taking in the numerous treasures they passed: gleaming suits of armour, statues and huge chunks of crystal. He glimpsed a number of rooms that were an odd mismatch of styles. Many of the rooms and passages frothed with white walls, soft-coloured furniture, and gilded mirrors and moulding. A few were decorated in a more monochrome palette of black, white, silver and purple.

'It was built by my great-grandfather over a hundred years ago now.' Lord Leyton waved his hand indifferently over his shoulder. 'Technically it is still my father's, but he is almost constantly abroad due to his health. He forbade me to touch a thing but I confess I made one or two changes to the decor. Once he finally dies, and the dukedom is bestowed on me, however, I intend to make some significant alterations.'

As they drew nearer, they could hear a great many voices and music gradually bubbling higher and higher. The music that was playing was not unlike a waltz, yet it seemed to have an unearthly resonance to it, plangent and hauntingly beautiful. It permeated and possessed one's body in a way that made it sway in time with the rhythm without the mind being aware of what it was doing. Douglas was familiar with the sensation; it was the unmistakable effect of Maestro's music. The gilt-framed doors parted without Lord Leyton needing to give a signal for his servants to open them. All three siblings were taken aback by the sight that greeted them. The Abernathys felt as if they were gazing at a ghost world of spectral dancers who shifted and twirled in time to the orchestra. The assembly was composed of the oddest and most lavishly dressed group of individuals any of the Abernathys had ever laid eyes upon. There were those who looked as if they'd had trouble deciding on a single article of dress and had resolved to tear several apart and stitch them back together into one garment. Some ladies wore enormous, bell-shaped skirts, but others wore far thinner gowns that showed their ankles – and more. Some were dressed in brightly coloured satin or silk with their stays worn over the top of their dresses; others wore trousers like the men. In fact, with a number of the dancing couples, there was a degree of uncertainty as to which was the gentleman and which the lady. There were people with their hair dyed unnatural colours, piled with flowers, jewels and feathers...and pieces of clock. All wore purple of some shade. The dresses of the female servants were unspeakably short, while the male servants wore trousers and plush waistcoats without shirt or collar beneath.

Some guests were seated around the perimeter of the room or stood conversing in clusters, while others swept across the ballroom floor. There was something eerily perfect in the way the dancers moved in almost faultless synchrony, as if they were each an extension of the same mechanism. The ballroom's architecture, with its ivory columns, dour archways and mismatched carvings, was a peculiar marriage of neoclassical and Gothic. A magnificent chandelier suspended from the lofty ceiling emanated a soft, blue sheen. A gallery ran around the top of the ballroom and the ballroom floor gleamed like glass below. The orchestra was on a raised platform. Leading them was Maestro, attired in magenta velvet breeches and a heliotrope tailcoat with wide lapels. Maestro saw little of what was going on around him, including the stares of the guests, since he was facing the musicians. He liked the lively atmosphere, however, and was satisfied that so many people were dancing to his music. He concluded that a ball was a very pleasant thing.

Several guests lifted their heads when the names of the three latest guests were announced. Seeing their host enter the room with his present company, many sharply turned to whisper to their companions or pointed to the two young men and the girl in the lavender gown. Douglas could practically feel the magnetic pull of their gaze. Lord Leyton stepped aside and addressed the crowd, his face glowing. The murmurs simmered down.

'My dear friends, may I present to you tonight's guests of honour.' He spread his arm like a white wing, his fingers uncurling one after another. 'The creators of my own dear Maestro.'

Douglas smiled freely and bowed to the crowd. Now he could observe the finer details of their dress more closely, he saw that a great number of them were wearing cogwheels or watch faces on some part of their dress, usually pinned onto their lapels or in their headdresses. Molly managed a curtsy, but deliberately hung back behind her brothers with her hands demurely placed in front of her, one enclosed inside the other. Her thumbnail was instinctively picking at the nail on her index finger, finding not a morsel of dirt to dislodge. George merely shifted his stance. Their actions set off excited murmurs from the crowd, several of whom quickly descended upon them as they stepped onto the ballroom floor. Two women in brightly printed dresses with no shoulders or sleeves sidled up to Douglas's side, their faces painted up and grinning like hyenas.

'Now, now.' Lord Leyton held up a hand to keep them all at bay, and smiled playfully. 'You will all get a chance to have your turn with them. But I reserve the right to their full attention first.'

The guests, including the women, melted away. A servant presented the Abernathys with a silver salver on which were three tall glass goblets of champagne. Molly found the champagne very dry and bitter-sweet, but she sipped it nonetheless, if only for some sort of distraction.

'Lord Leyton,' began Douglas, while looking about, 'why is everyone wearing pieces of clockwork on their clothes?'

'Hmm? Oh, it's the latest trend in fashionable parts of London. It is a sort of homage to Maestro. Most of the people who wear them do so to show they are dedicated followers of his.'

'Ridiculous,' muttered George under his breath, while tweaking his cravat. He took a swallow of champagne.

'I of course need not display my allegiance in such an uninspired fashion. But nevertheless, consider it a compliment to yourselves by the very finest of London society. Oh! Speaking of which, have you heard the most excellent news regarding Maestro?'

'No, I don't believe I have,' replied Douglas, lifting his gaze to the automaton, who was still at the helm of the orchestra of human musicians.

'I recently received a letter from a representative of the royal family requesting that Maestro give a concert before Queen Victoria and the Prince Consort next month!' Lord Leyton cried excitedly.

'That is fantastic news indeed!' Douglas looked over at George. 'I cannot begin to imagine what that will mean for Maestro.'

'Yes, we are all most terribly excited! Maestro had already expressed a desire to write an opera and now he could not have a better audience for it. It is a most charming little tale from what he has told me of the story. Maestro insists it is not quite right yet, but from what I have heard of it, it will be spec-*tacular* when it is finished! Now, my dear friends,' he said emphatically, as he clapped his hands together, 'there are some people whom I am simply *dying* to introduce you to. But first I want to know all about these mechanical animals that you have brought me. I'm curious to see what sort of bird you've made. I hope you heeded my request that it do something extraordinary, I have promised everyone quite a show for tonight!

But just as Lord Leyton was about to lead the Abernathys into the epicentre of the assembly, a footman appeared and bellowed, 'Monsieur and Mademoiselle Roux-Voclain.'

All eyes were riveted on the two figures entering the room. The man was tall, broad, and stiff in his gait. His skin had an odd pallor to it, like candle wax. His oiled hair was a pale red, almost yellow, mingled with steely grey at the roots, and his jaw square. He wore a dark green coat, an aubergine waistcoat and darker green trousers. The lady walked in front of him.

'Oh Lord.' Molly blinked as she watched the woman sashaying along. 'And I thought I was underdressed.'

Douglas snorted a laugh and almost choked on his champagne, hastily trying to check it by pressing his fist against his mouth.

The woman walked with her hips, moving slowly and fluidly as if she were underwater. Her elaborately piled red hair and rouged lips stood out boldly against her white skin but that was not the most striking thing about her, for she had on the most extraordinary dress of any woman in the room.

In fact she seemed to have neglected most of her dress altogether.

Suspended around her hips was a short crinoline cage that gaped open at the front, beneath which were layers of close-fitting, ruffled pink skirts that ended at least seven inches above the knee. Diaphanous material hung over the cage and fanned out behind her. The dark pink, silk bodice she wore exaggerated the narrowness of her waist and broadness of her hips and chest; a perfect hourglass. Its short sleeves hugged her shoulders and the neckline swooped down far below the collarbone, revealing a generous amount of her voluptuous chest. Something twinkled just above her right breast. Her ruby-red boots hugged her shapely calves, with heels an inch in height that clinked against the ballroom's glassy floor.

'Claudette! Oh, you look as ravishing as ever!' exclaimed Lord Leyton, as he rushed forward to meet the couple.

'Cephus.' She nodded coolly as he kissed her hand.

'But, my dear, I don't see a scrap of purple on you. Did you not read my invitation fully?'

'Do you not see my glove?' She held up her opposing hand, on which she wore a small purple glove.

'Oh, that is hardly any at all! But I will let you off this once.'

'I don't know why you insist on our being in heliotrope, Cephus. It is hardly an attractive colour,' she continued in the same poised manner, with her chin slightly raised. Her voluptuous voice was full and rich, enveloping every syllable that fell from her red lips. Her English was fluent with only a hint of the nasal accent of a native Parisian. There was an intensity in her eyes that Douglas could not help but be transfixed by. They were a peculiar purple-blue colour like forget-me-nots.

'Well, it is my birthday so you must do as I please. But I am so glad that you could come, my dear – and you too, of course, Gaston. It has been ever so long since I last saw you both! Another engagement fell through, I hear? Really, my dear, what are we to do with you?' He tutted.

'I got what I was owed. That is all that matters. It was all very civil.'

'How many is that now, five?'

'Six,' interjected her companion. He was lifting two goblets off a salver that was being offered by a servant.

'I do not count Cousin Louis,' she replied. 'He is family after all.'

'Oh, why would you not accept *me*, Claudette?' said Lord Leyton with vigour. 'Cruel girl! But no matter, I'd like to introduce the two of you to some new friends of mine.' He gestured to the three siblings with a sweep of his hand. 'May I present Mr George and Douglas Abernathy, and Miss Abernathy, their sister. These fine young men are the ones who built my dear Maestro.' Then turning to the other party, he said, 'This is Gaston and Claudette Roux-Voclain. They are old friends of mine whom I met in Paris many years ago.'

'*Enchantée.*' The French woman gave a shallow curtsy, her purple-blue eyes gliding over the two brothers from under her crinkled red hair. Douglas flinched as their penetrating gaze lingered on him. Surely Lord Leyton could not criticise her for her lack of purple when she had those striking eyes, he thought. He felt the roots of his hair at the nape of his neck prickle with perspiration. His face flustered ever so slightly and he looked down at his feet, something that did not escape Molly's notice. Gaston merely bowed, while retaining the same rigid, sombre demeanour.

'They are from an old, wealthy French family who managed to escape the fury of the Revolution,' Lord Leyton said, 'and retain the most magnificent collection of paintings and other treasures, which I have had the delight of exploring on more than one occasion. In fact, Gaston is quite the collector of automata and all sorts of other curiosities, is that not right, Gaston?'

'Indeed.' Gaston's voice and manner were both bland and apathetic as he continued to stare absently with colourless eyes set deep in their sockets.

'My brother is not one to boast about his wealth or taste. I hear some say he has too much pride and others say he has hardly any at all,' said Mademoiselle Roux-Voclain teasingly, tossing her head and sweeping back the liberated coils of hair that brushed against her white shoulders. She fixed Gaston with an expectant look as if she expected him to challenge her statement. When he did not so much as flicker a single facial muscle, she lifted the glass of champagne from his hand and sipped from it, sliding her glossy rouged lips over one another. 'So, will you be presenting us with any spectacular new inventions this evening?' This question she addressed to Douglas.

'They have constructed three ingenious mechanical animals, which I am promised will provide quite a show later,' chimed in Lord Leyton. 'And then Maestro will be playing a new waltz he has composed especially for tonight – his birthday gift to me.'

'How splendid.' She held her glass a little way from her body, its rim stained with a greasy pink smudge, and then aimed her forget-me-not eyes squarely at Douglas once more. There was a smile playing about their corners, a delicious delight in knowing the power they possessed. The heavy fumes of her perfume, dark musk and jasmine, started to seep into his senses.

As Douglas dragged his eyes away, he caught sight of a footman at the back of the ballroom whose coat and shirt were shredded to pieces, with his hair all disordered. He was wide-eyed, his mouth set in a grim expression of terror, his face ashen pale. That was save for the four red streaks running down the right side of his face. Several nearby guests noticed the poor man but cared to do nothing other than stare at him. He held onto the wall as he staggered along and soon vanished amongst the guests. Had he collapsed upon the floor?

Douglas sipped his champagne meekly and inclined his head towards George to whisper to him, but before he had the chance, George said, 'Yes, I see him,' out of the corner of his mouth without moving his head. 'They must have fooled around with one of the dials.'

'Oh, there's Marianne and Victor over there, Gaston.' Mademoiselle Roux-Voclain looked up at her brother. 'I suppose we ought to go exchange pleasantries with them. I am afraid you will have to excuse us, Cephus. It was pleasant making your acquaintance.' She shifted her eyes onto Douglas. 'Most pleasant, in fact.'

'The feeling is mutual, Mademoiselle,' stammered Douglas faintly.

'I hope I will have the pleasure of speaking with you once more before the evening is over,' she added, but whether to Lord Leyton or Douglas was unclear. Her crinoline swung hypnotically from side to side as she moved off. Gaston bowed stiffly before following closely after her. Lord Leyton looked after the two of them and shook his head.

'She has not changed one bit. Oh, what fool will attempt to tame her next? I almost regret that she turned me down so cruelly that night all those years ago. But I forget myself! So far, I have not shown you off to a single person!'

'Actually, Lord Leyton, perhaps we ought to prepare for the unveiling of the automata, since we arrived somewhat late, after all,' said Douglas.

'Oh. Oh, yes, of course. I am simply dying to see what you have come up with!' he cried shrilly and clapped his hands together.

'I assure you it will be quite spectacular, Lord Leyton.' Douglas looked down at his sister. 'Do you think you could stand to be by yourself a short while or do you wish to come?'

She raised her eyes skyward a moment as she considered the question. 'I think I could stand to be by myself a few minutes,' she conceded.

'But my dear, I will not allow you to remain by yourself! Perish the thought!' exclaimed Lord Leyton in protest. 'Why, I will personally act as your sister's guardian, rest assured, my dear sirs!' He entwined his arm gently around Molly's. She looked from him to her brothers with an alarmed expression. 'Your sister will be in good hands with me.'

'Hurry back,' she hissed through gritted teeth as Lord Leyton led her away. Craning her head, she strained to see her brothers, but they were swiftly consumed by the crowd. Lord Leyton talked away fervently and was extremely keen to know about how she managed to do all the things she did with flowers, until he was interrupted by some persons with whom he became engrossed in a loud and laughter-filled conversation, only acknowledging Molly once to introduce her. Gradually, his hold on her arm slackened so that she was able to slip free, her host being far too absent-minded to take notice. Unsure whether to retreat entirely or not, she hovered near him and contented herself looking about the ballroom, mentally detaching herself from the people around her as if they were no more real than their ghostly reflections upon the floor. There was still Maestro's music playing to soothe her and it was all a rather interesting spectacle to observe (and perhaps if she waited long enough and was tactful about it, Lord Leyton might recall his promise to show her that greenhouse of his). Yet gradually, without really noticing or caring, she drifted away from the earl and was entirely adrift amid the purple and gold sea of people. Her hot awkwardness and discomfort slowly subsided and she felt oddly at ease, enshrined by anonymity.

I can survive this, she told herself, taking a gulp of the bitter-sweet, lukewarm liquid in her half-empty glass, I can survive this easily.

Chapter Seventeen

Down in the servants' quarters, George and Douglas were checking the mechanisms inside of the mechanical tigers. One of the servants, overcome by sheer curiosity, had turned the dial on one of the tiger's collars, which, unbeknown to him, was the means by which it was activated. Had he not been so fast on his feet, he could have been torn to pieces. Instead he was merely nursing a wounded face and right arm and his pride.

'It was his own fault for being so foolish,' said George, as he finished his examination of the tiger, which, if one looked closely, had red-tipped claws on its left front paw.

'Poor devil. At least they were only flesh wounds it inflicted upon him. Who knows what Lord Leyton might have said if it had been otherwise,' returned Douglas, retrieving a spanner as he opened the tiger's jaws. He did not resume speaking until he had got a grip on one of the bolts inside the beast's mouth.

'You know, I'm actually rather proud of these "mechanimals" we constructed. I would certainly call it an extraordinary thing we got the bird to do...and the tigers.'

'Yes, as would I. Not that any of the company here will appreciate it.' A shadow of a smile passed over George's face. 'Are you ready?'

'It would appear so,' said his brother, as he closed the tiger's mouth.

Douglas wound the chain attached to the tigers' collars around his wrists and gave them a tug. George took hold of the ring-shaped gold handle that was attached to the birdcage. A velvet shroud had been placed over the six-feet-high cage. As well as being collapsible, the cage could easily be manoeuvred about on a set of four wheels. The tigers were to be pulled along on castors that popped out of the bottom of their paws when a stud on their collars was pressed.

'Uh, shouldn't we ask the servants to assist us with this?'

'And risk them causing further damage? We can manage on our own.'

'If you say so. Right, here we go.'

Douglas pulled the chains, but the beasts only budged a fraction. The shrouded cage practically sailed along the corridor in comparison. Douglas tried to reaffirm his grip on the chains, feeling the links sliding in his sweating hands. Heat seared along his arms and chest as he heaved on the chains to try to get the damned tigers to move. The one on his left arm budged along a lot easier, but the other, which was probably about two hundred pounds in all, refused to move a great deal. About halfway along the corridor, George stopped, rolled his eyes and offloaded one of the chains from Douglas, pulling both tiger and cage seemingly effortlessly until they reached the room adjoining the ballroom where supper was being laid out. The sound of the orchestra could be heard from the other side of the door. Douglas shook the chain from his hot, red hand and smoothed back his damp hair.

'That just about killed me!'

'I think you exaggerate,' said George unfeelingly, releasing his hold on his load and walking towards the doors between the supper room and the ballroom.

'How did you manage them both so easily?'

'I have my methods,' he said, his back towards Douglas as he opened the door a fraction. 'Once they have dimmed the lights, that's when we make our appearance.'

'George, I think it would be best if we followed the automata out. Let's get the footmen to assist us.'

'You just want to avoid pulling them.'

'No, I think it's best if we warm up the crowd first to build up their anticipation.'

'All right, although you will be doing the bulk of the talking as per usual.'

'As if I would allow it any other way. Besides, we have a script, remember?'

'Indeed. You have forced me to make a fool of myself acting it out enough times,' George muttered.

They caught the attention of two servants who had come in with plates of cakes and ices and requested they move the automata out under the cover of shadow when the next dance ceased and the lamps were turned low. George peered through the slit in the doors when the orchestra had stopped playing. The gold lighting gradually lowered and condensed into a cooler, dark blue glow. White spots of light drifted across the room like wandering moonbeams. The guests had solidified into a crescent-shaped mass, leaving the centre of the room free where the three shrouded automata were being conveyed at that moment. That was where the spots of light were converging. George looked up and saw a number of cylindrical lamps from which they were being emitted.

'What are they?' Douglas strained to look over George's shoulder. He was hastily wiping his sticky fingers on a napkin, having swiped a cake from the supper table.

'They appear to be Fresnel lenses like those we saw outside the house. I heard they were Monsieur Roux-Voclain's doing. Simple enough contraptions.'

'But it certainly adds to the drama.' He flashed a quick half-smile at George. 'Right. Showtime.'

They moved out under the cover of the inky blue darkness, Douglas leading. He had an odd sensation that he was hovering over his own body and watching himself move mechanically under the phantasmic blue and silver beams of light that fell across him. His legs positioned themselves before the assembly, which stared with one expectant, and perhaps a fraction hostile, gaze at him and George. George was standing on his left with perfect composure, his face as expressionless as ever. Douglas felt his heart racing and his hands becoming clammy. His fingers clenched into a ball and then relaxed. A shiver ran along his back as he felt himself sink back into his body, a flush of something like liquid mercury spiked the blood in his veins, and he addressed the crowd in a voice that was clear and commanding.

'Ladies and gentlemen, tonight you will witness a spectacle quite unlike anything you have seen before. Throughout the centuries, various attempts have been made to imitate nature's craftsmanship by machinery, stretching as far back as the age of antiquity. But all these attempts pale in comparison to the mechanical wonders that we have constructed especially for your pleasure...'

George came in directly on cue, nimbly spinning his cane as he lightly tapped one of the shrouded forms. 'For although they are forged from metal and moved by pure clockwork, these creatures possess extraordinary capabilities, and their sounds and movements are all but indistinguishable from any creature of flesh and blood.' George was inwardly cringing at having to recite this drivel Douglas had concocted, but anyone observing him would have commented that he possessed the self-assured air of a showman. Even Douglas was impressed as he took over from George.

'Thanks to the patronage of our distinguished host, Lord Leyton, we have humbly constructed three automata to mark this special occasion, including two tigers of copper and brass, sprung from the mind of man but seemingly surpassing the work of nature herself. If Mr Blake once asked, "What the hand dare seize the fire?", well, I would answer, "'twas us".' Douglas was in his element now, casting his spell over the crowd, reeling them in with his words, gestures and flash smile. Douglas spied Molly's face peering up attentively near the front of the crowd beside Lord Leyton. She smiled at him when he caught her eye.

'Prepare to be amazed and astonished, but do not be frightened. These creatures are for your entertainment only and we have gone to the utmost lengths to ensure that they present no danger whatsoever. So, without further ado, I present to you our three wondrous mechanimals!'

Douglas grasped one end of the velvet cover while George took hold of the other end and with a subtle mutual nod of the head, together they flung it back to reveal the gleaming gilded cage beneath, producing excited gasps from the crowd. Inside the cage, on a swing with gold vines climbing along its golden ropes, was a metallic purple and silver peacock. Each feather was forged of delicately thin metal, more like scales. A crop of curled silver wires tipped with purple crowned its head, and both its beak and long legs were of gleaming silver. A great tail of purple-blue feathers set with gold, turquoise and lapis lazuli discs hung down behind it.

Before the excitement generated by the peacock had died away, each of the brothers took hold of one of the purple silk sheets covering the other two shrouded forms and simultaneously swept them away. Two polished, bronze-skinned tigers with silver stripes sat on the ground in the pose of the sphinx, motionless as stone, their eyes closed. Wrapping their chains around a column, Douglas and George each turned the dial attached to the tigers' collars. The dials began to slowly spin, producing a buzzing noise, which set off a tinny whirring and clicking within the tigers' metal frames. A shudder convulsed the tigers' bodies and they rose onto their feet. Raising their great heads, they each let out a snarl that ripped through the air and sent the alarmed crowd receding like a purple tide.

'Now, there is no need to be frightened.' Douglas stepped forward before the mechanical beasts with his hands held up beseechingly. As he spoke, one of the tigers let out a growl and shook its head, pawing at the heavy chain and studded collar around its neck. The chains rattled and clanked, but the tigers found they could not free themselves and vocalised their frustration through a series of thunderous roars. 'The chains that bind them are made of exceptionally strong steel courtesy of our esteemed client, Mr Cobb. They will not break them easily.'

The tigers continued fruitlessly trying to chomp and claw their way through the chains. After finally giving up, they prowled along the edge of the circle formed around them and their makers, their sharp amber eyes shining fiercely. They followed the movements of their onlookers with a steady, protracted gaze, half-curious and half-livid. One got the impression they were waiting for something. Evidently growing bored with the humans, one of the tigers lay down and widened its great jaws in a yawn, revealing a huge grey tongue. Its mate sat down beside it and began licking its paw.

'However, as I will demonstrate to you, the chains are not really necessary as the tigers will obey any command we give them. Observe.'

Douglas turned to the supine tiger, his sudden attention causing it instantly to rise once more. It snarled at him, but he continued smiling broadly at it and, pointing his finger downward, said 'Sit, girl.'

The tiger instantly sat.

'Now roll over.'

The tiger rolled onto its side. Several of the guests' murmurs turned to laughter or applause.

'Adorable!' A small lady near the front batted her pink eyelashes and cooed over the tiger as if it were a kitten.

On an impulse, Douglas extended his hand towards her. 'Would you care to stroke her, madam? She won't bite you.'

The young lady blushed behind her fan, but allowed Douglas to take her hand and bring her right up to the seemingly docile beast.

'Now stay down, girl. Let this lady stroke your lovely head. Go on, madam, she is soothed for the time being.'

The lady glanced first at Douglas and then at the crowd, then her trembling, pearly silk-gloved hand hovered over the tiger's head until it made contact. She flinched on feeling the metal's heat. The tiger also contracted under her touch so that she instantly whipped her hand away.

'No, no, it's all right,' Douglas insisted. 'Just stroke her head, she will not stir again.'

The lady's lip quivered, but she once more moved her little hand along the bronze head. The tiger twitched its ear but made no other response. The lady's face glowed with pleasure and she gave a small curtsy to the applauding crowd before she rushed to rejoin her companions.

'But perhaps a further demonstration is needed to show that they really are under our control. George, if you would?'

George slowly approached the tiger that was still standing, careful in his movements but displaying no sign of fear. He reached out a hand to the mechanical beast, whose flashing, burning amber eyes were now fixed on George's cool sapphire eyes. It kept up a low growling like the chugging of a locomotive engine. Without breaking eye contact with the tiger, George lowered one hand near its neck and released the chain from the collar, hurling it onto the ground with a noisy clatter. Swiping the air around its neck, the tiger arched its long body and seemed prepared to pounce upon its maker, its eyes burning bright with orange fire. George swiftly stepped back several paces but appeared undaunted. Tensing itself, the tiger suddenly sprang at him with full force, but as it was in mid-lunge, George raised his cane and spoke in a firm and authoritative voice.

'Halt.'

The tiger's paws skimmed along the glassy floor as it drew to a stop just a few inches in front of George, its claws scratching thin white streaks into the floor and sending out yellow sparks. It bared its teeth and swished its tail from side to side as it watched George attentively.

He swung his cane through the air in a downward stroke and the tiger sat. The malignant purring and the look it aimed at him almost gave it the air of a misbehaving child.

'As you can see, even when the tiger was set on slaughtering George, George was able to control it with perfect ease.' Douglas grinned, although he cast a brief, troubled glance at the marks on the floor. They could expect a bill for that later.

After performing several more tricks with the tigers, and sensing that the audience's attention was wavering between intrigue and boredom, Douglas and George exchanged a look, which meant, *Now.*

'We will now present our third and final mechanical wonder – a bird able to fly with such majesty and beauty that, were a living bird to be placed beside it, it should seem the clumsy imitator.'

While Douglas was speaking, George disappeared around the back of the cage to wind up the bird, rolling his eyes now he was out of sight. The handle was like that on a music box. After only a few turns it became too stiff to continue winding, the pent-up energy travelling along the frame of the cage, twanging and rattling as the gears wakened into motion.

The flowers entwined around the cage opened their heads to reveal their clockwork centres, with small, intricate wheels spinning beneath their glass faces, a detail lost on the crowd, which was too far away to witness it. The bars of the cage gradually lowered and fanned out onto the ground.

The peacock slowly unfolded its magnificent, shimmering wings and let out a screech. It descended from its perch and strode forward with its proud head held high and its resplendent tail fanning out around it. Blinking its ebony eyes, it let out another shrill squawk that rang throughout the hall, then the tail feathers began to fold back on themselves. The peacock wafted its wings and raised itself into the air, creating a gust that swept Douglas's hair back and sent the skirts of his coat flying out behind him.

The bird shot up into the recesses of the ceiling and then swooped down low. It skimmed above the guests' heads, throwing up a whoosh of air that disarrayed headdresses and hats. People cried out Ah! and Eek! It flew close to Maestro, who was watching from the now dark and vacant platform, glad to not be the focus of attention for the present. His eyes widened as he beheld what happened next. The tips of the peacock's silver-purple feathers gleamed red as if they had been dipped into a furnace, and then suddenly the bird's entire body burst into colour like a firework, leaving a trail of rainbows in its wake as it glided around the ballroom. The crowd were now silent, utterly spellbound by the sheer beauty of the sight. When the rainbows began to melt away, Douglas let out a whistle and the peacock dipped down and circled around the crowd, although it showed no sign of slowing down. As it came in closer, one of its razor-sharp, glowing hot wings skimmed low against the ground and made contact with the recumbent tiger's chain, severing it clean in two. Douglas watched as it happened and his blood turned cold. The tiger shook its head and charged in the direction of the bird, its mate following closely behind it. People screamed and the crowd scattered like insects as the beasts came hurtling towards them.

'Stop! I said, stop!'

Douglas's words were drowned out by the screaming of the crowd and the roaring of the tigers. Meanwhile, the confused peacock hovered in mid-air, letting out horrible, bewildered screeches, not knowing which way to turn, even though it was well out of the tigers' reach. It landed on top of a curtain pole, but the tigers clawed at the wall and tore at the fabric until they brought the drapery down, the peacock taking flight just before the pole crashed to the floor. It soared up higher and came to rest atop the great gleaming chandelier, causing it to sway violently and a number of crystals to fall and smash on the hard floor like hail, sending nearby guests cowering.

'Oh dear,' remarked Lord Leyton, looking up at the gently rocking chandelier where the peacock could just about be seen wafting its wings. 'That's rather unfortunate, and that was my fifteenth-best chandelier too.'

'I'm awfully sorry, Lord Leyton,' said Douglas, at his side. 'This isn't part of the show. I'm not entirely sure what's causing the peacock to behave like this, it was working fine until the tigers tried to attack it. Of course we'll pay for any damages—' He felt a smart pain along his spine from George's cane pressing into the small of his back.

'Not unless he demands it,' George hissed.

'I hope it comes down, poor frightened thing! Do you reckon we could coax it down somehow?' said Lord Leyton.

'I'm not entirely sure,' said Douglas. 'It may need a bit of persuasion.'

'Bellamy, get a broom!'

The manservant bowed gracefully and swept out of the room.

'Pardon me, Lord Leyton, but that may not be wise.'

'Why ever not? Bellamy won't harm it. He is far too gentle.'

'But suppose we frighten it all the more? It might cause more crystals to fall from the chandelier too.'

'Oh, of course. Someone will have to intercept Bellamy. I see he has returned with the broom already.'

Douglas saw the manservant on the balcony of the gallery above with a broom. A long piece of thick rope was thrown out from the balcony to the gallery opposite where a short male servant almost failed to catch it and fasten it. Bellamy stepped off the balcony and, with incredible balance, walked nimbly along the rope towards the peacock with the broom carried like a lance. The peacock carefully watched his movements, flapping its wings in a show of defiance.

'Um, perhaps we had better move the guests to another room, Lord Leyton,' Douglas said, 'if you will pardon the suggestion.'

'No need. I was about to suggest the same thing myself. I will simply summon the party into the dining hall a little prematurely until they have cleared away all the glass.'

Lord Leyton snapped his fingers and two footmen instantly appeared by his side. 'Take the bottles of champagne off of the ice and into the supper room as soon as possible.'

'Yes, my lord.' They spoke and bowed simultaneously before dispersing.

'What about the tigers?' Lord Leyton asked Douglas.

The tigers had grown weary of waiting for the peacock to make a move and had spread themselves out on the floor, occasionally flicking their tails or ears. A falling shard of crystal plinked onto the floor and sent out tiny, iridescent splinters like water droplets. One of the tigers snarled and batted its paw in the air in response.

'George and I shouldn't have too much trouble with them now that it's quieter and they can hear our commands. We simply have to bid them to remain where they are so we can turn the dials on their necks that operate them.'

'Very well. I will trust you to see to it. That was a most spectacular display by all accounts! Do not worry about the slight, uh, disfigurements the ballroom might have suffered. They can easily be rectified, and my father will be none the wiser. As for the guests, well, a few glasses of champagne can smooth over all manner of sins and no one appears to have been harmed at all. It will certainly get people talking about this night for years to come! Tragedy often makes for a better story than triumph – ask Shakespeare.'

The doors to the supper room opened and the guests began to move. George approached the tigers, which appeared to have suddenly fallen asleep. At that moment the butler suddenly appeared, with an air of self-importance, and in a loud, although somewhat hollow, voice, announced Professor Charles Gottfried.

Heads instantly turned at the name. Standing in the doorway was a man in a long black greatcoat with a red waistcoat beneath. He was broad in shoulder with a trim waistline and gave the impression of largeness without being necessarily stout or particularly tall. In one hand he wielded a long, black cane. He entered the room, looking out over his audience with a keen, eagle-like gaze and a smile playing on his thin lips. He could have been anything from late thirties to early fifties. His hair was a light, dusty brown, sleeked back with oil and just beginning to recede away from the prominent, rounded forehead, with sideburns cut as fine as razor blades at the jaw bone. His face was smooth without beard or whiskers, making a feature of his cleft chin. Deep lines were etched into the skin on either side of the smiling mouth, and the hooded, sunken eyes cast deep smudges of shadow. Each firm, deliberate step from his black boots clipped the glassy floor and rang out clear and sharp in the silent hall. The only other sound came from the peacock letting out a sporadic squawk from above. When he reached the centre of the room he bowed graciously before the company.

Lord Leyton approached him at once and offered him a jewelled hand.

'Professor Gottfried, your reputation precedes you. I am grateful that you have honoured us with your presence.'

'And it was very gracious of you to request it, Lord Leyton.' The professor smiled as he cast his eyes up towards his host. He studied the offered hand as if it were a beetle turned on its back and did not raise either of his own from the head of his cane upon which they rested. His voice had a scratchy quality to it, but it was nonetheless authoritative and composed. There was something in the slate-blue eyes with their steady gaze, and the way he held himself, almost with the air of a military man, that commanded the complete attention of all about him, and subdued them into mystified awe in his presence.

'You must forgive me, sir.' Lord Leyton retracted his hand without an inch of awkwardness in his demeanour, making it look perfectly intentional as he pushed a lock of hair back behind his ear. 'The invitation I issued specifically requested that an item of purple was to be worn, and I see no purple on your person at all.'

'I was fully aware of the invitation, Lord Leyton. If you will only watch, you will see that I have indeed observed it.'

Gottfried stepped forward a few paces, the crowd parting before him like the Red, or rather purple, Sea. Every face was turned towards him. With a gleam in his eye and that same subtle smile upon his face, he held out his arms and the crowd watched as his greatcoat began to change colour and shrivel away before their eyes. It went from black to burgundy to brown, and then somewhere between brown and purple. Bits of material fell away from the bottom. It eventually settled on a bright heliotrope and was also now a frock coat. He spun around for all to see the transformation and was met with tremendous applause.

'Why, Professor, you do not disappoint!' cried Lord Leyton.

'Thank you, Lord Leyton. Although that of course was only a simple illusion, quite amateurish. I will be sure to go one better before the night is out.' His eyes flicked to George and Douglas. 'Ah! I trust these are the celebrated Abernathy brothers.'

'Yes, they are my honoured guests,' said Lord Leyton, as he followed the professor's gaze with a complacent smile.

'Please allow me to introduce myself to you, sirs.' He smiled as he shook first George's then Douglas's hand with vigour. 'I am Professor Charles Magnus Gottfried, professor of chemistry at the University of Cambridge, as well as a modern-day magus, inventor and collector.' He laughed as he reeled off this additional list of credentials, although Douglas reckoned he was very much in earnest. 'I believe we have a mutual acquaintance in Mr Clayton Cobb. I hear you have recently taken up a commission of his. Most interesting stuff!' he said ardently.

'Why thank you, Professor Gottfried. Yes, we have been consulting with Mr Cobb about the design of his new factory,' said Douglas.

'He himself told me of it only yesterday, when I had just returned from the Far East. Although one must go further than that not to have heard of the great Mechanical Maestro. Is that the android himself over there?' He pointed his cane at Maestro, who was still sitting on the stage. 'Ah! It is something to see it with one's own eyes, the papers scarcely do it justice! I would be most interested to hear about it over a glass of—'

Suddenly Gottfried's attention was arrested by something behind Douglas's head. Douglas followed his gaze and his eyes landed on Mademoiselle Roux-Voclain. 'Oh, she is an exquisite specimen,' muttered the professor under his breath. 'I will have to make a closer study of her. Excuse me, gentlemen,' he grunted, and adjusted his bow tie. 'I hope I will have another chance to speak with you later in the evening. *Au revoir.*' And he made his way straight towards Mademoiselle Roux-Voclain. The two of them disappeared into the crowd that was making its way towards the supper table.

With the professor gone, George examined a shrivelled shred of black fabric under his cane's lens, flipping it over to increase the magnification fivefold.

'I doubt you'll find much out that way,' said Molly, coming up behind him. She hitched up her skirt to reveal the small silk bag tied around her ankle. Widening the drawstring mouth, she pulled out a glass vial and a pair of small pliers.

Douglas folded his arms across his chest and shook his head at her.

'What?' she asked, as she uncorked the vial.

'Why on earth did you have that concealed under your dress?' asked George.

'Douglas said Lord Leyton might have some interesting plant specimens, in which case I thought it wouldn't hurt to take a few samples.' She shrugged, placing a sliver of fabric inside the glass tube. 'I can analyse the chemicals in the fabric when we get home.'

Having bottled her sample, she then refastened the bag and lowered her skirt.

'Only you would think to do that at a ball, Molly.' Douglas smiled, as he took her arm and led her towards the dining hall.

Chapter Eighteen

Molly felt that the supper had compensated somewhat for the company, even if the roast fowl was a little overdone. She mainly kept her eyes down on her plate, addressing only her brothers, although it was often hard to maintain George's attention as he would be conversing with other gentlemen and taking notes in his pocketbook. Douglas remained fixedly by her side. Upon his entering the room, all attention was momentarily diverted from them to the professor, who was performing seemingly impossible tricks to the guests' terrified amazement. When one guest asked in jest whether he had found the philosopher's stone and knew the secret of transforming base metals into gold, the man cocked his head and a knowing grin spread across his face. He then got up and walked over to the fireplace. Producing a small packet of blue powder from his coat, he sprinkled it over his cane as he suspended it over the smouldering fire. There was a puff of blue smoke accompanied by a pungent whiff of strong chemicals, and when he drew the cane back out, it was gleaming gold.

But the professor paid particular attention to Mademoiselle Roux-Voclain, who, like a panther observing a grazing antelope, gradually gravitated towards him, although she occasionally cast a glance at Douglas that made him shrink with mild embarrassment. The professor poured a measure of vinegar into a goblet and flicked the side of it with his fingers. A pool of deep, dark red swelled from the side of the glass he had touched and stretched out its burgundy tentacles, slowly spreading outwards and obliterating the bronzy vinegar. Swirling the liquid around in the goblet, he then deftly handed it to Mademoiselle Roux-Voclain. She eyed him with a simpering smile playing on her rouged lips as she lifted the goblet from his hand and sipped at it.

'Red wine,' she affirmed. 'Not the slightest hint of vinegar. Although it would have been more impressive if you had made it from water.'

'Ah, but that is old hat. Did Christ not do it almost two millennia ago? But in case I have disappointed you, Mademoiselle, perhaps my next marvel might compensate. This should interest you as well, sirs,' he added, casting a glance in George and Douglas's direction, before placing a metal box, heavily veined with engraving, onto the table.

'What is that?' asked Mademoiselle Roux-Voclain, eyeing it dubiously.

'This, Mademoiselle?' He slapped his hand over it and grinned slyly. 'This I will explain in good time. But first, I must ask you a simple, if rather peculiar, question. Do you care much for verse?'

'Some, although I confess not much. But that group over there, you see them?' She aimed her gloved finger in the direction of a group of men huddled together near the plates of jelly. 'They are your men.'

'Ah! Very well, Mademoiselle. You sirs,' he called with a whistle. They turned their heads sharply like sheepdogs. 'This exquisite lady informs me that you are appreciators of poetry.'

'Yes. And most of us are poets ourselves,' said one.

'Perfect.' The professor's hand dipped inside his coat and produced two thin pieces of pink paper. 'In that case I'm sure you won't object to taking a look at these two poems and telling me what you make of them, and which you prefer?'

Looking perplexed, the spokesman of the group accepted them and the poets closed in on themselves like a pack of dogs over two hunks of raw meat. After a few minutes, the spokesman faced the professor. 'It seems we are divided. Three of us prefer the first and three the second. I myself am of the latter party.'

The professor rested his elbows on the table and pressed the tips of his fingers together. 'And you are certain that is the one you found the most...human?'

'Yes, if you wish to phrase it in that manner. What is funny, sir?' he demanded as the professor began to snigger.

'Because *that* poem was in fact written by this machine.' He smacked his hand down on the box.

'What? That is preposterous.' The poet laughed. 'How can that little contraption compose verse?'

'Little contraption? Ah!' The professor took it up in his hand. 'Do not underestimate it because of its mere size.'

Twisting the box around in his hand, he showed the face, which had a round, red glass button in its centre, to the poets. After pressing the button, the box then sprang up from his hand. When it landed onto the hearthrug, it was five times its original size, and had sprouted all sorts of additional features.

'Allow me to explain.' The professor rose from his chair. 'This machine has been fed with millions and millions of words from what is considered to be the greatest poetry ever written. Chaucer, Donne, Milton, Shakespeare, Johnson, Blake, Wordsworth, Coleridge, Poe, Byron – they are all in there. It can then be made to compute a poem with a particular metre, rhyme or specific theme.' He turned to Mademoiselle Roux-Voclain. 'Mademoiselle, would you care to suggest a subject?'

'Beauty,' she said readily.

'Very well. Observe.' The professor went over to a blocky chunk of machinery studded with stubby brass keys and began typing on them. 'I will set it to write in couplets and generate a random metre. There!' His fingers curled tightly around a slender golden lever on the side of the machine. 'Let's see what it comes up with!'

He pulled down hard on the lever and a noise came from within the machine like a battalion's worth of pistols all being fired at once in rapid succession. Once the violent racket died down, the machine clacked away merrily. Expectation mounted in the air as all looked on. Even George let his pencil hover an inch above his notebook as he watched.

'What the machine is doing,' explained the professor above the noise, 'is its network of wheels and cams are continually checking what words it puts together, including some relating to beauty, while others are concerned with counting the syllables to ensure the metre remains consistent.' A long tongue of pale pink paper wriggled out from a reel above the rows of brass keys, and something went *ding*. 'It appears it is done.' The professor tore off the pink paper with a flourish and presented it to Mademoiselle Roux-Voclain. 'I'd be honoured if you would read it aloud to us in your melodious voice, Mademoiselle.'

She eyed him searchingly before taking the paper and reading in a clear and steady, if somewhat monotonous, tone:

A woman's blush is sure to pale
as certain as roses wilt.
The light in her eyes sure to fail
as a candle snuffed in silt.

The gold from her hair is sure to wane
and uncoil will her curls.
In vain she strives to smile and shows
two strings of blackened pearls.

The loss of her bloom man may rue,
as fleeting day fades into night,
but while the charms of flesh will never renew
her greatest beauty lies out of sight.

Around the room there was a chorus of assenting murmurs and nods, although there were many rude ejaculations emanating from the poets' corner.

'Rubbish! I don't believe that machine is genuine for a second! And besides, how can it be truly creative if it can only make patchwork poetry from what has come before it?' One of the poets crossed his arms over his chest and raised his chin.

'How is modern poetry any different?' challenged the professor. 'Is it not simply a tapestry of dead men's words?'

'You, sir, have no business talking of what you do not truly understand.'

The poet sniffed, although he looked slightly pale and deflated despite his defiant stance a moment ago.

After the conclusion of supper, the guests returned to the ballroom once more, where the dancing resumed. The dance was not a waltz exactly; it was far more rapid and heavier, the rhythm infused with something of a Spanish streak like a fandango. All three siblings, of course, abstained – one from indifference, one from lack of experience and the other from self-consciousness. Douglas had an opportunity to properly observe Maestro from his seat near a window. That was until Mademoiselle Roux-Voclain blazed into his vision. Before he consciously realised it, she had seized his hand and pulled him onto the dance floor. She was undoubtedly the one leading the dance, pulling him closer to her by the hand or raising his arm so that she might spin about him, her body rippling like a living flame. He did not remain with her long, however – when the professor smoothly cut in to relieve him of his unrequested partner, Douglas was allowed to drift back to his seat.

After the dance had concluded, Maestro prepared to give his solo performance, which was to consist of three movements, it was announced. The lamps were turned down low and he came forward to the front to the stage. He held in his hands a rather strange violin. It was an electrically bright azure, hollow in parts with a small brass horn sprouting from the neck. The first long note crackled through the hard silence like a streak of icy blue lightning; in fact crackles of electricity were visibly shooting from the violin. The violin's warbling voice was undeniably beautiful but somehow unnerving, like the kiss of a frozen maiden. Douglas felt an icy chill shoot down his spine. How had Maestro managed to construct such an instrument? He could guess roughly how it worked: the sound's source was most likely electrical wires, like telegraph wires, received by the horn, which filtered and amplified the sound. But the extent of the android's creativity astounded even him. The string section accompanied Maestro's violin and set the pulse racing of everyone who heard it. But then all of a sudden the other strings abruptly ceased, leaving only the sound of Maestro's violin. It sang out in a far slower, gentler and warmer tone that drew almost painful pangs from the heart and water from the eyes, before the strings trilled once more. It was like a pursuit of a maiden by a pack of fierce predators: the final note like the plunge for freedom, then silence reigned. The chase was at an end.

The assembly was in raptures as Maestro bowed modestly. But after the last patter of applause had died away, one very slow, deliberate set of handclaps still rang out. All heads turned towards a gentleman at the centre of the crowd, which parted in two to create a line between him and the android. He was dressed surprisingly plainly in a black coat, although the lapels were excessively wide, a purple waistcoat and bow tie. His face was lean, with a trim dark beard.

'Bravo, mechanical man, bravo indeed.' He folded his arms across his chest. 'But I do not believe that you are the brilliant composer that half of London says you are. In fact, I think you are a fraud.'

Gasps fluttered amongst the crowd. Maestro looked at the gentleman perplexedly, stepping down from the stage.

'Allow me to introduce myself. I am the revered music critic, Mr Merrill. I believe to call you a composer is an insult to the true great masters, and you, a mere machine, cannot possibly rival their brilliance. It is all trickery. You might be able to play a few clever tunes but it is all predetermined. I will prove that you cannot play anything on the spur of the moment. Here…' The gentleman's hand dipped into his coat and he pulled out a tattered scroll. He unravelled it before Maestro. 'Do you know what this is?'

Maestro peered at the parchment. His yellow eyes widened and blinked rapidly. He turned them to the gentleman's face and nodded.

'It's the Finale Sonata.' Mr Merrill smirked. 'By a great Italian composer whose name has been lost to history. This piece is notorious in that it is impossible to play. Many great musicians have tried and were left with either broken fingers or broken minds… I would like to see you attempt it.'

'Now, look here…' began George.

'What's the matter, clockmaker?' the gentleman sneered. 'Do you have so little confidence in your machine? You think it is beyond him?'

George stared at him disdainfully and took a step back. Lord Leyton watched the unfolding drama behind his fan with a look of fascination.

'Anyway, it is for your automaton to decide whether he will take up the challenge or not. What do you say?' Mr Merrill waved the scroll in front of Maestro's face. 'Do not look to your master to tell you what to do. You supposedly have a brain in that wooden head of yours. What do you say?'

Maestro's eyes flitted to his makers, to Master Josephus, and then to the assortment of guests before he looked the gentleman straight in the eye. He nodded firmly.

Mr Merrill sniggered most unpleasantly as he handed him the scroll.

'Bellamy!' called Lord Leyton. 'Fetch a music stand!'

The manservant swiftly set one up before Maestro, who laid the parchment on it and took up the blue violin once more. Making sure it was in tune, and adjusting the settings so it would sound like a regular violin, he brought it to his chin. His eyes flitted rapidly across the lines on the parchment. He had never seen anything so complex before. There were symbols he did not even recognise.

'Make haste!' said Mr Merrill, his foot rapidly striking the floor. 'We are waiting.'

The crowd did not speak a word. All heads were riveted on Maestro, who at that moment appeared rather small. Readjusting his stance, Maestro arched his arm, poised the bow at a precise angle and then, with a momentary glance at the shining crack on his hand, began. His fingers were a blur as they flew across the strings, the bow almost threatening to snap in two.

'Such speed!' someone cried, their voice a ghost.

'Such power!' cried another empty voice.

The power of Maestro's playing was unimaginable. The strained tension in the air became palpable, unbearably so, then suddenly the violin burst out into a long wail, letting the note ring out clear and strong until the glasses in the guests' hands shattered, as did some of the window panes. Maestro could feel the pressure building around the cylinder inside of his chest. Something was not quite right; every part of him was utterly straining in his effort to not let one single note slip. He felt as if he were about to crack into pieces – it was a wonder he hadn't already. It took every ounce of effort to keep his arm from jerking, although his body was doubled over and then thrown back with the effort of his playing. He had reached the final lines of the score. The song practically ripped through his body. He could feel his parts rattling away inside him and coming loose – he wouldn't reach the last note. His eyes and hands were desperately trying to keep up with one another as they danced along the final bars. But then he hit a blank. That was it, there was no more. When he hit the final note, he let his arms drop to his sides. The violin had actually broken in half, exposing its metal, wiry nerves. His entire body stooped. The crowd were speechless, their mouths hanging open. A gentleman's purple monocle had plopped into his glass but he hadn't seemed to notice. A lady had gripped her companion's sleeve so hard that she split the fabric at the shoulder. The gentleman himself stood pale and dumb, totally oblivious.

'Bravo!' Lord Leyton clapped loudly. 'Bravo, Maestro, that was beyond spectacular!'

'Im-impossible,' uttered Mr Merrill. 'That was impossible!'

But others followed Lord Leyton's example, drowning out the gentleman's babbling. Soon the whole room was erupting into ecstasies. But Maestro could feel something jarring inside him. He looked down at his fingers and saw the casing on both hands was riddled with cracks, the brass showing through beneath his padded fingertips.

Douglas saw what was happening. He stopped clapping and marched out into the semi-circle past the incoherent gentleman.

'Maestro, are you all right?'

Maestro wanted to say, *Yes, Master Douglas. It is only the casing that is badly damaged. Although I fear something is not quite right*, when his body jerked involuntarily as he felt a peculiar sensation in his chest.

'Maestro?' Lord Leyton approached them, his face ashen pale beneath his powder. 'What is the matter?'

'I think something is wrong.' Douglas looked across at George, who was surrounded by a crowd of gentlemen who were shaking him by the hand and grinning widely. 'I can take him into one of the rooms upstairs to see if I can fix him.'

'Please do. Oh, please do.' Lord Leyton wrung his hands. 'I should never forgive myself if anything were to happen to him.'

'I think the excessive playing he has been doing recently has been putting unnecessary strain on his parts. This was merely the final straw.'

'Oh, it is all my fault!' Lord Leyton hollered.

No, Master Josephus, Maestro wanted to tell him as he saw his anguished expression. *It is my own fault. I accepted the challenge. It was my decision.*

Then a sudden change came over Master Josephus's face and he whipped himself around towards Mr Merrill. 'You, sir!' Lord Leyton snapped. 'How dare you force him to take up your cruel challenge?'

'B – but—'

'I will have someone call a carriage for you and then I want you to leave my house, is that clear?'

The man seemed incapable of speech and was escorted away by two purple-clad footmen. Molly ran forward and assisted Douglas to lift Maestro onto his feet.

'I might be gone some time. Make sure George stays with you so you're not on your own,' Douglas told her.

'Never mind about me, you idiot,' she retorted. 'See to Maestro before he falls apart.'

'I should only be half an hour, unless the damage turns out to be worse than I'm anticipating.'

'Yes, half an hour. Fine. Now *go*!'

Douglas nodded to her, then turned to Maestro. 'Are you able to walk, Maestro? Perhaps we should try shutting you down in case anything else decides to come loose.'

Maestro assented and Douglas turned a dial in his chest that sent him limp. Molly watched as he was carried out of the room and then turned around, expecting to see George nearby. He wasn't there. Of course he wasn't, how stupid of her.

Chapter Nineteen

George had slunk away from the commotion and returned to the dining hall to examine the professor's machine. He flipped the lens of his cane over so that the image enlarged fivefold and George could make out the engraving on the case. When this turned up nothing, he twisted the cane's engraved middle, which broke into two. Around the rim of the exposed bottom half was a silver ring that was in fact a loupe. He found a small, circular hole in the case, which appeared to be a vent, and pressed the loupe against it. Inside he could see a long stack of what looked like small squares of thin metal with minute holes and raised veins on them. An acidic smell was seeping from the hole.

'Curious, Mr Abernathy?'

George turned his head and saw Professor Gottfried closing the door behind him as he entered. 'I knew you couldn't resist having a closer look, so I thought I'd take the opportunity of having a private word with you.'

Now that he was close to the man, and in the absence of the noise of the party, George noticed that his jaw clicked every time he ceased speaking. The professor pulled a chair back by hooking his foot around its leg and slid into it. He cocked his head to one side as his heavy, hooded eyes fixed on George's cane.

'That is quite an unusual cane you have there. I dare say it even outshines my own.' He held up his golden cane. The topper was in the shape of a wolf's head; its sparkling red eyes seemed to observe the onlooker. 'I knew I made the right decision by approaching you alone first instead of consulting you and your brother together. I feel we are more likely to see eye to eye.'

'What is it exactly that you're alluding to, Professor Gottfried? I don't see why dropping all these hints and allusions is necessary. You will not profit from it with me as you did with the rest.'

'It concerns your dealings with Mr Cobb. I know the particulars of what he is planning to do. A promising idea put to a poor use.' He shook his head sadly and picked over the remnants of some fruit in a glass dish. He plucked off a grape and rolled it between his thumb and finger as his eyes rolled onto George, glinting strangely. 'Which is why I want to offer you a proposition.'

'And what is the exact nature of this proposition?'

The professor lifted the grape as if he intended to swallow it but instead let it drop carelessly from his fingers onto the tablecloth.

'I want you to sabotage Cobb's factory.'

'You can't be in earnest.'

The professor raised his palm. 'Let me finish. I want you to sabotage the machines you are building for him, making him falsely believe that they do not work, and then come join me in an enterprise of my own. As a partner, of course – your brother too if you so desire. I'm developing a machine that can do far more than churn out paltry poems. It will make Babbage's difference engine seem like a mere abacus in comparison. Information on all manner of subjects will be fed into it via the metal disk system that you no doubt glimpsed just now. The machine is like a mechanical mind. Imagine all of the fun we could have with that.' His jaw clicked shut and his sedate eyes settled squarely on George as he leant back into the chair. There was undoubtedly an alteration in his demeanour, as if he had decided his exuberant outer layer was unnecessary and stripped it away.

'I could use the designs that Cobb has spoken to me so highly about,' the professor went on. '"Machines that can innovate" is what he said. "Machines that can learn". Combine that with my method of storing data and, well, who knows what then? You have seen for yourself what I am capable of.' He waved his hand towards the poetry machine. 'Don't you think inventions such as yours would be wasted in the hands of a bloated textiles manufacturer?'

'Yes,' said George deliberately, after a pause. 'I have seen what you are capable of, Professor, and quite frankly...' George looked down at him dourly. 'I think you are all show and no substance.'

Gottfried snickered. 'Then explain to me how I transformed this cane here from ebony to gold, and how I performed all my other feats of the impossible.'

'I am no chemist. But I imagine it was in fact a gold alloy all along that was simply coated in an oxidised layer, which the powder then stripped away. As for the other tricks, it would be useless for me to speculate.'

'Or do you simply fear what you don't understand?'

'I think it is all nothing but clever magic tricks.'

'Au contraire, Mr Abernathy! In my experience, the line between magic and science is so thin that it is practically transparent.' The professor smiled as he rose from his chair. He jostled the cane in his hand and the wolf opened its metallic jaws, which were clearly attached to a spring mechanism, and a thin square of card shot out from between its shining gold teeth. Gottfried plucked the card from the wolf's mouth and presented it to George. 'I'll leave my card with you while you think my proposal over. But that is what I offer you: equal recognition, equal profits and a far more worthwhile objective than pinching at the French share of the silk trade.'

George snatched the card from between the man's fingers and tucked it into his pocketbook. 'I will not promise to consider it.'

'Oh you already have, or else you would not have accepted my card.' Gottfried smiled as he turned to go, leaving George to contemplate what had just transpired.

Upstairs, Douglas had managed to restore Maestro, although it was only a temporary fix. The excessive wear on his parts had caused a number of gears inside his chest to come loose, leading to a whole other series of problems. A lever had even punctured one of the bellows in his chest.

Douglas had also noticed large cracks in his casing and places where the leather pads had become unstuck, which looked like older problems. Maestro would need to be brought back to the workshop for the damage to be repaired, but in the meantime he could continue running more or less as normal. Douglas had been cautious when Maestro insisted on playing still, although he eventually relented and warned him not to put himself under too much strain, and it was stringed instruments only from here on out.

He left Maestro in his chamber to practise playing more gently and made his way back through the labyrinth of luxurious rooms. Of course, Maestro couldn't see it – he was far too naive. He didn't realise when he was being manipulated or taken for granted. He was nothing but an amusement to them, a clever toy. And just like any child presented with a new toy, it was only a matter of time before they grew tired of it and dropped it, in search of something else to quench their curiosity. Even now Douglas could see that dull, glazed look that overcame some of them when they listened to him playing. Although there were many like Lord Leyton who genuinely revelled in and admired his music; that was true. At the other end of the scale were those who thought Maestro a monstrosity or a fake, like those damned SOAL fanatics.

His train of thought was interrupted by a rustling coming from the room on his right. As he drew nearer, the sound suddenly ceased, and the red-haired woman burst through the doorframe.

'Oh, it is you, Mr Abernathy,' she cried, pressing the fingers of her gloved hand to her bosom. 'You startled me.'

'Mademoiselle Roux-Voclain, what are you doing here?'

'I have lost my brooch. I thought I might have left it in here earlier this evening. You don't happen to recall seeing it anywhere at all, do you?'

'I'm afraid not, Mademoiselle.'

'You will help me look for it, won't you? I am certain that it is in this room somewhere.'

Before Douglas's brain could formulate a response, she had already disappeared back inside. He looked down each end of the corridor before reluctantly following her. He would do a quick sweep of the room out of courtesy but no more than that. He couldn't keep his sister waiting for much longer. Mademoiselle Roux-Voclain was stooping down by the hearth, or at least as much as her wire skirt would allow.

'I thought the most likely place would be near the sofa where I was sitting earlier,' she said as she straightened herself. 'I have looked there already, but perhaps a second pair of eyes would be beneficial.'

'All right, I will take a quick look.' Douglas went over to the spot she was indicating and knelt down on the rug. 'What sort of brooch is it?' he asked, as he began moving the sofa cushions around.

'A jewelled octopus,' she replied, softly shutting the door. He heard the clacking of her boots as she moved across the room, the sound becoming muffled as she stepped onto the rug. 'Oh!' she cried suddenly. Douglas was sure he heard a tinkling sound in the same instant. 'I hope it turns up. It is very precious to me.'

'I'm sure it will, Mademoiselle. I can't seem to find it anywhere around here.'

'I will check the far corner. I seem to remember standing there while I was looking over some of Cephus's books. You keep checking the rest of the room.'

She swept past him, leaving a fragrant trail of musk rose in her wake, and Douglas inched his way towards the top end of the room, deliberately working towards the door. From the corner of his eye, he caught a yellow, metallic glint of something by the leg of the sideboard.

'Aha!' Douglas swooped on it and held it aloft. 'I think this may be your brooch, Mademoiselle.'

'Bring it here and let me see it.'

He obliged her request and when she laid eyes on it, she enclosed both hands over her heart. 'Yes, that is it! *Merci*, Mr Abernathy. You have found it. I am ever so grateful.'

'It was nothing, Mademoiselle.' Relief swept through him. Now, how best to disengage himself from her?

'We should drink a toast to its safe return! I know where Cephus keeps his best brandy.' She went to the fireplace and lifted down the painting over the mantel. Inside the wall cavity was a bundle of dusty, burgundy velvet. She lifted it out and cradled it in her arm like an infant, peeling back a corner of the material to reveal a dark glass bottle.

'Why would someone stash it in a reading room?'

'For relaxation,' she answered simply, uncorking the bottle with a squeaky pop. 'And fear of dishonest servants.'

'Well, I suppose that makes sense. But Mademoiselle—'

'*Claudette*,' she said sharply, as she prepared the drinks by the sideboard with her back to him. 'I cannot bear formalities.'

'Well, Claudette, I am sorry to say this, but I really must be getting back—'

'Oh come now, surely you would not refuse a lady's request after you have shown yourself to be such a gentleman? It is only a toast after all.'

'Oh, very well, but then I really must hurry back.'

'Pray sit down a moment, Mr Abernathy. I am sure you have time enough for that.'

Douglas seated himself on the sofa and fumbled with the brooch in his hand. Claudette came over with two glasses of dark liquid and handed one to him.

'Urgh, I cannot move for this cage. *Un moment, s'il vous plaît*.' Her hand dipped behind her back and the metal cage suddenly folded in on itself. The transparent material enclosed her legs like a shroud, but he could still see their shifting, shadowy outlines as she seated herself beside him. The floaty material brushed against his trouser leg.

'To the brooch's safe return.' She smiled as she clinked his glass, eyeing him over her glass as she drank. Douglas smiled bashfully and took a swig of the dark, bronze-gold liquid, swallowing it hastily before placing his glass down on the table. It scorched his throat.

'It is a rather peculiar brooch,' he remarked, as he turned it over in his hand. It was a white and yellow diamond octopus with beady green eyes and a rectangular, orange gem set in its bulbous head like a crystalline brain. In one of its front tentacles it cradled a pearl.

'It was a gift from my father to my mother, so it is of sentimental value. Would you be so kind as to pin it on my dress for me?'

'I'm sorry, Mademoiselle?' The glass paused halfway to his lips. He had not even been aware that he had gone to drink from it again.

'Could you please pin the brooch onto my dress for me?'

'Oh, um, of course…if that is your wish. Claudette.'

He almost spilled the liquid in his glass as he put it down and shakily raised his hands to the spot she was indicating, with her finger above her left bosom. He blinked hard. He was starting to feel light-headed and his ears were burning.

'You said it was a gift from your father to your mother?' he said, in an attempt to distract himself from the feeling.

'Yes. She was an English actress, although not the sort that played at Drury Lane or Covent Garden. My father saw her performing in some dreadful melodrama one night and was instantly captivated by her. Ah, *merci*,' she said as he sharply retracted his hands, the jewelled octopus gleaming in its rightful place. 'He took her to Paris with him shortly after that. He was often chastised for marrying below his station.' She cast him a sidelong glance. 'Something I believe you can relate to.'

'You are familiar with my family's history?'

'The story happened to reach my ears earlier this evening.'

'It is common gossip amongst the social elite.' Douglas smiled with a downward glance.

'The social elite has nothing better to occupy itself with. They are as empty-headed as marionettes. Why should we rush to join them?' She sank back on the sofa and lifted one leg over the other, the pearly flesh surfacing through a slit in the fabric. 'I much prefer your company. I am sure your mind is occupied by far higher pursuits.'

'Will our host not mind our absence?'

'If I know Cephus, he will be far too drunk to care by now. This is a surprisingly tame celebration for him compared to some I have attended. At the last ball of his I went to, he was dressed as a maid and insisted we call him Cecily and then reckoned to serve us and play the fiddle all evening.'

'He certainly does seem to cultivate a taste for the eccentric.'

'He was not bad, I must admit.'

'As a maid or as a fiddle-player?'

'Both. He could balance a glass of champagne on his arm while still playing in tune.'

'Did he really ask you to marry him? And you refused him?'

'Yes, but I don't think he was at all serious about it. And don't believe him if he says he was heartbroken over it. He was serenading my cousin over the breakfast table the very next morning. But enough about Cephus.' She put down her glass. 'I would rather hear about you.'

'Me? Oh, I'm hardly an interesting topic for conversation.'

'Oh, I do not believe *that*.' She inclined herself towards him, with her cheek resting on her palm, as she looked up at him with her dazzling eyes. 'In fact, I find you rather fascinating. You know, I was simply enraptured by your automaton's performance earlier.'

'Thank you, Mademoiselle. Although I fear his parts have been under quite a lot of strain. In fact, I fear he is greatly being taken advantage of.' He spoke rapidly, words tumbling out from his mouth without his being fully conscious of what he was saying.

'Really? Oh, how awful,' she sighed.

Douglas felt a draught of her sweet breath skim across his cheek. 'Yes, not that it is of any consequence to anyone it seems. Least of all my brother.' Up came the hand that bore the glass once more. Douglas's latest sip was not quite as keen as the first couple had been. 'You know, Mademoiselle, your eyes are the most beautiful I have ever seen,' he blurted out, instantly regretting it. He quickly looked down, his face burning with shame. His eyes fell on her hand, which was brushing away the flimsy skirt so that even more of her thigh became visible. Douglas had never seen a great deal more than a woman's ankles before, and now here was this woman with her legs practically bare! His senses were thrown into confusion. The veins in his temples throbbed, he was sure, audibly.

He thought he had heard her say something in response to his last rash comment but he wasn't sure. 'George doesn't see Maestro for what he really is, or at least he claims not to.' The words came gushing from his mouth in a senseless torrent as he picked up the previous thread of conversation. 'George always acts as if he knows better than anyone else and that *he's* the only true genius – ever since we were boys. Even though I have proven countless times that I can produce machines every bit as good as *he* can. And whenever he does something reckless, it's always *me* who's left to deal with it.'

'I am sure you are every bit the genius he is, with the added benefit of modesty and a number of other exceptional qualities, which I dare say he lacks.'

'And then – ' Douglas swallowed breathlessly, ' – and then Maestro almost falls apart right before everyone's eyes, and George doesn't even turn his head.'

'But the automaton is quite all right now, I take it?'

'Yes, for now at least. Until the next incident.'

'And it will be you who is left to fix him?

'Precisely!' Douglas cried, a little too loudly.

Claudette nodded slowly and deliberately, showing she was in sympathy with him. 'Tell me…' She took his hand lightly in her own. 'How does it work? Your automaton?'

'Oh, I fear I would not do a terribly good job of explaining it. It is all rather complex. To tell the truth I only just about understand it all myself. It was George who built him originally.' Douglas laughed lightly.

'I am sure that you understand it all perfectly well, as much as your brother does. I would be fascinated to hear it from your own lips. I would relish every detail of what you had to say.' As she had been talking, her hand had crept around the side of his head and her fingers burrowed their way into his auburn locks.

'I doubt hearing it from my lips would be of much use,' he stammered.

'Do not speak at all then.'

The heavy fumes of perfume washed over his senses as she leant in closer towards him, her fingers locked into his hair. He was insensible to everything but her. The magnetic gaze of her eyes, the touch of her hair and skin brushing against his, and the pressure of her lips against his. At that moment, his mind appeared to be suspended outside of time, between the seconds. He was on the brink of yielding to her, like a stone before it succumbs to the pull of gravity and drives headlong down the mountainside. She had released her hold on his hand and pressed the gloved hand against his chest, right where the purple carnation sat. Whether it was this that sparked something in his brain or the Frenchwoman's kiss, which roused him from his dream-like stupor, it was impossible to tell for they both happened in the very same instant, but it called to mind one single thought, which brought him back into himself.

'Molly!' he exclaimed as he tore himself away. 'I'm sorry, Mademoiselle, but I must get back to my sister.'

He stumbled to his feet, but Claudette was quicker. She flitted past him and flattened herself against the door. 'But I will not let you leave.'

'Mademoiselle, I must warn you, I am not afraid to move you from my path if I must.'

Unfazed by his declaration, the smiling woman removed the clasp from the back of her head and shook free her long sheaf of red hair, which fell past her waist.

'You will have to do better than that if you hope to dissuade me, Mademoiselle.'

Without taking her eyes from his, and still with that same sumptuous smile on her shining lips, her hand deftly moved to the back of her dress, which then fell to the floor. 'Now are you still willing to move me, Mr Abernathy?' She smiled.

Douglas blinked hard. 'Why are you are not wearing any…'

'If you truly wish to leave, well, you will have to get past me first.'

Douglas's eyes flitted to the door. She stepped out of the puddle of fabric around her feet and fear shot through him as she was about to advance towards him. He desperately looked about for a way out or something to shield himself with.

Someone began banging on the door from outside. Claudette turned her head aside but did not seem terribly alarmed.

'What is going on in here?' a familiar voice demanded. The door burst open and Monsieur Roux-Voclain filled the doorframe, his eyes bulging in their deep-set sockets as he beheld the scene in front of him. He ground his teeth and stared hard at the two of them, his pallid, waxy face roused to colour a little. At the moment Douglas anticipated he would erupt, he seemed to recollect himself. The colour dissolved from his face and he lowered his eyes. When he spoke it was in a low, expressionless voice. 'I think you should rejoin the party, Mr Abernathy.'

Douglas hurried past Claudette with his eyes cast down onto his tripping feet. He hurried down the corridor, his head spinning and blood pulsing through his temples. He could faintly hear the monsieur's voice saying, 'Cover yourself.'

'Why must you always ruin my fun, Gaston?' was the distant-sounding reply.

Chapter Twenty

Douglas had been absent for well over thirty minutes. Bored of being either ignored or gawked at, Molly had become determined to explore the garden and find the fabled greenhouse Lord Leyton had spoken of. If Douglas wasn't going to uphold his promise, she would find a way to occupy herself for the remainder of the evening. The cool night air and light breeze were a welcome relief from the hot, sultry ballroom. The second she stepped outside she felt her head sway as if she had just boarded a boat on choppy waters, and she pressed her palm to her forehead. Two goblets of champagne on an empty stomach had not exactly been the best idea, and the food she'd eaten since had helped little. She peeled the stupid little lace gloves from her hands and cast them into the shrubbery as she crunched her way along the gravelled path, kicking up the stones with her shoe. She disliked gravel walks – there'd be no gravel walks in *her* garden. Lord Leyton's ornate garden was oppressively angular and symmetrical.

'Too much marble,' she muttered to herself as she wandered amongst the maze of neat, blocky hedgerows and human statues that were like unfortunate souls lost in the maze and petrified for eternity. There were a few rose bushes but they were not in full bloom yet. At the heart of the maze was a large water fountain. Molly sat down on one of the marble slabs beside the fountain and ran her fingers under the curtain of water flowing from a stone maiden's vase, its numbing coolness refreshingly pure. She'd been sweating right through those lace gloves. A few water lilies were bobbing about in the basin. Molly retrieved one and examined it. It was very sick. The yellow curling leaves and the pale bud beneath marked it as destined for the compost heap. A fungal disease. A common enough ailment but easily remedied. She had developed a fungicide that would cure it in an instant, but that was little use since the glass bottle was sitting on her desk at home.

'I'm sorry,' she said to the plant and dunked it back into the water. She caught sight of her rippling reflection. *Plain, dull, common, nothing but the eyes.* Such comments had been swirling around her head all evening. Did they think she was deaf as well as everything else? Of course George and Douglas had gotten such responses too, George obviously being oblivious to it all. In fact, he seemed to have been in his element all evening, conversing with intellectuals and men of distinction, constantly scribbling things down in his pocketbook.

Molly rubbed her heavy eyes. One of the cosmos in her hair fell into her lap. It was looking a little sorry for itself; the petals were starting to wilt. Pinning it back into place, Molly heard the far-off crunch of gravel and female voices. She darted behind a hedgerow just as two older ladies made their appearance and sat down on the marble seat that Molly had just vacated. They were rather plainly dressed in comparison to the other guests.

'Such relief! It was unbearably hot inside, wasn't it, Lady Ashton,' exclaimed the plump, squat one in the purple and green gown, waving her fan about listlessly.

'Yes, the temperature is much more agreeable out here,' returned her grey-haired companion coolly, taking out a small jewelled snuffbox. 'I don't know why my nephew insisted on inviting so many of those queer, detestable people. I sometimes think it a blessing that my poor sister is no longer here to see what has become of her eldest son. At least we were able to slip out unnoticed for a short while, although we must be sure to return before that mechanical man plays again.' She took a pinch of snuff and offered the box to her companion. 'Not that I care a great deal if we miss it.'

'Oh, I think it is rather wonderful!'

'It is ingenious, I will grant that, but I am in no doubt that there is some clever trickery at work. It might run unaided, but there will most surely be some human involvement somewhere. A well-known composer perhaps, who wishes to remain anonymous, whose melodies it plays.'

'Certainly, certainly, Lady Ashton.' Her companion nodded fiercely, the plume of purple feathers in her hair bobbing about wildly. 'The two clockmakers who built it for your nephew are here. Have you seen them?'

Molly had started to make her way back towards the house but retreated a few paces at hearing this turn in the conversation.

'Yes. Their sister is here with them.' Lady Ashton wafted her fan, not acknowledging the other lady's searching gaze.

'Oh, I saw her! She was wearing a lavender gown with flowers in her hair. She has hardly said a word to anyone or danced all evening. I dare say she is either a mute or incredibly simple-minded. I confess she has some beauty, in a rustic sort of way, like one of Fanny Burney's heroines – or Madame D'Arblay rather. I forgot she married.'

'Really, Mrs Dunn.' Lady Ashton snapped her fan shut. 'You do ramble on in such a trivial manner.'

'Oh, do you really think I do, Lady Ashton?'

'Indeed. Yes, the girl might possess some beauty, even though her manners are remarkably rude and peculiar.'

'Oh, I quite agree, my lady.' Mrs Dunn's feathers reeled dizzily from another bout of head bobbing. 'Dreadfully simple, dreadfully rude. And most peculiar.'

'It is hard to believe…' Lady Ashton leant her head closer to Mrs Dunn with her fan held up against her cheek, as if there were hidden eavesdroppers eager to devour their discourse. Aside from Molly that is, who was lurking nearby. '…it is hard to believe who her mother was.'

'Her mother? What of her mother?'

'You mean to say you don't know?'

'I declare I do not know what it is I do not know.'

'How dull you can be, Mrs Dunn.' Lady Ashton sharply pointed her fan at Mrs Dunn, who flinched as if it had been a dagger. 'Did you not see the dark-haired brother?'

'Yes. I would say he is rather handsome considering his class. A little grave and sullen-looking perhaps, but there was unmistakably something in his countenance and bearing that spoke of better breeding.'

'There you are at it again! You really do have an eye for the most trivial details. However, you have hit upon the essence of what I am getting at. Was there nothing else you noticed about his countenance?'

Mrs Dunn only widened her eyes in panic and effected to appear in deep thought, her bottom lip sticking out and her brow clouding.

'Did you not think he bore a striking resemblance to anyone of our acquaintance?' Lady Ashton prompted.

'No. Did you, my lady?'

'Why, Mrs Dunn, save for his eyes he is the spitting image of the Duke of Hereford.'

'The Duke of Hereford! My word, now you have said so, Lady Ashton, I see that you are right! But how can that possibly be?'

'Do you recall,' the lady said with great deliberation, 'the scandal involving the daughter of the previous duke, the current duke's elder sister, Lady Georgina Dennington?'

Molly hovered on the very edge of the hedgerow, almost risking making herself visible. She knew what was coming next.

'The one who eloped with the clockmaker? My dear Lady Ashton, it was the talk of the season back in thirty-one! Why do you mention it?'

'Really, are your wits that slow, Mrs Dunn? Those two clockmakers, and their sister, are the offspring that resulted from the ill-fated union.'

'My word! So the duke is their uncle!'

'Yes, but of course his father cut his sister off without a shilling as soon as he learnt of the marriage. She was ostracised from society.'

'Quite rightly so. You know, Lady Ashton,' Mrs Dunn put her finger to the corner of her mouth, where it sank into her doughy cheek, 'now that I think about it, the other brother and sister have the Denningtons' distinctive green eyes. The current duke's eyes, if I recall correctly, are brown. His nephew might resemble him very closely, but *his* eyes are a rather striking tint of blue. To think that I have seen the Duke of Hereford's nephews and niece this very night without knowing!'

'Indeed. I suppose we should go back inside. I am beginning to feel a chill,' said Lady Ashton crisply, as she rose from her seat.

'As am I, Lady Ashton. Yes, let us go,' Mrs Dunn concurred, rising after her.

They sauntered back towards the house, and Molly emerged into the clearing. The only sound now came from the trickling of water in the fountain. She was used to her family history being reduced to common gossip. It was known to every member of London's high society how Lady Georgina Dennington had been wooed by the clockmaker hired to fix a family heirloom and eloped with him in the dead of night. Molly had pieced together the particulars over the years. How her father had constructed wondrously beautiful and delicate mechanical trinkets (a few, such as the emerald-green beetle that doubled as a hairpin, were now in Molly's possession) to express his adoration for his raven-haired goddess. How he had plied her with promises of the fame and riches he would one day achieve when he was discovered, which she had believed all too readily, flattered as she was by his attention and the novelty of the gifts that he made her. And how, when it was too late, he had soon discovered the true nature of his goddess: haughty, proud and inflexible as steel. She had had him paper her a parlour, hire a maid and spend the far humbler income he now made on other small luxuries. He had offered no resistance and became resigned to her will. Yet as the family's fortunes gradually decayed, Mrs Abernathy showed herself to be extremely frugal and shrewd, maintaining an outward appearance of propriety but carefully monitoring every last penny that trickled in or out of the shop, and spending many nights with a huge ledger spread on her lap. Still bitter about her husband's unfulfilled promises, when she was expecting her third child, Mrs Abernathy sought consolation in her vision of an ideal daughter. She would be a miniature of her mother, a black-haired, green-eyed beauty. She would be a polite, obedient and accomplished little darling. Eventually she would marry advantageously and bring prosperity to her family. Instead of this ideal daughter, however, she got Molly. When her husband died and money became even scarcer, Mrs Abernathy's scheme to marry her fifteen-year-old daughter off to the first willing, well-to-do suitor was put into action. While preparations were underway for Mr Abernathy's funeral, his widow had noticed that the son of the local undertaker had taken a fancy to her daughter. Mrs Abernathy had then tactfully opened negotiations with Mr

Underwood about the terms of a union between their respective offspring. When Molly refused to marry Mr Uriah Underwood, her mother took no notice. Nor did she care for her sons' objections.

'Mother, the man is twenty years her senior and a brute. Did you not see how he was leering at her?'

'What else are we to do with a peculiar, plain girl such as she with not a penny to her name?' was Mrs Abernathy's brusque reply. In the end, she was forced to back down from her scheme when George had told her that if the marriage went ahead, they would quit the family business altogether, Douglas promptly backing him. It was perhaps the first and only time in her life that her indomitable will had been challenged.

Now, as Molly stood gazing up at the grand house before her, she wondered whether she should be so entirely resentful of her mother, seeing what a different world she had been born into. It wasn't where she belonged. Sighing, she trudged back up to the house, hearing the blend of music and lively chatter once more. As she made her way towards the ballroom, the first person she encountered happened to be George. (He'd sought a place of refuge, bored of having to make idle chatter with people who didn't interest him.) He was standing in the mouth of one of the archways leading to the ballroom with a glass of something bright amber in his hand when he noticed her.

'Molly?' He approached her at once. 'What have you been doing? Hasn't—'

George read plainly the crestfallen look in his sister's eye and put down his glass. Seeing his sister so neglected and unhappy was the final straw. 'Come, we are leaving.'

'What?' Molly jerked her head up in surprise.

'We will find Douglas first, and then we're going home. Come.' George wasted no time once he had resolved to quit the ball. He took her arm and strode purposefully into the ballroom, directing their course around the periphery, away from the dancers.

'But shouldn't we find our host and inform him that we're leaving?' Molly protested.

'It'll take too much time. I doubt he'll mind.'

A few people turned to them as they passed and looked set to address them, but George swept boldly past them with that resolved look on his face that no soul could dare challenge. Just then, they saw Douglas practically hurl himself into the room at the far end. He supported himself on the doorframe, and then on the back of a gentleman's chair, before he caught sight of them and began to stagger over to where they were, attempting to navigate the people who swam past him, as he had thoughtlessly cut straight across the dancers. When he did eventually join them, appearing breathless and flustered, Molly immediately caught a waft of the Frenchwoman's strong perfume and saw the pink, greasy smear printed over his mouth. None of them spoke above the sound of the applause as a dance finished, and it wasn't until they were back in the passageway that Molly kicked Douglas in the shin.

'What was that for?' he demanded, retracting his leg.

'You broke your promise,' she said flatly before striding off down the corridor, the hollow echo of her footsteps marching after her.

'But – what?' Douglas stood open-mouthed and dumbfounded. George fixed him with a fleeting stare and then followed Molly. Douglas lamely attempted to catch up with them. A servant fetched their cloaks, George having to wait for his to be located while his brother and sister got into the cab. When the cloak was eventually brought to him, George heard a voice behind him say, 'Leaving already? Are you not supposed to be tonight's honoured guests?'

He turned around to see the professor grinning at him.

'Large social gatherings are not entirely my forte,' returned George as he put on his hat.

'Humph, what a pity. And before the firework show to boot! But I encourage you to consider my offer. I think it would be mutually beneficial for the both of us.' He bowed smartly and then disappeared out of the room. George watched after him and then got into the cab. As they set off down the gravelled drive, Molly stared intently at Douglas with narrowed eyes, but then her brow smoothed and she turned her head towards the window. They were all silent until the cab pulled up outside their front door.

Chapter Twenty-One

The chiming of clocks woke Douglas with a start. Dream was still emulsified with reality; it took a few moments for the two to separate and for the latter to reassert itself at the surface. He had been dreaming about a mechanical and crystalline red octopus that'd had him trapped in its tentacles. He could still feel them constricting his chest. His heart was beating furiously and he felt slightly ill. When he threw back the bedclothes, he saw that he was still dressed in his clothes from the previous night. He changed into his day clothes and stuck his head out onto the landing. Silence hung in the air. Treading carefully, he hovered outside his sister's door. There wasn't a sound from within. He was about to try a tentative knock but, thinking better of it, made his way downstairs instead.

George was sprawled face down on the sofa in the parlour with a quarter-full decanter of brandy and an empty tumbler on the table next to him. He had never made it to bed. His hair was matted and his shirt creased, his collar and cravat cast onto the floor. The black frock coat was folded carelessly over the back of the sofa. A small, rotund automaton was setting the morning paper down at the other end of the table. It glanced up at Douglas and then hurriedly rolled out of the room on its steel wheels. Douglas sat in the armchair adjacent to the sofa and began idly flicking through the paper. The curtains were half closed, making the room a little dim. Douglas considered opening them so that the full force of the bright sunlight would be thrown on George, but he decided to show mercy. He was facing away from the window anyway. After some minutes there came a low rustling as George rolled over onto his side.

'What time is it?' he asked in a dull, groaning voice.

'Nearly eleven,' answered Douglas, behind the pages of the *Morning Post*.

'Molly will have something to say to you, you know. Where were you?'

'With Mademoiselle Roux-Voclain. She had me trapped.'

'That I find hard to believe,' he muttered faintly. When Douglas next looked up he saw George had dropped off to sleep again.

Douglas heard a creak on the stairs. 'Molly!' He laid the newspaper aside when she appeared at the threshold of the parlour. She had morphed back into the wild, unkempt sister he knew, wearing an old cotton dress; a few ripples in her loose hair remained from where the plaits had been.

'I'm sorry I broke my promise to you, Molly. I did mean to come find you but the Frenchwoman had me trapped in the reading room.'

'It's all right.' Molly shrugged. 'I'm not angry with you anymore. I realised, when I saw the state you were in when we got home last night, that she must have drugged you.'

'What?'

'I'd say a solution of cocaine most likely. She must have slipped it into your drink or something.'

'Oh, that explains why I felt so peculiar when I went to bed last night. I remember having bad convulsions and then passing out in a stupor.'

'It must have been a fairly strong dose she gave you. It's something of a miracle that you were able to resist her charms with that in your blood.'

'I think it's more of a miracle that George stayed relatively sober throughout the whole evening, although I dare say he made up for it when we got home.' Douglas smiled, kicking his brother as he lay there on the sofa. George swore at him.

'Yes, but he's used to it. He'll come round by dinnertime. As it happens, George actually came to my rescue last night when you failed to show. Now, do you have any other symptoms?' Molly approached him, searching his face critically. 'Any headaches or nausea?'

'No, I'm fine. My head does feel a little murky to tell the truth, but it's not as bad as when I fell into bed last night.' He half-smiled, lightly swatting her hand away. 'Although I still feel bad for not keeping my promise. I mean, I could have made some excuse and slipped away before she offered me a drink. I did try to get away.'

'I said – ' Her voice was tinged with mock annoyance and she put one hand on her hip ' – that I'd forgiven you. Now you can stop mentioning it. If you really want to make it up to me you can wash and press all our clothes for a week.'

'Well, if that's what it takes to let me off the hook I suppose I could…'

'Ah, not so eager now, are you?' She grinned and went to pick up George's frock coat. She shook her head at it and then threw it down again.

'So…' Molly folded her arms over the top of the sofa. '…what exactly happened between you and Mademoiselle while she had you locked up in the reading room?'

'Oh, um…' Douglas rubbed the back of his neck, and his face reddened. 'I don't remember much of it.' This was a half-truth. His memory of the previous night was quite hazy, although he did have flashes of images. Some very vivid images in fact. 'Just a couple of things.'

'Not that you're prepared to say what they were,' said George groggily, as he brought himself up into a sitting position. He leant forward and put his hand to his head. 'Did you manage to learn anything from the samples you took from the professor's coat?' he asked Molly.

'Not really, I'm afraid. I'm struggling to identify just about any of the chemicals he used in the material. I'll keep trying though.'

A sharp rap on the front door made them lift their heads in unison. Douglas got up to answer it. He saw the familiar grand black coach through the shop window. A chill ran though his blood. Had they done something to upset Lord Leyton? It must be bad for him to roll up on their doorstep before noon. Perhaps the cost of the damage to the ballroom had been greater than expected. Or perhaps, God forbid, the tigers had mauled a guest. When he pulled back the door he saw a servant in livery. Standing a little distance behind him was Maestro with his instrument case in hand.

'Good morning, sir. At the request of Lord Leyton, I have brought the automaton to you for repairs. His lordship asks that he be returned by tomorrow morning. He also expresses his disappointment at your prompt departure last night and hopes nothing was amiss.'

Something clicked in Douglas's brain. Of course, now he recalled telling Lord Leyton to send Maestro to them for inspection as soon as possible.

'Oh, send our compliments to his lordship, and our sincerest apologies for leaving the ball so suddenly. You may tell him that there was an urgent matter, which compelled us to leave at once. Thank you.'

The man tipped his hat and returned to the coach; there appeared to be nobody else inside it. Douglas ushered Maestro inside before the coach had driven away and shut the door. Maestro's eyes boggled at seeing the assemblage of automata before him.

'Oh, those are waiting to go out. Although it seems some people have failed to turn up to collect them. Um, shall we go up to the workshop, Maestro? It'll be a lot less crowded there. I'll see to your repairs myself. Master George isn't in much of a fit state for anything this morning. It'll give us a chance to have a proper conversation with one another, eh?' He opened the black door, swiftly raising his leg to avoid stepping on the little tin cleaner that was sweeping the shop. 'Come on through. You know the way.'

Maestro hesitantly trod across the floorboards. His path was suddenly blocked as Molly wordlessly flitted past them and hurried up the stairs, apparently bent on an urgent mission. Douglas looked across at George, who was standing at the side of the fireplace so that he was squarely facing them. He held up a warning finger.

Douglas could detect a faint scuffling from inside the chimney – and saw a weak cloud of coal dust curl out from the mouth of the fireplace. As his brain was processing the situation, the fireplace spewed out a cloud of black dust. George's arm shot out and grabbed hold of the writhing thing in the midst of the murk, holding it away from him at arm's length. It thrashed about kicking its legs before he threw it down onto the sofa and swiftly flicked the switch on the side of its head with impressive finesse. It instantly went limp.

Molly's footsteps came thundering down the stairs.

'Did you get it?' She hurried past Douglas with a bedsheet spread over her arms, looking down at the sooty little automaton. It was about two feet high and made of dull steel, with a blockish head almost as large as its body, out of the top of which sprouted a round brush like a sweep's.

'How on earth did it get up there in the first place?' Douglas glanced at the automaton and then at the chimney.

'I know I didn't switch it on,' said Molly. 'So I don't see how it managed to find its way up there.'

'Unless one of the other automata switched it on somehow and it climbed up inside the chimney.'

'Well it must have been there all night. I haven't seen it around this morning,' she said, as she slung the bedsheet over her shoulder.

'I don't see why you won't let it be dismantled and have done with it,' said George. 'It's caused us nothing but trouble, and if you think—'

His words were choked by a plume of coal dust coughed up by the automaton, which rained down over the three of them. George and Molly got the worst of it, being closer to the epicentre, and were both coated in black down their fronts. Molly wiped her screwed-up face with a corner of the sheet and looked down at the mess. Everything was coated in soot.

'I'm not cleaning that up,' she said, with a light shake of the head, and then disappeared back upstairs.

Douglas looked towards the stairs, then at the chimney sweep, at Maestro, and at the other automata crowding around the door to see what the commotion had been. 'We need a bigger place.'

George drew his arm across his soot-smeared face. 'Yes, I quite agree,' he said with a slight cough.

'There! You're all done now, Maestro. I've tightened everything up, replaced the warped metal and repaired the punctured bellow. Let's give it a test. Did you bring a woodwind instrument like I asked you to?'

In answer Maestro undid the clasps on the instrument case and held out an oboe, which he then proceeded to play a chirrupy tune upon with a flourish.

'Perfect. Once more?'

Maestro promptly obeyed, but a couple of notes in the instrument began to make a sour squeak. Bringing it away from his mouth, he saw the reed had broken.

'Never mind,' Douglas said, 'at least it's the reed and nothing inside you. You were quite fortunate that the damage wasn't half as bad as it could have been with the strain that playing the so-called Finale Sonata note-perfect produced on your parts. But it looks as though you've been having some trouble for a while now, Maestro, with all those cracks on your casing. Did you not say anything to Lord Leyton?'

Maestro put down the oboe and reached for the slate. *It did not seem important, Master Douglas.*

'Well, I'd say it was rather important, wouldn't you? The left hand was especially bad. Did you have some sort of accident?'

Maestro remained still a moment. He began shifting his feet about and then took up the chalk. He wrote line after line before finally holding up the slate to Douglas. Douglas's eyes widened as he scanned the block of writing.

'Mr Griffin really did all this to you?' Douglas looked at Maestro. 'And you said nothing of it to anyone?'

No.

'So he trapped your hand in a door and actually struck you in the head?'

Yes.

Douglas sat back in his chair aghast. He let out a sigh and rubbed his eyes. 'It isn't right, Maestro, don't you see? People like that treat you as if you're nothing but a wind-up toy. You shouldn't have to stand for it.'

There came the soft tapping of the chalk. *But what should I do, Master Douglas?*

Douglas opened his mouth and then hesitated. He looked pityingly at Maestro's frank, questioning eyes. The truth was there wasn't a great deal he could do to make them see that he was a living being and not just a mechanical toy. Douglas turned his gaze upwards and drummed his fingers on the tabletop thoughtfully. After a couple of minutes, his gaze absently wandered over to the oboe. He picked it up and tipped the faulty reed out into his hand. An idea entered his head.

'Actually, Maestro, there is one more adjustment that I'd like to make to you.' He instantly sprang up from his seat and retrieved a U-shaped iron clamp that widened its jaw when he wound round a screw on its side. He placed it on the edge of the table. 'Kneel down and rest your head in there for me, Maestro.'

When Maestro had his head securely wedged between the clamp's jaws, Douglas began rummaging through the piles of mangled metal and strange-looking instruments. 'Aha, here it is!' He held up a tool with a long handle connected to a steel disc with sharp, jagged edges.

'Now, it's important that you don't move, Maestro.' He pressed a button on the handle's side and the jagged head began spinning so fast that it formed a blurred circle, making a horribly fierce buzzing. 'Don't worry, this will all be over quickly.'

Maestro could only widen his eyes as Master Douglas came towards him with the cutter. He didn't think he liked the look in his master's eyes.

George held the professor's card between his fingers, going over the exchange in the supper room the night before in his mind (which was still slightly blunted by the brandy but rapidly regaining its faculties). The man was a fraud, he was sure of it. There was nothing to be gained by his proposal that could benefit them, and 'equal partners' in actual fact meant sacrificing creative and legal control. Placing the card on his bedside table, he went to his desk and resumed work on his machine from the previous evening.

Sabotage Cobb's factory. And the man had Cobb believe that he was a valued acquaintance. So what treachery was he capable of towards a business partner? What lengths would he go to?

George's hand reached for his screwdriver. It wasn't there. He felt through his desk drawers, but it wasn't there either. Douglas must have taken it. Sighing, George pushed back his chair and got up. Should he tell Douglas about the professor's proposition? No, it would only complicate matters further. It was best not to involve anyone else. Without bothering to knock, George opened the workshop door and glanced inside. His brother's voice instantly ceased. He'd had his head bent close to the android as if he had been confiding something to it, but instantly whipped his head up at hearing George enter. The expression on his face certainly suggested something covert had been taking place.

'I've been looking for my screwdriver. Have you taken it?'

'Possibly, although I've moved a lot of things around in here. You'll have to search for it.'

George ran his eyes over the piles of metal and sprinklings of what looked like sawdust strewn across the floor.

'So you've finished fixing it then?'

'Yes.'

George narrowed his eyes.

Douglas had that expression on his face that said he was up to something. He was grinning foolishly at George with his hands behind his back.

'So when is the earl sending someone for it?' George asked after a brief silence.

'Oh, tomorrow morning I should expect,' Douglas replied, his eyes flitting briefly to the android, which remained perfectly still, only blinking every now and then. George turned his back on them and went to retrieve what he had come for. He found the screwdriver carelessly buried under a pile of papers on the worktable.

Then he heard the android move a couple of steps forward.

'Good afternoon, Master George.'

George dropped the screwdriver and looked over his shoulder. The voice that had spoken was distinctively different from, lighter than, Douglas's. George had heard it as clearly as if another person had been standing a few feet away from him. He approached the android. 'What did you just say?'

'Good afternoon, Master George,' Maestro repeated.

'Ah – haha!' Douglas cried gleefully at George's mystified expression.

George glanced at Douglas questioningly and then returned his gaze to the android. 'How is it you are able to speak? Tell me.'

'Master Douglas inserted a reed into my throat and constructed a tongue made from rubber, sir. Gradually, I learnt to manipulate the air flow from the bellows in my chest until I was able to speak freely.'

George's frown deepened, and then he thrust Maestro's head back, seeing the line where the jaw had been cut and a nut bolted at either side.

He then tilted Maestro's mouth open and peered inside. Sure enough, there was a rubber tongue attached to the back of the mouth, and a set of wooden teeth rimmed each jaw. By dragging the android over to the window, he was able to catch a glimpse of the reed deep down in its throat cavity.

'That is remarkable,' said George. 'I don't doubt there isn't a hidden recording-device somewhere on it, since it was able to answer my question just now. Unless of course you anticipated that I would ask it… No, I don't think you would have had that much foresight. I admit it's quite impressive that you managed to give it speech, but I fail to understand why you took such trouble when we have so many outstanding commissions. This one is finished with. Did Lord Leyton request that you do this?'

'No, but I thought it would benefit Maestro if he could actually speak for himself.'

'Could what? Oh, I see what you're getting at. You believe that by bestowing it with a voice, it will appear more human-like. Well, you won't prove it can think for itself merely by giving it speech. Tell me, Maestro…' George folded his arms across his chest as he addressed the android, although he eyed Douglas all the while. He spoke the android's name with bitter sarcasm. '…how do you like being able to speak for yourself?'

Maestro seemed to ponder the question. 'It is…it is far more convenient than having to write my thoughts down all of the time, Master George. I can express my thoughts with much greater ease.'

'But how does it *feel*?'

Maestro blinked his yellow eyes. 'I am afraid I do not quite understand.'

'Do you feel at all *liberated*?'

Douglas frowned at the contemptuous tone George had adopted, the same he used when pronouncing the android's name.

Maestro glanced at Douglas a moment and then answered. 'Well, I find that I can make my meaning understood a lot clearer and much more rapidly, which is highly beneficial and much more efficient. It might prevent miscommunications in the future, as I have previously experienced.'

'Well, you aren't wrong, Maestro,' said Douglas. 'But I hope you'll soon find that there are other advantages your new voice will give you besides mere convenience and efficiency.'

'It certainly presents a commercial advantage, now it can speak as well as play music. I wonder perhaps if it can sing in tune. That would help prolong public interest in it,' said George.

'I haven't tried getting him to sing, nor do I mean to make a further spectacle of him.'

'I believe I could sing, Master,' said Maestro, unwittingly aiding George's cause. 'The mechanics of singing are almost the same as those of speech, and I am able to match pitch. I can demonstrate for you if you wish.'

'No, Maestro. That's not necessary.' Douglas stared at George. 'I did this so he could be taken more seriously and to have a better means of self-expression. Then perhaps people will stop taking advantage of him.'

'You're imprinting human wants onto an android that has no true understanding of them.'

'That theatre manager Lord Leyton is acquainted with treated him like a malicious child would treat their doll. He struck him in the head.'

'That is none of our concern. If the android gets damaged that is not our responsibility, and if the earl wants it fixing then we will do so.' George shrugged and retrieved his tool. 'I have said all of this to you before, and I won't waste my breath on the subject anymore.'

George walked past his brother and shut the door behind him. Douglas was expecting the sound of the shutting door to be louder than it was.

'Master Douglas?' Maestro was pointing towards an unfinished automaton that was slumped against the back wall. 'What is this automaton meant to do, Master Douglas?'

'He is to be an acrobat when he's finished.'

'Will he be given a voice too, Master?'

'No, Maestro, an acrobat doesn't really need a voice, you see? It would have no use for one.'

'But, if you will forgive me, you insisted to Master George just now that I needed a voice, even though a musician does not strictly need one. Is it not the same for this automaton?'

'He is different from you.' Douglas was slightly taken aback by how Maestro managed to construct a well-formed chain of reason. 'His mind, and those of all the other automata that were built after you, is nowhere near as advanced as yours. They all possess intelligence, yes, but none are fully aware like you are. You are exceptional.'

'But why did you and Master George make me so?'

'Oh, many reasons,' said Douglas vaguely.

'So...there are no others like me?'

'That's right. But that is nothing to dwell on. Being the exception to the rule is hardly a bad thing,' Douglas said brightly. 'After all, that is why half of London is going wild over you. They've never seen anything like you before. Although the end of the season will soon be in sight, then they will all go back to the country and your parts won't sustain wear as quickly from playing at all these balls and dinners.'

'But that will not matter soon, Master Douglas.'

'What do you mean, Maestro?'

'Master Josephus is planning on taking me with him to the Continent next month.'

'*What?*'

'He says he is bored of the society of London and craves a warmer climate. He intends to show me to the rest of the world, he says.'

'But...' Douglas faltered. What would it mean if Lord Leyton really did intend to take Maestro on tour abroad? It would do wonders for the Abernathy name if Maestro were to travel the world, but would his parts last that long? How much wear could they sustain? It wouldn't be like it was now when Lord Leyton could have Maestro sent back to the shop at a moment's choosing. Here in London he was safe. He was nearby at least. Douglas could still communicate with him easily and monitor how he progressed in the world. He would be exposed to all sorts of places and people who may wish to acquire him, and his secrets. And no doubt there would be others like the SOAL. There was also the matter of the sorts of people Maestro would be mixing with, which, judging from the assortment of Lord Leyton's friends at the ball the previous night, was a possible cause for concern. Maestro's nature was so open and innocent, it would be a shame if it were to be so easily corrupted. Lord Leyton was not exactly an ideal mentor as it was.

'But what if you need repairing again? The Continent is a very long way away.'

'It is quite all right, Master Douglas. Master Josephus can write to you if anything is wrong. He says he will even pay to have you come to Italy or Vienna if needed.'

'There may be many…risks to going abroad when you don't really know that much of the world, Maestro. I don't think you should go.'

'Why, Master Douglas? Am I not to obey the wishes of Master Josephus? You yourself told me I must do so.'

'Oh, well, that is true. But what of your own wishes?'

'I was built to perform.' Maestro blinked. 'So would I not be fulfilling my primary purpose?'

'Well, I suppose so. Never mind, we'll let the matter rest for now,' Douglas said lightly, giving it up. 'Now, let's go call on Molly. She said she wanted to hear you play before you went, and we'll give her quite the surprise when she hears your new voice.'

Chapter Twenty-Two

Rehearsals for the opera that he had written commenced alarmingly soon after Maestro had completed the score, with one or two minor alterations. At the story's centre was an automaton, wandering all alone through a large city with no memory of how he was created, by whom, or for what purpose. Perhaps it wasn't very original, but the way it was told, Maestro hoped, would be. The plot was the canvas on which to paint his musical masterpiece. The songs would bring the story truly to life. Master Josephus had seen to it that the very best musicians from all over the world were selected to form the orchestra, although Maestro of course had the final authority on all aspects of production. There had been some minor controversy over his introduction of unconventional elements; he had chosen music-hall singers to sing alongside recognised opera stars, and insisted on allowing the little man from the street corner with the battered accordion and other street musicians to form part of the orchestra.

'This will upset certain people, you know, my dear Maestro,' Master Josephus had remarked when he came to observe how rehearsals were coming along.

'But what is it that separates them from the professionals, Master?'

'Many years of training at the Royal Academy, or some such place, not to mention what would be considered good breeding. Those people you introduced are not exactly...clean, in more than one sense of the word.'

'But, forgive me, Master, you yourself once said that talent cannot be taught. The street musicians know how to generate harmonious sound by what you might call instinct. Why should they be excluded because of external circumstances they cannot help?'

Master Josephus looked at him strangely as he twisted his moustache in his customary way. Oh dear, had he said something wrong? But then Master Josephus smiled and chuckled in his throat as he closed his eyes. 'How remarkable you are, Maestro. You never cease to amaze me. Indeed, perhaps after they have been given a good wash and a haircut, who will be any the wiser? It will be an interesting experience.'

The professional musicians had complained at having to learn the entire thing in only a matter of weeks, but Master Josephus said a little extra money would soon quieten them, and indeed he was right.

Maestro found his new position of authority rather strange. He had led an orchestra once before at Master Josephus's birthday celebration, but this was something different. He wasn't entirely sure what he made of the experience. How curious it was, that all he needed to do was wave the baton in his hand a certain way and the brass or woodwind section would respond, almost as if they were the ones driven by clockwork and not he. Each section carried out a particular function. The strings carried the melody while the others provided various harmonies. Yet he was ultimately in control of the flow of the music, save when one of the musicians faltered or improvised something of their own, which he did not discourage – although he was sure one or two of the humans deliberately hit wrong notes or played out of time, fixing him with a malevolent glare. Some submitted gladly to his direction, others continued to resist. Where discord persisted, so too did it persist in the music. He'd overheard the musicians talking amongst themselves backstage on a number of occasions. One conversation was particularly memorable.

'A machine directing human musicians in an opera about machines who are played by humans? Makes your head spin, doesn't it?'

'It isn't right,' affirmed the pianist.

'That reverend wasn't wrong, was he? Today it's this – tomorrow they'll be bloody ruling us. He says it's in the Book of Revelations, you know.'

‘My brother recently joined the SOAL, the Sons of Adam League. He says the movement is starting to splinter between the religious faction and those like him who are just worried that their livelihood is going to be taken from them by the Abernathys’ machines.’

‘Is that so? Maybe we ought to join.’ His tone suggested he meant this in jest, but Maestro wasn’t entirely sure.

Gradually, harmony began to descend, but Maestro still felt the opera was missing an element somehow. What that was precisely, he was not quite certain. His mind was busily at work on the problem as he held one of the books he had retrieved from Master Josephus’s library open before him. He remembered what Master Douglas had once said about being receptive to new thoughts and ideas, so he had formed the habit of regularly taking out books from the library. There were books on all kinds of things in there.

He found that a lot of the larger volumes on the bottom shelves were atlases. His eyes brushed over them. But there were also books on history and mythology, and science journals. Most of the latter he was quite baffled by, although the writer managed to imprint the faintest impression of the idea he was explaining onto Maestro’s mind. There were also a great number of books by a man called William Shakespeare whom he had heard Master Josephus refer to before. How the speech of the characters carried a melody, how the playwright could make music with only his pen, was quite ingenious, Maestro thought – the way the rhythm of the words mimicked the *tee-tum* of the human heartbeat. He particularly liked *A Midsummer Night’s Dream*, which he had read three times. But now he found his gaze was redirected to the painting of the girl above him. Seeing that he could gain no inspiration from reading at present, he decided to return the book to one of the stacks on his bureau, when Master Josephus entered. He was wearing a short black and white pinstripe coat with no tail; neither was he wearing a waistcoat and his neck was entirely bare, the front of his lilac silk shirt wide open. His narrow trousers matched the coat perfectly.

‘Good afternoon, Maestro,’ he said, smiling expectantly.

‘Good afternoon, Master Josephus,’ Maestro replied, perceiving his master press a hand over his quivering mouth, a slight titter escaping from either corner. Master Josephus had been rather astonished when Maestro had greeted him verbally upon his return from the clockmakers' house. After recovering from the surprise, he had laughed brightly and since then was forever entreating him to speak. 'Say something, Maestro. Oh please do, let me hear you speak.' Maestro would of course oblige him, much to his master's unceasing delight.

'How are you getting on with the opera? Did you find anything of use in the library?'

'Yes, Master Josephus. Quite a few things in fact, although I confess I still don't know what it is that is missing.'

Master Josephus glided his hand over the piano keys, playing a few bars of Handel, and approached Maestro's bureau. He took the topmost volume from a stack and turned it over in his hand.

'Ah! Homer's *Odyssey*. I remember studying this when I read Classics at Oxford in my youth – not that it is spent just yet,' he added quickly, replacing the book.

He turned his silver eyes up to the portrait of the lady in white and wound his moustache around his smallest finger. 'If you are experiencing creative difficulties, why not do as Homer and the great Greek poets did and ask your muse up there to lend you inspiration?'

'Muse, sir?' Maestro came and stood beside Master Josephus in front of the painting.

'Oh, you did not know that is Euterpe smiling so prettily up there? She is one of the Nine Muses – goddesses who are guardians of the arts and sciences. She is the muse of music. So perhaps, if you ask nicely, she will provide you with inspiration for your opera.'

Maestro gazed up at her with fresh reverence. He wondered whether the girl, who was most likely only a human girl made to dress in white robes for the painting, really possessed such power. In spite of himself, he couldn't help hoping that perhaps it really was true. 'Please, most gracious Muse, could you grant me your aid?' he whispered, too delicately for his master to hear. He heard no female voices, other than the housekeeper three rooms away.

'How long does it take for the muse to grant her favour, Master?'

'Be patient, dear Maestro. If the goddess favours you then inspiration will present itself soon enough. Now, I came to discuss with you the matter of your attire for the Royal Performance.' He snapped his fingers and Bellamy entered with a number of garments draped neatly over his arm, which he began spreading out on the chairs and chaise longue. 'I could not decide which of my designs I liked the most so I had my tailor make up all four of them. I will have a far better idea of which suits you the best once I actually see them on you.' He was reaching for the first garment, which was of black silk embellished with a gold pattern like waves, when his smile suddenly faded and he looked at Maestro thoughtfully. 'Actually, Maestro, do you have a preference? It will be your moment of glory after all; it is only right that you wear what you feel suits best.'

Maestro widened his eyes at his master in surprise. 'Thank you, Master Josephus. That is most generous of you.' He cast his eyes over the garments before him. Some were bright or pastel pale, but all were heavily patterned, with lace or gold trimming. 'Please do not think me impertinent, Master, but… I think I should like to wear the red coat I wore the first time I performed at Mr Griffin's theatre.'

'You would wear something *old*? Although…' – he rubbed the end of his moustache – 'yes, I can see that working. Clearly you have absorbed some of my taste for aesthetics. Take the other garments away, Bellamy.' Master Josephus smiled as he looked at Maestro. 'Maestro has made his choice. Although you must have a new cravat. I will not allow you to step foot on stage without a new cravat.'

'Very well, Master.' Maestro bowed. If he was truly honest, he did not care a great deal about how he was dressed. What concerned him more was the sound of the music itself. He could only hope his muse would grant him his request.

The string of the guitar (a recent present from Master Josephus), which Maestro had struck last, hummed faintly, overlaid by a smatter of applause. There were three guests in the drawing room that evening: Monsieur and Mademoiselle Roux-Voclain, and Professor Gottfried.

'Remarkable, even more so when one sees it up close,' said the professor. His jaw made a click as it shut. Maestro imagined that it was spring-loaded. 'I just wish you would permit me to have a good look inside of him, Lord Leyton. Are you sure you will not permit more than a peek?'

'I am afraid not, Professor.' Master Josephus shook his head, although he smiled as he did so.

Mademoiselle Roux-Voclain, or Claudette, as they all addressed her, laid a hand on the professor's arm. She was wearing a very unusual dress made entirely of red lace, which was very tight against her skin. The lace ran all along her arms and up to her throat. The skirt trailed to the floor, unsupported by any sort of petticoat. 'You know why Cephus will not let you look, Charles. It is because he is afraid you will deduce how the automaton works and make one of your own, so then his Maestro will no longer be one of a kind.'

'I think you will find that Maestro *is* truly one of a kind, Claudette,' said Master Josephus with one hand on his hip and a glass of dark liquid in the other. 'And I defy anyone to prove me wrong.'

Monsieur Roux-Voclain, who had remained mostly silent all evening, put down his own glass and cleared his throat. 'Well, Josephus, what if I were to tell you that your android isn't quite as unique as you think it is?'

'What on earth do you mean, Gaston?'

'I happen to have in my possession an android, which I recently acquired for my collection, made by a little-known French engineer and builder of automata. It too can compose music by itself, although it is limited to the flute. It can also sing.'

'Oh?' Master Josephus coolly arched an eyebrow.

'In fact it is in the adjoining room at this very moment. I had it brought into the house along with our other boxes when we arrived earlier.'

'Well,' said Master Josephus in a slightly piqued tone, 'can we see this automaton of yours then?'

Nodding at his host, Monsieur Roux-Voclain snapped his fingers. All eyes were directed towards the doorway. Maestro's superior hearing could already detect the light, regular footsteps long before the figure appeared. Standing there was a female automaton, petite in stature and made entirely out of silver. She was clad in a dress of silver silk that fell to her knees and in one hand she held a silver flute. Even the flowers entwined in her silver hair were of the same hue. Maestro could hear the delicate ticking of clockwork coming from within her. She came to a stop in the middle of the room and curtsied elegantly.

'*Bonsoir, mademoiselle et messieurs*,' she said in a honeysuckle voice with a sweet smile on her face.

'Pretty little girl, isn't she?' said Claudette. 'I call her Céline, although my brother thinks it silly that I name her.'

'I simply don't see why she needs a name. She is pure clockwork like your android, Josephus, and like him, she comprehends human speech. I will bid her to play for us, if you wish.'

'Yes, yes, please do,' said Master Josephus with a brisk flick of his hand.

Nodding solemnly, Monsieur Roux-Voclain turned to the silver girl and said something in French, which Maestro did not entirely understand, unable as he was to discern where one word began or ended so all the man's speech was conjoined in his ear. But the girl understood it perfectly, for her eyelids fluttered and she nodded her head in her master's direction before twirling around on one leg. Maestro watched as the silver girl sang a pretty little song in French, swaying and rotating her body as she sang. Her limbs and torso glimmered and twinkled in the brightly lit drawing room. Her movements were slow and fluid like liquid metal, like a real human girl's only perhaps with a touch more grace. Then as she reached the climax of her song, she lifted the flute to her lips and played a sweet melody upon it. Her delicate fingers clicked as they danced nimbly back and forth across the holes, and she continued to sway and twirl with faultless measure. At this point, moved by some unnameable impulse, Maestro came in with his guitar and matched her harmony with one of his own. The voices of the two instruments entwined together, producing one unnervingly beautiful song. Eventually Maestro receded away and left her to sing unaccompanied, and at last, she finally signalled the close of her song with another curtsy. As she rose, her eyes fell upon him and she batted her delicate, pale lashes. Maestro's applause was undoubtedly the most enthusiastic of all of the company, although they themselves were not lacking in it, save perhaps Master Josephus.

'Most original,' said the professor, leaning towards Gaston Roux-Voclain. 'Pray, will *you* enlighten us as to how *she* works, sir?' It was strange that he addressed this remark to Monsieur Roux-Voclain, but he looked at Master Josephus all the while. Maestro guessed he was making some sort of point. Nevertheless, Gaston Roux-Voclain rose and walked over to the silver girl. He opened a panel in her back and spun her around to show them.

'You see this dial, here?' He pointed to a golden wheel in her middle, ringed with teeth that were marked with what looked like individual notes. 'Each of these cogs are codes for a particular note to be played upon the flute, which can be executed in an almost infinite number of sequences.' He then pointed to the three stacks of golden cams that ran up her spine. 'The stacks of cams within her contain the code for a particular algorithm that the engineer devised, which ensures that whatever sequence the girl selects to play will be harmonious to the human ear. Essentially, it is like a patchwork of song, taking sequences found in most forms of music, which can be mathematically proven to be melodious, and then rearranging them. That is the essence of it as far as my understanding goes. I am afraid no detailed drawings or documents accompanied the automaton, and the mechanisms inside of it are far too complex for my understanding.'

'And what would it take for you to let me cut it up to see how it works?' The professor grinned, his gold tooth glinting, and he chortled gruffly.

'Now, now, Charles.' Claudette slid her hand around the inside of his arm. 'Don't go breaking Gaston's little toy, although goodness knows how many of my dolls I found in pieces as a girl!' She let out a velvety laugh.

'That was your own doing.' Her brother frowned. 'You took apart my toy soldiers.'

'Oh it was all mere childish foolishness.' She waved her hand and rolled her eyes. 'But if you ask nicely, Charles, then maybe Gaston might let you try to decipher how she works. Maybe you can expand her repertoire.'

'I'll have her playing more than one instrument, and singing in English, German, Italian and even Hindi by tomorrow!' he declared. There went the clicking jaw, harsher this time. 'And you see if I don't. Of course, if you *were* serious about letting me borrow her for a short while, I could really make some serious modifications.'

'Don't get overexcited, Charles, or else she'll have a leg sticking out from the side of her head and her hands for feet or goodness knows what. Well, Gaston? What do you say? Are you willing to let Charles gratify himself?'

'I suppose,' he muttered as he sat back down. 'Since you are so keen for me to do so.'

'I merely want everyone to be friends. Is that really such a bad thing, brother?'

'Although I do have a gentleman here in London who is very eager to buy it. If Professor Gottfried tampers with it, then it will decrease its value drastically.'

'Tell me what this gentleman has offered for it and I will match it! I bet I know who it is. Is it Babbage? I bet anything it is.'

'I cannot disclose the man's identity,' replied Gaston coolly. 'And I am still in the process of negotiating a price for it.'

'Well, be sure to tell me the figure once it is fixed. In the meantime, I promise to restrain myself and return the little lady to you exactly as she stands at this very minute.' The professor's mouth arched into a wide smile.

'Well, I must say,' cut in their host sharply, 'I think your search will not turn up much, Professor. It will take a lot more than that little demonstration to convince *me* of this automaton's authenticity. Forgive me, Gaston, I don't mean to insult your connoisseur's eye, but I think you have been deceived. I mean, if this French engineer is so brilliant, why is it that he is nowhere near as famous as Vacaunson?' He was referring to the man who had invented the automatic loom, Maestro knew.

'No one would take him seriously.' Gaston shrugged. 'They thought he was a fraud and chased him out of Paris. His wares turn up at private auctions from time to time and are highly sought after. Only a few expert collectors such as myself know of him.'

'Or more likely he never even existed.' Master Josephus sniffed, as if the wine in his glass had been turned to vinegar all of a sudden by the professor.

'Enough. We shall not have any petty squabbling spoiling our evening,' interposed Claudette. 'Was this not meant to be a long-overdue reunion, after all?'

'You are right, my darling,' said Master Josephus in softer tones. 'For this may be the last time I get you under my roof for many a year! And the professor, I know, was courteous enough to find time for us in his busy schedule. Although of course, I will soon follow the both of you to the Continent.'

'Why not come to Paris and stay with us, Cephus?' Claudette smiled. 'Have you been reading the latest novel by Flaubert? It is most engrossing. If you come to stay there is a chance I may be able to acquaint you with him.' Maestro did not heed the rest of the conversation. His gaze and thoughts were absorbed by the now silent silver girl.

As soon as Maestro was back in his room, he seized his pen and began writing everything down that had been forming in the back of his mind since he first beheld the silver singer. It flowed out of him almost too quickly for him to trap onto the paper. He wrote unceasingly, only pausing once to wind himself up again. He was glad Master Josephus had given him possession of his own key. The night was always the best time for him to work as there were no disturbances from the house's human inhabitants, and now he could keep going for as long as he liked. He had to make a slight revision to the opera's plot, into which he incorporated several new songs. One day his automaton is given a spyglass by an old man in the market square and, aiming it at an old lofty tower, sees a female automaton, created by a wicked old inventor who keeps her locked away inside her room. After secretly communicating with her, he frees her and they run from the city. However, the wicked inventor discovers her absence and sends a monstrous machine after them to recapture her. The attempt fails; the automata defeat the machine with the aid of the old man from the market, who then reveals himself to be the automaton's creator. He explains how his creation was stolen from him and believed lost long ago. The two automata are reunited and live happily with the old man.

The clock on the mantel chimed three times before he finally laid down his pen and stared at the wad of papers before him on his writing desk.

He finally had the missing element.

The sheets were blotched and smeared in places and, as he shuffled them into a neater arrangement, they proved to be of a considerable weight. Twisting himself around in his chair, he glanced up at Euterpe.

'Thank you,' he said softly, doubting whether she had actually heard him. Even so, he felt she had helped him somehow and deserved his thanks. In ancient times, Master Josephus said, people would honour the gods with sacrifices, but he had assured him that this was no longer necessary. Maestro turned and lifted the first sheet from the pile, humming the tune to himself in a mellow voice.

A silvery beam of moonlight fell upon the table. Maestro flexed his fingers beneath the disc of ghostly light and looked up to the open window. A gentle breeze was lapping the gauzy blind with a little *whoosh*, veiling the view. In the same instant that he had lifted his head, the peal of a sweet, shimmering note broke through the still night air, carried along by the breeze. It was unmistakably a flute.

Maestro was instantly on his feet. He drew back the blind and there, perched on a chimney top and little more than an inky silhouette against the full moon, was the flute-player.

The first note was followed by another, and another, all seamlessly sliding over one another in sequence. Retrieving his violin, and without much consideration of what he was doing, Maestro opened the window wider so the curtains billowed inwards like tails of white vapour in the night air, and tentatively planted one foot onto the window ledge. He curled his fingers around the edge of the window frame to steady himself as he stood there on the square stone slab. Below him he saw the shifting forms of the two tigers, which shimmered in the weak pool of moonlight, occasionally issuing low, murmuring growls. The wind blew the tails of his coat and moaned against the sides of his head but it also brought the silver girl's sweet melody to him. Maestro reaffirmed his grip on the violin tucked under his arm, his fingers firmly locked around its neck. He eyed the ledge above his window. A swift leap was all that was needed to reach it. From there he could reach the balcony running along the roof. Tucking the violin into his breeches, and giving himself a few turns of his key, he sprang up with a fresh surge of energy. His fingers just caught the ledge. He dragged himself onto it, finding the ledge was just wide enough to stand on. As he rose, he wobbled precariously and almost lost his footing. He swiftly swung his legs over the parapet and hopped down onto the roof, hardly processing his movements. He had made it.

From there on he simply made his way from roof to roof of the white stone and red-brick houses, which, fortunately, were wedged tightly together. Gradually he made his way towards the flute-player in this manner, guided by the song. At last she was within reach, for she was on the roof of the building next to him, only this proved to be far higher and further apart than any of the others he had encountered, and left him obscured in its shadowy gloom. He was unsure whether it was too far for him to jump across onto the window terrace or not. As he stared down into the gulf between the buildings, Maestro wished that Master George and Master Douglas had built him with extendable legs. He went up to the very edge of the roof and felt a tile he was stepping on break away and fall into the gulf. He heard it smash. The scintillating silver girl had stopped playing and stepped down from her perch atop the chimney. Bathed in the moon's full light, she gave off a brilliant glow, as if enshrined in a silver halo like an angel.

Backing out of the shadow, Maestro called out to her tentatively.

'Céline? Céline? It is I, Maestro.'

She did not reply but continued beaming down at him with her radiant smile, and blinked slowly. Then she raised her flute to her lips and held it there. Understanding at once, Maestro positioned his own instrument and bowed to her to take the lead. She resumed playing her song and Maestro waited for the right moment before he also began to play with vehement force. The two harmonies instantly slid into accord with one another. It was a process of to and fro, the violin answering the flute as one melody matched the other, like silver and golden waves spreading across the night, or two butterflies fluttering their wings in play. The girl twirled and sang at intervals. Although he did not understand the words, Maestro sang along with her when she reached the chorus, and found that the notes spontaneously emanating from the strings of his violin were so perfectly in line with those pouring from her throat, that it was as if he were reading them from spectral sheet music. He wondered if he had ever heard anything so powerful and pure. He was sure this was what bliss sounded like. He wished for the song to go on forever, but eventually the silver girl fell silent. She called out, '*Bonne nuit, mon ami*,' and slipped behind the chimney top. Maestro waited in the feeble hope that she would reappear. It was only as dawn threatened to break and the black night sky melted into a deep, inky blue that he hastened back over the rooftops the way he had come. He made it back to his own room just as the sky began to pale into blue and gold over the horizon. The night's encounter already seemed like some brilliant fantasy.

Chapter Twenty-Three

It hadn't taken half the effort to coax George into getting into the airship again that Douglas had anticipated. He'd found him in his bedroom, hunched over the accounts. He sat down on the side of the bed behind him, unsure how to divert George's attention from *that* riveting occupation (George always insisted on doing them, to quieten his mind, he said). All Douglas had to do was expand upon the potential logistical and financial advantages of flying their prototype to Cobb's factory as opposed to any other method. Although he'd doubted whether George had really been listening to what he'd said at all, suddenly George waved his hand as if he were swatting some pesky insect and said, 'Fine, now *get out*.'

Anyhow, George had made no complaints in the first five minutes of their journey. In fact, he hardly spoke at all. The only word he uttered was 'chimney' just before they'd felt a sharp bump beneath them. He simply sat there in the passenger seat with his arms folded over his chest the remainder of the time.

'Fine flying weather,' remarked Douglas amiably, as he pulled a glass lever overhead. 'Hardly a cloud in the sky. We'll make good time.'

'Just keep flying at this altitude and try to avoid church steeples. We don't want to risk damaging our prototype.'

Said prototype was strapped to the roof of the ship, safely inside a large wooden box.

'I will, I will. And no, not after all the effort we put into making it. When you told Cobb we would make it in less than four weeks I thought you were mad, but I'm just hoping that he won't be too vexed that what we have to show him is very different to what he had in mind.'

'He won't object, you'll see.'

'Hmm.' Douglas gently swerved to avoid a tall, red-brick chimney on the top of a factory.

George lapsed back into silence.

'Are you all right?'

'Hmm? Why?'

'You just seem somewhat…' Douglas let his shoulders fall. 'Like you have something on your mind.'

'What are you insinuating?'

'Nothing. It's just that you've been even more distant and evasive than usual as of late. Ever since Lord Leyton's ball.'

'I can assure you I'm fine. If there is a problem, it resides in *your* mind. There's the factory – bring the ship in lower.'

Before them was a rather rundown, brick building with three storeys. Most of the windows were smashed. It was surrounded by warehouses along the edge of a murky canal. They were met at the factory gate by a shabby man dressed like a clerk, who ushered them inside and told them to remain on the factory floor while he went to retrieve Mr Cobb. Douglas shivered the moment they stepped over the threshold of the factory. They were standing in a long, bare room. One or two remnants of old machinery were still scattered around. Two poor wretches were sweeping the floor at the far end of the room. Mr Cobb appeared promptly, his lips peeled back in a grin, which was intended to be inviting, but appeared slightly menacing.

'Good afternoon, gentlemen,' he said, with as much cordiality as his dry, husky voice would allow, as if silk fibres were scratching his throat.

'Good afternoon, Mr Cobb. It is quite a…promising establishment you have here.' Douglas was relieved there wasn't a repeat of the handshaking episode.

'I trust you have something to show me?' asked Cobb bluntly. He smacked his big hands and rubbed them together, like a man in anticipation of a good dinner, Douglas fancied.

'We certainly have, Mr Cobb. Although...' Douglas hesitated. 'We may have made a...slight alternation to the proposed design.'

Cobb's wide smile deflated. 'How slight?'

'Well...' Douglas clapped a hand on the back of his neck. 'Instead of creating a series of machines, we condensed all of their various functions into one single machine.'

Cobb fixed him with an incredulous look. 'Are you serious? After all this time you have only managed to produce *one* machine? I expected a lot more for the advance I gave you.'

'Yes, but it's a machine that is practically several machines in one.'

'That is not what I asked you to do. You were asked to work to *my* concept and *my* designs. That was the agreement. There are all sorts of stages that you need to go through to produce silk – turning the raw silk into yarn, weaving it, dyeing it, finishing it. Are you really telling me you managed to get one machine to do all *that*?'

'Yes. It will perform every stage of the process from start to finish. We deemed it far more efficient *and* cost-effective,' said Douglas emphatically. Funny how that was the second time in one day he'd had to practise that argument. Hopefully it would prove as successful the second time.

'And where is this machine then? I'm assuming you brought it to show me,' challenged Cobb, as he swept the flap of his greatcoat back and wedged his fingers in his waistcoat pocket.

Nodding at their indignant client, Douglas put two fingers to his mouth and whistled. After a moment there appeared the wooden box, fitted with a square, rectangular frame around its middle, with two spindly mechanical legs, or feelers, on the front and back, which crept steadily along. Cobb's eyes widened as the box settled down on the ground and the legs folded in on themselves. George pressed a button on the frame, which fell away in two pieces. The box itself then fell apart and each face slammed onto the ground, the sound echoing across the empty factory floor. Inside was something laid in a nest of straw.

'A spider?' said Cobb. That was the best available description for it, for the machine resembled an enormous, almost primitive, steel spider.

'You object?' George straightened himself and faced Cobb squarely.

'Well, it's just – it's just not what I 'ad in mind for a spinning machine.'

'Spiders are naturally adept at spinning silk. It was pointless to develop an entirely new design when there was a perfectly suitable template before us to work from.'

'If you have reservations about the design, Mr Cobb,' put in Douglas, 'then we can always modify the look of the machine. Might I suggest however that you see it in action first? If you are still not satisfied afterwards, we will change the design of the machines to whatever suits your fancy.'

Cobb's brow furrowed, the rings below his chin multiplying. He smoothed down the front of his waistcoat and crammed his fingers into the pocket. 'Well, I suppose so,' he muttered, although the words were muffled on account of him rubbing his finger over his rubbery top lip.

As Douglas made a move to set the silk spinner in motion, George caught his arm and tugged it down so they were at eye level with one another. 'We are *not* modifying the design just because he doesn't like the look of it,' he hissed into Douglas's ear.

'Relax.' Douglas wrestled his arm free from his brother's hold. 'We won't need to touch a thing once he's seen it at work. You promised me that, remember?'

'Is there a problem?' Cobb demanded keenly.

'Not at all, Mr Cobb,' said Douglas brightly at normal volume, spinning around on his heels. 'We were simply discussing what speed to set the machine at.'

'Full speed,' he said firmly. 'I want to see what it's fully capable of.'

'If we were to set it going at full pelt, Mr Cobb, I fear you wouldn't be able to appreciate the intricacy and elegance with which the mechanical creature goes about its craft.'

'Oh, set it at whatever speed you please and get going.' Cobb waved his hand dismissively and began lighting a cigar.

'Right away. I just need to tweak this here and...here we go!'

Douglas sprang back as the spinner's steely legs shot out so suddenly that Cobb made a surprisingly swift movement backwards despite his bulk. The machine raised itself up on its four back legs. Its head emerged from its bulbous body, with two small blank eyes and steely pincers that clicked open and shut. A long, thin, silvery thread came shooting up from its rear and it hoisted itself up a few metres into the air along the string. It sprayed multiple strands of the fine silk in a continuous flow, which its two hind legs started working rapidly as the strands fanned out, eventually at such great speed that they could hardly be seen. But there began to emerge a long trail of metallic fabric that inched slowly towards the ground.

'Tougher than steel.' Douglas caught the tail end of the sheet of shimmering, silvery fabric with a flourish and brought it before Cobb. 'But as soft as the caress of a dove's wing.' He spread it carefully over his hands and offered it to Cobb as though it were a sacred tapestry. The man eyed the silver mantle dubiously, tossing the butt of his cigar onto the floor and trampling it under his foot. He rubbed the fabric between his thick fingers. His eyebrows shot up. A shiver ran through him, and a strange wave of emotion crossed his face, which seemed to be melting.

'Incredible!' He took the fabric from Douglas's hands into his own as gently as if it were a newborn infant.

'That silk is in its purest form, although we can set the machines to produce any sort of pattern or colour. Say you wanted to reproduce *The Last Supper* in cloth form...' As Douglas said those words, there was a change in the rhythm of the machine's clacking, and the trail of white silk took on a kaleidoscope of different shades. After a few moments Douglas caught the edges of the coloured rectangle so to stretch out the image, and there was Christ surrounded by all his disciples, stippled sublimely so that even from close up, the quality was more approximate to a photograph than a painting. 'They basically work in a similar way to a Jacquard loom, only a lot more complicated and without the cards with holes punched through them, not exactly anyway.'

'Try to keep explanations in layman's terms, if you will. So can they be taught new weaves? And learn off one another?'

'Ah, that is where the clever part comes in.' Douglas smiled, having resumed his usual confident manner now that he could see Cobb's resistance wavering. 'For you see, what we intend to do is implant a device inside each machine that will allow them to communicate with each other using electromagnetic waves, in a sort of "web" if you will. These machines will be produced and presided over by a "queen" machine. I know it's not in keeping with a spider's physiology exactly, but I suppose we can bend nature's rules a little bit more.' Douglas shrugged. 'The information each spinner learns will be passed back along the "web" to the "queen" and then each spinner she subsequently produces will already know the new weave or innovation. That's putting it simply.'

Cobb looked thoroughly baffled. He stared up at the now dormant machine, which had ceased spinning, and then delicately stroked the fabric in his hand. Douglas bit his lip. George only coolly studied the man's face. Cobb suddenly looked up sharply and his words came rushing out, along with minute droplets of spittle.

'I want twenty of 'em up and running as soon as you can manage. And I want to see this "queen" of yours. Have you built it already?'

'Not yet, Mr Cobb. We have the plans and the means but not the space. She would have to be constructed within the factory itself.'

'I'll provide you with it then, as long as you're quick about putting it together.'

'We certainly can be.'

'It's still not what I asked for,' he mumbled, stroking his chins. 'And a bit queer, but if it works, I think we could both stand to gain rather handsomely from this scheme.' Again came the cracked grin. 'What do you say we go upstairs to my office and we'll sort out the necessary paperwork?' Cobb thrust the newly spun silk at Douglas and made his way to the staircase.

Douglas genuinely doubted whether the man would make it up the stairs without collapsing into a drenched heap. Nonetheless, he hastily bundled up the silk and followed him. George was waiting for his brother near the foot of the stairs.

'Oh, but there is one thing I neglected to mention.' Cobb stopped and turned as he rested his hand on the rail. 'I wish to slightly amend my terms.'

'How so, Mr Cobb?' asked George.

'I want a share of your business.'

'I beg your pardon?'

'Rather than merely being your patron, I want to take you on as partners in my firm.' He smiled broadly. 'Just consider what good my name could do for you. What will happen when those barons and lords of yours go back to the country in a few months' time? Surely your demand will slump. But with my backing, you would receive regular commissions all year round from some of the wealthiest manufacturers in the county. In fact, I have a couple of investors coming here tomorrow and I mean to show them your machine. I could introduce them to you. I could even set you up in one of my factories to provide you with a proper space in which to work.'

'And our designs?' said George sharply. 'Who will have ownership over those?'

'Well, naturally, if it was a shared enterprise, then the ownership would also be shared.'

'So effectively you'd be taking credit for our inventions?' George fixed him with an icy stare. Douglas saw Cobb visibly tremble under the gaze. His expression confirmed George's accusation.

'We don't accept, Mr Cobb.'

'You won't even give it some thought?' said Cobb indignantly, not even faintly disguising the offence George's forthright reply had aroused in him.

'The terms of our arrangement stand as they were. We provide you with the machines while retaining the designs, but the finished product is yours. You may do as you please with that.'

Cobb wiped a finger below his nose with a loud sniff and replaced his fingers in his waistcoat pocket. 'Very well.' He grunted. 'Don't think I'll offer this again though.'

'Don't think you are the first to make us such an offer, Mr Cobb. Nor will you be the last. But let me be clear on this point – we will not compromise our control over our designs or what work we choose to accept or decline. And no amount of money, contacts or resources will alter that.'

Cobb only shrugged his shoulders and turned his back.

George could feel Douglas fixing him with a disapproving stare. 'Would you have said anything different?' he asked in a low voice, without turning around, as he waited for their client to haul himself up the second step.

'No, but did you have to put it so bluntly?'

'Unlike you, I don't soften my words or make lavish speeches. I don't see the point in it.'

'I know you don't,' Douglas muttered.

Cobb did manage to lumber his way up the stairs with great effort, although he was panting and wheezing so heavily after several steps that Douglas really did believe his prediction was about to come true. But after a brief reprieve, he mopped his brow with his handkerchief and resumed climbing until he eventually conquered the final step. He negotiated his way back down with greater ease once the papers had been signed, although he was still painfully slow and deliberate in his every step.

When he was only three steps from the ground, an unmistakably distinctive voice arrested the brothers' attention.

'Marvellous place you've got here, Clayton! Although it was a hard job finding it!'

Standing in the entrance was Professor Gottfried, wearing a brilliant black greatcoat with large, stiff lapels. The coat was unbuttoned to expose the red lining. His top hat perched proudly on his great, prominent head. Beside him stood Monsieur Roux-Voclain looking as grave as George remembered him being when they spoke at the ball. He proved equally as laconic, scarcely uttering more than 'Good afternoon'.

'I fear we have come too early. I see you haven't quite concluded your appointment yet. Good to see you again, sirs.' The professor tipped his hat to them.

'Likewise, Professor,' Douglas acknowledged.

The professor drew a black-gloved hand from the great heavy folds of his coat that grasped the gold cane, pointing the wolf in the direction of the Frenchman. 'I brought a friend with me. Hope you don't mind, Clayton. Monsieur Roux-Voclain here is only in England a short while longer and I wanted to show him what progress we English have made in the world of commerce.'

'Not at all, Professor,' said Cobb, regarding Monsieur Roux-Voclain in a manner that thinly veiled his disdain. The Monsieur performed a stiff, but most dignified bow.

'Ah! I see we have arrived at a good time, after all. Is that your machine, sirs?' asked the professor, pointing towards the silk spinner with the end of his cane.

'Yes, Professor,' said Douglas. 'That is the prototype for a new silk-spinning machine.'

'And so you have given it the form of a spider? Now, there's a thing! Oh, I say, my good fellow, will you please tell the cab driver that we'll be a little longer than expected and to return in half an hour?'

Monsieur Roux-Voclain nodded with great seriousness and gave George a brief, meaningful stare before departing.

'Now, I know your opinion on the people of his nation, Clayton. But think, what if he reports back to his fellow Frenchmen what progress we English have managed to accomplish in a trade that they have prided themselves on mastering with their precious Jacquard loom? Won't that set them trembling in their boots?'

'Or set them trying to copy it for themselves. You've as good as admitted a spy into my factory, Charles,' growled Cobb.

'Pooh! Do you seriously think they could duplicate the work of our friends here? I wager they won't catch up for another century! The only real threat that exists is if they drop the duty on importing French silks, which I highly doubt they'll do anytime soon. Well, if it helps at all, the fellow is actually half-English. It's a long tale, which I won't trouble you with. Yet seeing as our good friends happen to be here, perhaps I might trouble them for an explanation about how this silk-spinning machine works, before you give me that promised tour of the factory?'

'As a matter of fact, we were just on our way out,' Douglas admitted, feigning sounding apologetic.

'Really? Dashing off again, I see! But you are busy gentlemen. Perhaps another time, although I will be leaving England myself very shortly. Unless you'd be willing to satisfy me with a quick explanation now?' His predatory eyes, lurking beneath their heavy lids, were aimed at George as he spoke.

'Since you are so keen, Professor, I could oblige you by sparing five minutes of my time,' said George, with remarkable civility. 'If my brother does not mind waiting for me?'

'Oh, no, that is fine. There are one or two things Mr Cobb wanted to discuss about the queen. I'll wait for you outside when you're finished,' Douglas conceded, shooting his brother a puzzled look.

As Douglas went to speak to Cobb in one corner, the professor led George over to where the spinner was hanging, his head bent low.

'I received your letter this morning.' He held it up between his fingers. 'I admit, you surprise me. I wasn't expecting you to respond to my proposal in the manner you did.'

'You obviously aren't well acquainted with my character.'

'That may change. My offer still stands.' The paper seemed to vanish into air from between his fingers and he pulled out a gold pocket watch. 'Although I suggest you be quick about it. You are a master of time, aren't you? You know how it is prone to slipping away.' He held up the watch meaningfully before George. 'One of yours, isn't it? I had it given as a gift not long ago, although I did not know at the time the significance of the maker's mark. I just thought it a very beautiful watch.'

'I am not one for flattery.'

'That much of your character I do know. But I'm hoping to appeal to your reason, not your vanity.' The watch disappeared inside the professor's coat. 'My tour with Cobb should not be long. No more than thirty minutes I should imagine, if those stairs don't kill him.'

'I think I understand your meaning.'

'Then I will leave it with you to consider.' He drew away from George with a knowing grin and tipped his hat to him once more before he went to join Cobb. Douglas was nowhere to be seen.

George found his brother outside with his back resting against the airship and his arms folded over his chest. 'You took your time. That was closer to ten minutes than five. What did you and the professor talk about? George?'

George was gazing up at the factory. Out of the corner of his eye he could see Monsieur Roux-Voclain standing beside a growler some distance away. 'Actually, you go on home. I want to stop somewhere first. I'll take a cab.'

'You're not intent on finding the nearest watering hole, are you?'

'It's none of your business what I intend to do,' snapped George readily.

‘Fine.’ Douglas shrugged. ‘Suit yourself.’

Douglas climbed into the airship. He watched George’s dark figure rapidly shrink and then disappear out of sight as he ascended.

When George finally did come through the front door that evening he was without his coat or shoes. Douglas knew better than to ask what had become of them.

Chapter Twenty-Four

The following day was unusual in that Douglas and George actually kept the shop open the entire day, an increasingly rare occurrence, as they were usually at meetings with clients or forced to close early to work on commissions. They had declined at the last minute to attend Cobb's meeting with investors, much to his annoyance. But they had been busy; there'd been a continuous stream of people coming either to place or pick up an order. They'd sold a few odd inventions too. Now it was approaching five o'clock and Douglas was sitting at the counter with a newspaper and a cup of tea quite contentedly after the day's proceedings. Although he frowned at seeing Reverend Clarke's latest offering printed in the Letters section.

Dear Sir,

It saddens me that my continued warnings against the so-called 'automaton craze' have gone unheeded by the masses. Only yesterday did I see a bill advertising that 'The Mechanical Maestro' is to perform before Her Royal Highness and the Prince Consort tomorrow night. That this machine is to perform before Royalty is indicative of how far this mechanical menace has polluted the heart of our dear nation!

While some only view these automata as an amusement, the threat they pose is a serious one. Mr George and Mr Douglas Abernathy commit a blasphemy by bestowing upon themselves the status of our divine Creator, by claiming not only to duplicate but outshine his work! Do not be fooled! I urge you to consult the Scriptures and see whether it does not say

Douglas made a pfft noise and tore the page out. The automaton sorting through a pile of screws at his feet picked it up and folded it into a paper hat, which it then went about wearing. Well, it was hardly surprising, he thought. When you attempted to replicate something as intricate as the human brain, some were bound to have a few loose screws of their own. He was amusedly watching the automaton strut about in its paper hat when the shop bell tinkled.

It was Mr Spencer. He had been coming to their shop for just about as long as Douglas could remember. He was a man of modest manners, quiet, soft-spoken and never fast in his movements, possibly on account of being painfully short-sighted. He had been a rifleman in the army once, so it was said. Douglas didn't see it. He couldn't imagine him roused to spear another man with a bayonet, nor able to shoot with any degree of accuracy (or to even see that the enemy was approaching).

'Ah, good afternoon, young Abernathy.' It had been 'young Abernathy' or 'my boy' since Douglas wasn't even tall enough to peer over the counter without standing on his tiptoes. Mr Spencer closed the door behind him with great deliberation so as not to slam it. He had once told Douglas that he detested loud noises on account of a cannon having once exploded next to him, and now any loud noise exacerbated the ringing that was constantly in his left ear.

'It has been a while since I've seen you, Mr Spencer.' Douglas smiled as he leant forward and rested his arms on the counter. 'How are you and Mrs Spencer?'

'Oh, both my wife and I are in fine health, my dear boy. How is your sister? I swear I have just seen her in town. Still fixated with breeding flowers, is she?'

'Very much so, anything that comes out of the soil really.'

'Ah, that is, eh, good. Practical occupation for a young lady. Nurturing things. I was wondering if you might be able to take a look at something for me. It's this old watch of mine that doesn't seem to be working any longer.'

He took a pocket watch from his coat with a trembling hand. Douglas saw the raised, blue veins on the old man's brown hand as he placed the warm watch in the younger man's palm. The smell of his particular brand of tobacco on his clothes carried Douglas back through time to his boyhood for an instant. It was one of their early watches, from back when their father finally let them do more than simple repairs or assist him in making watches. It used to be a contest between them to see whose watches sold better. Yes, he definitely remembered this one. It was George's. It was matte silver, possibly dulled with age. The lid was embossed with a silver, diamond-studded moon that encircled a golden sun, its waving arms like a sunflower. The clock face could be seen beneath. Inside there was a semi-circular aperture in the upper half of the watch through which the inky-blue steel disc was visible. The disc was inlaid with a golden-orange sun that would travel around the semi-circle as the day wore on. But, Douglas knew, as the disc gradually rotated, the blue deepened to almost black and a silver moon and fine white stars would appear. The correspondence with the day or night outside would be, of course, perfectly precise. But that wasn't the most impressive thing about the watch, for the moon would change from full to new moon, and follow the lunar month. The moon was created by a small, round hole that acted as a window onto the second silver disc below the first, on which, painted in line with the hole, were images of the moon in each of its phases. Whether it worked according to the seasons, Douglas didn't know. George wouldn't say, although Mr Spencer claimed that it did. George must have been no older than eight or nine when he had made it. A mere trinket for him, but for many watchmakers, something like this would have been perhaps the grandest timepiece they ever produced.

'It may take a while to repair, I'm afraid, as we have an awful lot of orders to get through. But I'll make sure you're near the top of the list. You are an old friend of the shop, after all.'

While Douglas wrote out a ticket for the watch, the old man's gaze travelled around the shop. 'You and your brother have made quite a name for yourselves with all these, uh, marvellous machines of yours. Your father would have been very proud.'

'Thank you, Mr Spencer. It means more to hear it from someone like you than the London journalists. Although not everyone feels that way unfortunately. I think there's a great many who would like to see us made a laughing stock.' He handed Mr Spencer his ticket.

The automaton in the paper hat, which had been strutting back and forth in a corner of the shop, suddenly veered off course and went straight up to Mr Spencer. Without any warning, it thrust its arms around his leg and its hat fell off as it looked up at him.

'I apologise about him, Mr Spencer.' Douglas winced. 'He doesn't understand what he is doing really. He is simply acting out a predetermined gesture.' Although precisely what gesture, Douglas wasn't sure of. Perhaps he thought the old man was a stack of boxes to be moved that was too heavy to lift.

'Affectionate little fellow, isn't he?' said Mr Spencer, as he spread his arms out wide and raised his other leg in the air to balance himself, sounding more bemused than annoyed.

'A shopkeeper requested it. He thought it would be useful to have an automaton that could serve customers when business was heaving. I know we certainly could. It was meant to sort through change, only it isn't functioning properly at the moment. It can sort through screws or buttons but not coins for some reason.'

'My wife could use a button-sorter. She collects them, you see. Big jars full of them. *And* he's about the size of a young child, your machine. My wife is desperate for a grandchild but our only son seems intent on remaining a bachelor. It is becoming a sort of monomania with her lately. When she's not sorting through her buttons, she sits there crocheting quilts and making clothes for phantom babies. I wonder if something like this might pacify her.' He bent down on one knee to look at the little automaton, which had withdrawn its hold on his leg, at its own level.

'Take him if you like. We're building a new automaton for the shopkeeper and we're running out of screws for him to sort through.'

'That's awfully kind of you, but I couldn't possibly afford it.' Mr Spencer raised himself up with some difficulty, leaning heavily on his umbrella.

'When I said take him, Mr Spencer, I meant *take* him. You have long been a loyal customer to both my father and then to my brother and me.'

'Are you quite sure, my boy?' Mr Spencer twisted his hands around his umbrella.

'Absolutely. How about this? Take him home with you for two weeks and if your wife doesn't take to him, you can simply return him.'

Douglas watched his eyes, like two small soft-boiled eggs trembling in their sockets behind his thick spectacles, turn upwards.

'Well, I don't see what harm it'd do. I'm at a loss to know what to do other than force my stubborn son to marry, which is a battle I'd rather avoid if possible.'

'Of course, it can never take the place of an actual child,' Douglas cautioned. This automaton, he knew, was not like Maestro. It could learn, yes, but it could not truly comprehend the world around it or really think for itself – in the same way a dog can be taught to respond to the command 'sit' without really understanding the concept of sitting. Mrs Spencer could have it sorting through a whole barrel of buttons while wearing a white frock and cap, and it would think nothing of it.

'Well she has a morbid abhorrence towards animals, which I for the life of me cannot comprehend, so I see little other alternative. I very much appreciate this, young Abernathy.'

'Think nothing of it, Mr Spencer. And I'll have that watch ready for you in no time,' Douglas assured him as he held the shop door open. Mr Spencer gently led the little automaton out by the hand. Douglas shut the door after him, locked it and flipped the sign around from 'Open' to 'Closed'. He sat back down, turning the watch over in his hand. With one cheek resting against his knuckles, he half-smiled to himself. It was somehow comforting in its smoothness and familiarity. He couldn't remember the last time he'd made a watch repair. How much their lives had changed in only a few short months! Then again, when had their lives ever been unaffected by madcap machines? It was the natural order of things for them. He certainly wouldn't wish to go back to the way things were before Maestro was brought into being.

His thoughts had begun to drift into a channel of days gone by when the sound of George's approach made him raise his head alertly. 'You just missed Mr Spencer. He took the sorting machine with him.' George had appeared from behind the black door.

'Good. It was becoming a nuisance.' He didn't take his eyes off the letter in his hand.

Douglas leant back on the creaky chair and strained his neck towards his brother. 'Problem?'

'The agent has written back about the estate. It seems they have decided—'

A very demanding knocking on the door, which caused it to rattle in its frame, silenced George. The bell gave a nervous tinkle.

They looked at one another with the same confused expression, and Douglas shrugged his shoulders before rising from his chair. When he unlocked the front door, he was startled to see a man standing there flanked on either side by a police officer.

'Mr Douglas Abernathy?'

'Yes. Is there something the matter, officer?' Douglas asked, sensing George right behind him.

'I am Inspector Lyell of the Metropolitan Police. I understand that you've recently had dealings with a Mr Clayton Cobb, is that correct?

'Yes. Why? Is he in some sort of trouble with the law?'

'Oh, he's in trouble in a sense, but not with the law.' The contemptuous tone of the inspector's voice set Douglas on his guard. 'There was an incident at his factory earlier this afternoon. Seems a machine you built for him exploded right next to him. Nearly killed him.'

One of the two younger officers in the background muttered, 'Probably all that fat of his what shielded him,' as Inspector Lyell continued.

'His two associates who were present at the time of the incident are also in hospital. It took at least three men to cut through the spider web stuff they were covered in.'

'My God!' exclaimed Douglas. 'Are you sure that's what happened? That it exploded?'

'First it tried to attack them. Went at them with its pincers and shot webs over them like they were flies it was going to make a meal out of.

Then the thing exploded into a pile of scrap metal.'

'But it can't have done.' George frowned, pushing past Douglas. 'For a fault that drastic to occur, it simply isn't possible.'

'And do you know of anyone who would be capable of tampering with it? Or have reason to?'

Douglas immediately thought of the professor.

'No one else knew how it worked,' said George promptly, before Douglas had a chance to answer.

'Only yourselves?'

'Yes.'

'Because from where I'm standing...' The inspector smirked. 'This is a straight-up case of sabotage, and the two of you are the most likely culprits.'

'What are you driving at?'

'George.' Douglas gripped hold of his brother's shoulder but George fiercely shrugged him off.

'Here's what I think happened: Cobb wanted to make a deal with you to go into partnership with him, which you refused. I have a witness, a man who claims he's Cobb's clerk, who said a rather heated exchange took place between the two of you at around four o'clock yesterday afternoon. You relented and agreed to the deal, but were then concerned that Cobb might swindle you. So while Cobb was otherwise occupied, you deliberately tampered with your own machine, planning on disguising it as a fault, and setting it to murder Cobb so you could get out of the contract you had just signed with him and ensure he wouldn't pass off your machine as his own.'

'That is preposterous.'

'I have seen men do worse things for less. Nevertheless, I'm arresting the two of you for the attempted murder of Mr Clayton Cobb, as well as for wounding two other persons.'

'What?' Douglas suddenly felt sick in the heart.

'Don't do anything clever. It'll only make things worse for you, although I don't see how.' He inclined his head towards the two young officers.

'Don't try anything,' Douglas warned his brother, setting the example by coming forward and allowing one of the officers to fasten his hands behind his back. 'Just do as they say.'

The man then placed his other hand on Douglas's shoulder before leading him towards the waiting police vehicle. George's fingers curled inward on themselves as he calculated his chances against the two officers. One was stocky and the other was no weakling. Even so, he could easily take them both; he knew precisely which points to strike at. The detective was no real obstacle to overcome. But then his mind ran ahead to the ensuing chain of events. He would be a wanted man, hunted down relentlessly. In the brief second of time that all of this rushed through his brain, he looked at the police officers and at his brother. He could not leave Douglas to face this ordeal alone. They would most likely be better off together. But was he sure? Would he be more use to him if he were outside the walls of a prison cell? If he allowed Douglas to escape, he'd be making him a wanted criminal too.

George slowly raised his hand. An officer clamped hold of his wrist. It was only as he was being bundled into the back of the vehicle that he realised he had not thought to set the alarm system.

'Molly.' Douglas's head jerked up, speaking George's thought aloud as he sharply turned to look at him. 'George, what on earth are we going to do?'

For once, George found it difficult to offer a solution.

Chapter Twenty-Five

The opera was undoubtedly much better now he had worked in his missing element. This had meant several last-minute revisions but there had not been as much resistance as Maestro had anticipated from any of the humans. His soprano, the female automaton in the story, was a young woman whom Maestro had frequently heard singing on a street corner when Master Josephus's coach passed her by. She had something of a timid air about her as she walked onto the stage during the first few rehearsals, and peered out anxiously from under her long hair, with her hands clasped demurely over her chest. But when the first few bars of her song sounded, she shattered the air with the force of her voice, powerful and sweet as a nightingale's. It seemed impossible that the small, slight body of the human girl was the vessel containing that magnificent voice. Now her timidity was simply a guise she wore for the character of the female automaton, which she stripped away the moment the final note had rung out and she skipped down from her place in the middle of the stage with a smile as bright as starlight.

But as the opera began to come together, his muse seemed to have vanished altogether.

When Maestro had come down to the drawing room the evening after his encounter with the silver singer, he had anticipated that she would be there. All the same guests were there, but as the night wore on, it seemed less and less likely that she would appear. Several more nights had passed but he had seen nothing of her. Maestro had even been making rapid progress mastering French in anticipation of seeing her. If he could converse with her in her own tongue, for she did not appear to understand English, then it would overcome a great many difficulties. Master Josephus found nothing suspicious in his enquiries about how to speak the language, in light of their forthcoming journey. In fact, he even went as far as to hire a private tutor to teach Maestro French, despite the rapid approach of their departure in just over a fortnight's time. Fortunately, the automaton's mind, unhindered by the many shortcomings of the human brain, was receptive to his teachings; neither was he subject to the bouts of lamenting and weeping that many human pupils display when they repeatedly fail to comprehend something. Although, of course, Maestro also possessed the advantage of having a natural aptitude for grasping the mechanics of sound. And more or less everything he learnt, he retained. The tutor remarked that he had never encountered such a brilliant pupil. Maestro also supplemented the tutor's lessons by reading certain words in books in his free time throughout the night hours, and by hearing them spoken by the Roux-Voclains or Master Josephus. The result was that he had achieved an alarmingly fluent grasp of the language in the space of only a week, even if it was by no means perfect. Master Josephus seemed most pleased with his progress, and spoke of getting him to learn German and, perhaps, Latin next.

'Master those three languages, Maestro,' he said, 'and you will have mastered the world.'

Maestro consented to this future project, which would no doubt be highly beneficial, although he still had not revealed the true reason for his initially wanting to expand his linguistic repertoire. Master Josephus did not seem to like the silver girl an awful lot, so perhaps he might discontinue the lessons if he were to find out their objective. And so, for the first time, he had unintentionally practised a deception against his master.

Yet Maestro's determination dwindled away little by little each night. Master Josephus even enquired whether there was something the matter with him after he hit his third wrong note in the space of an evening, for his eyes habitually drifted towards the drawing room door. However, it was also Master Josephus who was indirectly responsible for providing an explanation as to the singer's whereabouts.

'Will your flute-player be joining us this evening, Gaston?' he said in a somewhat mocking tone one night. 'Or has she run out of melodies to play for us?'

Monsieur Roux-Voclain said nothing; he merely directed his eyes towards the professor, who tapped the side of his nose and grinned horribly. The professor left the following day, but the Roux-Voclains remained for another two days before insisting they had other acquaintances with whom they had promised to stay while they remained in London. It was on the night before their departure that a peculiar event occurred.

Maestro was on his way back to his room in the early hours of the morning, softly humming a tune to himself as he placed his hand on the door handle. He paused. He was certain that he had just heard the mechanical girl's flute from somewhere distant. When he hastily flung open the door to his room, he saw all was as he had left it; his books were lying open on the table and the window was open slightly (the summer heat did not affect him, of course, but the housekeeper insisted on airing every room in the house).

But no, there had been one minor alteration, or rather, addition. For on his writing-table was a silver flower head, and pinned beneath it a slip of curled paper with two lines of immaculately neat writing in fine letters.

Come to the top floor of the Duke's Hotel just after midnight tomorrow.
Tell no one.

The note must be from her! Perhaps she had escaped the professor's clutches and sought Maestro's aid, in which case he would undoubtedly help her. But why did she request that he tell no one? Unless she thought there was a chance that the professor, or Monsieur Roux-Voclain even, was still residing with Master Josephus and might attempt to recapture her. He should have liked to consult with Master Josephus on the matter, but he could not betray a lady's confidence – that would be unthinkable. He had no choice but to act on his own for the time being.

*

The following day happened to be the final day of rehearsal before the Royal Performance. Maestro had spent all day at Drury Lane. It was, he honestly thought, just about there. The duet between the two automata upon their first meeting in the clocktower had sounded its best yet. All of the disparate elements had slid into place and, although there was still the occasional baleful look directed at himself or at the unprofessional musicians, the tension in the air had all but melted away and the music benefited greatly from it. The set design was remarkable – they had constructed a fictitious city from canvas and wood. For the clocktower scenes they had constructed an enormous yellow glass screen with numerals and hands in reverse on the other side.

He thought he should be able to make his appointment with the singer (he carried her flower and note safely about with him in his coat pocket at all times) without any obstacles, as Master Josephus did not have any company, and he had talked of going to the theatre that night. But when Maestro arrived back at the house, Gilbert informed him that his master had been taken ill and had gone to his bedchamber. He had requested that upon his return, Maestro was to go straight up to the sickroom. There Maestro remained, attempting to restore his master in whatever way possible, playing to him hour after hour. He did not notice the passing of time at first as his attention was wholly devoted to this end, his meeting with the singer at the back of his mind. Master Josephus looked dreadful. His face was chalk-white, almost grey, and his eyes red and watery. When he attempted to speak, it was in little more than a hoarse whimper, and he complained of being plagued by headaches. He repeatedly said that he was certain he was developing a fever. A doctor had been sent for earlier in the afternoon and had declared that it was nothing but a bad cold, but Master Josephus was convinced it was far worse and refused to take the medicines the doctor recommended. Yet after what seemed like a very long time to Maestro, he appeared to revive a little and, with Maestro's assistance, rose from his bed and seated himself at his dressing-table.

'It is this city air, I am sure of it,' he affirmed as he ran a comb through his hair with surprising vigour, sniffing practically between every word. 'My constitution, I admit, was never the best, but prolonged exposure to this foul air worsens it tenfold—' Here he was cut off by a fit of coughing.

Maestro hastily retrieved the water jug beside the bed that Master Josephus had gestured towards as he pressed his silk handkerchief over his mouth. He wondered to himself where the servant Bellamy was. Normally, he was constantly at Master Josephus's side, but every now and again he would have a brief spell of absence. Nobody in the house remarked on it.

'You'll see the difference, Maestro,' said Master Josephus raspily, after taking a sip of water from a glass, 'that it makes to me once we are past France and on our way towards Rome. I promise you, you'll hardly recognise that I am your same master. Urgh, just look at what a state I am in. No, don't look! I am not fit to be seen!' Master Josephus gazed into the mirror, his reflection's expression progressively softening. He turned his head to the side and brushed his fingertips along the corner of his eye. 'You don't know how fortunate you are, Maestro,' he said, as he ran his slender hand along his sallow cheek. 'That you don't have to worry about ageing.'

As Maestro sought for a suitable reply, his master attempted to laugh, although it came out very strained and Maestro feared it would set off another fit of coughing. 'You should not worry about such things yet, Master Josephus,' he ventured, as he refilled the glass. 'And I will rust and rot as time passes, only slower.'

'Oh, you will still be in your prime a century or more from now when I am nothing but dust and ashes! And you will never know the absolute joys of ill-health,' he muttered over the glass. 'But I'll see to it that I summon the strength to attend the performance tomorrow. I would not miss it for the world!'

'I would not want you to endanger your health, Master.'

'Oh tsk! I'll even risk swallowing the doctor's potions if that is what it takes.'

Maestro was about to protest when the chiming of the clock on the mantel distracted him. It was already eleven o'clock. But it was another half hour before Master Josephus decided he would attempt to sleep and allowed Maestro to leave. Maestro stood in the music room listening. Some members of the household were still awake; he could hear closing doors and feet walking about. There he remained with his eyes alternatively on

Euterpe or on the mantel clock as the minute hand inched ever closer to twelve. The house gradually became stiller and stiller, with only the faintest ripple of human motion. The housekeeper, with her trouble sleeping in the summer heat, was barely turning about in her bed. She began to snore. He was sure all of the human inmates were now asleep. To the human ear, excluding the clock's ticking, all was perfectly silent, but not to Maestro. There was extreme quiet, but never silence. Silence was an unknown concept to him.

The clock struck twelve.

Maestro made his way towards the window on almost noiseless feet, picking up his violin as he went. He had the singer's flower in his coat as a buttonhole, the note remaining curled inside his pocket – he felt it to make sure. Widening the window a fraction, he repeated his actions from their previous encounter with a little less hesitation. He knew clearly in which direction the hotel was; he had passed it in Master Josephus's coach many times. All he had to do was simply make his way along the rooftops as he had done before. Once more, the haunting sound of the flute began again, rising to a radiant crescendo and acting as his guide. He could tell it was coming from the open window on the hotel's fourth floor. But to enter it, he would have to climb his way down the building's exterior. He peered over the balcony. It was at least five storeys from the roof to the ground. If he fell, he was sure not even his old masters could fix him then. He dangled himself over the edge of the balcony so that he was in line with the open window, intending to swing through it. Only he released his hold too quickly and frantically grasped the window casement, remaining suspended in the frame. The room was unlit save for the light of a single candle that burned upon the table. In the recesses of the opulent-looking room (from the little he could see of it), was a figure, faintly gleaming with a silver glow from the candlelight, with its back turned away from the window.

Maestro dropped down into the room and cautiously began to approach her. 'Hello? Céline?' he said, sotto voce. 'It is I, Maestro. I received your note.'

She made no response. It struck him that she obviously would not have understood him in English. How thoughtless of him. He repeated his last words in French, but still she made no response. She seemed to tilt her head forward and then raise it again. He heard the twang of the spring.

'J'ai apporté mon violon. Je pensais que nous pourrions jouer ensemble – comme nous l'avons fait avant?'

He went as close to her as he thought he ought to and waited for some show of acknowledgment. Was she broken? Or had she wound down? She had been moving just a moment ago, he was sure. And he could still hear the clockwork ticking inside of her.

'Céline?' He walked around to the side of her to try to look into her face, but she sharply turned her head away. Had the professor done something to her that she did not wish him to see?

But then the rest of her body twisted to follow the inclination of her head. She gracefully rose and gave a curtsy, still facing away from him.

'*Bonsoir, mademoiselle et messieurs.*' She drew herself upright. '*Je jouerai pour votre divertissement une mélodie que j'ai composée moi-même.*'

She then put her lips to her flute and began to play, just as she had in the drawing room that first night he had seen her. The exact same melody. The same words, the same gestures.

Maestro swept right around so that he might look her plainly in the face. His body slumped. The moonlight slid over her glassy eyes that looked out blankly at nothing.

She was nothing but a soulless puppet after all.

Maestro hung his head. So he really was alone, the only one of his kind. He had so sincerely wanted to have another who understood what it was like, whom he might speak to and who might help him understand his own nature better, without even really understanding why. Once she had finished her tune and curtsied once more, he lifted his head and addressed her in a quiet, cautious voice. He did not even realise that he had slipped back into English.

'Can you – can you really not speak to me at all?'

The girl said nothing, the silvery little mouth smiling all the while.

Maestro gingerly reached out to touch her limp hand. 'Can you not respond to me... Céline?'

At the precise moment he uttered those words, her hand shot out and tightly clamped his wrist. Maestro involuntarily released his hold on his violin as she tightened her grip. He could hear the crackle of his casing splitting. She seemed to grow to almost twice her height and sprouted long arms that entwined themselves like silvery pythons around his arms. The instant he managed to free one arm, more tentacles simply latched onto him again and constricted him with an even greater force. By now they had hold of each of his legs, pinning him helplessly no matter how he struggled. She lowered her head and looked down at him, still with that same blank look and smiling mouth. Suddenly her eyes rolled back in her head, she opened her mouth, and more silver, mechanical tentacles shot out. He glimpsed one tentacle waver before his eyes, like a snake charmer's cobra, and then it plunged into his chest. In one instant he felt a great pressure and a bursting sensation behind the cylinder in his chest. The next, nothing.

Chapter Twenty-Six

Strange, thought Molly, as she took a cutting from her specimen and placed it on a thin glass tile. Strange that George and Douglas had been out all evening. The house had been empty when she'd come in through the back door and called out hello. She thought she'd heard signs of movement from Douglas's room upstairs, but it turned out to be the mechanical mouse nibbling a hole in one of his pillows. The automata downstairs were all wound down and the shop had been shut up. Perhaps her brothers had a meeting with a client or something. It wasn't as if she were aware of every single one of their engagements; it wasn't her business to know. They never insisted on knowing where she was every minute of the day either.

Shrugging off the matter, she placed the glass tile under a microscope and adjusted the lens until the blurry image became crisp and clear. She could see the squarish cells floating about, the building blocks of all plant life. Seeing the sample was healthy, she placed the specimen in a flat, circular glass container and heard the satisfying snap of the glass lid as it neatly slotted over it. She then labelled the dish and placed it beside its two now filmy companions on the shelf beside her. One was beginning to sprout blue spores on the inside of the glass. On the shelf below them was a plant with pink leaves like a five-pointed star inside a glass tank half-filled with soil and bathed in warm, reddish light. A thick pipe on the lid snaked down towards a square metal box, the generator, which hummed merrily. Molly could feel it through her bare feet. It was her main birthday present from her brothers, designed to replicate the warm, sultry climate of a tropical jungle. She had been highly delighted when they presented it to her, having lost many a good specimen to English frosts, and lacking an orangery as she did. It made her room a little sweltering at times though, especially now that the weather was getting warmer.

Well, that was the main task of the night done. Now she just had to water, and feed, everything. An advantage of keeping so many carnivorous plants was that her room was virtually free of flies throughout the summer.

As she began to clear away her apparatus, she heard the front door open downstairs and the bell tinkle. Ah, they were back. She went out onto the landing to greet them, but something she heard plugged her voice inside her throat before she could holler down the stairs. The tread of the footsteps was wrong. She knew her brothers' gaits: George's was light, deliberate and measured; Douglas's slightly more brisk, buoyant and elastic. These steps were lethargic and heavy.

'I wanted to do a bit of smashing. It ain't no fun when it's too easy,' said a whining voice that sounded as though the speaker had a lisp.

'Quit your yapping. You want the entire bloody street to hear? You've no style whatsoever, my boy,' replied a deeper, gruffer voice.

'And I don't like all them things we had to pass on the way in,' he replied sulkily. 'All those mechanical dolls. It makes me shiver!'

'Well, at least you'll get to smash some of them up. Mr G said to make sure we smash them up good and proper before we burn the place.'

'*And* I don't trust this Mr G. I mean, why's he insisting on us calling him "Mr G" in the first place?'

'It's discretion, ain't it? Probably some person of distinction who don't want to get his hands dirty. Thinks we'd squeal on him if he told us his real name. Most of these men in high society have aliases – keeps people thinking they're more proper than they actually are.'

Molly crept noiselessly along the first flight of stairs and listened to the two voices down below her as the men entered the kitchen.

'So what we looking for again?' asked the one with the slight lisp.

'Drawings, like Mr G said,' replied his companion.

Molly grew bolder and inched down the second flight of stairs so that she could see the intruders. The one who had spoken last was taller and burlier than the other, with mottled, warty skin like a potato's, with a little purple stub nose. His hat was rather battered. His younger companion was as tall and reedy as his voice. Both were dressed in dark, greasy, shabby coats and had a smell of general filth that clogged her nostrils.

'Drawings of what?' said the younger one as the other helped himself to the contents of the larder.

'Not drawings like pictures. He used a fancy word to describe them. *Die-a-grams* or something like that. They're drawings of how that music-playing machine works.'

'And we're to clear everything out of the shop too before we burn the house down?'

'Every last clock and watch, he said. Just the mechanical dolls want smashing. Did you not hear anything he said, Sharp?'

'You know I'm a bit hard of hearing, Murray. Ever since that bobby whacked me round the head with that club of his.' Sharp winced as he touched the side of his head.

'It's a wonder he didn't bash some of your brains out too, although I sometimes think he did.'

'Did Mr G say anything about the money in the till?'

'No, he didn't mention anything about it. But there's no sense in letting it burn though. Just keep quiet about it, mind.'

'And the girl who lives here?' persisted Sharp. 'What do we do about her if she's upstairs somewhere?'

'Mr G said we can do what we like with her.'

The men exchanged a knowing look and let out horrible, snickering laugher as they vanished into the parlour.

Molly shrank away to her bedroom, her heart pounding and her mind racing. 'All right, keep calm, keep calm,' she muttered faintly to herself as she moved around her room. 'You need a plan. You can get yourself out of this.'

Down below, the two men took out the sacks they had stuffed inside their overcoat pockets and began filling them with whatever they deemed to be of value.

'How much do you reckon these'd be worth?' Sharp held up a pair of silver candlesticks, having tipped their candles onto the floor.

'I reckon they'd be worth a couple of pounds. Might as well take them.' Murray shrugged, pausing from his work to help himself to the brandy in the decanter.

'Mr G said those two inventors were locked up earlier this evening.' He smacked his wet, smiling lips together.

'Imagine if they put them in our old cell, Murray. That would be a mighty fine coincidence, eh?'

'Nah, they aren't in the same place we were.' He swigged directly from the decanter and swallowed loudly. He turned his waxy brown eyes up towards the ceiling. 'The girl has probably gone to bed. She must be a heavy sleeper.'

'It'll make it all the easier,' returned his companion with a cackle. He took up a vase from the mantel. 'You think this is real?'

'Hard to say.' Murray put down the brandy and took the vase from his companion. 'Looks fake to me.'

'Nah, I think it's genuine antique, that is.'

'Looks too fresh – not many cracks or chips in it.'

'Oh I can assure you, gentlemen, that it's quite real.'

Both men turned their heads to see the girl standing in the doorway, smiling sweetly at them. 'Might I ask, sirs, what you are doing in my house?'

'This is your house, is it, miss?' Murray grinned, setting the vase aside. 'We just happened to call at your brothers' shop and noticed that the front door was unlocked but nobody was in, so we thought we'd see if anything was amiss.'

'Oh, is that right?' said Molly in an almost disinterested tone. 'So why is it that you're stuffing my mother's heirlooms into a sack?'

'Don't try to pretend you're not afraid of us,' said Murray, his charming demeanour starting to give way to impatience and annoyance. 'We'll soon get you to show how afraid you really are.'

'I never said I wasn't afraid.' Molly flicked something from under her nail and looked at them from beneath her wild hair. Both men were starting to advance towards her. 'But I never said I was helpless either.'

The colour of Murray's face darkened so that he resembled a swede rather than a potato. As his lips peeled back, revealing rows of yellow teeth, Sharp grabbed his sleeve and shook him.

'Murray! Look!'

Around Molly's feet, green vegetation was sprouting before their very eyes and rapidly spreading out along the floor and walls, so that in under a minute the doorway to the parlour was like a gateway to the Garden of Eden. As Molly extended her arms outward, leafy vines entwined themselves around her arms and sprouted orange flowers.

'You think you're going to scare us with some clever magic trick?' said Murray, calling her a rather vicious name.

'No, I don't.' Molly raised her hand with her palm outstretched towards her two assailants.

Murray twisted his thick neck around as Sharp broke out into an impossibly high-pitched scream. A vine had wrapped itself tightly around his leg, anchoring him to the ground. He took out a knife from his boot to try to cut it, but it was far too thick. He desperately tried clawing at it with his nails, yet it only constricted him all the more. All of a sudden, his body went rigid and he crumpled to the floor, the grassy turf cushioning his fall.

'Why you – ' Murray drew out a long knife and raised it above his head, ready to strike the girl, who was regarding him with a calm, collected stare. The orange flowers along her arms and back sent out bursts of green spores and Murray's twisted features instantly relaxed as they wafted over him. The fury evaporated from his eyes, which took on a glassy, doll-like quality, and he stooped to his knees. The knife fell to the floor. Molly made circular motions with her finger and the vines swiftly wrapped themselves around his body, completely covering him right up to his head.

'Don't worry about your sight. The toxins' effect will pass. Your friend has only been paralysed. He'll be quite all right.'

'What have you done to me, you little witch?' He spat as Molly took a step towards him. A drop of the foam at the corner of his mouth had flicked onto her dress. At least it was one of her old ones.

'I'm no witch. What you see here isn't magic. Only science.'

A green plant head with red lips curled its way around Molly's wrist like an asp and raised its head, leaning towards the fallen man.

'Tell me where my brothers are being held, or else I'll do more than paralyse you.'

Murray cursed at her.

'I'd consider the position I was in if I were you,' said Molly sternly, as the vines visibly tightened around him and squeezed his windpipe. 'You have witnessed what I am capable of *and* you are currently blind. You cannot predict what I'll do next. So I'll say it once more – tell me where my brothers are.'

Sweat ran down Murray's lumpy forehead and his lips smacked together wordlessly like a fish's.

'They – they're in…Newgate,' he wheezed feebly, his face now a violent, plum-tomato red.

'Thank you.'

The hold of the vines slackened.

'I promise you this won't hurt. In fact you won't feel a thing for the next twelve hours.' The little plant lightly kissed Murray's forehead.

Chapter Twenty-Seven

Maestro opened his eyes, or at least he imagined he had, for everything was still dark. He heard the sound of his eyelids snapping open and shut. What had happened? He was lying on his back with his arms and legs fastened by the wrists and ankles. He tried raising them, but they were fixed firmly in place, struggle as he might. But he was still free to move his head, not that it was much use. All around him was pure darkness. No, not entirely. There was one far-off dot of bright yellow light, winking like a star, when he turned his head to the left. Another thing that puzzled him as he lay there trying to make sense of everything was the odd resonance of the parts within his chest, which sounded clearer and sharper than usual, like they weren't dampened by his chest casing.

'This will all be very bewildering to you no doubt, but you are in no immediate danger,' said a familiar voice nearby. The echo it produced suggested that the place he was in was of considerable size, although not as big as some of the rooms in Master Josephus's house. The yellow dot, he now noticed, had swelled in size. A hand materialised from out of the darkness, glowing pink as it passed over the dot and adjusted the dial on the side of the lamp which now burned with a bright yellow-white flame. It rapidly grew in strength and cast a halo of soft, liquid light around the shapely form of Mademoiselle Roux-Voclain.

She was dressed very differently from how he had seen her before. Her red hair was tied back at the base of her skull and her lips were not quite so red. She wore a dark pink bodice with padded shoulders, buttoned up to the throat. Over this she wore a crimson corset, and her legs were clad in tight-fitting, burgundy trousers, similar to those Master Josephus often wore.

'Do not fear.' She smiled as she came nearer. 'I will not take you apart. Well, not yet. Hopefully Gottfried's men will save me the trouble. It would be an act of sheer vandalism to destroy something as marvellous as you,' she continued in her melodious voice, the clack of her heels resounding across the room (it was largely empty, Maestro judged from the feedback) as she leant over the table he was strapped to.

Looking down at himself, he saw his chest plate had been removed, exposing his clockwork through his torn shirt.

'But I confess I grew more than a little impatient.' Her hand hovered over his chest and slowly made its way upward. 'I am simply dying to find out what…makes…you…tick.' She tapped her finger against his forehead as she spoke each word, before abruptly snatching her hand away. 'Say something to me. Just so I know nothing was damaged in the recovery process.'

'I can speak just fine,' answered Maestro, eyeing the metal rings fastened around his ankles. 'The only damage I sustained was to my left hand, and that is nothing serious.' He couldn't see his hand as his arms were raised above his head, but knew from the loose feel of the joints when he flexed his fingers that something was not right. The smallest finger he could not even move at all.

'Good. I confess she was a little rough with you. How unladylike! You like my flute-player?'

She raised the lamp and lifted her extraordinary eyes away from Maestro. Far off in a shadowy corner, the form of the flute-player glittered in the lamp's light. She was sat slumped against a chipped pillar with much of its bare plaster exposed, perfectly still – her eyes wide open.

'I modelled her after Vacaunson's machine, although I confess I made a considerable number of modifications of my own, the voice box, for example, making the movements more natural and so on. She is pretty, no?

You made it so easy for me, Maestro!' she chuckled, moving the lamp so that the light receded from the flute-player. 'But she is completely dumb. She has no mind of her own. The composing apparatus Gaston explained – I made him rehearse *that* a good deal – is genuine. But otherwise, she performed exactly as I instructed her to. You will not find a better little actress than she.'

There had been a change in her manner of speaking, which now possessed a gravity it had lacked before. Gone was the toying, airy aspect of the speech that she had used with Master Josephus and the professor.

'But how – how were you able to—?'

'To make her? You think your creators are the only ones who have attempted to create artificial life?'

She adjusted the dial on the side of the lamp once more and raised it high above her head. The darkness lifted from the theatre stage, for that's what they were standing on, and Maestro could also now clearly see what was hanging from the high ceiling above him.

Bodies.

Rusted, twisted bodies with their lifeless limbs dangling limply, and their heads drooping. Some had strange glass chambers inside their heads and torsos, filled with murky-coloured fluid. Maestro stared wide-eyed at them.

'Failed experiments,' Mademoiselle explained. 'Nothing but poor puppets.'

Maestro turned his head to the side, although he still caught sight of them in the corner of his eye. But a movement of Mademoiselle Roux-Voclain's drew his attention. She was twirling a silver instrument, like a surgeon's scalpel, between her fingers as she smiled at him.

'For years I've tried to create a being such as yourself. Not specifically a composer as such, but a being who is entirely mechanical. I thought the solution might lie in a synergy between the organic and the mechanical. But looking at you, I realise that I was mistaken. It *is* possible to construct a conscious being from pure clockwork after all.' A tremor of excitement in her voice had been steadily climbing while she was speaking. But as it threatened to break, she closed her eyes a moment, pressed a hand to her chest and cleared her throat.

'You stole me so that you could learn how I worked? said Maestro. 'And the professor was working in concert with you all along?'

'Correct. People always assume it is the man who is the mastermind, when in reality, behind almost every great man in history, there is a woman pulling the strings. Gottfried is nothing but my puppet,' she said, her voice taking on a hard edge when she spoke of the professor. 'He was a perfect decoy, and his chemical knowledge was of some value to me, otherwise I wouldn't have tolerated him for so long. He calls me his *joli rubis*, his pretty ruby, as if I am something to be worn. Sickening, isn't it? There were so many times I wanted to burst into laughter when he reckoned to know things about machinery. Hah! A schoolboy knows more! He had no hope of uncovering your secrets for himself, although he has no idea what I am capable of. He thinks it is Gaston who is the one with the knowledge. My dear brother does not mind acting as my go-between. After all, I compensate him well enough with former fiancés' payments to keep matters out of the court, and the money from the inventions I provide him with to sell to collectors. He claims they are by so-called anonymous inventors. The inventions are all my own, of course.'

'Is that why you pursued Master Douglas – to obtain his money?'

'Money? No, if it was only money I wanted, there are richer Englishmen I could try my luck with. Besides, I have enough of it. What I sought from your master was your secrets. When I first encountered your two masters at Cephus's ball, I instantly knew I would be wasting my time with the dark-haired brother. Cold, brilliant and impenetrable as a diamond, he is much like Gaston in many ways, I thought. I could tell that your Master Douglas would be far more responsive.' She smiled wickedly and pressed her lips together. He watched the blood rush rapidly back into them. 'But when he resisted me, in spite of the amount of powder I slipped him, I decided I would have to try other means.'

'Master George and Douglas are very clever, you know. They will deduce somehow that you have taken me.'

'They might. Which is why I saw to it that they had a very unfortunate accident at their meeting with Mr Cobb's investors. No doubt they'll be in hospital by now, where they can give me no trouble.'

'An accident!'

'Don't think I underestimated them. I knew I'd have to ensure that they were out of the way. So I may have made a few...adjustments to Mr Cobb's silk spinner to cause it to misbehave.'

'You mean you tried to murder them?'

'Oh, such harsh words. But no, I didn't intend to injure them enough to kill them. It is done now anyhow. Enough talk.' She ceased twirling the scalpel. 'I can abide no longer.'

Maestro watched as the nib of the scalpel came down towards his eyes and bit into his casing just above the right eye. With one hand on the side of his head, she sawed into the casing – the sound of the wood splitting was like thunder in his ears – until the pressure suddenly dispelled. When the scalpel was retracted, he saw it had excised a chunk of wood from his forehead.

'Oh!' she exclaimed breathily and seized a looking glass. Her eye appeared blurry and bug-like under the lens. He could see every flicker of movement of the iris.

'*C'est magnifique*!' She began muttering rapidly in her native tongue. 'Some of this is far too complex for even my understanding.' She set the glass down. 'Hopefully, I will not have to cause too much damage to you to determine how you work.'

The sound of heavy footsteps entered Maestro's ear – as if they were coming from backstage, from behind the cobwebby and dust-encrusted lopsided curtain. Mademoiselle Roux-Voclain seemed oblivious to them until her brother burst onto the stage, half-cast in shadow. He addressed her in French.

'There may be a problem.'

'May be a problem or is a problem?' she said irritably as she turned her back on Maestro to face her brother, putting her hands on her hips.

'Gottfried's men have not yet returned. It should not have taken them this long to have acquired the plans for the automaton.'

'I told you to keep watch on them. Has there been any communication from Gottfried himself?'

'None.'

'Fine. I will come.' Mademoiselle Roux-Voclain sighed, casting a glance back at Maestro. 'It is not as if he can go anywhere.'

'I don't know why you insist on returning to this place.' Her brother frowned as she slipped behind the curtain. He followed swiftly after her.

'It is as good as any other,' Maestro heard her reply offhandedly. 'And it provides, I suppose you could call it a sense of…theatricality?'

'It is hardly taking *prac*ticality into consideration.'

The sound of their voices and footsteps died away. Mademoiselle had taken the lamp with her, leaving Maestro in total darkness. At least he could no longer see the dangling feet of the decaying automata, although he still felt their presence.

Chapter Twenty-Eight

'Right, so if we were to acquire a sufficiently powerful spring,' said Douglas, as he rapidly chalked equations along the prison wall, which was more or less now covered in figures and symbols, 'then that should generate enough force to punch a hole right through the wall!' He drew a ring around the solution with a flourish and turned around to George, who was sitting on a stool with his legs set slightly apart and his arms across his lap. His head was sunk low so Douglas could only see the top of his dark crown. He knew if he were able to see George's eyes, they would have taken on that glassy, but unsettlingly intense, look that meant he was in deep thought. Douglas snapped his fingers near George's ear several times until a hand shot out and seized his wrist.

'Will you stop that infernal clicking?'

'I'm sorry, but I need you to be here right now and help me think of a way to escape from this place.'

'I was in the process of doing so until you interrupted my train of thought.'

'Well, could you retrace it?' Douglas wrenched himself free of George's grasp. 'It'd be helpful to know what it was.'

'Perhaps, although I can't recollect it at present.' There was a steely edge to George's voice as he eyed Douglas. His blue irises had an almost phosphorescent glow in the half-shadow of the receiving ward, like cat's eyes. They were the only two inmates in the receiving ward, where all new prisoners were brought.

'You were making me anxious. How was I meant to know what on earth you were thinking?'

Douglas sat on the cold, hard floor and started idly drawing with the piece of stone in his hand, the nib a clean white. He assumed George had lapsed back into thought until he spoke.

'I cannot recall it. I doubt it would have had a high chance of success anyhow.'

'If they hadn't stripped us of everything but the clothes on our backs as we passed through the yard, we could have used our pocket devices.'

'And how could we have used them?' George leant back against the whitewashed wall. Streaks of moonlight from the gridded window on the far wall fell across his chest. 'Even if we could pick the lock to the door or somehow break the bars off the window, what then? How far would we get before we were apprehended?'

'Well, I still think it would have helped.' Douglas shrugged, tossing away his stone and letting out a sigh. 'Then it looks like we're stuck here for the time being. We'll miss the Royal Performance for certain.'

'That is the least of our concerns. You do realise that if we are convicted we will more than likely get the death penalty,' said George, having shut his eyes.

'Yes, only I was trying not to let my mind enlarge on that possibility,' said Douglas irritably. 'What do you think about the solution I wrote out over there? You think it'll work?'

Opening his eyes, George rapidly scanned the wall. 'No.'

'Urgh, then it is hopeless.' Douglas slumped back against the wall opposite George and drew his knees up against his chest. His eyes landed on the sleeping mats hanging from hooks on the wall.

He shuddered.

Attempting not to acknowledge his fear, he tried to direct his thoughts towards anything other than the very real prospect of imminent death, which was unfolding before him like a horrible, black mist. His concern for his sister's future was like a rope thrown down to him that he clung to eagerly. No, he couldn't give up hope. He must be objective about things. It was not the eleventh hour yet, or even the tenth or the ninth. Since calculating the chances of a reprieve was futile, which depended largely on Cobb's chances of recovery, escape was a more definite route. Either way, they would be damned if they left Molly all alone in the world. They'd sworn to their mother on her deathbed and to themselves never to do so. After a minute, Douglas looked around the ward with new eyes and let out a brief laugh.

'You know, in a way this reminds me a lot of when we were boys and Mother or Snell would take away our inventions and lock us up in our room all night without supper.'

'Usually for abetting our sister's escape from her own confinement,' said George.

Douglas may have imagined the hint of amusement in his voice. 'Yet we always managed to find a way to give them the slip then.'

'Yes, and face an even more severe punishment as a consequence.'

'Not that it ever deterred us from trying.'

'No, quite the opposite I should think.'

'So what has changed now then?'

George looked at him incredulously. 'There's a difference between a prison ward and our old bedroom.'

'Is there?' Douglas cocked his head and half-grinned. 'Because I'd say this actually feels a lot like our old room. Maybe not quite as cold.' It was difficult to see in the weak light, but he could have sworn George actually smiled.

'Perhaps you're right.' George stood upright with a resolute look. 'In which case I might have an idea. If we can just—'

At that moment, there came the sound of heavy boots and a man's voice on the other side of the thick iron door to the receiving ward. 'You needn't be so rough with me.'

'Shut it!' barked a policeman. He sounded like the same one who had escorted Douglas and George to the ward earlier. Both brothers watched as the door opened and two burly officers dragged a man inside.

'I didn't steal it!' bellowed the man pitifully, as they released their hold on him.

Ignoring him, one of the officers caught sight of George and Douglas, and said, almost gloating, 'Your music-making machine was reported missing a few hours ago. Stolen. Your client, Lord Leyton, identified this man as the culprit, only he won't say what he's done with it.'

Douglas caught the tattoo on his hand. An inverted triangle inside a circle with a cross running through it. The mark of the SOAL.

'But I didn't steal it!' repeated the man, as the officer and the turnkey turned to go, deaf to his pleas.

'We found ropes, a sack and a bill from a locksmith in your lodgings. It's obvious you were planning on stealing it,' said the officer over his shoulder.

'But I never actually *did* steal it!' the man said desperately. 'Someone else stole the machine before I had a chance to! I mean, not that I was thinking of – I didn't mean—'

'Save it for the trial, Griffin.' He smirked. 'I'm sure the judge will be more interested in what you have to say.'

'Please!' Griffin threw out his hands like some begging animal, but they locked the door again. Their boots could be heard clomping back down the gallery. Griffin continued pleading, cursing and striking the door with his fist until the sound of the gate further along slamming shut rang out. Then, he sharply turned his attention to George and Douglas.

'Please, I beg you! Help them see I'm innocent!'

'How are we to do that exactly?' said George from his stool. 'We appear to be in the same position as you, and even if we were to protest on your behalf, our words would be met with nothing but contempt. But tell us, just to be clear, has our automaton really gone missing from the earl's home?'

'Yes, but not because of me. That fool Cephus found it missing from its room and immediately concluded I had stolen it. He alerted the police and they threw me in here.'

'But you admit you were planning on stealing Maestro?' said Douglas.

'Cephus owed me that automaton!' he burst out angrily. 'It isn't theft if what you are taking is rightfully yours. Cephus agreed to let me show it at my theatre. *I* was the one who made it famous! I even have a document proving Cephus transferred it over to me!'

'And did you tell that to the police?'

'Yes, only they took no notice. I'm just a lowly theatre manager,' he sneered. 'What is my word against his lordship's?'

'So you are the one who made Maestro perform unceasingly and make a spectacle of himself,' said Douglas. 'And the one who mistreated him.'

'Mistreated? It's a bloody wind-up doll!'

'Maestro told me all about what you did to him. Had Maestro been human, it would have been considered assault.'

'Oh, damn that accursed automaton! It's brought me nothing but trouble! And now I'm going to rot in here for the rest of my days for something I never even did.' He put his face in his hands and began moaning, sinking down onto a vacant mat on the floor. Douglas watched him a moment and then turned back to George.

'Whatever that plan of yours was that you were about to tell me a few minutes ago, you had better have held onto it. If what he says is true and someone really has taken Maestro, we need to find out who and what they intend to do with him.'

'That plan would have taken until morning. It's useless under the present circumstances.'

'Then think harder! We can't leave the police to deal with this, not if they think they already have their man.'

'But to establish a clear course of action, first we must determine who really has taken the automaton, if that is indeed what happened. All we know for certain is that it is not in its room in the earl's house where it was earlier this evening.'

'Do you think Maestro may have run away?'

'Why on earth would it do that?'

'Lord Leyton was planning on taking him to the Continent in two weeks or so, wasn't he? Perhaps Maestro didn't wish to go and so he fled.'

'I'm not even going to attempt to explain what's foolish about that idea. That someone has taken it seems the most plausible scenario. And someone familiar with the house's interior, or who has been colluding with someone who is.'

'Given just how many people that could include, since you know how Lord Leyton likes to entertain his many friends, I doubt we could rule out half of London.'

'I am only stating the facts as they appear. Although there are several likely suspects that come to my mind.'

'Professor Gottfried seems the most likely of them. He knew Cobb, so it makes sense that he would use our mutual acquaintance to his advantage. By tampering with the machine and framing us for it, that left the way clear for him to take Maestro. He probably didn't mean for Cobb to be severely injured in the process, just for the machine to appear to be a failure and to get us out of his way.'

'No,' said George, 'Gottfried might have had the willingness to sabotage Cobb's enterprise, but I don't believe he truly possesses the knowledge to construct machines of his own from our designs. He is colluding with somebody else.'

'But didn't you say Gottfried himself asked you to sabotage Cobb's factory?'

'Yes. And I refused him, as I told you in the police vehicle.'

'So when you went off on your own yesterday, you really did go off to the public house?'

'No.'

'Then where did you go?

George stared hard at the ground with an opaque expression. 'I went to Spitalfields to see the dwellings of the weavers for myself. For what reason,' he shrugged, 'I cannot say. It was a vile place – one of the worst slums I have ever set foot in.'

'Did the poor wretches steal your coat and shoes?'

'No. I happened to see a family through a broken window, gathered around the body of a man that was spread out on the floor without a shroud or coffin. So I knocked on the door and offered my coat to the woman who answered as a means of covering it. She accepted. There was a boy standing beside her, clad in ragged clothes and with no shoes. His feet were deep purple and covered in filth, so I provided him with something to cover *them* with. I also gave the woman a banknote before I went. I think it was at that point she started weeping. I didn't turn back to see.'

Douglas only stared at him, half-stupefied and half beside himself. 'Did you not think that this family could serve as witnesses to place you at the time of the crime?'

'And how would we go about reaching them? Although it was my very last resort for when the case came to trial.'

'Because heaven forbid the world should know George Abernathy did a charitable deed for once in his life. I dare say you'd rather put the hangman's noose around your own neck.'

'Can we please return to the matter at hand? My point is that if I refused Gottfried help, he must have sought it from another source. The prototype and plans would be useless to him otherwise.'

'But how do you know he *is* a fraud?'

'Numerous reasons. But what confirmed my suspicions was when I received a note from him this morning in response to my refusal of his request. The poor scrawl it was written in suggested his control of his hand was affected by palsy. I first perceived a delicate tremor in his hand when I encountered him at Lord Leyton's ball. He would therefore be incapable of carrying out delicate work such as tampering with the automated silk spinner.'

'So Gottfried isn't our man then. Which brings us back to the question of who he is working with, or for.'

'Someone who has demonstrated ingenuity and knowledge of mechanics, and who would profit from acquiring the android.'

'Gaston Roux-Voclain springs to mind.'

'No. *Think*. I see why you think him the obvious choice, but he is not the correct one. Try to imagine alternative possibilities.'

Douglas's eyes scrutinised his brother's face as if the answers were written there. Why was George putting him through this test of wits? Why could he not simply speak his mind? Suddenly, his searching look broke.

'Claudette could have been acting as an agent for her brother, seeing as he is supposedly a collector of automata. Or...'

'Or she was the one working the strings the entire time.' George completed the thought.

'Are you sure?'

'Not entirely. But for one thing, we can rule out the brother. It was obvious when I was conversing with him at the ball that he only possessed a surface knowledge of automata, and an even weaker grasp of basic physics and mathematics. He didn't really bring a great deal of enthusiasm to the conversation either, as one might expect from an avid collector of automata. More likely he has been acting on behalf of his sister's interests.'

'It would explain why she was so keen to know about Maestro when she had me trapped in the reading room. She must have hoped the cocaine or whatever it was would loosen my tongue so I'd give away the secrets to how he worked without my being aware of what I was doing.'

'Yes, it seems more than likely that was the case.'

'Not to mention the cage she was wearing. There was a mechanism that could make it fold in on itself, which might show she has some skill with mechanics.'

'That is hardly much to go on, but it is highly suggestive.'

'So the Roux-Voclain siblings are, we have to assume, our most likely suspects for the present. Unless you can think of anyone else?'

'None with a probability of more than five per cent by my estimation. Assuming it is the Roux-Voclains, we need to work out where they would take the android.'

'George, she could have Maestro on a ship bound for France right now,' said Douglas dejectedly.

'I don't think so. I heard a good many stories from the other guests at the ball about that woman. Scandal has a habit of following her wherever she goes. She and her brother had to leave Paris after some dalliance of hers with a member of the Foreign Office. They have few friends and many enemies in their native land. She wouldn't risk taking the android there, not when there are so many who would wish to pry it from her by way of revenge. Here they are obscure and safe from suspicion.'

'So, she'll have him hidden somewhere in the city then…'

Douglas snapped his fingers. 'Yes, I remember what she told me about her family history.' He turned his head and saw the theatre manager still in the same position, sitting dejectedly on the edge of the mat moaning to himself. 'Mr Griffin?' Douglas hissed sharply.

Mr Griffin instantly quit moaning and raised his head.

'Do you know anything about an English actress who married a French lord many years ago?'

'Why yes, I do! I do!' He sprang to his feet. 'But what of it? Is it worth something to you?'

'It might just be worth the price of your freedom. If you answer satisfyingly that is.'

Douglas hated having to deal with him in this way but he knew he would have to cast his own personal dislike of the man for his treatment of Maestro aside if they were to ultimately aid the automaton in any way.

'Her name was Alice Conway,' Griffin said hurriedly. 'She used to perform at a theatre near Wych Street about twenty years or so ago. Then this French nobleman fell madly in love with her and she ran away with him to Paris. I think he married her and a child was born not long after.'

'Is the theatre in Wych Street still open?'

'No. It has been shut up for the best part of ten years now.'

'That'll do, Mr Griffin.' Douglas nodded. 'You have my word that I'll do whatever is in my power to secure your release.' Ignoring the man's rapturous thanks, he faced his brother.

'You really think she's taken it to an old theatre purely based on *that* man's testimony?'

'I admit it's not much, but it makes sense she'd take Maestro somewhere quiet and secluded that she's familiar with. Let's face it, it's as good a lead as we can get while we're stuck here.'

George was about to speak when there came the sound of the door being opened once more. A portly officer appeared with a wicker basket in his hand, covered with a spotted cloth.

'A young lady came by carrying this for you. Said she was your sister. She was in a bit of a state, weeping and wailing about her poor brothers and how she couldn't bear the thought of them going without a decent meal.'

There came the familiar rattle of keys as he inched the door open and set the basket down, quickly locking it again. 'It would have been utterly heartless of us not to comply with her request that we deliver it to you, even if it is outside the usual time for visitors. I personally took it from her hands and promised to see that it got to you. A meat pie and fruit "to keep rickets at bay", she said. I've never seen a pie as nice as that one.' He let out a deep, guttural belch and patted his gut. 'It was very tasty.'

He laughed to himself all the way back down the passage.

Douglas and George eyed the basket and then one another.

'You really think it was Molly?' Douglas asked.

'Possibly. But I suspect there's more to this than meets the eye.'

George knelt beside the basket and knocked back the cloth. Inside were two red apples and an orange, a scrap of paper half-soaked in grease and a scattering of crumbs. George shook the crumbs from the paper and lifted it towards the light. The paper was transparent where it had absorbed the grease from the pie. He could see there was something written on the back of it in Molly's hand: *Enjoy the pie and the fruit. Be careful not to spill any of the precious juices. M.* He glanced at Douglas, who was contemplating the exceedingly rosy apple in his hand, like one he had seen before. He retrieved his stone and stuck the nib into the apple, twisting it back and forth to burrow it deeper into the flesh. There was a faint, acidic hissing and frothing. When he removed the stone, it had been half eaten away. A tail of white vapour rose from it. His face lit up.

'Aha! Brilliant! Even if they read the note, they'd have had no idea what it really meant.'

He quickly went over to the window and, stretching up, dashed the apple against the rusty bars on the side where the hole was. The metal instantly began to fizz and melt away where the juice had touched it. He bade George pass him the orange, which he rammed against another bar until the skin broke and the juice bled out from the pulp and streamed down the bar. George followed suit and, after grating the second apple against a bar, dripped juice along the bottom and top of it, catching it as it fell away.

'That's one, but we should hurry. The wardsman could be back at any moment.'

'It seemed as if he was rather intoxicated when he came in earlier. He's most likely sound asleep somewhere,' replied George, getting to work on the next bar. Once all of the bars had been removed, Douglas cautiously inched his head out of the window.

He could hear the chugging of the airship before he saw its shape amid the black night, its half-closed eyes shining sleepily so as not to attract much attention. Snatching the spotted cloth from the floor, he waved it frantically out of the window. The flying machine hovered closer to the window but then drew up. Had she not seen him signalling?

A thick rope dropped down past the window, and Douglas reeled it in. 'Could you give me a boost?' he called to George.

'And how am I supposed to get up?'

'I'm sure you'll manage it. Don't fret, I'll be quick, then you can follow on after.'

'You'd better be.'

'Take me with you!' Griffin cried. 'Take me with you or I'll alert the guards!'

'You do that and you'll be damaging your own chances of escape,' George told him flatly, as he gave Douglas a leg up and watched his brother's feet slide out of the window. 'We'll be able to secure your freedom by legal means if we are outside, and our escape will divert attention away from you in the meantime.'

The man scowled sulkily at George and then turned his back on him.

George gripped the rope firmly in his hands and hurled himself up onto it, trapping the end between his legs. Pulling himself up a couple of inches, he braced his feet against the window ledge before swooping out of the window, feeling a sting along his arms as the corroded metal brushed against him. The noise from the flying machine suddenly became much louder. The air whooshed past his ears and his black hair whipped up before his eyes as he found himself dangling maybe forty feet above the ground. Douglas had just reached the top and was dragging himself through the open porthole door. The rope burned George's palms and forearms as he pulled himself up along it. He could see Douglas calling down to him, but his words were drowned beneath the noise of the flying machine. When he was near the top, Douglas extended his hand out towards him. George timed the precise moment to let go of the rope with one hand and grab hold of his brother's hand. With one last surge of determination, and the additional force of Douglas pulling on his arm, he managed to climb into the airship. As the porthole closed, he became aware of his own exhaustion; his arm muscles shuddered and were searing with pain, his heart rate was elevated and every pulse in his body throbbed. But it was quick to subside, and after a matter of seconds, he was master of himself again. Douglas was more affected and was still panting heavily beside him.

'Are the two of you all right back there?' Molly shouted from the driver's seat, although her mouth arched in a half-grin as she twisted her head over her shoulder. The edges of her eyes were slightly red. 'Not bad for a botanist and a woman, eh?'

'Not bad? That was brilliant, Molly!' Douglas threw his arms around his sister's neck and kissed her cheek forcefully.

'Well, it was a risk, I'll say that much. The entire plan hinged on them leaving the fruit and going for the pie.'

'Well, it worked! Risky or not, it was still pure genius!'

'But it isn't over yet,' said George, drawing himself up in his seat. 'We need to get away from here. Fast.'

'Right. You want to take over?' she asked Douglas.

'I'd feel more comfortable if you kept your place rather than have Douglas drive,' said George.

'Fine. I'll steer, you direct. This GPS thing of yours took me a stupidly convoluted way to get here.'

Douglas climbed over into the passenger seat, noticing Molly had tied two wooden blocks to the bottoms of her shoes in order to reach the pedals.

'Right, Spuggy!' She expertly flicked a lever overhead. 'Let's see what else you've got in you!'

'Spuggy?!' cried Douglas. 'The name I decided on was the Sparrowhawk.'

'But to me it's more like a garden bird than a bird of prey, so I shortened it.'

'But—'

'Is this really the time or place to be having this debate?' demanded George impatiently. 'Every second we waste bickering, the more time is lost in which to recover the android.'

'All right, all right. Head west, Mol, as fast as you can.'

She promptly pulled the largest lever and they shot off across the night sky, Douglas silently praying they weren't already too late.

Chapter Twenty-Nine

Neither Maestro nor Mademoiselle Roux-Voclain had spoken in a while. Her brother had been dispatched to Gottfried's residence and she had resumed her examination, occasionally asking Maestro a question. She was, he had to admit, beautifully delicate in handling his parts (the ones he could continue to function without) as she removed them, like they were eggs plucked from a bird's nest, putting everything back as it was afterwards. The important thing, as he had explained, was that she did not touch either of the two cylinders rotating inside of his head and chest. The serene, concentrated look in her eyes and the fluid movements of her hands suggested they were well practised at this sort of work, like how his own hands (one of which she had detached to examine the finger joints, before replacing it) moved across the keys of a piano with seemingly little input from his mind, the knowledge residing in the bone (or brass in his case).

'These bellows,' she indicated, with the tool she was holding, 'are they purely decorative or do they serve a function?'

'They function in a similar way to the human lungs. I require them for playing woodwind instruments.'

'As I suspected. Although they are hardly the most interesting thing compared to the rest of what's inside you. I could content myself studying you for years!' Then after a pause she added, 'I also assume that's how you are able to speak now?'

'Yes.'

'You weren't able to at Cephus's ball, I recall.'

'Master Douglas inserted a reed into my throat to act like a larynx.'

'And he also put a tongue inside your head, so you can sing as well as play. How clever of him. That will have stopped Josephus tiring of you for a little while longer. Humph, what a fool he is. He possesses the first conscious machine in mankind's history and what does he do with it? Parades it before London's idiotic aristocracy and dresses it up like a little girl does her doll.' She muttered the words more to herself in an undertone, switching between French and English. 'You should be thankful I delivered you from Cephus. He is nothing but an indulgent fool and a degenerate.'

'Master Josephus might be a little strange but he is not bad.'

Mademoiselle Roux-Voclain raised her eyebrows. One corner of her mouth slid upwards. 'Oh? You feel a sense of loyalty to your master, do you?'

'I believe him to be a good master. At least, he has never treated me unkindly and has come to my defence on a number of occasions. But, I do not quite understand. . .you made every appearance of being his friend, and yet you deceived him.'

'And what about you sneaking away in the dead of night to see that silly little girl?' She held up a finger and tutted. 'How naughty! You know he will be absolutely distraught not knowing what has become of you? Well, until the next plaything comes along to divert his attention.'

Maestro averted his eyes from her. He had not considered it in that light before.

'And as for my deceiving him, as you call it, that does not weigh heavily on my conscience in the slightest. Many years ago, an opportunity presented itself to me to become acquainted with Josephus and knowing how well connected he was, I seized it. My luck at encountering the professor at the ball was only the latest example of how that acquaintance has served me well, trying as it has been at times. Oh, Cephus can be charming and highly entertaining, but he is not a *true* man, and his presence grates on one after a while.'

'So you don't have any regard for him?'

'Not a great deal,' she sighed, somewhat impatiently.

'And you don't possess any feelings of affection towards the professor at all either?'

'*Mon foi*! You are naive, aren't you? Pah! As I said, I only sought his chemical knowledge to further my research, although he also presented a useful decoy to divert the police's suspicion away from my brother and me.'

'Is that what you do? You make intelligent men become infatuated with you so you can steal their secrets?'

'How is that any different from the deception men have practised towards my own sex for countless generations? They pour their amorous words like honey into our ears and press their fevered lips against our hands with promises of undying love and devotion, only once the wedding band is on the unsuspecting wench's finger, she finds herself not the adored idol, but an object. A trinket. Everything we possess becomes theirs – body, fortune and all. They are free to do what they wish with us. Even beat us. So one deception for another, I say. I am playing the same game as them, only I'm playing it better.'

'But what you are doing is still not right, Mademoiselle. No matter what others may do to you.'

'Who are you to preach morals to me? You know nothing of the world of man, nor have you seen the dark underbelly of human nature as I have. You have never known hardship or betrayal. Do not speak about what you truly don't, and cannot, understand. You are not quite as human as that.'

Her voice had gradually become more affected as she spoke. She suddenly checked herself, smoothed back her hair and resumed her examination of Maestro as if nothing had occurred, although he could hear plainly that it took a little while before her elevated heartbeat slowed to a normal pace. He could still hear the minor movements of the automata above him, and every now and then there would be a complaining creak from some part of the building up in the shadows of the fly tower, as if protesting against the dead weight it was made to support. Every slight action of Mademoiselle's, even the slightest recalibration of a muscle, caused the strands of her hair to rustle against one another. After a while, her eyes flickered onto his and her face became taut with some suppressed emotion. As her hands continued their work, she began to speak in a steady, unwavering manner, never once lifting her eyes from what she was engaged in as her words unfolded seamlessly.

'Let me tell you a little story,' she began, 'about a girl born in Paris many years ago. Her father was from an old, wealthy family, but her mother had been nothing but a humble, English actress who was scorned by her husband's relations and acquaintances. And so the family did not receive many callers and the little girl had no playmates. Her brother was often away at school. Once or twice she was sent to school in England, only to be soon brought back again for no reason obvious to her. But she was bright and curious. She taught herself from books and things that she saw. She would develop a fierce interest in whatever it was she came across, whether it be astronomy, entomology, deciphering Latin texts, the theories of Newton, but only for a time, and when she had exhausted one subject, she moved on to the next. But then she found her true vocation. To compensate for the lack of real little girls to play with (not that she greatly felt their absence as she grew older; she even grew to despise their intrusion, at least in the case of an irritable younger cousin and her equally irritable brother's occasional presence), her father substituted them with mechanical dolls and trinkets. But instead of dressing them in pretty frocks, she took them apart to see how they worked. She would do this at night when her nurse was sound asleep, and then put them back together again before sunrise so no one was any the wiser. Later on, she used pieces from different dolls to make moving clockwork figures of her own design. They could walk, sing, dance and sketch in a manner that made them indistinguishable to humans, and far outstripped anything churned out from the workshops of the automaton-making families lining the streets of the capital. Yet as she grew older, she became ever more frustrated. Her knowledge of mechanics was, by that time, unrivalled. But still she longed to know more. Of course, she had no hope of being admitted to the Académie des Sciences. She was hindered by society on two accounts: her mixed parentage and her sex. Having red hair did little to help matters either; it only marked her out as an anomaly even more. But she noticed that men were beginning to pay her greater notice. She had, by this time, developed fully into a woman. Her father had also died and left her with a modest fortune. She had been made to understand her duty from an early age – she was to accept one of these drooling dogs as her husband. That was the only means of securing herself a respectable future. They cared nothing for the content of her mind when she attempted to communicate with them at social gatherings she attended with her mother. They only prattled on about her beauty and virtue, to which she was meant to repeat the same few stock words or to blush. No more than that. So she came up with an idea. If it was a doll they wanted her to be, then she would play the part of the doll. Her mother had taught her the tricks of her craft, and Mother Nature had provided her with the rest. Her victims were scholars, philosophers or engineers. Anyone she felt she could learn from. The procedure was simple. She would capture their attention until they proposed; she would accept, force them to break it off once she had learnt all she could from them (which was surprisingly not too difficult since most men have secrets), and extract the money owed to her for the breaking of the agreement, which helped fund her projects. The perfect arrangement. That was until a slight miscalculation resulted in her being caught in the process of wooing a politician who initially studied the sciences before switching to politics, and had recently been dabbling in electromagnetism after hearing about a Frenchman's failed attempt to improve on Jacquard's loom two years ago. She used the money he had given her to enable her and her brother to escape to London for the present. Only, as luck would have it, within a day of stepping off the boat, she learnt of the existence of what appeared to be an automaton that could think for itself. It was the ultimate prize, which she then directed her attention towards gaining. And here we are.' She smiled. 'So perhaps now you understand better, little Maestro, and you will not be so quick to judge. Or perhaps not. Either way, it makes no difference.'

Maestro made no immediate reply. He was still attempting to formulate a response to the extraordinary story she had just related to him when the distinct ring of Monsieur Roux-Voclain's steps returned. A few moments afterwards, he reappeared from behind the curtain. The light from the lamp impressed sharp shadows in the groves of his stiff, waxen face, particularly below the eyes and along the lines of the forehead, intensifying his strikingly grave expression, although his heartbeat, peculiarly sedate and shallow as it usually was, remained unchanged.

'There's been a complication,' he announced. 'The explosion you caused in Cobb's factory was far more powerful than you meant it to be. Cobb and two other men were very badly injured. Perhaps mortally. The clockmakers were not at the meeting as the professor said they would be. They are to be tried for attempted murder.'

'*What?* And Gottfried?'

'Gone. He is not at his lodgings. What has become of him is anyone's guess. I got nothing out of the servants.'

'Damn him!' She thrust down her tools. 'We must leave London. Now.' She had already begun hastily unfastening Maestro's restraints as she was speaking.

'We'll travel north. I'll go—'

There was a creak from above. Louder this time. So loud that even Maestro's captors looked skyward. The chains shook and visibly disturbed some of the automata. Was someone there? Crawling amongst the shadows? Was it someone coming to rescue him maybe?

But then there came another sound. Not a creaking, but a cracking. No sooner had he detected the sound than the calamity it signified struck. Everything seemed to happen at once so Maestro had trouble arranging the sequence of events and disentangling the various sounds that overlaid each other. A beam came crashing down, and a number of the automata along with it, directly above the spot where Mademoiselle was standing. But the instant before they reached the ground, her brother knocked her away and the whole tangled mess came crashing down on top of him with a terrible cacophony. Mademoiselle Roux-Voclain shrieked her brother's name. As he had pushed her out of the beam's path, the lamp had smashed on the stage. In the next instant, the chemical chambers inside the automata had also been dashed into a million shards of glass, spilling the fleshy matter and discoloured liquid they contained. The puddles of spilt liquid instantly ignited into pools of orange flame. The fire spread outwards with alarming rapidity, beginning to climb the stage curtain.

Maestro looked in bewilderment at the unfolding scene. He could see the theatre's interior a lot clearer now. It was in a dilapidated state, its insides torn up. The stalls were filled with all manner of machines and automata. It was a workshop, like Master George and Douglas's. But he had no time to dwell on this revelation as more pieces of the roof began to fall. Sprinklings of plaster dusted his coat and thick coils of rope descended from above. Grey smoke was beginning to curl up from the burning stage. He heard someone choking. Mademoiselle. She was stooped over her brother, desperately trying to move the debris that he was half-buried under. Maestro leapt down from the table and as his feet made contact with the ground, he heard a sound like more glass smashing. The flames had continued on past the curtain and stretched up into the recesses of the ceiling. What ensued afterwards was a rather spectacular sight. One after another, the chemical chambers in each of the automata exploded, sending glass, droplets of liquid and gears raining down. The bodies dropped like ripe fruit from a tree, some taking parts of the ceiling with them. He could no longer see Mademoiselle clearly through the screen of smoke and fallen debris. Nor could he hear her. Stumbling down from the stage, Maestro fought his way through the wreckage to where he anticipated the exit would be, being familiar with the layout of such theatres as this. Yes, there was the door! It had not been greatly touched by the fire. He struck it with his foot and it banged open, throwing up a burst of cinders like fireflies. His means of escape was clear. He was about to take his first step towards freedom when he hesitated. He glanced back and forth between the open doorway and the stage, then hastily ran back towards the latter. He began frantically shifting the piles of broken metal bodies and shards of wood until he had fully unearthed his two captors. Mademoiselle was lying beside her brother, her eyes closed, covered in dust and dirt. He was certain he detected her shallow breathing, but as for the brother, he could hear nothing. The path to the exit was still relatively clear; if he was quick about it, he could make it out unscathed yet. It would have been the logical thing to abandon any hope of recovering the two humans and to preserve himself given the circumstances. The chances of them surviving were small. Instead, he heaved the beam off the man's body so he was free and then went over to the curtain. He tore off the portion that had, amazingly, remained unscathed, and spread it out beside them, quickly swaddling them inside it like a makeshift sack, which he bundled together and hauled over his shoulder.

The fire had now reached the pit and was wasting no time in spreading. Now everywhere he looked there were crackling, orange flames and black curls of smoke. It took a great deal of effort to drag the bundled curtain along without being too rough. Time seemed to pass slower; it took an age to cover the distance that he had crossed in a matter of seconds only minutes ago. And every second, the flames drew in closer around his path. The material on his clothing burned away, but when the flames licked his wooden casing, they didn't even so much as smoulder it. But the metal inside his exposed chest was growing hot – he could feel it vibrating. It was a wonder his brass and iron parts had not melted. How much could they withstand? His steps became even more lumbering. Had his legs softened? Or was this a consequence of Mademoiselle's meddling? Whatever the cause, he began to doubt whether he could make it out of the theatre in time.

Chapter Thirty

Molly yelled, 'Are you sure it's around here, Douglas?' She squinted down at the bunched-together buildings below. 'I can't see anything that looks remotely like a theatre! It's just all houses!'

'It's definitely here. This is where Mr Griffin said it was,' Douglas insisted. Spuggy's lights were aimed down below but although they were flying at a low altitude, the weak light did little to illuminate their surroundings.

'I told you he lied to us,' said George, as he looked down from his own window. 'I say we circle around at the end of this row and turn back on ourselves. If we don't see it a second time then we give it up. I'm willing to bet this theatre doesn't even exist.' For once he genuinely seemed to be offering an opinion, rather than attempting to spite his brother.

'All right, but as long as we definitely know we've done a thorough sweep.' Most of the antique buildings on the street below seemed neglected and uninhabited, save for the odd open window. They were seventeenth-century at least and were just waiting to be torn down. None resembled a theatre. Douglas had to admit to himself that it looked bad. And if there was nothing here, what then? Where was best to redirect their search? Probably the professor's residence. George claimed he'd memorised the address.

'Wait, do you see that?' said George urgently. 'Molly, turn the ship to the left.'

She did as instructed and brought the thing George was indicating into full view of the front window. The theatre stood on a street corner, marking one point of a square. It was also on fire.

'Good God!' Douglas exclaimed at the flames furiously blazing away. 'Molly, take us down!'

'I'm sorry, you want to go *towards* the very large fire down there?'

'Maestro might be caught up in it. Take us down!'

'All right, down we go then.' She prepared to land and gave her brother a sad, pitying look. 'Although I really don't see what we can do if that's true.'

'I know, but do you really want to turn back around and go home?'

'*No.*' She sounded somewhat affronted. 'I'd rather attempt a futile rescue than sit at home sipping tea beside the hearth any day.'

'She's right though,' said George. 'I fear there's a good chance the android may be lost, if your hypothesis that it is being held here is correct.'

'I'm really hoping it isn't.'

They bumped to the ground a little roughly in the middle of the square. George manually opened the door without waiting for Molly to locate the necessary controls. The three of them hastened out of the airship and instantly felt the intense heat rush at their faces. What had been the old theatre was now totally engulfed by flames that snapped and crackled furiously. Several bystanders were gathered around the theatrical scene of the burning building. George began walking forward, Douglas thinking for one alarming moment that he was intent on entering the building, but then he veered off down a small side street to the left.

Douglas called, 'George! Where are you going?', but he didn't turn around or slow his brisk pace. Exchanging a look with one another, Douglas and Molly chased after him. By the time they had caught up with him, he had come to a stop, and now they saw what his objective had been. Before them was an abandoned hansom without a horse, tipped over on its side. Most likely the poor creature had become frightened at the sight of the flames and fled. George reached his hand inside the box and pulled out a travelling cloak.

'This is Mademoiselle Roux-Voclain's,' he said. 'I recall seeing her wearing it when she was waiting in the professor's cab yesterday.'

'Are you sure?'

'Without a doubt.'

'No,' said Douglas weakly, his worst fears confirmed.

The three of them could only watch the blazing inferno in despair. The other bystanders in the square had vanished, perhaps bored of the spectacle. The building was now little more than a blackened, hollow husk, its front doorway like an open mouth, wide and horror-stricken, as if howling out in agony. Tongues of flame shot out of its many eyes. It was a wonder it hadn't yet collapsed. Molly raised her hands over her mouth and her wide, glistening eyes trembled, although no tears fell. George's intense, strained expression told plainly that he was not wholly unaffected by what was transpiring around them. Douglas's heart was lead in his chest as he stood stock-still beside him. What chance did they have of any sort of rescue? It was too late. Maestro was gone, and most likely the Roux-Voclains. They had not escaped, that much was obvious from the upturned hansom. And he doubted she'd have left Maestro behind. He couldn't deny that he did feel something at the thought of her being engulfed in the blaze, whatever that may be. Possibly nothing beyond the bounds of human sympathy at her having met such a horrible end. He could not imagine how Lord Leyton would react when they told him that his automaton was no more. But now was not the time to mourn; they were probably being hunted by the police at that very minute. His sorrow became mingled with anger and he tightened his fist. Yes, it was all they could do to clear their name and make sure no one was mistaken as to who the true culprits of this devastation were. And that scoundrel Gottfried, they would see to it that he paid for his share in the affair if nothing else. And there was still Maestro's music – that would be his legacy. It would far outlive any of them.

He was so caught up in thoughts of retribution that he flinched violently when he felt someone shaking his arm. 'Douglas, look.' George's head was turned towards the eastern side of the building.

A moving figure was emerging from around the side of the building, wavering like a demonic spectre in the fire's heat. (It certainly looked like it had emerged from a gateway to hell.) It was dragging something behind it, clearly struggling. It had made its way around to the front of the building before they could clearly discern its identity.

'Maestro!'

Douglas sprinted towards him with George and Molly following closely at his heels. On seeing them approach, the automaton lowered the bundle he was hauling over his shoulder and leapt, or rather hobbled, forward to meet them.

'Master Douglas! How is it that you are here? I thought Mademoiselle Roux-Voclain had you put away in prison!'

'Never mind that, Maestro!' Douglas took the automaton by the shoulders. 'We thought we'd lost you! It was a miracle you didn't burn!'

'It certainly is, Master. I was sure I was done for.'

Molly bounded forward and looked as if she were about to throw her arms around him, but on feeling the heat that was coming from the glowing metal in his chest, thought better of it and hastily retreated at the last moment.

'But what of the Roux-Voclains? Did they…'

'Perish? Not at all, Master.' Maestro threw back the corner of the bundle. Wrapped up inside were Claudette and Gaston. 'I made sure I got them out as well as myself. They are quite all right, Master Douglas. At least, I think so. I thought I could still detect their breathing. It was rather confusing in there with everything that was happening around me.'

George knelt down and leant his head close to Claudette's. 'The woman is breathing. She has most likely inhaled a lot of smoke but she'll live.' He conducted a brief examination of her before turning his attention to Monsieur Roux-Voclain. 'Her brother is slightly worse off. I can feel several broken bones. We'll need to seek medical treatment. But why did you retrieve them?' George was frowning. 'It was not necessary for you to do that.'

'I couldn't leave them there, Master George.'

'But what compelled you? Given the unlikely chance of their survival and the fact they were a threat, your first prerogative should have been to preserve yourself.'

'Because…it was the right thing to do.' Maestro shrugged almost bashfully. 'I am afraid I really cannot explain it any better than that, Master George.'

'Now are you finally convinced, George?' Douglas smiled. 'That Maestro is more than just a music-making machine? What better proof is there that he is a fully conscious being than his being capable of compassion?'

George looked utterly nonplussed. Not a single muscle in his face flinched. When he did become animated once more, he shut his eyes as he spoke, his head lowered and his manner stiff. 'I suppose that whether a mind is constructed from flesh or metal is immaterial. In which case, there is no reason why this machine cannot possess something akin to consciousness.'

Douglas threw back his head and chortled heartily. 'Ha!' he cried out triumphantly. 'Oh, I wish I could have recorded what you just said now. That's two impossible things that have happened in the space of two days! First you show an ounce of compassion towards another human being, and then you actually own up to being in the wrong—' Douglas found himself landing flat on his back on the ground, sharply winded.

George had swept his foot under Douglas's feet. 'Shut up.'

Before Douglas could recover his voice enough to remonstrate with him, Claudette began to stir and half-dragged herself up, slowly lifting her head. She coughed violently.

'Tell me, is my brother all right?' she asked hoarsely from beneath her thick hair, which was matted with blood and plaster.

'He's unconscious but he'll live,' said George.

Her face took on a calm, relieved aspect and she closed her eyes. She allowed her head to sink. 'So what do you mean to do with me now?' she asked rather indifferently.

'We'll hand you over to the authorities,' said Douglas, kneeling down beside her. 'And then it'll be for them to decide what to do with you.'

'You wouldn't consider letting us go?' She lifted her eyes, reddened from the fire but losing none of their intensity, to Douglas, who felt a shudder along his spine in spite of himself. 'You would never hear from us again. There are places we could go where we can live quietly.'

'And you'll give up your pursuit of Maestro?'

'If I promised to, would you believe it?'

'Probably not. Don't worry about your brother, we'll see to it he gets to a doctor. George?' But George already had the unconscious man propped against his shoulder and was making his way back towards the airship.

'How is it that you managed to escape?' she asked him.

'Because of something you didn't account for – our younger sister happens to be a genius.'

'Hmm, I suppose I should have anticipated as much. You really were the most intelligent and truest gentleman that I ever pursued, you know,' she told him, as Molly came and assisted her in getting onto her feet.

'I'm sure I am not the first you have spoken those words to, Mademoiselle.'

She held her hand out towards him and he instinctively reached out to accept it.

'Oh no, Mademoiselle,' said Molly, as she bound the woman's wrists. 'We're not having you try any of your tricks.' A length of vine slithered down Molly's arm and wound itself around Claudette's wrists.

'That really isn't necessary. I will go willingly.'

'Yes, but it never hurts to err on the side of caution. I could easily blind you too if I wanted, but I'm feeling generous.'

'You do credit to your sex, my girl. Not many would show such self-possession and ingenuity as you.'

'I might say the same of you, if you hadn't had both my brothers locked up in Newgate and all the rest of it.'

'That is fair.' She briefly tossed her head over her shoulder and addressed Douglas before Molly led her away. 'You may do with it what you please.'

Molly had not quite been quick enough to snatch Mademoiselle Roux-Voclain's hand away from Douglas's; she had managed to slip something into it. Douglas unclasped his hand and stared down at the octopus brooch sitting in his palm, its red jewel burning blood red in the fire's light, although its fire was perhaps the more brilliant and intense of the two. Yes, she might be cunning and manipulative to the highest degree but all the same, what an extraordinary woman.

Douglas tucked the brooch into his pocket before going to stand beside Maestro, who was intently watching the still raging fire.

'You know, Maestro,' Douglas began, 'you could just slip away if you wanted to. Everyone will assume you were destroyed in the fire and you'll just be another one of history's lost relics. You'd forever be safe from harm then. What do you say?'

Maestro pondered this as he turned his eyes away from his master's face back to the burning theatre. He did not have to turn the question over in his mind for very long.

'I think… I think perhaps history has enough lost relics, don't you Master Douglas?'

Douglas smiled and chuckled as the roof of the theatre began to collapse in on itself.

Chapter Thirty-One

Molly smiled to herself as she slipped into the house by the back door. The day had been exceptionally fine. A soft breeze blew, carrying the sweet, creamy perfumes being emitted by her flowers, which hung in baskets on either side of the door outside. Summer had finally arrived. The afternoon sun warmed her back as she plucked a few dead flower heads. She closed her eyes and let her skin drink in the warm, honey-gold light. Behind her closed lids, she could see flashes of colour, but in her mind's eye she was envisioning the scene she had just witnessed as she had passed by the little church nearby. There had been a wedding on – the bride and groom were just emerging from the church. Who should she have seen but Laura Blakeslee on the arm of Uriah Underwood! Both looked very grave and serious as they made their way past the well-wishers and climbed into the waiting carriage drawn by four horses, three white and one pearly grey. Molly had spied old Mr Underwood watching them with an almost melancholy serenity in his sombre black coat, with his hands folded meekly before him. Perhaps it was habit. Mrs Blakeslee was daubing her streaming, puffy eyes with a lace handkerchief. What a funny sight it had been. Molly still couldn't help smiling a little at picturing the odd couple who looked as if they had just stepped out of a funeral service rather than their own wedding ceremony. She did pity

Laura in some way or another, although in many respects she and Uriah Underwood were a perfect match, and she would certainly put him in his place should he try to act as if he were in charge. At least Douglas was safe from her advances.

The sound of a voice roused her from the stupor she had sunk into, half-drunk as she was from the late afternoon sun and the fumes from the flowers. It had come from upstairs. She closed the door behind her and paused to listen.

Silence. Apart from the ever-present ticking of clocks, of course.

Puzzled, she went and stood at the foot of the stairs. She could hear Douglas's voice, she was sure of it. George's too. Strange – it didn't sound as though they were arguing. She crept upstairs as quietly as she could and hovered outside Douglas's door where their voices were coming from.

'Hah!' Douglas cried out. 'That makes two.'

'Out of twenty,' said George.

'But it means the first time wasn't a fluke, and that I *can* beat you. So that makes the exact odds one in ten. How about we confirm it? Best out of thirty? Perhaps you'll find the odds are even higher in my favour.'

'No, I've just about had enough of this game.' There came the sound of chair legs scraping across the floor.

'Just because I beat you there's no need to be upset.'

'We didn't close the shop today to play games. We were supposed to be working, since we have an extensively large back catalogue of orders in need of completing. Then you went and uncovered *that* thing in the workshop. "One game", you said, just to prove you could win against me without me holding back. You've proved your point and I concede defeat. What more do you want?'

George opened the door and his eyes briefly skated over Molly as he paused in the doorway. Behind him, Molly saw Douglas leaning back in a wooden chair, opposite a chessboard arranged on a little table, and a vacant chair.

'Well, I did offer to stop at ten. It was you who insisted we go up to twenty,' Douglas called out to George, as he made his way towards the stairs.

Molly obstructed George's path. 'Did you let him win?' she said quietly.

'Only the first time. The second defeat, I admit, was genuine,' he muttered in a low voice and made his way up to his room.

Molly shook her head, then surveyed Douglas's room with her hands on her hips. 'It's a mess in here, and after all the times you've complained about my room being bad.'

'Well, I was waiting for you to do the laundry this week. I'm rapidly running out of clean shirts.'

'Oh no, if you want your shirts washing, you can either fix that damned machine or do it yourself.' She jerked her thumb over her shoulder and then crossed her arms over her chest, although her face showed she wasn't truly cross.

'What happened to you earning your keep?' he asked, feigning shock.

'Well, I reasoned I'd done enough to justify my continued presence, seeing as if it weren't for me then you and George might have – well, you know.' She theatrically raised her clenched hand above her head and jerked her head to one side while making a gargled, hacking sound.

'All right, Mol. I understand well enough.'

She instantly dropped out of character and let out a laugh, then pattered back down the stairs.

Douglas began gathering up the chess pieces. It was fortunate that Cobb had recovered from the worst of his injuries, otherwise they might not have been let off so easily for escaping from Newgate. He stowed the chessboard away inside the chest beneath his bedroom window, then glanced down into the street. 'Um, George?' he called out. 'I think Lord Leyton's coach is parked outside.'

'What?'

Seemingly in an instant, George came and stood beside his brother. It was unmistakably the earl's coach below the bedroom window. Wasting no time, George flew from the room and down the stairs, Douglas's footsteps juddering after him. Molly gave an exclamation of surprise as they passed her in the hallway, staring after them as they passed through into the shop and tore open the front door. Trunks and boxes were strapped onto the earl's coach, most of which were instrument cases judging by their shape. The peacock was caged on the back of the coach, virtually dormant save for the odd puff of its wings. Bellamy alighted from the coach and handed down his master, who was holding a bronze tiger cub under one arm. Lord Leyton wore a short, pale yellow coat that hung in neat pleats, a thick, navy waistband with a large square buckle nipping his waist. His trousers were narrow and dove-white, teamed with white pointed shoes. A straw hat shielded his face from their view.

'My dears!' cried Lord Leyton, as he raised his head. Douglas advanced to meet him with Molly tagging alongside. George hung back in the doorway.

'Lord Leyton! I thought you were leaving this afternoon.'

'I am, only I thought we would pay a quick call on our way to the dock, seeing as there was time. Maestro?' The automaton emerged from the coach and hastily shuffled himself down to the ground to join his master. He was dressed in a cobalt blue coat with gold trimming and his casing had been polished to a shine. 'I thought he might wish to say farewell. He is ever so excited to be going to the Continent. I have promised to take him to all of the grandest opera houses and galleries. No, Tiberius!' He tapped the tiger cub's paw as it tried to swipe a butterfly that came fluttering by. 'Naughty thing! Bellamy, will you take Tiberius?'

'When shall I have the driver return with the coach, my lord?' he asked in hushed, silvery tones as Lord Leyton deposited the tiger cub into his waiting hands.

'Oh, half an hour will do. Perhaps forty minutes.'

'As you wish, my lord.' He bowed, before returning to the coach, which drew away down the street.

'Do come in, Lord Leyton,' offered Douglas, leading him into the house.

Molly hastily retreated inside. George had already vanished. Douglas kicked a metal leg out of the way as they passed through the shop. It was in a bit of a state. The half-finished automaton still lay on the floor.

'Oh, the house is smaller than I remember it being the first time that I was here!' remarked the nobleman, as Douglas held the black door open, rolling his eyes as he heard Lord Leyton exclaim, 'Oh my! This certainly has changed! I do not recall it being like this!'

Douglas heard a clatter from the kitchen and the whiny whistle of the kettle. Of course, the one time George made tea for someone other than himself was as an escape from being in the same room as Lord Leyton. The earl seated himself in the green armchair beside the hearth and Douglas sat in the upholstered chair opposite. Maestro stood behind his master's chair. Although there was a vacant chair, Molly preferred to sit cross-legged on the hearthrug, her back being gently warmed by the sunlight that was pouring in through the window. George entered with the tea tray, which he deposited on the table, and then sat down in their father's old chair. Seeing George had neglected the sugar, Molly uncurled herself and went to fetch it. The earl did not seem to mind that no one made a move to serve the tea and chatted amicably as he poured his own.

'Yes, I am planning on showing him all the best sights I witnessed when I took the Tour.' He chinked the spoon on the side of his cup and waved it through the air with a flourish as he spoke.

'We will sail to France and then work our way eastwards to Spain, Italy, Greece – oh, thank you, my dear girl,' he said, as Molly set down the little bowl of sugar and then retreated to her spot.

'I am looking forward to seeing Italy the most,' said Maestro, 'since that's where all the greatest operas come from.'

'And you haven't had any problems at all, have you, Maestro?' asked Douglas, as he took up his own teacup. 'No loose joints or anything?'

'No, Master Douglas. All my parts have been working just fine since you and Master George repaired me.'

'Oh, when I think what a dreadful state he was in after what Claudette had done to him!' Lord Leyton pressed one hand to his chest, and he shook his head. 'They still haven't found a trace of her or Gaston. The French authorities have insisted they are doing everything in their power, as if *they* will recover them. It was thanks to them that they were able to slip away and avoid punishment. Although I confess, I still cannot get over the shock of their being the culprits behind Maestro being taken and almost reduced to a pile of ashes. I was so certain that Basil Griffin was the one behind it all, although I don't feel at all sorry that his name is in the mud, even if the law let him off lightly.'

Douglas had been true to his word and seen to it that Mr Griffin was granted bail, although public opinion of him swiftly soured. After all, there was bound to be someone in every dress circle acquainted with

Lord Leyton. The professor, however, had disappeared completely. Most likely he had sensed something had gone wrong with the plot and fled abroad. They would probably never know. Douglas glimpsed the newspaper lying near the foot of George's chair. Reverend Clarke had fallen oddly silent around about the time of the Royal Performance (which was generally deemed by the critics to have been a great success), but his work was done. They could expect a lot more trouble from the SOAL in future.

'Well, I doubt Claudette and Gaston will be brought to justice. But at least the extent of their crimes has been made public, and Maestro is none the worse for the whole adventure,' said Douglas, looking past Lord Leyton towards Maestro. 'And perhaps we had best give you a quick examination, just to be on the safe side, Maestro. We wouldn't want you going abroad in anything less than perfect condition – and it will be difficult for us to reach you there.'

'Absolutely,' Lord Leyton assented with a nod. 'I want him to be in pristine condition. Oh yes, there is another thing I wished to ask of *you*, my dear girl.' He turned his head towards Molly. 'I should like a nosegay of those flowers of yours to brighten up my cabin on the voyage. You know the ones you sent me last have held their scent and colour. Everyone who calls at my house in town remarks upon them.'

'Of course, Lord Leyton.' Molly sprang to her feet. 'I'll go pick a dozen of the most radiant ones for you right this minute.' She smiled sweetly and curtsied before bounding out of the room.

'Oh, splendid girl!' Lord Leyton smiled after her, before taking a sip of tea and swiping a straggling pale lock of hair away from his right eye with his long, slender, jewelled fingers.

'So, you are planning to move, I take it?' he said to Douglas.

'Yes, and very soon if all goes to plan. Nothing has been signed yet, although the house is as good as ours. It is a mansion about thirty miles out of London on the border of Hertfordshire.'

'Your ancestral residence?'

'Yes, although not the house that the family currently use. George graciously gave that up to some second cousin, along with the title.'

They had received word that their uncle had passed away about a month ago, with no heir. It appeared that the duke had relented on his deathbed, forgiven his sister and instructed his lawyer that her eldest son was to have the dukedom. When George had refused it, they had offered it to a distant relation, who was no doubt delighted at his unexpected good fortune. What they had asked for, however, was the ancient family house that George also stood to inherit.

'I cannot believe that I did not make the connection! Who has not heard the story of the Dennington daughter's elopement with the clockmaker? But are you sure you will not reconsider, sir?' he asked George. 'You would, after all, be a duke nonetheless! You would even stand higher than myself in the peerage,' he added, as he set his cup and saucer down on the table with a feeble rattle.

Douglas said, 'George is too modest for grand titles and houses. I can't imagine him as a duke.' George turned his face away from his brother. 'The house that we wanted had been out of use by the family for some time after they built a newer, grander residence in the neighbouring county. It is plenty big enough for what we intend to do with it. We could have twenty studies and two dozen workshops if we chose. And there's two hundred and fifty acres of land for Molly to grow her garden in.'

'Well, I am sure it will suit in that case. Consider it a blank canvas to make your mark upon.' He craned his head around to Maestro. 'Shall you let them examine you then, my dear Maestro? I want to be left in no doubt that you will not fall to pieces as soon as we reach Venice.'

'Of course, Master Josephus. Oh! Master Douglas, I believe I left my violin when I was last here for repairs. Might I please retrieve it?'

'Oh yes, it is still where you left it. I had forgotten to mention it to you. Go and get it, Maestro.'

The mechanical man bowed briefly and then made his way upstairs. The door to the workshop let out a long creak as he peered inside. Sure enough, amongst the pieces of machinery and various other things, there was his violin on the tabletop by the window. Having retrieved it, Maestro paused in the doorway to have one last look at the place that was bound up with the nascent days of his existence. This had been his entire world at one time. His very earliest recollections were a confusion of sound and light that he gradually came to disentangle: the sound of his own clockwork ticking from within him and Master George's voice, the soft flush of pale yellow candlelight and Master George's face looking down over him. He shut the door softly and made his way back downstairs. There was the soft creak of the back door being opened and not fully shut. It made a long whinge, as if wondering why it was suspended ajar. Reaching the ground floor, he saw Miss Molly sitting on a tree stump by the back door with a small bunch of flowers set down beside her, her eyes closed and her face lifted up to the bright sunlight that fell over her. Strands of her hair waved about in the sharp light.

'Have you come to enjoy the evening as well, Maestro?' She opened her eyes and smiled at him. The fabric of her dress rustled as she raised one of her feet onto the stump. 'I couldn't resist staying out here a little longer with it being so warm and sunny.'

'It certainly is, Miss Molly,' agreed Maestro, as he came closer to her. She carefully lifted the flowers onto her lap and patted the stump, inviting him to sit down beside her. The stump was just wide enough for him to perch on the edge.

'You know this was the tree Douglas harvested your wood from?' she said, as she rubbed its smooth surface. 'It was a bit of a shame to see him chop it down, but there's enough maple left to replace your casing three times over.'

'That reminds me, Miss Molly, there was something I wished to ask you. Forgive me, but did you…did you change the tree in any other way besides making it grow faster?'

'Ah.' Molly winked. 'I might have done, but what if I were to reveal all my little secrets? Where would the fun be in that? Was there actually a reason you came out here, by the way?'

'I came to get my violin from the workshop. I should not have liked to have left it behind,' Maestro said, as he made sure it was still in tune. 'I am sure Master Josephus would have gotten me another. He has insisted that he will get me a Stradivarius a number of times, but I prefer to play this one. It produces a superior sound somehow; perhaps it is something to do with its shape.'

'Hmm, are you sure it isn't because it was your first instrument that you're so attached to it?' Molly chuckled, and her fingers began to weave a flower through her hair, almost as if she wasn't aware of them doing so.

'Are you glad to be going to the Continent, Maestro?' she asked buoyantly, after a pause.

'I think I am, Miss Molly. There are so many things I wish to see and experience. I feel perhaps one should endeavour to go beyond the bounds of what one knows. Although,' he cast a brief look back towards the house and then up at the lavender sky, 'I confess it is somewhat…unsettling.'

'I know what you mean. I thought I couldn't wait to finally leave this pokey old house behind and get a proper garden of my own. But now it's happening, I keep thinking about all the little things that I'll miss. *Pfft.* Sentimental drivel, I know. Change will be good for you, Maestro, you'll see. Things can only get better from here, for you and for my brothers. Hopefully.'

She patted the flower to make sure it would stay and sighed contentedly to herself, letting an agreeable silence fall over them. Insects croaked and hummed around them, and birds tweeted as they skittered across the sky. Maestro heard the delicate rustle of flower petals and leaves rubbing against one another. Molly reached her hand up to the flowers in one of the hanging baskets and stroked them. The delicate breeze made it appear as if they were affectionately rubbing their heads against her hand.

'The flowers do like to hear your music, Maestro. It always makes them grow so much better,' she said dreamily, lifting her distinctive green eyes to his. 'Won't you play something for them just one last time? Just a little tune will do.'

'Why of course, Miss Molly. I would be honoured to.'

He raised his violin and let the bow rest on the strings as he allowed the song to build itself up inside of him, feeling the wheels moving inside his head and his cylinders turning. He wanted it to sound like Miss Molly, and he fancied it did, although she was difficult to capture. He would try to capture her as he saw her there, with her gaze attentively bestowed on the flowers and with a blossom in her hair. A cascade of warm, bright notes fell from the violin, which sang with a cheerful, chirrupy voice. Miss Molly, her eyes closed once more, swayed gently in time with the music, smiling irresistibly. But then sweeter, softer notes were introduced into the melody, like a scattering of bright blossoms on the air, and were carried across the city, gradually giving way to far more dulcet tones, and the song seemed to guide itself. Around them, all other sounds seemed to fade away. The insects lay quiet, and even the flowers ceased their rustling. The summer breeze grew stronger, like a bid to hush, and then died away altogether. The entire evening lay in an attentive silence, as all listened to the greatest composer that the world had ever known.

Lightning Source UK Ltd.
Milton Keynes UK
UKHW011841030520
362639UK00002B/210

9 781781 329672